DEATH ON TELEGRAPH HILL

ALSO BY SHIRLEY TALLMAN

Scandal on Rincon Hill

The Cliff House Strangler

The Russian Hill Murders

Murder on Nob Hill

DEATH ON TELEGRAPH HILL

SHIRLEY TALLMAN

Minotaur Books 〰 New York

www.minotaurbooks.com

ISBN 978-1-250-01043-8 (hardcover)
ISBN 978-1-250-01524-2 (e-book)

First Edition: October 2012

10   9   8   7   6   5   4   3   2   1

In loving memory of our beautiful and courageous
daughter Karen. You will be with us forever in our hearts.
And to H.P., who is always there for me.

ACKNOWLEDGMENTS

I owe a debt of thanks to Patrick Buscovich, San Francisco structural engineer, and Edgar Oropeza of the San Francisco Planning Department, for their assistance in helping Sarah defeat Ricardo Ruiz's proposed bullfighting arena. Also, many thanks to the San Francisco office of the Society for the Prevention of Cruelty to Animals. Your help is greatly appreciated.

DEATH ON TELEGRAPH HILL

CHAPTER ONE

A sudden gust of wind hit me full in the face, nearly causing me to lose my footing on the wooden steps leading up the east slope of San Francisco's Telegraph Hill. Burrowing my head farther inside my hood, I hastened to catch up with my brother Samuel, who was several stairs ahead of me. He was obviously as eager as was I to be done with this precipitous climb.

It was a cold, clear evening late in March 1882. In addition to the gusting wind, the approaching dusk was making our hike up the Filbert Street Steps more arduous than if undertaken during daylight hours. Had I known what lay in store for us that night, the efforts of this ascent would have seemed very trivial indeed. But I am getting ahead of my story.

Our destination was the home of Mortimer Remy, a friend of my brother's and publisher of the *San Francisco Weekly,* a popular newspaper that often bought Samuel's crime articles. Mr. Remy had invited a group of local authors to meet the young Irish poet Oscar Wilde, who was touring the United States to publicize a book of poetry he had published the previous year.

At least that was the ostensive reason given for his visit. It was hardly a secret that the actual purpose of the trip was to tout the so-called Aesthetic Movement, which comprised artists, poets, and writers who argued that art need not be practical or useful, but should exist solely for its own sake. Mr. Wilde, the self-proclaimed champion of this philosophy, announced that it was his mission "to make this artistic movement the basis for a new civilization." Curious to meet the colorful personality, I had readily accepted Samuel's invitation to accompany him to the reading.

Tonight's clear view demonstrated how Telegraph Hill had received its name some thirty-two years earlier: it possessed an excellent vantage point for sighting ships entering the bay. In order to alert the town to these much-anticipated arrivals—bearing mail and necessary goods—a windmill-like structure called a semaphore had been erected atop the Hill. The contraption had long since disappeared, but its brief existence had permanently established the hill's identity.

Mortimer Remy's home was located on a narrow dirt-and-gravel street, perhaps more correctly labeled a "byway." It was a modest, gabled-roof cottage, probably dating from the late 1850s or early 1860s. Houses along this lane were all but impossible to reach by one-horse, sometimes even two-horse, carriages. A real estate man by the name of Frederick O. Layman had recently applied for a city franchise to run a cable car line up Telegraph Hill. Reportedly, Mr. Layman's ultimate plan was to construct an observatory atop the hill and required the cable car line to transport visitors to and from what was already being described, and ridiculed, as a "German Castle." If the cable car line was eventually built, Telegraph Hill's inhabitants would benefit from its convenience. On the other hand, it would almost certainly increase housing prices, which for now remained affordable because of the hill's unfriendly grade.

Mr. Remy himself opened the door and greeted us with hearty cheer, then led us into a front parlor where seats had been arranged to face the front of the room. Built into one wall was a large hearth, the crackling fire giving out rather more heat than I found comfortable. Opposite the fireplace was an ever-popular bay window, outside which I glimpsed a small copse of trees.

The parlor was simply arranged with functional, rather than decorative, furniture. About half a dozen people were already seated there, and our host directed us to a settee located toward the back of the room. Stephen Parke, a friend of my brother's and an aspiring writer, stood and smiled as we approached. He was a taller than average man in his late twenties, blessed with a head of curly brown hair, a fair complexion, and cheerful hazel eyes that twinkled as he assisted me into a seat beside him on the sofa.

"I'm charmed to meet you again, Miss Woolson," he said. He shook Samuel's hand, then sank back into his own seat.

"It is very good to see you, Mr. Parke," I replied, pleased we had been placed next to such an agreeable companion. "It promises to be an interesting evening."

"That's what I'm hoping, since I was unable to attend Wilde's lecture at Platt's Hall yesterday," he said. "Opinions about Wilde differ considerably."

Samuel lowered his voice. "Judging by the man's photograph in today's papers, he certainly is a distinctive-looking fellow."

"Not many men have the nerve to appear in public wearing turbans and knee breeches," said Parke with amusement.

My brother chuckled. "It makes good fodder for the newspapers. By the way, have you read his book of poems?"

"Not yet," Parke answered. "But I hope to purchase one tonight. I assume he'll bring copies."

This time Samuel laughed aloud. "Have you ever known an author who didn't drag around a trunk crammed full of his scribblings?" He had the good grace to look sheepish. "Not to say that I wouldn't behave the same if my own book were to be published."

"Not *if,* Samuel, but *when* it is published," Parke corrected.

"And your book as well, Stephen," said Samuel. "You're correct, we must remain optimistic."

"Yes, but your manuscript is nearly finished," Parke pointed out with a wry smile, "whereas mine is still in a very rough state."

Stephen Parke referred to the political treatise he was writing that dealt with San Francisco's frequently corrupt city administrations.

The necessity to eat regular meals and keep a roof over his head, however, obliged him to sell articles to Remy's *San Francisco Weekly,* as well as to any other publications willing to accept his work. Parke lived farther down Telegraph Hill, as did a small colony of writers struggling to make their names in the literary world.

Even as I was pondering this, another member of that community was making his way over to speak to us. I had met Emmett Gardiner on several previous occasions, when I had accompanied Samuel to various literary functions. He was a tall, blond-haired man of thirty, with a strong, handsome face, steady brown eyes, and a genial personality. Emmett contributed regular stories and poems to *The Californian,* a literary periodical that had evolved out of the old *Overland Monthly.* I seemed to remember my brother telling me that Emmett, too, was writing a novel, although I could not for the life of me recall the subject matter.

"Samuel, Stephen," said Gardiner, shaking their hands with his usual good cheer. "And Miss Woolson, it is always a pleasure to see you. Did any of you attend Wilde's lecture at Platt's Hall last night?"

When we indicated that we had not, he went on, "Neither did I. Which was why I was delighted when Uncle Mortimer arranged tonight's reading."

"I keep forgetting that Remy is your uncle," Samuel said. "You don't sound anything like him."

"That's because he hails from Louisiana, while my mother, his eldest sister, moved with her family to San Francisco when I was just five. She still lives here in the city."

"That explains it, then," Stephen commented. "By the way, how is your book progressing?"

As the three would-be authors discussed their various projects, Tull O'Hara, who also lived on Telegraph Hill, entered the parlor. A short man in his fifties, he had a long crooked nose, critical gray eyes, and a perpetually dour expression on his weathered face. O'Hara worked for Mortimer Remy's newspaper, and although he was touted as one of the best typesetters in the city, he was even better known for his disagreeable personality. He certainly lived up to his reputation tonight, giving his employer the barest nod and studiously ignoring the rest of us as he took a seat behind our own.

"Who is that sitting next to Tull O'Hara?" I asked Samuel, nodding toward the large, ruddy-cheeked man frowning at the typesetter.

"Claude Dunn," my brother whispered, "yet another hopeful author. He spends his days writing while his wife, Lucy, the pregnant girl sitting next to him, cooks and cleans for anyone on the Hill who will pay her."

Discreetly, I examined the young woman seated beside her husband. She could not have been more than nineteen or twenty, but her sallow skin and straggly blond hair gave her the appearance of a much older, world-weary woman. I was shocked to note that despite the huge swell of her belly, the bony line of her shoulders was clearly visible from beneath her worn cotton dress. She should be at home tucked into bed, I thought indignantly, not forced to sit here in an overheated room, clearly fighting a losing battle to keep her eyes open!

Mrs. Dunn suddenly looked up, and loath to be caught staring, I hastily turned my gaze on a couple who were sitting in front of us. The man looked to be in his fifties and had a long, gray-streaked beard, dark eyes, and a yarmulke atop his balding head.

"That's Solomon Freiberg and his daughter, Isabel," Stephen informed me, following my gaze. "They live down the hill. Miss Freiberg teaches piano, and her father works as a diamond cutter."

Isabel Freiberg was remarkably pretty. She had a small oval face, creamy skin, intelligent brown eyes, and silky brown hair fashioned into a neat bun at the nape of her slender neck. Although she made a show of listening attentively as her father spoke to her, I noticed her steal several unobtrusive glances over her shoulder at Stephen. Just as interesting were the looks he returned when he thought no one was watching. Unless I was mistaken, those two shared more than a casual friendship.

Shortly after eight o'clock, Mortimer Remy strode to the front of the room, clearing his throat to attract his guests' attention. Our host was not an imposing man, but he possessed a steady brown-eyed gaze that co-workers boasted could burrow with uncanny precision into the heart of a story. Perhaps his most notable feature was a full head of white hair that curled about his face in disarray. By contrast, his shaggy eyebrows remained a dark brown, drawing even more attention to those penetrating eyes.

While Remy waited for the last whispers to quiet, I saw him suddenly grimace and touch the right side of his face. Looking closer, I noticed a slight swelling along his jawline . . . from a toothache? I wondered. If so, the man had my sincere sympathy. Above all things, I dreaded the thankfully infrequent occasions when one of my own teeth caused me distress. There was so little one could do to alleviate the pain. Even my physician brother, Charles, was usually forced to resort to age-old remedies such as holding whiskey in the mouth or applying concoctions composed of red oak bark, camphor, cinnamon, or clove oil to the tooth and gum. Even then, relief was fleeting. The only permanent solution, of course, was to have the afflicted tooth extracted, a recourse even the heartiest of men dreaded!

Remy gingerly moved his jaw from side to side, then gave a labored smile. "Welcome, everyone. I am pleased you could join us this evening."

Despite his obvious discomfort, our host's voice was pleasant, carrying a strong flavor of the Deep South. I was aware that he had traveled to San Francisco from New Orleans a decade or so earlier and had brought with him a number of old world customs, including a penchant for long, and in my opinion disagreeable, green cigars and Zydeco music. Although I had met him only once or twice, I had come to appreciate his affability and easy charm.

"Tonight we are in for a rare treat," he continued, smiling at the tall young man who came to stand behind him. "Mr. Oscar Wilde, author of a recently published collection of poetry, and a forerunner in the Aesthetic Movement, has graciously agreed to meet with us here in my home for a more informal visit than his appearance last night at Platt's Hall."

Wilde smiled and executed a small, somewhat affected bow, which precipitated a murmur from the audience.

"Too utterly utter," came a man's low, sarcastic voice from behind me. There was a smattering of laughter, and I knew at once that the remark had come from Claude Dunn. Not that the comment was original; the expression had been reported with great humor in newspapers throughout the poet's American tour, along with other so-called Wildean expressions.

Mortimer Remy shot Dunn a censuring look, then turned his attention back to the guest of honor. "Considering Mr. Wilde's views concerning architectural design and household furnishings, I pray that he will overlook the many deficiencies to be found in my own humble abode. I entreat him to turn his attention instead to literary matters, commencing, if he will be so kind, with how he came to produce such a fine volume of poetry at the tender age of twenty-seven."

There was polite applause as the publisher stood aside to allow Mr. Wilde to take his place in front of the audience. I had, of course, read newspaper articles describing the Irish poet, but it was nonetheless startling to meet him in person. Wilde was already known across two continents as an opinionated dandy with a cutting, sometimes treacherous, wit. He had a long, somewhat fleshy face, full lips, and heavy-lidded eyes placed to either side of a prominent nose. Attired in a maroon velvet smoking jacket edged with braid, a lavender silk shirt, flowing green cravat, knee breeches, and black shoes with silver buckles, he looked as if he had just stepped out of an eighteenth-century French drawing room. A few muffled laughs once again rippled through the room, and Dunn made more acerbic remarks. Remy's piercing expression finally silenced the annoying man.

Whether or not he had come to Remy's house with the intention of speaking about the Aesthetic Movement, Wilde seemed happy enough to accede to the publisher's request that he confine his discussion to his literary efforts. Having produced a slim volume of the book, titled simply *Poems,* he commenced reading in a dull, rather nasal voice. I must say I found his manner surprisingly languorous, as if he were bored by the necessity to speak to us at all.

Wilde had been reciting for only a few minutes when his performance was interrupted by the sound of the front door opening. A moment later, an elderly woman in a wheelchair was rolled into the room. She was small and very wrinkled, her wispy white hair tucked beneath a black hat with a short black veil. She was wearing a black dress with ivory-colored lace at the neck and wrists and a simple mourning brooch pinned to her bodice. Despite her advanced years, she had bright blue eyes that appeared to miss nothing as they swept over the room. A muscular man in his fifties, dressed in dark livery and a battered gray felt cap, pushed her squeaky conveyance into the room. He had a craggy face and black eyes that looked out suspiciously from beneath bushy black-and-white eyebrows. A long scar ran from his right jawline down his throat until it was lost beneath his shirt collar.

"Who is that woman?" I whispered to Samuel.

"That's Mrs. Montgomery, a wealthy widow who lives in the large house at the top of the hill. I don't know the name of the man pushing her wheelchair, but—"

"His name is Bruno Studds," said Emmett Gardiner, leaning over so that he could address us in hushed tones. "And you're right, Samuel, Mrs. Montgomery is quite well-to-do. Her late husband owned the largest lumber business in the city. She's been a particularly generous benefactor to the writers living here on the Hill. It was she who financed the launch of the *San Francisco Weekly* when Uncle Mortimer founded it ten years ago."

"Doesn't she sponsor the Butter Ball Literary Competition each year?" I asked, referring to the much-sought-after literary award.

"She does indeed," Gardiner answered, his eyes dancing in the gleam of the room's gaslights. "Not only does the winner receive a sizable monetary prize, but Mrs. Montgomery publishes his book at her own expense."

"I've never understood what 'Butter Ball' stands for," I said.

"I've heard rumors that it was the name of her only son's favorite pony," Gardiner explained. "Lawrence was an aspiring writer who died quite young. A year or two after his death, Mrs. Montgomery established the award in his honor."

Our conversation was cut short as Mortimer Remy greeted the latest arrival. "Mrs. Montgomery," he drawled, his manners at their southern best, "I am so pleased that you could come. I regret any inconvenience it may have caused you."

"Thank you, Mr. Remy," Mrs. Montgomery replied, holding out a slightly trembling hand. Remy took her frail fingers and brought them to his lips.

"Please, do make yourself comfortable, dear lady. You're just in time to hear Mr. Wilde read from his volume of poetry." Smiling, he indicated an area in front of the fire that had evidently been reserved for her wheelchair.

Mrs. Montgomery returned her host's smile, and without being told, Studds wheeled his mistress to the designated place. As soon as she was settled, he rearranged the blanket covering her lap, although I couldn't imagine how she would tolerate it considering the heat emanating from the hearth. The man then went to stand stoically behind his mistress's chair.

Before Wilde could resume reading, there was yet another disturbance in the foyer, and an arrogant-looking man wearing a topcoat and bowler hat stepped into the room. I recognized him at once as Jonathan Aleric, a celebrity of sorts and owner and editor of the *Bay Area Express,* a recently established local newspaper.

Despite his haughty demeanor, I thought Aleric to be a rather ordinary-looking individual: in his early forties, he was of average height and build, with graying hair, a large and rather untidy salt-and-pepper mustache, a pocked complexion, and washed-out blue eyes. Some twelve years earlier, Aleric had gained international fame by penning *An Uncivil War,* an immensely popular book describing General Grant's 1863 march on Vicksburg. In mere weeks, the book had sold out across the nation—surprisingly, sales were brisk even in the South—casting Aleric as the defining voice of the horrendous War Between the States.

In the years following the book's publication, his devoted readers waited expectantly for more stirring words to issue from the great author's pen. When none were forthcoming, Aleric's name gradually faded but never disappeared completely from the literary scene. He was still regarded as one of the finest American writers of our time and gave occasional lectures on the war, and his craft, throughout the country. Two years ago he migrated to San Francisco, determined to reinvent himself in the field of journalism. According to Samuel, the relationship between Aleric and Mortimer Remy had been strained from the beginning, both professionally and personally. Over the past year, Aleric seemed to have made it his life's purpose to put Remy's newspaper out of business.

Had that goal been his only sin, Remy probably would have been able to cope with it as one more example of journalistic rivalry in an extremely competitive town. But Aleric had not contented himself with stealing Remy's readership; he had also stolen the affections of his lovely wife, dealing the southerner a devastating, and humbling, blow. When Remy's wife succumbed to a lung disease just months after she had scandalously deserted her husband, a war hardly less intense than that between the states broke out between the two men.

"Aleric!" Remy's face had flushed red with fury. "Good God, man, have you no sense of decency? This is my home, and you most certainly were not invited!"

Ignoring his host, Aleric stepped casually inside the parlor. His angular, sharp-featured face was creased in a self-satisfied smile, as if Remy's reaction were everything he had hoped for.

"I said what are you doing here?" Remy again demanded. His brown eyes bulged, and his hands were balled into fists. I honestly feared he might be angry enough to strike the inter-loper.

"Calm down, Mortimer, you'll do yourself an injury," Aleric said calmly. If anything, his smile grew even more taunting. "I came to meet Mr. Wilde, of course. Isn't that the purpose of to-night's little get-together?"

"You bast . . ." Remy stopped, fighting to collect himself. He glanced uncomfortably at Wilde, who was watching the episode with quiet amusement, then at his tense guests. He took one or two steadying breaths before continuing in a more composed voice. "As I said, you were not invited, Aleric. I will thank you to leave my home. At once, if you please."

Aleric laughed, dismissing Remy's words with a careless wave of his hand. "Nonsense. I'm here to make Mr. Wilde's acquain-tance, and I shall not leave until I have done so." He gave the Irish poet a little bow. "I was privileged to hear your lecture on art decoration at Pratt's Hall last night, Mr. Wilde. It was truly inspira-tional. With you as their representative, the Aesthetic Movement cannot fail to be a grand success."

Wilde studied Aleric for a long moment and then nodded his coiffed head as if to an admiring subject.

"That is kind of you to say, Mr. . . . ?" He looked questioningly at his host. "Aleric, was it?" He paused a moment, then his lazy eyes suddenly brightened. "Jonathan Aleric! You are the author of *An Uncivil War,* are you not? I remember reading it as a young lad. A marvelous book. It was quite popular in Ireland after your War Between the States."

Aleric beamed. "How kind of you to say so, Mr. Wilde. I'm honored that you enjoyed my book."

Remy's face had grown very red, and I saw his jaw muscles clench as he tried to regain control of the situation. "I apologize for this rude interruption, Mr. Wilde. I am sure Mr. Aleric will do the gentlemanly thing and retire, immediately, from my home."

"Come now, Mr. Remy," Wilde protested. "Mr. Aleric is a noted author—indeed, a kindred spirit. And he has traveled all this way—" He fixed his gaze on the newcomer. "I assume you *have* come from some distance to see me, Mr. Aleric? The walk alone up all those stairs must, in any sane man's opinion, constitute a journey of inestimable miles."

I truly feared our host might explode. He opened his mouth to speak, but Wilde cut him off. "After all, life is too important to be taken seriously, don't you agree? For myself, I make it a point to avoid arguments; they are always vulgar and all too often convincing."

Wilde's languid eyes turned to Remy, as if awaiting his agreement. Our host took another deep breath, but there was little he could do but accede to his guest's wishes. He gave a curt nod of his head, then wordlessly motioned for his nemesis to take a seat. Several people moved aside so that the author could make his way to a vacant chair next to Tull O'Hara, but Aleric held up a hand as if to signify that he wished to cause no inconvenience. Instead, he settled in the seat Remy had occupied prior to his arrival.

Our host's face grew even darker, but after catching sight of Wilde's obvious amusement, he placed a chair to Aleric's left and sat down. Stone-faced, he indicated that Wilde should resume reading.

"That is good of you, Mr. Remy," Wilde said, once again picking up his book of poems. He gave a rueful smile. "Life is never fair, and perhaps it is a good thing for most of us that it is not."

The tension triggered by Aleric's arrival never truly dissipated as the long evening marched drearily onward. Wilde continued to read, but I sensed a general unrest in the room as one desultory poem followed another. I enjoy good poetry, but these offerings were rather too morose for my taste.

When at long last the Irishman brought his recitation to a close, there was polite applause and one or two thinly disguised sighs of relief, one of them coming from Claude Dunn's expectant wife, Lucy. But it appeared that the poet was not yet finished, and to my dismay he went on to lecture us for another hour on the "house beautiful" and how his opinion of Americans as barbaric was reinforced each time he was introduced to yet another "ill-looking room in an ill-built house."

Finally, mercifully, he concluded his talk by instructing us on how to build and furnish houses that would "live in song and tradition, and delight the hearts of generations of aesthetes yet unborn."

This time, the applause was less enthusiastic. Even Mortimer Remy seemed visibly dismayed that Wilde had veered from his request to focus on his literary career. I must admit that I was more than ready to take my leave of the gathering and return home. I turned to say as much to Samuel but found him engaged in a heated conversation with Emmett Gardiner and Claude Dunn. Dunn's wife, I noticed, remained in her seat, looking resigned and clearly exhausted.

Out of the corner of my eye, I noticed Stephen Parke slip away to share a few words with the attractive Isabel Freiberg. It was a brief meeting, but it was clear from the way they looked at each other that I had correctly assessed their feelings. When the girl's father pulled on his topcoat and made toward the door, the young couple quickly drew apart, Stephen looking flustered, the young woman's face flushing a becoming pink. Taking her arm, the man nodded curtly at the writer, then led the girl none too gently out the door.

Stephen watched the two make their way down the hill, then reluctantly turned back to the room. He and my brother spoke quietly for several moments, then Stephen paid his respects to our host. After bidding me farewell, he departed the cottage.

As Samuel and I approached Remy to say our own good-byes, we found that he had joined Emmett Gardiner and Jonathan Aleric, who were chatting with Oscar Wilde. Mrs. Montgomery sat in her wheelchair in front of the fireplace, speaking quietly to Claude Dunn. Looking toward his weary wife, he seemed to question something she had said. The elderly widow smiled at Lucy, then nodded her head at Dunn. I sincerely hoped she was suggesting that the man take his poor wife home and put her to bed!

Unfortunately, that did not appear to be the case. Despite his earlier disparaging remarks, Dunn moved to join the others clustered about Wilde, followed a moment later by Mrs. Montgomery, wheeled there by her man, Bruno Studds. Clearly, the poet was in his element.

Mortimer Remy, on the other hand, looked miserable. He was once again holding his swollen jaw, all the while darting hostile looks at Jonathan Aleric, who was chatting with the poet as if they were long-lost friends. Finally, he seemed unable to bear it any longer.

"Come, everyone," he said, forcing a painful smile. "Our guest has had a long journey, and I am sure that he is weary. We must allow him to return to his hotel."

"Don't be ridiculous, Mortimer, the evening is still young," Aleric put in with a patronizing smile. "Were you aware that Mr. Wilde plans to write a stage play? We were just discussing—"

To my surprise, Mrs. Montgomery spoke up from her wheelchair. "Mortimer is quite right, Mr. Aleric. Mr. Wilde is obviously fatigued after entertaining us with his splendid poetry." Before Aleric could object, she turned to the faithful man standing silently behind her chair. "It is a clear evening and the moon is out, but the path can be treacherous at night. Please light Mr. Remy's guests down the steps, Bruno."

"I won't hear of it, Mrs. Montgomery," Remy protested. "Bruno must take you back up to your house. I will see my guests down the hill."

"Nonsense," she replied, waving a dismissive hand. "You have put up a brave front all evening, Mortimer, but you are obviously suffering a toothache. Soak it in whiskey and get a good night's sleep. That's the ticket."

Remy looked at her in dismay. "But—"

"I'll hear no more argument." She looked at Remy's gruff typesetter, who was silently making his way toward the front door. "Your man O'Hara will take me home, will you not, Tull?"

The crotchety man stared at the woman in sullen surprise. I feared he might be about to refuse when Remy sighed.

14

"I suppose if Tull is willing . . ."

"His willingness is neither here nor there," the old woman said with acerbity. "He is your employee and naturally will be happy to accede to your wishes. In truth, it is past time we all made our way home."

Her tone was so resolute that even Oscar Wilde was forced to stop talking, appearing affronted that someone had had the effrontery to interrupt his discourse.

"My dear madam, you speak of time," he said in a droll voice, peering at her down his long nose. "As the brilliant Brendan Francis put it, 'When you are deeply absorbed in what you are doing, time gives itself to you like a warm and willing lover.'"

Mrs. Montgomery did not appear impressed. "I'm confident that even Mr. Francis eventually learned not to overstay his welcome, Mr. Wilde. It is a lesson worth cultivating."

Before the poet could object, the widow motioned for Studds to take up his lantern and lead the way out of the cottage. Mortimer Remy shrugged in resignation. No doubt his toothache was finally getting the better of him.

Without further comment, Wilde donned his oversize fur-trimmed coat and followed Mrs. Montgomery's man toward the door, Jonathan Aleric close upon his heels. After bidding our host a good evening, Samuel and I trailed the group out of the cottage, pausing a moment to wish Emmett Gardiner good night before he turned to walk to his own home.

Studds led the way, lantern held above his head. Wilde and Aleric followed behind him, while Samuel and I brought up the rear. Mrs. Montgomery's man was obviously familiar with the path, for he set a brisk pace.

We had nearly reached the top of the Filbert Street Steps when Aleric lost his footing and started to fall. Samuel bent over and caught him by the arm. As I, too, stepped forward to lend a hand, the quiet night was shattered by a loud explosion.

Time seemed to hang suspended as I looked around, searching for what had caused the boom. I heard my brother utter a single muffled gasp and turned to find him standing perfectly still beside me, his expression one of astonishment.

Then, suddenly, his legs seemed to give way from beneath him. I watched in horror as, without another sound, he crumpled to the ground like a rag doll.

CHAPTER TWO

For a long, horrible moment I stood frozen, unable to move. I was in shock; I realized this even as a voice in my head shouted, *For God's sake, do something!*

Shaking myself out of this momentary paralysis, I knelt beside my brother, horrified to find blood flowing far too freely from beneath his topcoat. Adding to the nightmare, Aleric kept yelling that we were under attack, while Wilde wailed that the American West was as wild as he'd been warned.

"Damn it all, be quiet!" I snapped, heedless of my language. "Your caterwauling isn't helping my brother."

The men fell into stunned silence. As I tore apart my brother's cravat and starched white shirt, I came upon a gaping wound just above his left breast. I am ashamed to admit that when I stared down at this sickening defilement to my brother's body, I experienced a moment's light-headedness. Closing my eyes, I took in a deep gulp of cold night air to clear my head, then ripped several strips of longcloth from my petticoats and bound each one as tightly as I dared around his chest. As I worked, I murmured soft words of reassurance, all the while praying that the bullet had not lodged near his heart.

Once I had staunched Samuel's bleeding as best I could, I attempted to minimize his shock by tucking my cape snugly about his body. Getting to my feet, I ordered Aleric and Studds to carry him as quickly, but gently, as possible down the hill. Without comment, the two men dutifully lifted my brother from the dirt, Studds hoisting him from beneath his shoulders, Aleric bearing his weight from the knees down.

Despite my brother's slender frame, it seemed to take the two men forever to navigate their way down the steep wooden stairs. I had grabbed hold of Studds's lantern to light the way, but I was all too aware of how badly my feckless hand trembled as I held on to the handle. Behind me, I could hear Samuel's ragged breathing and cringed every time he groaned in pain when one of the men tripped or fumbled to regain his grip. Bringing up the rear, Wilde continued to look over his shoulder, declaring that he was too young to meet a violent death in such a barbaric land.

To my profound relief, the Irish poet managed to pull himself together by the time we reached the street, offering his waiting carriage to rush my brother to St. Mary's Hospital. Adding to this act of chivalry, Wilde insisted on accompanying us. To my surprise, Jonathan Aleric also joined us in the carriage. After helping us lift Samuel into the cab, Bruno Studds closed the carriage door and without a backward glance made his way back up the stairs.

The rest of the night passed in a terrifying blur. I'm sure we must have arrived at the hospital faster than it seemed at the time, but the bumps and jolts of the racing vehicle did nothing to ease my poor brother's pain. I maintained a constant pressure on the wound, but the flow of blood continued to be alarming. Most frightening was the sight of his dear face appearing so deathly pale when it was caught in the spill of passing gaslights. I found myself counting each of his short, shallow breaths, as if by doing so I could ensure that they did not stop. I surely prayed more for his survival during that ride than I had prayed for anything in my entire twenty-eight years.

Once we reached the hospital, Aleric and a somewhat clumsy Wilde managed to carry Samuel into the building, where he was hastily transported into the dark bowels of the building. I recall a feeling of profound relief to realize that the doctor on duty was a colleague of my brother Charles, although his patience must have been sorely tested when I demanded to be allowed to accompany Samuel.

In the end my objections were overridden, and I was forced to adjourn to a dreary room with few amenities, occupied by an elderly man dozing fitfully in one of the room's half-dozen chairs. I had, of course, scribbled a quick note to my family alerting them of the attack on Samuel and sent it by way of Wilde and Aleric when they departed the hospital. I tried to ease my family's fears by describing my brother's condition as stable. There would be time enough to face the reality of his condition when Samuel was out of surgery. Even so, I worried that my mother would suffer one of her nervous attacks upon hearing that her youngest son had been shot.

After I had discharged this duty, the minutes began to drag by, and the fear I had worked so hard to keep at bay returned with a vengeance. Now that there was nothing to do but wait, my entire body began to shake as though I had been immersed in a vat of icy water.

Far too unsettled to even consider joining my snoring companion in one of the straight-backed chairs, I paced back and forth across the room. How serious was Samuel's wound? I kept asking myself. How much blood had he lost? How close had the bullet come to his heart? Even if it had missed his heart, had it punctured other vital organs?

With a pain so acute it felt like a knife piercing my chest, I could no longer avoid facing the unimaginable. What if Samuel's wound proved fatal? Dear Lord, it wasn't possible. It had all happened so quickly and without warning. Surely I would awaken to discover it had all been a terrible dream. My entire world could not be turned upside down in a single moment. Samuel was my best friend, an eager accomplice to all the mischief we'd gotten up to throughout our childhood. I wasn't sure I could bear a world without him.

As I continued my restless pacing, my fear gradually gave way to anger. Why would anyone do such a terrible thing? Who hated my brother enough to hide in the dark and deliberately shoot him? I was unaware that I had balled my hands into fists until my nails pressed into my palms with such fury that they broke the skin. Then and there I vowed that I would find my brother's assassin and bring him to justice, no matter how long it took or how tedious the trail. In the heat of that moment, I had no thoughts of whether I could even succeed at such an undertaking. The idea of failure did not enter my mind!

With grim determination, I gathered myself together by the time my family arrived at the hospital. Papa pushed through the door first, hair still mussed from bed, brown eyes wide in alarm. My mother followed, her white face strained and taut with dread. My brother Charles, and his wife, Celia, entered last, their expressions equally anxious.

"Sarah, what happened?" Mama said, rushing into the waiting room to grasp me in an almost suffocating embrace. "How is he?"

The rest of my family quickly joined us. Taking a deep breath, I did my utmost to look more confident than I felt.

"They took him into surgery nearly two hours ago," I said. "As yet there's been no news."

"Where was he wounded?" asked Charles before Mama could venture another question.

"Just below his left shoulder," I told him.

"Shot," Papa repeated slowly, as if trying to process such a preposterous idea. "Why would anybody shoot at Samuel?"

"I have no idea, Papa," I said bleakly. "It was so sudden. The shot seemed to come out of nowhere."

"Where did it happen?" my sister-in-law Celia asked in a quiet voice.

"On the east side of Telegraph Hill," I told her. "Just above the Filbert Street Steps."

Celia placed a small hand across her mouth as if to stifle a cry. "Who would do such a dreadful thing?"

Once again I shook my head. "I've been asking myself that same question. I can only think it must have been someone from the reading at Mr. Remy's house. Although I can't imagine who, or why."

"Didn't Oscar Wilde speak there tonight?" Papa asked.

"Yes, he—"

I stopped when Mama gave a little cry and buried her face in her hands, her shoulders heaving in silent sobs.

"You said in your message that it was nothing serious, Sarah," she said, looking at me through her tears. "Why didn't you tell us the truth?"

I shook my head, too miserable to speak. Perhaps I should have been more frank in my note, but my only thought had been to postpone my mother's pain for as long as possible.

"Don't fret, my girl," Papa said, recognizing my wretchedness. "Trying to explain what happened in a note would only have made matters worse." Holding Mama by the shoulders, he led her toward a chair opposite the elderly man, who had awakened to watch our little group with ill-concealed curiosity.

Charles waited until they were out of earshot. A lump formed in my throat to see the lines of tension around his mouth and the deep furrow between his eyes.

"Sarah, I want an honest answer," he said. "How close is the wound to Samuel's heart?"

"I don't know," I said, voicing the fear that had been plaguing me for hours. "I think it missed his heart—I pray it did. But there was so much blood." I felt hot tears stinging my eyes. Taking a deep, ragged breath, I fought them back. The last thing Mama needed was to see me dissolve into tears. "I should have done more to stop the bleeding!"

"I'll hear no more of that," Charles said, pulling me into his

21

arms and giving me a fierce hug. "I know you, my dear sister. I'm certain you did everything possible for him."

"Of course you did," said Celia, her sweet voice comforting.

"But why is he still in surgery?" I asked. It was an enormous relief to have Charles here. Finally someone who might be able to answer some of my countless questions, who could allay my fears. "Why is it taking so long?"

"Wounds of that sort require a steady hand, Sarah," he told me. "It can be very delicate surgery. Did they tell you which doctor is attending him?"

So confused were my thoughts that it was several moments before I could recall the man's name. "It's Dr. Ludlum. One of your friends from medical school."

Charles's somber face brightened with relief. "But that's excellent news, Sarah. Thomas Ludlum is a first-rate surgeon."

I closed my eyes, feeling as if a huge weight had been lifted off my shoulders. While I had met the man once or twice, I had no knowledge of Ludlum's medical expertise. "Thank God," I said in little more than a whisper.

Celia gave my arm a reassuring squeeze, her expression equally grateful. "Thank God indeed, Sarah."

"Why don't you both take a seat while I inquire about his progress?" Charles nodded us toward two vacant seats by my parents. "It's late, so I'm not sure how much staff is on duty, but I'll do my best to bring back news."

Unfortunately, when my brother returned to the waiting room some twenty minutes later, he could report only that Dr. Ludlum was indeed performing the surgery, although no one would tell him how it was proceeding. He reassured us again that Samuel was in good hands, but I was disheartened to see the lines of worry still etched across his tense face.

We continued our desultory wait for another two hours. We had fallen into an apprehensive silence as the unbearably slow moments crawled by. Sometime around three o'clock in the morning, a man whom I took to be a physician stepped into the waiting room and we all sat up expectantly. The newcomer, however, passed by our little group and made his way over to the old man dozing in the chair opposite ours. He gently touched the man's bony shoulder to wake him, then bent to whisper something we couldn't hear. Bad news, it appeared, for the elderly gentleman's wrinkled face seemed to melt into itself, and his pale eyes glistened with tears. I glanced at my mother to find her staring at him, her expression a mix of sympathy and dread, surely wondering if it would soon be our turn to receive such appalling news.

Papa took my mother's hand in his and patted it reassuringly. "It's going to be all right," he told her softly. "You heard Charles. Our son is in capable hands."

Mama nodded bleakly but said nothing. Since she was normally reticent in public, I was surprised to see her lean her head on my father's shoulder and close her eyes. Celia met my gaze and managed a wan smile. My sister-in-law was the kindest and gentlest of women, and I knew she was doing her utmost to be strong for my parents' sakes. However, she could not entirely mask her own fears, and again I sensed the tears she was holding back by sheer force of will. I blinked hard to contain the flood threatening my own eyes and tried not to stare as the physician helped the elderly gentleman from the room.

Without the old man, the room seemed smaller somehow, and I had the irrational feeling that the walls were closing in on us. I scolded myself. Such imaginings were surely brought on by anxiety and fatigue. I could hear my father encouraging my mother to sleep, but this was beyond the power of any of us to achieve. I had never known time to pass so slowly.

Shortly before dawn I was surprised to see Sergeant George Lewis, Samuel's boxing partner and good friend on the San Francisco police force, standing in the waiting room door. He started forward, then hesitated as he took in our forlorn little group, including my silently weeping mother. I quickly stood and joined him in the outer hallway.

"How is he, Miss Sarah?" he asked without preamble. I knew

that George considered Samuel to be one of his best friends, and realized that he must be equally shocked by this senseless attack. "I've been told that he was shot in the left shoulder."

"Yes. Far too close to his heart. He's been in surgery for hours. We won't know his condition until we speak to the doctor."

George shook his head and sighed heavily. "I can't make any sense of this. Why would anyone want to shoot Samuel? You were with him when it happened?"

I nodded, then went on to briefly relate the events leading up to the shooting. As I spoke, he jotted details into a small notebook. At his request, I went on to list everyone who had been present at Mr. Remy's house for Oscar Wilde's talk.

I had just started to describe what I knew about Remy's neighbors on the Hill, when Dr. Ludlum, a short man in his mid-thirties, joined my family in the waiting room. He looked weary, but his dark eyes were clear and his step brisk. George and I followed him into the room.

Charles immediately stood, and the two physicians spoke quietly for several minutes. When my brother led his colleague over to us, I thought the furrow between his eyes looked less pronounced.

"Mother, Father, Celia, allow me to introduce my friend and colleague Dr. Thomas Ludlum, the surgeon who operated on Samuel. I believe you've already spoken to my sister, Sarah, Tom."

Before the doctor could answer, Mama asked him anxiously, "How is my son, Doctor?"

Dr. Ludlum smiled down at her, his eyes sensitive to her distress. "It was a difficult procedure, Mrs. Woolson, but your son is young and strong, factors which weigh heavily in his favor." He glanced at Charles, who gave a little nod. "I won't lie to you, Mrs. Woolson. Samuel has lost a great deal of blood. Whoever bound the wound most likely saved his life." He looked at me. "I understand that person was you, Miss Woolson."

I nodded but did not attempt to speak.

"I must also applaud your good sense in using your cloak to

cover your brother once you had staunched the bleeding," the doctor continued. "It is an unusually cold night, and he was in shock. May I inquire if you have had medical training?"

"No, I have not received formal training, Doctor." I smiled at Charles. "But I was blessed with a brother who ensured that his family were well versed in the basics."

"We are in your debt, Dr. Ludlum," Papa said, rising to shake the surgeon's hand. "Charles assured us that Samuel was in the best hands possible."

Ludlum's full face flushed. "That is high praise indeed, Judge Woolson, coming as it did from your son." He cleared his throat, his tone growing serious. "I must warn you that the worst may be yet to come. As I say, Samuel is in excellent health, but he is a long way from being out of the woods. He'll require steadfast care if he is to pull through this ordeal." He smiled at Charles. "It's far too early to predict when he'll be able to leave the hospital, but fortunately you have a most competent doctor in the house to monitor his recovery. Charles's presence will allow me to release your young son sooner than I might consider under different circumstances."

"Don't worry, Thomas," Charles told the physician, looking at Mama, and his wife, Celia. "I will be assisted by two of the finest nurses in the city." He adopted a cheerful smile that I suspected was mainly for Mama's benefit. "In fact, I don't doubt that my little brother will be spoiled beyond redemption by the time he has recovered."

Thankfully, it was not until early afternoon that my eldest brother, Frederick, and his stiff-backed wife, Henrietta, paid a visit to the hospital. I say "thankfully," since the couple was hardly likely to bring comfort and good cheer to any patient's bedside.

Papa and I had attempted in vain to talk my mother into going home and getting some rest after the long night's ordeal, but naturally we were wasting our breath. Indeed, she would leave Samuel's room only when Dr. Ludlum or one of the nurses inspected his wounds or changed his bedding. Celia did return to Rincon Hill to help her children's nanny, Mary Douglas, feed and tend to her three young charges, but even she promised to return to the hospital as soon as she could reasonably get away.

Despite Dr. Ludlum's encouraging words, it was a shock to see my brother's white face when they brought him into the room after surgery. He was so still that my heart practically stopped beating for fear that there was not enough blood left in his poor body to sustain life. From my mother's quick gasp, I knew the same dreadful thought had occurred to her. She watched helplessly as two male attendants, under the matron's supervision, settled him in bed. Then, as soon as they left, she approached the bed and lovingly rearranged the bedding to her motherly satisfaction. When she was certain that he was as comfortable as she could make him, she brushed the blond hair from his forehead, clucking in fearful, hushed tones about his damp, cold skin.

"His hands are like ice," she cried, and gently placed them beneath the covers. When she looked up, her eyes pleaded with my father for reassurance that their son was going to be all right.

Papa went to her side and placed his arm around her waist, allowing her to cry against his shoulder. "We can but put him in God's hands, Elizabeth," he told her softly. "Thankfully, we can rest assured that he is receiving the best care possible."

For the most part, Samuel passed the day in a deep sleep, moaning a few times when he half awoke, then drifting off again. I was pleased when, despite her anxiety, my mother finally dozed in a chair. Papa located a blanket and draped it across her shoulders, indicating with a nod that we should be quiet and leave her to get whatever rest was possible under the circumstances.

My father and I were half-asleep ourselves when Frederick and Henrietta unceremoniously arrived shortly after one o'clock that afternoon.

"Good Lord, how did a thing like this happen?" Frederick demanded, forgoing pleasantries as he marched into the room with a heavy tread and a face as dark as a thundercloud. He turned his outraged gaze onto me. "What tomfoolery have the two of you been up to this time?"

"I'd hardly call getting shot at by some homicidal maniac tomfoolery," I said, unable to control my temper at my eldest brother's insensitivity. "And for heaven's sake, be quiet. Mama is exhausted."

Naturally, my warning came too late. Mama jumped at Frederick's sharp voice and her eyes flew open as Papa reached out to prevent her from falling out of the chair.

"What is it?" she murmured, a bit dazed. "Oh, Frederick, it's you. And Henrietta. It was good of you both to come."

"Good afternoon, Mother, Father," Frederick said, kissing Mama lightly on the cheek. "You should be at home resting in your own bed." This time his eyes went to Papa. "It is unforgivable that Sarah and Samuel have caused you this grief."

Coming to stand beside her husband, Henrietta gave a loud sniff. "The story was on the front page of every newspaper in town this morning. Your name was mentioned as well, Father Woolson. Most distressing for a superior court judge."

My father's face suffused with anger. "Don't be idiotic, Henrietta," he snapped, surprising my sister-in-law with his sharp tone. Although he was outspoken by nature, Papa generally made at least a token attempt to treat Frederick's wife with civility. The events of the last twelve hours had obviously affected him more than he had let on. "Losing my son would have been distressing. Finding my name plastered in some rag sheet is no more than empty babble, picayune nonsense of no interest to me. Nor should it be to you."

Henrietta took a step back, her normally sallow cheeks coloring. She opened her mouth to speak but was forestalled by her husband.

"Really, Father, that is shortsighted of you," he blustered, his own face turning red. "You may consider the city's newspapers to be of little importance, but they are popularly read. Moreover, despite your disdain, the puerile public generally accepts the articles they contain at face value. When Sarah's or Samuel's name appears within those pages—as each has far too frequently over the past year—it reflects badly upon the entire family, and especially you in your role as a distinguished judge."

"And you in your role as a state senator," I added, far too furious over his callous behavior to police my remarks. "Our brother was shot, Frederick. Shot! Had the bullet entered his shoulder even a fraction of an inch lower, we might well have lost him. Yet you behave as if Samuel deliberately threw himself in the shooter's path for the sole purpose of causing you aggravation. Sometimes I think you forgot to pack your brain, much less your heart, if you've ever possessed one, when you moved to that mausoleum on Nob Hill."

My eldest brother drew himself up to his full height, his unfortunate jowls, which had become more pronounced of late, quivering like a bowl of Cook's gelatin. Before he could speak, however, our mother rose, took hold of his arm, and led him toward the door.

"I am sure you meant well by coming here, Frederick," she told him with unaccustomed resolve. "But as you see, your brother is seriously ill and cannot be disturbed. I think it would be best if you and Henrietta came back in a few days, when he is on the mend."

She stopped at the door, regarding the couple gravely. "And when you do return, Frederick, I expect you to behave civilly, and without flinging about hurtful recriminations. Sarah has been through quite enough without you and Henrietta adding to her distress." Without another word, she hustled her son and his wife out of the room, then closed the door firmly on their incredulous faces.

Before returning to her seat, Mama walked to the bed and gazed down at Samuel, who had blessedly slept through the entire event. Only when she had assured herself that he seemed peaceful, and in no pain, did she look up to realize that both her husband and her daughter were staring at her as if a stranger had somehow taken possession of her body. Mama's face colored, causing her to appear younger and more animated than she had since Samuel's attack.

"What is it? Why are the two of you looking at me like that?" She straightened her skirts and sank back onto her chair. "I apologize if my tone was sharp. It pains me to speak ill of my eldest son, but I fear that he occasionally behaves tactlessly, speaking before he fully considers the consequences. I simply cannot have Samuel disturbed in that way, nor you, Sarah."

Mama reached out a slim hand to pat my knee reassuringly. As she did, I spied fresh tears glistening in her eyes. "If not for you, my dear, Samuel might have—" She faltered, attempted to speak again, but seemed to have lost her voice.

Using his handkerchief, Papa gently wiped away the tears that were now rolling freely down her cheeks.

"I couldn't have dealt better with Frederick myself, Elizabeth," he told her with loving pride. "And I'm sure it made considerably more of an impression on him coming from you." He turned to me. "Sarah, would you please see if you can find your mother a glass of water?"

I nodded and left the room, still marveling that my mother had finally put my pompous brother in his place. I vowed to describe the scene in every detail to Samuel when he awoke. *If* he awoke, I thought, then immediately gave myself a mental shake. Not if, but *when* he awoke, I told myself defiantly. He would return to us, even if I had to pull him back from the gates of heaven myself!

Recalling my errand, I located the matron who had been attending Samuel. She was speaking to a young boy in the corridor, a street urchin, I guessed, from the way he was dressed. Hearing my approach, she turned to look at me, and I recognized the waif to be none other than my young cabbie friend Eddie Cooper. Cap in hand, he had obviously been doing his utmost to charm his way into the hospital. When he saw me, his thin face broke into a broad grin.

"Miss Sarah," he said, circling quickly around the surprised matron, "I've been trying to tell this lady that Mr. Samuel is my friend." When he saw my face, his smile vanished, and I realized that after all that had happened, I must look a sight. "I been real busy all day. Didn't find out what happened till I come to your office and Mrs. Goodman showed me the newspapers. I got here quick as I could. Do you know who done it? Is he . . . I mean—"

"He's resting," I told him, experiencing a pang of remorse. I should have sent word to him during the day, as well as to Fanny Goodman, the woman who ran the millinery shop situated below my office. Eddie idolized the ground Samuel walked upon, while Fanny had long since succumbed to my brother's considerable charms. It was unforgivable that they had had to learn of his attack in the newspapers. I had sent a note to my friend and colleague Robert Campbell, only to learn that he was out of town until this evening.

"We can't disturb him, Eddie," I said. "But if you'd like to take a quick peek in his room . . ."

His dirty face lit with relief. "Yes, ma'am, I'd like that a lot."

Ignoring the matron's frown of disapproval, I requested that she bring a glass of water to my mother, then led the lad down the hall and quietly opened Samuel's door. Mama and Papa looked up, startled to see Samuel's unexpected visitor, his brown eyes huge with fear.

"You remember Eddie Cooper," I told them quietly. "I told him it would be all right if he came in for just a few minutes to see Samuel."

My father looked none too pleased, but my mother instantly understood the boy's helpless expression. She rose from her chair and led Eddie to her son's bedside.

"He's just asleep, dear," she told the boy gently, causing me to marvel yet again at Mama's kind nature. In spite of all she had been through, she could still find a place in her heart for this distraught young boy.

If possible, Eddie's eyes had grown even larger, and he stared down at Samuel as if unsure that he truly was alive.

Mama put her arm around the lad's thin shoulders and gave them a little squeeze. "Sleep is the best way for the body to heal, Eddie. Tomorrow . . ." She swallowed, then managed a wan smile. "Tomorrow I'm certain he will be much improved. You must return then to visit."

"Yes, ma'am, I'll come back," Eddie told her, careful to keep his voice equally quiet. "Mr. Samuel's a real rip-staver. He's not gonna let a little bullet stop him. Not in a month of Sundays." He nodded politely to my parents, then turned and tiptoed toward the door. As if remembering something, he stopped. "Dang it all, Miss Sarah, I almost forgot. Mrs. Goodman said I was to give you a message."

I motioned the boy out into the hall. "What is it, Eddie?"

"She says a man and woman come to yer office this morning sayin' they wanted to see you right away. She told 'em to come back this afternoon, and wants to know if you'll be comin' in today."

"Did the couple leave their names? Or state the nature of their business?" I asked, surprised by this news. I had not been expecting any clients this morning, or anytime in the near future, for that matter. As usual, my law practice was perched precariously on the brink of financial disaster.

Eddie shook his head. "Mrs. Goodman only said they didn't look like no mudsills." At my bewildered expression, he added, "They weren't no tinkers. They got the money to pay yer fee, Miss Sarah," he finally explained, appearing a tad exasperated.

"Oh," I replied rather lamely. Just when I thought my knowledge of the vernacular was fairly comprehensive, Eddie once again broadened my education.

"So, kin I tell her yer gonna be comin' in this afternoon?"

I thought about this for a long moment. While I was loath to leave Samuel, there was little I could do here while he slept. I knew that he would be the first person to tell me not to squander the prospect of new clients, especially those with the wherewithal to pay.

I made up my mind. "Yes, Eddie," I told him, ignoring my weariness. "Give me a few minutes to inform my parents, then I would be grateful if you would drive me to Sutter Street."

CHAPTER THREE

Eddie reined to a stop in front of my office, assisted me out of the brougham, and then took off at his usual breakneck speed to catch as many fares as possible before the end of the day. Eddie was the eldest of four children. His sickly, overworked mother tended her brood as best she could—cursed as she was with a husband who drank away any money that came into his hands. Eddie did his best to keep his own slim wages out of his father's clutches, paying the rent himself and whenever possible purchasing the family's groceries. Any small cash that might be left over he kept stashed beneath a loose floorboard behind his cot. Despite these precautions, his drunken father had more than once waylaid him before he'd had an opportunity to hide his earnings, leaving the family with a threatening landlord and empty cupboards until the lad's next payday. Not for the first time, I heartily wished that my business were on a firm financial footing so that I might more adequately reimburse Eddie for his services.

I was still pondering the unfortunate plight of the Cooper family when I spied my downstairs neighbor, Fanny Goodman, standing just inside the entrance to her millinery store. Strands of gray hair had escaped her usually neat bun, and her eyes were red-rimmed from crying. At my approach, she rushed outside to pull me into her ample arms.

"Sarah, I'm so glad to see you," she exclaimed, giving me a ferocious hug, then pulling away far enough to study my face with an anxious expression. "How is poor Samuel? How badly was he hurt? Those horrible newspapers said next to nothing, only that Judge Horace Woolson's youngest son had been shot last night." She took my arm and tugged me inside her shop. "Come in, dear, please. I've been worried half out of my mind. Tell me how such an awful thing could have happened. There's a fresh pot of coffee on the stove."

"I'm so sorry, Fanny," I said, following her into the homey kitchen that was the heart of the small apartment behind her shop. "I should have sent you a message from the hospital. It was extremely thoughtless of me."

"Oh, but I don't blame you, dear, not for one moment," she said, looking abashed to think she might have given me such an impression. "It must have been horrible for you. My goodness, Sarah, you had far more important matters to think about than getting word to me." She pulled out a chair. "Sit down, dear. I want to hear every word of what happened, especially how that dear boy is doing. I'll just pour the coffee."

With a contented sigh, I took my usual seat at Fanny's small table. Being here always had a calming effect on my nerves; her kitchen was a peaceful refuge where I was treated as a beloved member of my friend's own family. A meticulously clean and pressed, if much mended, red-and-white cloth covered the table, and a simple spray of wildflowers, arranged in a preserves jar, had been placed in the center. Their homey colors, and the warmth from the woodstove, added to the tranquil atmosphere, as did the ever-present mouthwatering smells of home-baked confections emanating from Fanny's oven.

As she placed a cup of steaming coffee and a plate of shortbread cookies in front of me, I remembered Eddie's message.

"I hear that I had visitors this morning," I said, stirring cream and sugar into my cup. "Eddie said some people were here seeking my help. Do you know if they're coming back?"

"Good gracious," she exclaimed, taking a seat across from me at the table. "In all the excitement I completely forgot about them. It was a couple in their fifties, and they did seem eager to see you. I suggested they return here this afternoon at three o'clock."

I checked my timepiece. It was nearly two thirty. "It appears that I had arrived just in time."

"I wasn't sure if you would even be here, after what happened to Samuel." She stirred cream and sugar into her own coffee. "But they were nicely dressed and seemed well-off, so I hated to send them away. I know you need the business."

"I certainly do," I admitted. "Did they happen to mention the reason for their visit?"

"All they said was that their situation was a matter of some urgency." She gave a little harrumph. "Truth to tell, they were a bit uppity. You know the type, act as if they're just a little better than the rest of us ordinary folk. Not that they put it in so many words, mind you, but I understood well enough what they were thinking. Especially the wife."

"That's interesting." I sipped my coffee, thinking it was strange that people of that caliber would choose to see me at all, not when there were dozens of better-known law firms in town. Firms run by *male* attorneys.

As if reading my mind, Fanny smiled. "Like I said, I could tell right off that they weren't the sort to trust their business with a lowly shopkeeper." She pushed the cookie plate closer to me. "I'll wager you haven't had a bite to eat since Samuel was . . ." She hesitated, as if finding it impossible to put what had happened into words. "Eat up, Sarah. You've got to keep up your strength. And don't you mind about those two, you'll meet them soon enough. First, tell me about Samuel. I thought I would die when I saw the article this morning. Went right out and bought two more newspapers, but as usual none of them had any real details to report.

How is he doing? Where was he shot? Dear Lord, who could have done such a monstrous thing?"

"My goodness, Fanny," I protested. "I can only answer one question at a time."

"I'm sorry, Sarah, it's just that I've been so—"

"I know," I said. "I'm truly sorry you had to read about it in the newspapers."

"Never mind that, dear. Just tell me how the dear boy is doing. That's all that matters."

Briefly I described the events of the night before. "The doctor says the bullet missed any vital organs, but he lost a great deal of blood, and he's very weak. We hope to know more by this evening."

"But who could have shot him? And why?"

"I wish I knew," I answered grimly, a shiver sliding down my spine. I feared that the sight of my brother lying there so pale and still, with all that blood pouring from his chest, would be forever etched into my memory.

Fanny put a plump hand over mine. Not until I felt the warmth of her skin did I realize how cold my own flesh was.

"It must have been terrifying," she said, an expression of profound sympathy filling her eyes. "I swarn I don't know what this city is coming to. I just can't understand anyone wanting to hurt that dear boy. Do the police have any idea who was responsible?"

"Sergeant Lewis came to the hospital last night, but there was little I could tell him. We could see little beyond the light cast by our lantern as we made our way down the hill."

I started to tell her about Oscar Wilde's kindness in driving us to the hospital in his carriage, but I was interrupted by the sound of the bell atop the millinery shop door jingling, indicating that a customer had entered Fanny's store.

Both of us stood. "I'll tell you more later," I promised. "Thank you for the coffee. Perhaps it will help keep me awake when I meet with the couple who visited this morning. That is, if they return."

35

Once upstairs in my office, I had barely time to remove my wrap and settle down behind my cherrywood desk when there was a sharp knock on the door.

"Come in," I answered, rising and preparing to greet my visitors.

The door opened and a plump, tightly corseted woman entered my office. I heard a noisy yip as she stepped inside and was surprised to see that she was holding a tiny brown dog tucked against her ample bosom. I could make out little of the dog except for its face, but I doubt that I would have recognized the breed even if it had been in full view. I could, however, clearly make out two button-black eyes regarding me suspiciously from over the woman's left sleeve. Perhaps I imagined it, but the dog seemed to regard me with as much disapproval as did its mistress.

The woman appeared rather too formally attired for an afternoon call, wearing a gown of deep blue cashmere and satin merveilleux, which must have cost more money than I had earned since opening my law practice. Her matching blue hat was so large, and so overcrowded with feathers, ribbons, and stuffed wildlife, that it completely overwhelmed her sadly fleshy face.

Her most commanding—nay, unsettling—feature, however, were her steel-gray eyes, which, like her pet's, seemed to fasten on to me like a predator about to pounce on its prey. She looked me over with barely disguised disdain, her expression uncompromising in its implied superiority, as if I were hardly worth the effort of an acknowledgment.

A tall man with thinning hair and a wiry graying mustache followed in her wake, closing the door quietly behind him. Like the children's nursery rhyme "Jack Sprat," he was as thin as his wife was stout. His large brown eyes darted quickly about the room, then rested on me as I once again took my seat behind the desk. He made no move to advance farther into the room, as if unsure whether his wife would decide to stay.

The woman showed no such reserve. Marching over to my desk, she announced in a loud, commanding voice, "We are here to see Mr. S. L. Woolson. The shopkeeper downstairs said he would be available for consultation at three o'clock." She consulted the gold watch pinned to her shirtwaist and nodded, as if pleased to find the time to be exactly as it should be. "We were informed that Mr. Woolson's father is a noted San Francisco judge."

"That is correct," I told the woman courteously. "Horace Woolson is superior court judge for the county of San Francisco. However, I am the S. L. Woolson you are seeking."

The man gave a little start, blinking at me in surprise. "I beg your pardon?"

It seemed he was about to say more when his wife gave him a silencing look. She eyed me frostily. "If that is intended as a joke, it is not in the least humorous, young woman. Moreover, my husband and I are in no mood for levity." She stared pointedly at the door leading into the second room of my compact suite, which was currently utilized as a small law library and sitting room. "Will you kindly inform Mr. Woolson that Mr. and Mrs. Bernard Dinwitty are waiting to consult him on a matter of some importance."

"Mrs. Dinwitty," I said, making an effort to keep my voice gracious, "I assure you that I am the only attorney on these premises. My name is Sarah Woolson, and my father is the Judge Woolson you mentioned upon your arrival." I nodded to the two chairs positioned in front of my desk that I reserved for clients. "If you'd care to take a seat and tell me how I may—"

"A *female* attorney!" she exclaimed, looking aggrieved that I should make such an outlandish claim. "Well, I never. The woman downstairs referred to you once or twice as a woman, but since that was clearly impossible, I assumed she was addlebrained."

"Believe me, Mrs. Dinwitty, Fanny Goodman is anything but addlebrained." Sadly, I was all too accustomed to this reaction when people first learned of my profession—and it pained me to find that women were every bit as guilty of this prejudice as were men. "I am indeed a licensed attorney. In fact, I am one of three female lawyers currently practicing law in this state. Now if you will please tell me why you have come to my office, I'll—"

"That is out of the question!" Mrs. Dinwitty arched her back until it became so erect, I feared she might snap in two at the waist. After subjecting me to a final disdainful look—delivered down an unfortunately pudgy nose, which rather spoiled the effect—she made a move toward the door. "Come, Mr. Dinwitty. We shall go elsewhere." Once again, the little dog gave a loud yip, as if heartily endorsing its mistress's command.

Her husband, who had observed this exchange with a worried look on his long, thin face, finally came to life. Taking hold of her arm, he said, "Be reasonable, Celestia. There is nowhere else to go. We have exhausted the possibilities." Turning to me, he explained, "The truth is that my wife and I have already been to half a dozen law firms in the city. Every one of them has declined to represent our case. If you will permit, we would like to discuss this business with you."

"Mr. Dinwitty!" his wife protested, pulling her arm out of his grip and causing the dog to wriggle and whine its objection. "I'll have no truck with a woman who has the temerity to pawn herself off as an attorney. We have been cruelly misled by Mrs. Hardy."

"Mrs. Hardy?" I inquired, the name sounding a bell in my memory.

"Mrs. Jane Hardy," Mr. Dinwitty answered. "She claims to have made your acquaintance several months ago, in connection with a neighbor of hers whom you were representing."

"Ah, yes," I said, able now to put a face to the name. Jane Hardy was the kindly woman I had met during the case I have come to refer to as the Cliff House Strangler. She had generously offered sanctuary to one of my clients, who was being physically abused by her husband. Although I could not understand why Jane chose not to clarify the Dinwittys' misconception concerning my gender. "You say Mrs. Hardy suggested that you consult me? About what, may I ask?"

"That need not concern you," Mrs. Dinwitty said, moving toward the door. "We shall entrust this matter to a proper attorney."

"Please, Celestia, we are here now. We can at least describe the situation to Miss Woolson," Mr. Dinwitty implored.

Almost tentatively, he took his wife's arm and guided her to one of the chairs. Reluctantly, she complied, rearranging the dog against her protruding bosom until both of them were in a position to fix me with baleful eyes. Obviously relieved that she had allowed herself to be seated, the man sank his long frame into the second chair. He regarded me expectantly, but when I said nothing he seemed to realize that it was up to him to begin the conversation.

"My wife and I are members of the San Francisco Society for the Prevention of Cruelty to Animals," he said a bit self-consciously, as if not accustomed to taking control of a discussion when his wife was present. "You have perhaps heard of us?"

"I have indeed," I replied, aware that the much-needed group had been founded in the city some fourteen years earlier. "I am an admirer of the organization. It provides a valuable service to the community."

He smiled, looking pleased with this praise. "We like to think that we have made a difference in the lives of countless mistreated animals in San Francisco. Until our group was established, unscrupulous owners savagely beat their horses on these very streets. Not to mention the cruelty inflicted on dogs—"

His wife shifted in annoyance. "Oh, do get on with it, Mr. Dinwitty. If you insist on consulting with this . . . *woman*"—she shot me a distasteful look—"then by all means get to the point."

"Yes, my dear, quite right," he murmured, and cleared his throat. Regarding me with large, solemn eyes, which I realized somewhat humorously reminded me of the very dogs he was pledged to protect, he said, "When it became apparent that our society required legal representation, Mrs. Hardy, who is a volunteer member of our group, suggested we seek your services." Dropping his gaze, he once again cleared his throat. "She neglected to inform us that you were a woman."

"I see," I said, and waited patiently for him to go on.

He glanced at his wife, but when she stonily refused to return his look, he continued. "As I said, circumstances have left us with little choice but to consult an attorney."

"Yes?" I prompted. Would this man ever come to the point? On this matter, at least, I was forced to agree with Mrs. Dinwitty. "May I inquire the nature of these circumstances?"

Once again, the man shot his wife an imploring look. This time she made a disgusted sound and said, "Oh, for heaven's sake. It has recently come to our attention that a Mexican landowner is planning to build a bullring here in San Francisco. Our organization has vowed to fight the construction of this atrocity, and we are seeking legal representation to guide us in this endeavor."

I stared at the woman; surely I could not have heard her correctly. "Excuse me, Mrs. Dinwitty, did you say a *bullring*?"

"That is exactly what I said, Miss Woolson," she replied, her look indicating that she would be more than pleased to add the sin of stupidity to that of my having claimed to be an attorney.

"Actually, it would not be the first bullring to be housed in San Francisco," her husband put in. "Some forty years ago, a similar arena was erected opposite the Mission Dolores, where it remained until the early 1850s." He gave a wry smile. "One can only imagine the reaction of churchgoers as they departed Sunday services, to be subjected to such a drunken spectacle."

"I had no idea," I admitted, still trying to digest the astonishing notion that a bullring had ever been allowed to exist within the city of San Francisco. "And now you say that a group wants to erect a second bullring?"

"Unfortunately, that is true," he said, his long, angular face once again solemn. "We have it on good authority that City Hall is seriously considering approving the plan."

"This is the first time I've heard about such a project," I replied. "Certainly nothing has been written about it in the newspapers."

"No, you wouldn't have read about it in the papers," Mrs. Dinwitty put in, a sour expression pinching her thin lips. "The forces behind the plan have gone to great lengths to keep the nasty affair hidden behind closed doors. In fact, our organization first heard about it only last week. We have attempted to speak to Mr. Ruiz, but our efforts have been shamelessly thwarted."

"Mr. Ruiz?" I inquired.

"Ricardo Ruiz," Mr. Dinwitty explained. "He is the gentleman behind the scheme."

His wife gave him a disparaging look. "I would hardly call the brute a gentleman, Mr. Dinwitty. He is a crude, ruthless, arrogant Mexican."

Her gray eyes narrowed and glinted like tempered steel. "Unfortunately, although the man is dreadfully common, he comes from a family of vulgar, suspiciously obtained wealth. From what we have been able to ascertain, the Ruiz dynasty wields nearly absolute power in their native Mexico, including a disgraceful group of corrupt government officials. Ricardo Ruiz is using that ill-gained money to buy our own City Hall, in order to erect this temple dedicated to the worship of pagan atrocities." She gave a nod of self-satisfaction, as if pleased to have presented such an accurate and succinct account of the situation.

I found myself at an unusual loss for words. Although I could well understand the SPCA objecting to the construction of a bull-ring in the city, I was unnerved that Mrs. Dinwitty appeared more displeased by Ricardo Ruiz's ethnicity than by the cruelty the project would inflict on the poor bulls.

As if sensing the reason for my hesitation, Mr. Dinwitty hurried to explain, "What my wife means is that our group finds it incomprehensible that City Hall would approve a project which would result in the butchering of innocent animals." He patted her hand. "Isn't that right, my dear?"

His wife did not reply; she merely moved her arm out of his reach and rolled her eyes as if such a statement completely missed the point.

"You say that you've attempted to speak to Mr. Ruiz?" I asked, directing my question to Mr. Dinwitty.

"Yes, several times. As my wife mentioned, each time we try to see him we are subjected to a long, and frankly unsatisfactory, list of excuses why the man is unavailable to meet with us. All of them undoubtedly duplicitous."

"What about City Hall?" I asked. "Have you made inquiries there concerning Mr. Ruiz's project?"

Before her husband could respond, Celestia Dinwitty made a contemptuous gesture with her bejeweled hands. "Of course we have, although not surprisingly it has gotten us nowhere. It's obvious that you know little about the nature of politics, Miss Woolson, but our city government is composed of fools and lackeys who will sign their name to any scheme which will pad their own pockets."

"Celestia, please," protested her husband, regarding me in embarrassment. "Miss Woolson is an attorney. I'm sure she is accustomed to dealing with—"

"Don't be obtuse," his wife declared, cutting him off. "Just because a donkey calls itself a horse, that doesn't make it one." Abruptly, she rose from her chair, rearranged the dog in her arms, and motioned to her husband. "Come, Mr. Dinwitty, we have wasted more than enough of our valuable time here."

The poor man's face suffused with color, but he dutifully prepared to take his leave of my office.

"When it comes to your assessment of city government, Mrs. Dinwitty," I said calmly, "I'm inclined to agree with you. I'm sure there are many honest politicians, but I fear the few bad apples tend to ruin the barrel."

I rose from my seat and circled my desk. Clearly this meeting was over. Although I felt a profound sympathy for Mr. Dinwitty, and more than a little empathy for their cause, I had had my fill of his wife. If City Hall were truly committed to Ricardo Ruiz's planned bullring, I feared there was little the SPCA would be able to do to halt the proposed construction.

"I wish you well in finding satisfactory legal representation for your case," I told them civilly enough, although I doubted any law firm in town would take what appeared to be a hopeless case.

Ignoring Mrs. Dinwitty's derisive sniff, as well as her dog's menacing growl as I moved past her to open the door, I saw the couple firmly out of my office.

CHAPTER FOUR

After my meeting with the Dinwittys, I succumbed to a brief nap, then returned to St. Mary's Hospital shortly after eight o'clock that evening. My parents and Celia were keeping a quiet vigil by my sleeping brother's bedside when I arrived. Hoping to find that Samuel had awakened from the surgery, I was disheartened to learn that his condition had not improved since I'd left for my office that afternoon.

Papa, Celia, and I were trying to convince my mother that she should return home for a good night's sleep when we heard the sound of a booming voice loud enough to carry through my brother's open door. I would have recognized that Scottish burr anywhere: Robert Campbell had arrived!

A string of rolling *r*'s reached us several moments before my friend and colleague actually entered Samuel's room. Behind him marched the matron, her equally strident tones admonishing him to kindly lower his voice. Between the two of them, I daresay they had managed to arouse every patient on the floor.

"No one will tell me a bloody thing," Robert declared, glaring at the matron's retreating back. "What the blazes has happened to Samuel?" He came to an abrupt halt as he spied my mother and

44

Celia, his sunburned face turning an even darker shade of red at his unfortunate choice of language.

"That's what—I'd like to know," came a weak voice from the bed.

As one, five sets of eyes flew to my brother's bed. To our amazement, he was gazing at Robert, a bewildered expression on his pale face. His blue eyes were slightly unfocused and rimmed with dark circles, but thank God, they were open! Several locks of blond hair covered his damp forehead, and deep creases were etched between his brows. But as far as I was concerned, no angel in all the heavens was nearly as beautiful.

When he attempted to lift his head off the pillow, he gasped and winced in sudden pain. Mama and Celia instantly flew to his bedside.

"Don't try to move, dear," my mother told him, examining his bandages to ensure that the movement hadn't opened the wound.

"Yes, Samuel," Celia said, tears of relief coursing down her cheeks. "You must lie still." Gently, she plumped his pillow while my mother wiped the strands of hair off his brow.

"But what hap—" he again attempted, but couldn't find the breath to finish.

"You were injured, my darling," Mama told him, smiling at him through her tears. This time, happily, they were tears of joy. "But thank God, you're going to be all right—" Despite her obvious efforts to remain calm, her voice broke. "You had us all so worried."

Unable to move his head, my brother attempted as best he could to take in the group gathered around his bed. He looked very weak and still confused. "Where am I?"

"You're in the hospital, son," Papa told him, coming to stand next to my mother. "You were hurt last night, and Sarah brought you here, to St. Mary's."

If anything, this seemed to deepen Samuel's puzzlement. The two furrowed lines between his brows grew more pronounced as he fought to make sense of what had happened to him. "St. Mary's? But why?" With growing agitation, he again tried to raise his head.

"Shh," Mama soothed, lightly pushing his head back onto the pillow. "There's no need to talk about that now. Please, dear, you need your rest."

I couldn't resist a smile of relief when I saw that stubborn look come over my brother's wan face, the one I'd known so well since childhood. It would require more than Mama's determined coddling to overcome her youngest son's obstinacy. He turned his eyes on me. "Need to know—what happened. Sarah?"

I glanced at my father, who sighed, then gave a resigned nod of his head. "I suppose he'll refuse to rest until he knows. You might as well tell him, my girl."

"Finally," Robert said, drawing closer to the bed. "There are all sorts of crazy rumors circulating around town. One even claims you were mauled by a mountain lion!"

Despite the seriousness of the occasion, I found myself giggling at this. Dear Lord! I never giggled. Clapping a hand over my mouth, I looked at the others in chagrin. To my surprise, everyone except Robert—who clearly had no idea what he had said that was so amusing—was also smiling.

"Can't—remember much," my brother said haltingly, struggling with every breath he drew, "but—don't think it was a lion." His pleading eyes once again met mine.

Gently, I took a seat on the edge of Samuel's bed. Taking his hand, which was frighteningly cold, I said, "We attended a poetry reading at Mortimer Remy's house on Telegraph Hill last night, Samuel. We were making our way back down the hill when—"

I was interrupted as a tall, flamboyant figure swept into the room, followed by the protesting matron. I was surprised to recognize the newcomer as Oscar Wilde, outrageously decked out this evening in a purple velvet smoking jacket, matching turban, knee breeches, and black silk stockings.

"I tried to stop this—this man," the matron complained, eyeing Wilde's eccentric attire with obvious skepticism, "but he refused to be turned away. Claims he's a poet, or some such nonsense, as if that gives him the license to barge in wherever he pleases." She unhappily took in the five people already gathered around my brother's bed and gave a snort of annoyance. "No. Absolutely not! This will never do. This is a hospital, not a meeting hall. Mr. Woolson needs his rest."

"It's—all right," came my brother's weak voice.

The woman opened her mouth to argue, then suddenly realized that this comment had come from her patient. A gratified expression softened the stern lines of her face, and she elbowed her way to the bed, felt my brother's pulse, and examined his eyes.

"Well, that's better," she proclaimed, straightening his already perfectly arranged pillow and bedcovers. "I'll tell Dr. Ludlum you're awake."

With that, she hustled from the room, stopping only long enough to announce over her shoulder that she would give all of us exactly fifteen minutes to vacate the room. And that meant every one of us. Even the poet!

I turned from watching the matron's retreating back to find my parents eyeing Wilde with expressions ranging from astonishment to outright disbelief. Robert looked as if a wild peacock had pranced into the room and needed to be shooed straight out again. Before my outspoken friend could blurt out something we all might regret, I hastened to introduce my family and Robert to the newcomer.

"Everyone, this is Mr. Oscar Wilde, the Irish poet who addressed us last night at Mr. Remy's house. After Samuel's, er, injury, he kindly offered his carriage to transport him to the hospital. It is thanks to him that Samuel received such prompt medical care."

Wilde bowed with flowery courtesy, then reached for my mother's hand, bringing it to his lips for a decidedly overdramatic (to my mind, anyway) kiss. Mama's face turned pink, but I could tell that she was impressed by this gallant, if theatrical, gesture.

47

Papa's eyes lingered perhaps several moments longer than was polite on the Irishman's turban and then he held out his hand.

"My wife and I are in your debt, Mr. Wilde," he told him, his voice sincere despite any misgivings he might entertain about the headgear. "Your generosity may well have saved our son's life."

"Indeed, Mr. Wilde," my mother put in, her eyes once again filling with tears. "I hardly know how to thank you. If it hadn't been for your kindness, Samuel might have . . ."

I was surprised to see the poet's customary sardonic expression soften as my father placed his arm around Mama's shoulder, offering her a handkerchief and a gentle kiss on the cheek. Wilde appeared touched, if a bit uncomfortable, by this display of self-effacing affection.

Clearing his throat, he walked to my brother's bedside. "I am relieved to see you looking much improved, Mr. Woolson. I admit that I was more than a little concerned by your condition when I took my leave of the hospital last night—or should I say early this morning?" His gaze traveled around the room, stopping at me. "I heard stories about the American 'Wild West' before my departure from London, Miss Woolson, but I hardly credited them with any substance. I must say that your city has far exceeded my expectations. Is it common for ordinary citizens to be shot at of an evening?"

"It certainly is not," Robert said, taking umbrage at this remark. "For all the ridiculous rumors you've heard concerning what you term 'the Wild West,' San Francisco is as cultured and civilized a city as you'll find anywhere in your travels."

I regarded my friend in surprise. Robert had immigrated to San Francisco six years earlier from Edinburgh, Scotland, primarily to escape being constantly compared with his father, who was one of the country's premier trial attorneys. I assumed he bore some degree of fondness for his new home, but I had never before known him to defend it quite so vehemently.

Wilde gave him an apologetic little bow. "I am sorry if I have offended you . . . Mr. Campbell, was it? I meant no disrespect. Indeed, for the most part I have found your fair city to be most urbane. You must forgive me if I overreacted to Mr. Woolson's ordeal, but I confess that I have never before witnessed an actual shooting."

This apology did not completely mollify Robert, but at my father's look, he refrained from saying anything else, simply offering a curt nod of acknowledgment.

Always the peacemaker, Celia smiled at the poet, clearly deciding a change of subject was in order. "I understand you have been in our country three months now, Mr. Wilde. How are you enjoying America?"

"Actually, it has been most enlightening, Mrs. Woolson," he said, returning her smile. "When I was in Leadville, a mining town in the Rocky Mountains, I spoke of the early Florentines, and the town slept through it as though no crime had ever stained the ravines of their mountain home."

Celia's smile faltered just a bit as she attempted to understand this curious statement.

Oblivious to her dilemma, Wilde continued, "While I was there, I descended to the bottom of a silver mine in a pail. I, of course, remained true to my principle of being graceful even in a bucket."

Vaguely aware that this was meant to be amusing, Celia laughed a bit self-consciously. "I am happy to hear that you have been well received on your journey, Mr. Wilde. I have never left the state of California myself, but I've been told that visiting a strange country can be daunting."

"Ah, madam," the poet replied, "we really have everything in common with America nowadays except, of course, for the language."

Once again, Celia looked a bit baffled, while Papa blinked and Robert's face displayed renewed annoyance. Both, however, remained silent. Apparently satisfied that he had succinctly summed up his travels to date, Wilde turned back to Samuel.

"Now that I have seen for myself that you are on the road to recovery, I confess that the events of last night may turn out to be the highlight of my American tour." Wilde smiled as if struck by an idea. "In fact, I may immortalize this adventure in a book. I've long had the desire to write a novel. Indeed, Mr. Woolson, it may well be *I* who am in *your* debt."

Before any of us could find words to respond, Oscar Wilde bowed to the assemblage, and with a dramatic swirl of his oversize coat, he jauntily departed my brother's room.

Robert was the first to speak. "Good Lord, what a supercilious fop. And what a lot of dribble comes out of his mouth. I don't care if he's the finest poet in the world, he looks a complete buffoon who—"

He was cut off in midtirade as the matron returned to send everyone on their way. I crossed to the bed to bid good-bye to my brother, but during Wilde's leavetaking, he had once again lapsed into sleep. He still appeared far too pale for my liking, but at least he seemed to be resting more naturally now. I kissed him lightly on his forehead, then followed Celia and Robert to the door. After a few private moments with their sleeping son, Mama and Papa followed us out of the room.

Relieved to see my parents at last departing for home and, I trusted, some well-deserved rest, I was left alone with Robert. He was complaining that he still knew next to nothing about how Samuel had gotten himself shot and was demanding to hear the story. I led him into the room where we had spent so many long hours the night before. Once we were seated, I related the events of the previous evening, starting with the reading at Mortimer Remy's cottage and ending with Bruno Studds leading Wilde, Jonathan Aleric, Samuel, and me down the hill.

"That is the most bizarre story I've ever heard," he said when I had finished. "Why would anyone want to shoot your brother?"

"Those are my thoughts exactly," came a familiar voice.

Robert and I looked up to find Sergeant George Lewis, walking over to where we were seated.

"George," I exclaimed as both Robert and I rose from our chairs. "Is there any news on the shooter?"

Lewis motioned for us to resume our seats and then pulled over another chair for himself. He sank onto it wearily, and I wondered how much sleep he had been able to snatch since I'd seen him the night before. As one of Samuel's best friends, I could well imagine his determination to find the villain who had nearly taken his life.

George gave a sigh of frustration. "I wish I could report that I had news, Miss Sarah, but I'm afraid we're no closer to an answer than we were last night. We've questioned everyone who was at Mortimer Remy's house, and they all claim to have gone directly to their own homes after the poetry reading."

"What about the residents who live near the road leading down the hill?" I asked. "Perhaps one of them saw or heard something."

"We interviewed them as well," George said. "They all claim to have seen nothing out of the ordinary. Several people who live close to the Filbert Street Steps admit to hearing a gun go off, but it's not all that unusual on Telegraph Hill, so they thought nothing about it."

Robert gave a little snort. "Yet someone took a shot at Samuel. Do you know if he has any other acquaintances living there who might wish him harm, Sarah?"

I shook my head. "I don't know. A small colony of writers and artists live there, and Samuel knows most of them. But I can't imagine why they would want to see him dead." Just saying this awful word made my blood run cold, and once again I shuddered to think how close I'd come to losing my brother.

"I hoped to see him tonight to ask him those very questions," George put in. "But the matron was adamant that he'd had more than enough visitors for one day, and that he needed to rest."

"She's right, he does," I said. "At least he finally woke up this evening, if only for a short while."

George looked immensely relieved. "Thank God for that. I'm going to try to speak to him again tomorrow."

"Yes," I replied vaguely, distracted by a sudden thought. It must have been a sign of my shock that I hadn't considered the possibility earlier. "George, what if Samuel wasn't the intended target last night? Granted the moon had risen, but the trees along the path blocked out a good deal of the light. What if the shooter intended to hit someone else in our group?"

George sat up straighter in his chair, suddenly more alert than he had seemed only a moment ago.

Before he could reply, however, Robert exclaimed, "There you are, Lewis! That's a much more logical explanation. You need to change your focus and concentrate on the other individuals who were walking with Samuel. Sarah's right, I'm sure one of them was the intended target."

"That's not what I meant, Robert," I protested. "I only offered the idea as a possibility. It's just as likely that someone was shooting at a gray fox, or a possum, which I understand is not uncommon."

"Miss Sarah," George said, holding up a hand to prevent Robert from once again offering his opinion, "I know we've been over this before, but could you please tell me again exactly what happened on your way down the hill from Mr. Remy's house? You say Bruno Studds led you along the path." He consulted his ever-present notebook. "Let me see . . . he's Mrs. Katherine Montgomery's handyman, is that right?"

"Yes," I replied. "As I told you, despite the moon, the path was dark in places. Mr. Studds was in the lead, carrying his lantern. Mr. Wilde, Jonathan Aleric, Samuel, and I followed."

"Did the four of you walk in any particular order?" George asked. "Close your eyes and try to imagine it again for me, if you would. It's very important."

It was on my lips to snap at him for insulting my excellent memory when, to my surprise, I comprehended that I would be forced to do just that. Although I clearly remembered Samuel falling to the ground, the events leading up to the gunshot retort were a bit hazy. Obediently, I closed my eyes and attempted to bring to mind every step of that walk down the hill.

At length I said, "I am sure that Mr. Wilde was directly behind Mr. Studds. I recall his complaining of the hazardous going, and he seemed to scuttle as closely behind the handyman and his lantern as possible. Samuel and I followed, as did Jonathan Aleric, the author of *An Uncivil War* and publisher of the *Bay Area Express* newspaper."

"The three of you walked together?" Lewis asked, scribbling in his notebook. "In what order?"

"Let me see . . . I walked to Samuel's right, and Aleric to his left," I told him, confident now of my recollection.

"Good, that gives me a much clearer picture," George said, noting this in his book. "At what point did you hear the shot ring out, then?"

This memory required no hesitation. "The gun went off just before we reached the Filbert Street Steps," I told him with an involuntary shudder, then suddenly recalled a detail I'd forgotten until that very minute. "Wait, George, we had nearly reached the top landing of the steps when Mr. Aleric stumbled. I remember Samuel reaching down to help him. That's when we heard the gunshot, and my brother fell to the ground."

The two men silently considered this last piece of information. For my part, I chided myself for forgetting such a vital detail. I knew, of course, that witnesses to a crime all too frequently gave muddled accounts of what they had seen, but I had not expected my own memory to fail me in such a way.

"What do you know about Mr. Aleric?" George asked, breaking into these unhappy musings. "Is there any reason to believe he has enemies who might want to see him dead?"

Once again I was struck by my failure to think more clearly, especially when clarity was of such importance. Only now did I recall the hostility I'd witnessed between Aleric and Mortimer Remy.

"What is it, Sarah?" Robert demanded, watching me with narrowed blue-green eyes. "You're obviously chewing something over in that busy brain of yours."

I glanced at Lewis, who was also watching inquiringly, pencil poised above his notebook. "Yes, Miss Sarah," he urged quietly. "What is it you've remembered?"

Realizing I could not withhold such a potentially vital piece of information, I reluctantly described the animosity that existed between Mortimer Remy and Jonathan Aleric, along with the angry scene between them the night before.

"It's no secret the two men have a long-standing dislike of each other," I said, doing my best to put the feud in the proper perspective. The publisher of the *San Francisco Weekly* had been good to Samuel over the past five years, not only printing his articles, but also assigning him as an independent reporter to cover special crimes and other pieces that paid generously. Moreover, competition among the city's newspapers was hardly unusual. As far as I knew, no one had been killed over such rivalry.

"George, Samuel has known Mr. Remy for years," I went on. "He's always been treated fairly and with respect. Neither my brother nor I have ever known him to be a violent man. Quite the contrary."

"Tell me, Miss Sarah," George said, refusing to be sidetracked by my assessment of the publisher, "why didn't Mr. Remy see his own guests down the hill? How did it happen that Mrs. Montgomery's man led you instead?"

"Mr. Remy was suffering from a toothache," I told him. "Mrs. Montgomery realized that he was in pain, and insisted that he remain in his cottage and treat it. She volunteered Mr. Studds to show us the way with his lantern."

"That would give Remy a good excuse to stay behind and take a shot at Aleric," Robert put in, much to my dismay. "The lantern probably provided him with a good target."

I shot Robert an angry look. "Pay no attention to him, George. That's a wild theory at best. Mortimer couldn't know ahead of time that Mrs. Montgomery would notice his toothache or, even if she did, that she'd offer her man to escort us down the hill."

George did not immediately reply as he scribbled busily in his notebook. "That's as may be, Miss Sarah," he said, closing the pad. Absently he pushed back the lock of brown hair that habitually fell across his forehead, giving him the appearance of a man younger than his thirty-two years. "But Mr. Campbell makes a good point. As I see it, either the shooter was aiming at a fox, or some other small animal, and the shot went wild, or he intentionally aimed at Samuel or Jonathan Aleric. You indicated that Bruno Studds and Oscar Wilde were walking in front of you, so in order to hit one of them, he would have had to shoot through the three of you, which would have been risky. I'm assuming, of course, that the bullet came from the grove of trees to the rear. Because of the way the bullet entered Samuel's chest, he could not have been shot from down the hill, and there was little cover to either side of the grade."

Robert, who had been listening attentively to George's reconstruction of the crime, rose to his feet in obvious agitation.

"Wait a minute! We've been assuming that Samuel or Aleric was the intended victim. But what if the shooter was aiming at Sarah? She was standing as close to Samuel as was this Aleric fellow." He looked at me in horror. "Good God, Sarah, who have you annoyed sufficiently enough that they might want to see you dead?"

"Oh, for heaven's sake, Robert," I exclaimed. "That's ridiculous. Why would anyone want to shoot me?"

I looked to George for support, only to find him shaking his head thoughtfully. "I don't know, Miss Sarah. As unlikely as it seems, we must take all possibilities into consideration. Unless it really was a shot gone wild, we must assume that Samuel, Aleric, or yes, even you, were the intended victim."

I rose to my feet, refusing even to discuss such a nonsensical idea. "Don't be foolish, George. There is a potential killer on the loose. You can ill afford to waste your time on absurd speculation!"

"Sarah, sit down, and for once stop being so dashed stubborn," Robert said. "You just told us that Mortimer Remy wouldn't hurt a fly, even if he can't stand the sight of Aleric. And you can't name a single person who might want to murder Samuel. So, who is left?"

I was spared having to come up with a rejoinder when a short, tubby little man came through the hospital's front door. He started across the lobby, then spied Robert, George, and me talking in the waiting room.

Oh, no, I thought in dismay. It was that pesky reporter Ozzie Foldger. I required no crystal ball to know why he was here.

"Aha, Miss Woolson, what a stroke of luck finding you here," he said, whipping out his notebook and pencil as he walked toward our little group. "I tried to see your brother this afternoon, but some bear of a nurse refused to let me in."

For a moment, I was tempted to simply ignore him and walk out of the hospital. But of course that would be cowardly and in the end would solve nothing. Better to face him now and be done with it.

"You were sent away on doctor's orders, Mr. Foldger," I told him, doing my best to keep my voice civil. A hospital was hardly the place to tell the irksome reporter what I thought of him. "Samuel is far too ill to see you, of all people."

Foldger gave me an ingratiating smile as false as his words, and I felt my hackles rise. The man was no better than a troublesome toad, and I had yet to forgive him for writing a number of disparaging articles about me several months ago, as I sought to bring the Rincon Hill murderer to justice. Naturally, my actions during that case had been completely justified, considering that a ruthless killer was terrorizing our quiet San Francisco neighborhood. However, the nasty little reporter had twisted my motives, generating a spate of disagreeable publicity not only for me, but for my entire family. My brother Frederick was still complaining about Foldger's disclosure that I had paid several visits to one of the city's high-end brothels. Frederick claimed that these inflammatory stories were weakening his credibility as California's newest state senator, an assertion I found laughable. As far as I was concerned, my eldest brother required no outside help to weaken his credibility.

Beside me, Robert took a step closer to the reporter, fists clenched at his sides. At well over six feet tall, he towered over Foldger.

"Even when Samuel recovers, you'll be the last man in this city he'll want to speak to," he snapped.

Foldger flinched as he stared up at the muscular Scot, but he was nothing if not persistent. "You misunderstand me, Mr. Campbell," he said in that irritatingly saccharine tone he employed when he was after a story. "I wouldn't dream of disturbing Mr. Woolson. I simply wish to verify one or two facts about the incident."

Robert snorted. "And why would you want to do that? You wouldn't recognize a fact if it hit you square in the face."

Foldger opened his mouth to retort, then seemed to think better of it. Turning his back on Robert, he tried the same smile on George Lewis. "Sergeant, you're in charge of the case. Surely you can spare me a few minutes of your valuable time."

I gave George a meaningful glance, which Foldger caught, but the policeman required no prompting. He cared no more for the little weasel than did Samuel or I.

"The matter is under investigation, Mr. Foldger," George told him. "I have no information to give you at this time."

Foldger shot me a glaring look, all pretense of affability now gone from his sharp face. "Dad-blast it!" he spat. "You Woolsons think you're the biggest toads in the puddle. But I'll fix your flint, just see if I don't."

"Watch your language, Foldger," Robert exclaimed, somewhat ironically, I thought, considering his own fondness for expletives. "There's a lady present."

The reporter looked me over derisively. "Ha! That's a rich one. No *lady* snoops around like a bloodhound, poking her nose into men's affairs. And she sure as hell doesn't visit brothels and befriend strumpets."

George gasped and took a step toward the little man, but Robert reached him first. He grabbed the scruff of Foldger's collar with one large hand and pulled him nearly off his feet.

"Listen to me, you little guttersnipe," my colleague hissed. "You aren't good enough to polish this lady's shoes. Miss Woolson's methods may not always be conventional, but she's done more to help the poor and downtrodden citizens of this city than you could do if you lived to be a hundred." Abruptly, he released the reporter, giving him a hard push toward the door. "Now get out of here. And don't come back!"

Foldger stumbled and nearly fell before catching his balance. "You may have won this time, Campbell," he snarled when he was safely out of my colleague's reach. He looked defiantly at each of us in turn. "But upon my oath, I'll get answers about this shooting one way or the other!"

Before any of us could react to this threat, Foldger was out the door and disappearing into the night.

CHAPTER FIVE

By a stroke of luck, Eddie was just reining up in front of the hospital as Robert, George, and I came out onto the street. The boy hardly brought his dappled-gray to a stop before hopping off his seat like a jack-in-the-box.

"How is he, Miss Sarah?" he asked, his expression creased with worry. "I came here right after my last fare. Ken I go in and see him? Mr. Samuel, I mean?"

"I'm sorry, Eddie," I told the boy, regretting that he had been unable to arrive earlier. Though even if he had, the stolid matron who guarded my brother like an avenging angel would undoubtedly have forestalled yet another visitor to the already crowded room. Especially, I thought, this ragamuffin of a boy. "Samuel is resting now, and no one is allowed in," I went on. "But he did awaken earlier, which is a very good sign."

Eddie heaved a sigh of relief. "I'm mighty glad to hear that, Miss Sarah. He didn't look none too good when I seen him last night." Such had been his apprehension that he appeared to notice the men for the first time. He nodded a brief hello to Robert and then focused intense brown eyes on George. "Have you caught the bloke what shot Mr. Samuel yet?"

I shuddered at the boy's massacre of the English language, but before I could correct it, George answered. "Not yet, son, but we're sure to find the man soon."

"They oughta have a necktie sociable and string the rounder up, that's what they should do," Eddie proclaimed, his eyes blazing. "That bast—" He shot me a sheepish look. "I mean, that blasted idiot blame near killed Mr. Samuel."

"Eddie!" I exclaimed, horrified that he would espouse such an unlawful act, particularly in front of a police officer.

"Don't be too hard on him, Sarah," Robert said, laying a hand on the boy's shoulder. "He's very fond of Samuel, and it certainly was a close thing. The shooting has shocked us all."

Eddie, who perhaps because of Robert's imposing size and abrupt demeanor invariably treated him with wary respect, beamed up at his benefactor. "That's right, Mr. Campbell. I surely thought he was a goner. The sooner the leatherheads catch the ornery devil, the better."

Good heavens! Before I could berate the boy for uttering such profanities, George inquired whether we would be kind enough to drop him off at the police station before Eddie took us to our own homes. Naturally, I was happy to oblige, and the three of us were soon seated in the brougham.

I was amused to note that having a policeman as a passenger aboard his carriage was accomplishing what Samuel, Robert, and I had tried unsuccessfully to achieve for over a year: Eddie was actually driving at a moderately sedate speed. We even took the first turn on all four wheels. Amazing!

Once we had dropped George off at the station, Robert turned in his seat to face me, his expression too grave for my liking.

"This has got to stop," he began without preamble, indeed without my having the least idea of what he was going on about.

My face must have reflected my confusion, for he continued solemnly, "You might have been killed, Sarah. That could be you lying in that hospital instead of Samuel. Or worse," he went on, his voice breaking slightly, "you could be lying in a pine box."

For a moment, I could think of nothing to say. The first words that came to mind were overly harsh. I could see that he was serious. He truly feared for my life, and I was touched, even if such fears were unfounded.

"Robert, don't you think you're overreacting? I'm perfectly fine, after all."

"Yes, but another few inches and that bullet could have hit you." An uncomfortable silence stretched into several minutes. "I don't know what I would do if anything happened to you, Sarah," he said at length, his voice so soft that I had to strain to hear him over the noise of traffic outside. Once again I was at a loss for words, wondering if I had even heard him correctly.

"Sarah?"

"Robert, I—I don't know what to say," I answered uneasily.

"You need say nothing." Underlying his words I detected embarrassment, as if he had said more than he'd intended. "Just promise me that you'll be careful. I know you too well. You can leave no mystery unsolved, no questions unanswered, even if it puts your life in danger. And now with Samuel injured, I'm afraid you'll stop at nothing until this villain is caught."

He reached out to take my hand in his. "Please, my dear, leave this matter to the police. You heard Lewis, they're doing everything possible to locate that madman. There's no need for you to become involved."

This surprised me. "I've said nothing about becoming involved, Robert. I have my doubts about the police department in general, but I'm sure George is doing his best to find the shooter." I hesitated, not wanting to make a promise I might not be able to keep. "On the other hand, I cannot turn a blind eye, or ear, for that matter, to any information that should come my way."

He dropped my hand as if it had suddenly caught on fire. "I knew it! You have every intention of getting involved in this."

I felt my temper rising. "I said I could not ignore any evidence I should happen upon. And neither should you. It is every citizen's duty to aid the police in their inquiries."

"Every citizen's duty—!" He broke off as if too angry to go on. His eyes were reflected briefly in the light of a lamppost, the deep blue-green color appearing nearly black as we quickly passed back into darkness. "If your behavior weren't so bloody dangerous, I'd laugh at such an absurd statement. Ugh!" he exclaimed, sliding hard against me as our carriage took a sharp right onto Pine Street. Now that we were alone in the brougham, the lad was back to his hair-raising two-wheel turns.

"You worry too much, Robert," I told him, mildly annoyed that he remained pressed against me instead of moving back to his own place on the seat. I decided it was time to change the subject and told him about the visitors to my office that afternoon.

"A bullring!" he exclaimed. He was regarding me as if I were pulling his leg. "In San Francisco?"

"Yes, outrageous, isn't it? According to Mr. Dinwitty, it would not be the first structure of its kind in the city. He says one stood across from the Mission Dolores in the 1840s and early '50s."

"But that was over thirty years ago, when San Francisco was little more than an oversized mining town. Surely City Hall would never allow such a barbaric scheme today."

"That's what I thought after learning of the plan. But according to the Dinwittys, Ricardo Ruiz has most of the city council in his pocket. Evidently he comes from an old and very wealthy Mexican family."

"Even so," Robert protested, "no one would sell him the land needed for such a structure."

"He already owns the land, I'm afraid. I'm not entirely sure what structures occupy the property now, but I gather Ruiz has no problem tearing everything down."

"It's insanity," he proclaimed. "Why haven't I heard of this scheme before now? You'd think it would be plastered on the front page of every newspaper in town."

"The Dinwittys said that Ruiz and his associates have gone to a great deal of trouble to keep the matter a secret. Now that the SPCA has learned of the proposal, though, I'm sure it will soon become public knowledge."

"Don't take this the wrong way, Sarah, but why did those people come to you? There are many prominent firms in town, with far more influence than you possess when it comes to City Hall."

"I appreciate your high opinion of me," I said dryly.

He sputtered an apology, but I cut him off. "Never mind, I know exactly what you mean. As it turns out, the Dinwittys have already visited a number of larger firms. They were turned down by one and all. I presume no one is willing to take on city government."

He shook his head. "This is bizarre. I cannot imagine a bull-ring being constructed in the center of San Francisco."

"Neither can I, Robert," I agreed. "Neither can I."

After spending the morning with Samuel, Celia, and my mother at the hospital the next day, I arrived at my office in the early afternoon. There were some odds and ends I wished to attend to before Robert and Eddie arrived to return with me to the hospital. I had hardly settled behind my desk, however, when there was a knock at the door.

"Come in," I replied, wondering who it could be. I was expecting no visitors, although the idea that it might be a new client was a welcome thought.

I left off further speculation when a darkly handsome gentleman entered the room. He appeared to be in his mid-thirties and was obviously of Latin heritage. He was dressed impeccably in dark brown trousers and a tan day coat, with a colorful cravat tied flamboyantly about his neck. He was nearly six feet, I judged, and was possessed of a slender but well-toned build. His curly black hair was unfashionably long but neatly combed and worn beneath a stylish top hat.

After little more than a cursory inspection of these details, however, I was drawn to the man's eyes: they were very dark and intense, and heavily framed by long black lashes. His eyebrows were thick and gently arched, his nose slightly hooked, which gave it a roguish look and prevented it from appearing too feminine. His lips were well shaped and full; indeed, I blush to say this, but the only term that seemed adequately to describe them was "sensual."

But my gaze kept returning to his eyes. They were intelligent and almost disconcertingly piercing. Good Lord, I thought with an involuntary little chill, my visitor was altogether too handsome for his own good. And dangerous? I wondered, although I wasn't sure why that thought should have entered my mind.

As I was examining him, he was looking boldly about my office, as if judging whether or not my rooms were up to his standards. He then took a long moment to subject me to the same rude scrutiny, after which he nodded, turned his head, and called out something in rapid Spanish. Immediately, two more men followed him into my office, closing the door behind them.

Still regarding me speculatively, the impertinent fellow finally removed his hat, performed a stiff little bow, and said in a precise, if accented, voice, "*Buenos días, señorita*. I am Ricardo Ruiz. You have heard of me?"

Perhaps it was because I was put off by his haughty manner, but I found myself loath to admit that I had indeed heard of him, in fact only the day before. And since he was standing here in my office, I assumed he must already know my name.

Instead of answering his question, I adopted my most professional air and inquired, "How may I help you, Señor Ruiz?"

If anything, the man drew himself up even straighter, trying, but not quite succeeding, to hide his annoyance that I refused to play his little game. Almost insolently, his all-too-direct eyes raked me over.

"Señorita Sarah Woolson? But you are *una mujer bella*! I must ask myself why a lovely young woman like yourself would make

64

a claim so *imposible*. An attorney, of all *idiocies*! When I was informed of this, I vowed to see for myself. Now that I behold your beauty, I find the charade even more *atroz*."

With a great deal of effort, I reined in my temper. Ignoring this chauvinistic folderol, I said with measured courtesy, "You are correct, I am Miss Woolson. However, I do not merely *claim* to be a lawyer, Señor Ruiz. I am, in point of fact, a licensed attorney in the state of California."

"Ah," he said, raising one dark eyebrow. He did not bother to hide a smile. I did not bother to hide my annoyance.

From beneath those long black lashes, his eyes burned into mine. I was certain that this practiced look was calculated to turn my emotions into mush, as they undoubtedly had many women before me. I am ashamed to admit to experiencing a small flutter in my bosom. Despite my body's involuntary betrayal, however, I succeeded in keeping my face impassive.

"What may I do for you, Señor Ruiz?" I once more inquired levelly.

His full lips curved into a suggestive smile, causing me to instantly regret my choice of words.

"*Sí*, but I understand, señorita," he purred, his velvety voice encircling me with an uncomfortable wave of heat. He leaned across my desk until his face was but a few inches from my own. His eyes glistened, and up close I noticed a small white scar that ran from his left temple nearly to his patrician nose.

"It is but a silly game you play until such time as you are married, is that not correct, señorita? To amuse yourself?" He shook his head, making a little clicking sound with his tongue as if to indicate that I was behaving like a naughty little girl. Again, he gave me that syrupy smile. "You modern American women. In Mexico such a thing would be unheard of."

"What may I do for you, Señor Ruiz?" I repeated for the third time, not bothering to hide my impatience. I was growing weary of the taunts and skepticism I had experienced since becoming an attorney. Occasionally, I was forced to ignore these gibes due to professional considerations. This was not one of those times, especially not when they issued from a man who obviously expected me to flutter my eyes and swoon over him with desire.

"I presume you have come to discuss the bullring you are planning to construct here in San Francisco, señor," I said matter-of-factly. I moved as far back in my chair as was possible, to allow more space between our faces. "If so, I have no interest in debating its merits or its obvious shortcomings with you."

"Ah, you come directly to the point, señorita," he said, appearing not the least put off by my stern tone. "And I see that you are also well-informed." He gave a little sigh, as if finally resigned to the fact that I did indeed possess all the unfortunate characteristics of the American woman. "Yes, you speak your mind. I have heard that said of you. On the other hand, I have also been told that you are a fair woman. The Dinwittys will have given you their opinion of my plan. But I said to myself, surely this independent Señorita Woolson will be willing to hear my side of the undertaking—if only for the sake of justice."

"Since I am not representing Mr. and Mrs. Dinwitty, I fail to see how justice comes into it, Señor Ruiz. I suggest you discuss this matter with the attorneys they have engaged."

I pulled some paperwork from my desk drawer—the month's budget, which I had been studiously attempting to avoid—and laid out the ledger before me as if it revealed something other than the unhappy fact that my practice was losing money.

I looked back up at him when he didn't move. "I'm sorry, Señor Ruiz"—a last vestige of courtesy prompted me to utter this untruth—"but I'm afraid there is nothing I can do to help you."

To my intense annoyance, he flicked his hand over the seat of one of the chairs in front of my desk, as if brushing aside invisible flecks of dust; then, uninvited, he took a seat. Without being told, his two men shifted their positions until they stood facing us, backs against the opposite wall.

Ruiz reclined in his chair and crossed one immaculately pressed trouser leg over the other, regarding me with that same frank appraisal. His demeanor was that of a man confident that he was in charge of the interview, not the other way around. And in my own office!

"In that regard you are incorrect, Señorita Woolson. As a matter of fact, I look forward to spending a great deal of time discussing this matter with you. My people are rarely wrong, and they tell me that you will soon receive a second visit from the Dinwittys. This time they will come with the intention of offering you the position as their attorney."

I regarded him in surprise. "How can you, or your *people,* possibly claim to know Mr. and Mrs. Dinwitty's plans?" I demanded. "They seemed intent on finding other representation. However, even if they did hire me to represent their case, what leads you to believe I would discuss the matter with you?"

Again that smile, an expression I was rapidly coming to abhor. Short of outright insolence, I wondered how I might get this arrogant man, and his two overmuscled guards, out of my office.

"Oh, I think you will be more than eager to go over the finer points of the project with me, my dear Señorita Woolson. You are a native of this city, are you not?"

"Yes, I am, but I fail to see—"

"Then as a daughter of San Francisco, you must understand that this project will bring a great deal of money into the city coffers."

"In view of the violence which will take place in your arena, I am hardly concerned with the question of profit, no matter how large that might prove to be."

"I see you are also a woman of principle, señorita," he said. "In fact, it is that very quality which will endear you to my cause. Your dealings with the Chinese are very well-known, you see."

"The Chinese?" I said, now totally confused. "What do the Chinese have to do with your plans for constructing a bullring in our city?"

"As I say, you are well-known for being a fair woman," he replied. "That lack of prejudice extends to women and individuals of other races, as demonstrated by the Chinese cook charged with murder you defended in court last year. Just before Christmas, I understand you represented two young Chinese boys also accused of murder. And of course there are your dealings with the powerful tong leader Li Ying." He made a tower with his long fingers. "Yes, I would say your reputation for protecting the oppressed is richly deserved."

I did my best to hide my astonishment that he knew so much about my professional and personal activities. Li Ying in particular would be considerably annoyed to discover that our dealings— indeed, our friendship—had been so well documented.

"Clearly the sources you referred to earlier have been actively engaged in prying into my affairs," I said with acerbity. "However, I cannot imagine what my past cases can have to do with your project."

He rested his chin against the steeple he had constructed with his fingers, as if considering his words carefully. "Are you aware, Miss Woolson, that San Francisco's SPCA is not the only group contesting my bullring?" When I did not reply, he went on, "I thought not. Perhaps you would be interested to learn that Denis Kearney and his band of sandlotters are violently opposed to the construction."

This took me by surprise. Ruiz was referring to the leader of California's Workingmen's Party. During the 1870s, Denis Kearney had called for the expulsion of Chinese immigrants from the country, arguing that they were willing to work for lower wages, thereby taking jobs away from Americans. He was one of the leaders of a mob that attacked and set fire to a number of Chinese immigrants living in tents. I admit I held Mr. Kearney and his cohorts, now generally referred to as "sandlotters," in utter disdain.

Mr. Ruiz smiled. "I see that I have touched upon a tender nerve, señorita. So you have heard of the man."

"Yes, Mr. Ruiz, I have." Of course Kearney would be against any project proposed by a Mexican, I thought, although his opposition would have nothing to do with the poor animals that would be killed in the man's bullring. "However, I believe you will find that Mr. Kearney is no longer the political force he was in the seventies."

"Ah, but there you would be surprised," he said, seemingly pleased to have an opportunity to further my political education. "Mr. Kearney may not wield the same power that he did during the past decade, that is true. But I assure you that he remains active behind the political scene. He still has the ability to inflame men against members of what he considers to be inferior races." His face hardened. "Even people who held land in California for a great many years before he entered this country. Long ago, my father purchased thousands of acres of land in southern California. As it happened, he also came into possession of a more modest holding here in your fair city. It is upon this land that I will erect my grand *corrida de toros*. I assure you, I will not permit Denis Kearney to obstruct my plans."

I was at a loss for words. What Ruiz said was true. Kearney was a bigot who had been responsible for a great deal of anger and dissension in the city. However, despite my dislike for the man, Ruiz was mistaken if he thought that Kearney's opposition would be sufficient incentive for me to support his project.

"I'm sorry to hear that Mr. Kearney is continuing to cause trouble, Señor Ruiz. Despite that, it's impossible for me to muster sympathy for an arena which will be dedicated to the slaughter of defenseless animals."

My visitor scoffed. "That is utter nonsense, a rank debasement of our national sport. You eat meat, do you not, señorita? Do you imagine that the cows and pigs that provide you with their flesh obligingly hop onto the butcher's block when you or your countrymen desire a steak or pork chops? Of course not. All over the world animals are slaughtered for food, many of them far more painfully than are our bulls."

"That may be true, but they are not slaughtered to provide entertainment for a crowd of bloodthirsty spectators," I retorted. "And I would hardly call it 'sport' when the poor bull has no

69

chance to survive, but is doomed to a painful death before he ever enters the ring."

"But señorita, you miss the point. *Corrida de toros* has been an honored tradition in Mexico for over three hundred and fifty years. In Spain, it has flourished for thousands of years. It is part of our culture, a graceful ballet, a dance with death, if you will, measuring the courage and heart of the matador."

"I very much doubt that the bulls enjoy their role in the dance, señor," I replied. "Quite frankly, it—"

I was interrupted when my office door flew open and Robert stepped into the room, as usual without bothering to knock. He stopped short at the sight of my visitors.

"What in blazes?" he exclaimed as Ruiz's two companions moved in to flank him on either side. "Sarah—Miss Woolson, who are these men?"

At my colleague's abrupt entrance, I had risen from my chair. "Mr. Campbell, this is Señor Ricardo Ruiz. Señor Ruiz, may I present Mr. Robert Campbell, who is also an attorney. I cannot introduce Señor Ruiz's friends, since I have not been told their names. But that hardly matters since they were all about to leave."

To my surprise, Ruiz did not stand as I performed these introductions. Taking note of this, Robert turned to me as if seeking an explanation for such rude behavior. Finally, almost languidly, Ruiz rose from his chair and reached out his hand.

"A pleasure to meet you, Mr. Campbell," he said with a lazy smile.

"Señor Ruiz," Robert replied, barely returning the handshake. He regarded the Mexican suspiciously, obviously sensing the tension in the room but not comprehending its meaning.

"We will take our leave, Señorita Woolson," Ruiz said. Without warning, he took my hand and brought it to his lips. His eyes never left mine as he executed a formal bow and leisurely kissed my fingers. Even when he straightened, he did not release my hand until I pulled it free with a little tug. "Ah, yes, you are far too *en-*

cantadora to make your way in a man's world, señorita. I beg you to consider carefully the matter we discussed."

"And what matter is that?" Robert demanded, glaring at the man. "What business do you have with Miss Woolson? Legitimate business, that is."

"Please, Robert, it's nothing," I told him, anxious to have Ruiz and his companions out of my office before my colleague exploded.

Ruiz gave me an unperturbed smile, donned his hat, and started for the door. "Until we meet again, señorita."

Robert opened his mouth to respond to this remark, but I poked him in the side with my elbow. By the time he finished glaring at me, Ruiz and his two *compañeros* were out the door, closing it sharply behind them.

"What in God's name was that all about?" he demanded, appearing all too ready to follow the men out onto the street. "That Ruiz fellow was damnably rude!"

"Do calm down, Robert," I told him, walking around the desk to collect my cloak. "Is Eddie outside? If so, we should leave for the hospital. I promised him he could see Samuel this evening."

"But that loutish man was—I mean, he seemed to be devouring you with his—" He sputtered to a stop, either unwilling or unable to find words to express his feelings. "Don't tell me you didn't notice the way he was looking at you!"

"It was all a ploy to get me to support his bullring, that's all," I said, deliberately making light of what I, too, considered boorish behavior. "And it failed to work, so there's an end to it."

He looked at me in surprise, then laughed. "That's the man with the ridiculous plan to build a bullfighting arena in the city? Ha! Then he truly is a fool."

"It may be a foolish idea," I agreed, "but according to Mr. and Mrs. Dinwitty, City Hall is close to allowing the construction to go forward. Come, let's not keep Eddie waiting."

Robert, Eddie, and I spent a pleasant hour visiting with Samuel in his hospital room, Mama and Celia having left several hours earlier. I was greatly relieved to see Samuel able to sit up in bed, at least for a short time. Most heartening of all, his color was vastly improved.

Eddie spent the first few minutes peppering my poor brother with questions about the shooting, then tried to disguise his disappointment when Samuel could remember virtually nothing of the incident.

"It happened so fast," I told the boy. "Even I've had difficulty recalling every detail. That sometimes happens when people witness a violent event."

"But you remember everything, Miss Sarah," he said, looking at me with an expression that indicated I had let him down. "Mr. Campbell here says you got a mind like a steel trap."

Robert cleared his throat and shifted awkwardly in his chair. "Have you heard if they've made any progress on the case, Samuel?" he said in an obvious attempt to get the conversation back on track.

"George was here this afternoon," Samuel said in a weak voice, and I could see that he was still having difficulty catching his breath. He smiled at Eddie. "He quizzed me about what happened that night, too. But I couldn't tell him anything more than I've told you."

"I sure hope they catch the feller what done this to you, Mr. Samuel," Eddie said, his thin face pinched in anger. "That rounder is savage as a meat ax. It just ain't right fer him to get away with such a damned awful thing!"

"Eddie!" I exclaimed. Despite the circumstances, I could not sit idly by and tolerate this sort of language.

"That's all right, Sarah," Samuel said, smiling at the boy. "He's upset for my sake, and I'm grateful to have such a loyal friend."

"We're all upset, Samuel," I said, unable to allow the matter to pass without a correction. After all, we three had set ourselves the task of educating the boy for the betterment of his future. "Yet that doesn't mean we can completely ignore propriety."

I heard approaching footsteps and turned to see my brother Charles enter the room. I was startled to note how tired he looked, and deflated, as if it had been a particularly difficult day. He set down his medical bag and went to stand by Samuel's bed.

"How is our prize patient?" he said, giving his younger brother a smile. "You're sitting up, that's a good sign."

Samuel returned the smile. "I'm doing much better. In fact, I'm eager to leave this place and return home. They're good to me, but I long for my own bed and especially Cook's food. The meals here are awful."

"I've just spoken to Dr. Ludlum," Charles told him. "He says that if you continue to improve, and there's no sign of infection, he might release you in two or three days."

Samuel groaned. "But I have a perfectly good doctor in my own home. You! And I can't think of two better nurses than Mama and Celia."

Charles passed a hand over his brow, then sank wearily onto the chair that Robert had vacated at his arrival. "Perhaps," he promised. "We'll see how you're doing in the morning."

I regarded my elder brother with concern. "Charles, what's the matter? You looked exhausted."

He regarded me sadly. "I lost a patient this afternoon, on Telegraph Hill, actually. I think you and Samuel met her, Sarah, at Mr. Remy's house. Young Mrs. Dunn died in childbirth. The midwife waited too long to call me in, and when I got there it was too late."

"Mrs. Dunn?" I said, stunned. "You mean Lucy Dunn?"

He nodded.

"And the baby?"

"A healthy boy," Charles said, this time with a genuine smile. "Although how that worthless husband of hers is going to raise the child on his own is anybody's guess."

CHAPTER SIX

Two days later, Samuel was allowed to come home from the hospital. Since Papa's study was located on the ground floor and within convenient proximity to the family, Mama, Celia, and I converted it into a temporary sickroom. There, the patient was settled into a daybed and supplied with books, newspapers, hearty soup, tea, and a variety of sweets from Cook's kitchen. Although he was being more than adequately cared for by a doting staff, Mama hovered over him like a maternal angel, ministering to his every need, whether real or imagined.

After two days of this, my brother took advantage of a few minutes we shared alone late the next evening to beg me to get Mama out of the house, if only for the afternoon.

"She's smothering me, Sarah," he said. "She bathes my wounds and changes the bandages so often, I fear I'll have no skin left to heal. When I try to read, she offers to read to me, then as often as not complains about my selection of reading material. I am then brought the Bible, along with some miracle potion a friend has recommended. My pillows have been poked and fluffed so many times it's a wonder there are any feathers left in them. Please, little sister," he begged, "I've got to get some rest."

Since I, too, had been laid up with an injury some months before, which resulted in my being subjected to my mother's untiring ministrations, I sympathized with my poor brother. Mama belonged to the school of nursing that dictated a patient be under constant supervision, preserved from drafts, filled with food and wholesome, if unsavory, liquids, and not permitted to strain his eyes lest it unsettle the body humors. Charles had more than once attempted to convince her that there was little validity in this ancient theory, which held that sickness resulted from a disproportion of the four body humors—blood, phlegm, yellow bile, and black bile. Unfortunately, old habits die hard, and although she was careful to assign the affliction alternate names, her treatment remained unchanged. It made for an exhausting recovery.

After promising Samuel to do my best, I had a quiet talk with Celia, and the following morning we put together a couple of baskets that we planned to take to Claude Dunn and his new baby son on Telegraph Hill. The hamper was filled with infant robes, bonnets, soft cloths, and various creams and lotions, as well as some mutton, cooked vegetables, and a loaf of bread, compliments of our sympathetic cook. As part of the conspiracy, we said nothing to Mama, only ensuring she would be in the general vicinity of the foyer when we collected our coats and set out on our errand of mercy.

I must admit that I fostered ulterior motives for suggesting that we perform this duty. I had not, you see, given up on my vow to uncover the coward who had shot my brother. If anything, my resolve had grown stronger with each day I was forced to watch Samuel languish helplessly in his bed, suffering pain that his pride would not permit him to acknowledge. The best place to start my investigation, of course, was at the scene of the crime: Telegraph Hill. Ignoring any pangs of conscience, I vowed to use any excuse that came to hand in order to facilitate this scrutiny, including Lucy Dunn's tragic death.

Our plan to involve Mama in this effort worked to perfection. On her way to deliver yet another foul-smelling concoction to the sickroom, she spied our butler, Edis, helping us out the front door with our hampers. When we explained the nature of our mission, she turned Samuel's miracle potion over to our maid, Ina Corks, to deliver, quickly donned her own coat and gloves, and set off with us for Telegraph Hill.

Neither of my companions voiced a complaint about the steep wooden stairs leading up the side of the hill. At least it was daylight, I thought, which made the trek much easier than it had been the night of Remy's get-together. But I truly believed that both my mother and my sister-in-law would walk through a blizzard, if necessary, to help someone in need.

When we reached the Dunn house, we were invited inside by Isabel Freiberg, the young woman I had seen with her father at Mortimer Remy's house. She informed us that she was caring for little Billy, Lucy Dunn's baby son, while his father was at his desk in the back room, attempting to write a story for one of the local newspapers. I introduced my mother and sister-in-law, who passed over the baskets we had prepared for the widower and his motherless baby.

"That is exceedingly kind of you," the young woman told us, gratefully accepting our offering. "Especially the food you've brought for Mr. Dunn's dinner tonight. I must return to my own home in a few minutes, as I have piano lessons planned for this afternoon, and there is very little to eat in this house. One of the neighbors has been bringing over meals when she can, but this will be most welcome."

She looked about the sad, poorly furnished cottage, bare of any real comforts except a worn wooden table and two straight chairs. There was a fireplace, but it contained only one log of any size, surrounded by a collection of twigs and branches. And despite the coolness of the day, it was unlit.

For the first time, I noticed a cradle had been placed beside the hearth. Walking closer, Mama, Celia, and I peered inside to see a tiny face, eyes screwed shut in sleep, snugly wrapped inside several hand-sewn coverings. The cradle had been decorated using the simplest of materials, with a small yellow bow fastened neatly at its head. My eyes filled with unexpected tears. I wondered if poor Lucy Dunn had been able to hold, or even see, her baby before she'd succumbed to one of the many perils of childbirth. I heard my mother sniff and saw that both she and Celia were also crying. How could one not at such a heartrending sight?

At least the infant had survived, I told myself, trying to find even the shadow of a rainbow at such a dark time. True, Claude Dunn had lost his young wife, but having a healthy son should bring the widower some degree of comfort.

I half expected to find Lucy Dunn's body prepared and laid out, awaiting her funeral, as was the usual custom for a family of humble means. To my surprise, Miss Freiberg informed me that Mrs. Katherine Montgomery, the elderly widow who lived in the big house atop the hill, was assuming responsibility for the funeral expenses. Lucy had been taken to a local mortuary and would be laid to rest the following morning.

"That was most kind of her," Mama said, using her lace handkerchief to dab away tears that had appeared on her cheeks. "But what is to become of the baby? How are you feeding him now that his mother is . . . is gone?"

"A neighbor, Mrs. Sullivan, has generously volunteered to wet-nurse him along with her own baby," Isabel Freiberg told us. "Her fifth. It's just a temporary arrangement since she and her husband are moving to Los Angeles next month, but it will give the poor little tyke a good start. After that . . . well, I have heard that hand feeding by sucking bottle has been much improved over the past decade. They now come with an artificial nipple made of India rubber, of all things. That may provide a more long-lasting solution."

Looking down fondly at the peacefully sleeping baby, the young woman pulled on her coat, obviously preparing to return to her home.

"How is poor Mr. Dunn taking this tragic loss?" Celia asked, her lovely face creased with concern. My sister-in-law was a devoted mother to her own three small children, and the thought of a newborn babe deprived of such maternal love obviously broke her tender heart.

Before Isabel could answer, the widower himself joined us in the main room of the cottage. He looked terrible, nothing like the robust, outspoken man I had met the night of Oscar Wilde's reading. His eyes were red and ringed beneath with dark circles. His strong face was pale and drawn into deep lines of worry. Although I hadn't been particularly impressed with him the night we'd first met, I couldn't help feeling a deep pang of sympathy for him now, given his terrible loss. This feeling of sympathy, I am sorry to say, lasted only until the brute opened his mouth to speak.

"Don't tell me you're leaving, Isabel," he cried in a voice so loud that it startled and woke the baby. He glanced fearfully at the fussing infant. "You can't go. What am I to do with—with that?"

Three sets of astonished eyes stared at him. Isabel quickly crossed to the cradle. Bending down, she cooed at the infant, gently rocking the cradle in an effort to soothe him back to sleep.

"Please lower your voice, Mr. Dunn," she urged the child's father. "You're upsetting the baby."

"Upsetting him!" he bellowed even louder. "What about me? Lucy is gone, leaving me to raise a child on my own. How am I supposed to take care of him? That was going to be Lucy's job. I didn't want him in the first place. How in hell am I supposed to do my work when there'll be no more money coming in?"

"Mr. Dunn, please, these ladies . . . ," Isabel said, her voice trailing off as she nodded pointedly at Mama, Celia, and me. "I'm truly sorry that I must leave, but I have students who will be arriving shortly, and I must prepare for their lessons. Mrs. Montgomery promised to care for little Billy until I return this evening. If you like, I can take him home with me for the night so that you can get some rest. I'll bring him back in the morning."

"Don't bother, you can keep him at your house if you like," he told her curtly. "I have an important story to write, and all he does is cry. In fact, keep him for good if you want. Don't know what in hell I'm supposed to do with the brat. If it weren't for him, Lucy would still be here, taking care of things like she always did."

This was too much for Mama. "Mr. Dunn," she admonished, her face red with anger and ill-disguised contempt. "I understand that you have sustained a terrible shock, and have obviously not yet come to terms with your loss. It is only to be expected." She turned to the tiny figure once again quiet in his cradle. "But you have been blessed with a beautiful, healthy baby boy. Surely you must put his well-being before any other considerations. You are all that poor motherless little boy has left."

Dunn looked at my mother as if she were a strange creature from another planet. "Who are you, and what are you doing in my house?" he demanded, his voice once again disturbing his sleeping son. "You were not invited here, but since you are, I'll thank you to keep your infernal opinions to yourself."

Celia gave a little gasp at this, while my face blazed hot with fury. "How dare you speak to a lady in that disgraceful manner, Mr. Dunn? My mother, sister-in-law, and I came bearing clothes for your new baby, and food for your dinner. In light of your un-forgivable behavior, I regret that we included anything for you in those baskets. You certainly don't deserve it."

The awful man glared at me in rage. "Listen to me, you bit—"

"No, you listen to me!" I said, cutting off the vile word before it could escape his mouth. "I had your measure the first time I set eyes upon you. And you have done nothing since then to prove me wrong. You are a sorry excuse for a man, and an even sorrier ex-cuse for a father. God help your unfortunate son!"

I would not have been surprised if the terrible man had come at me intending physical violence. Instead, he simply muttered an oath, turned on his heels, and slammed through the door into the back room.

By now, little Billy was wailing pitifully in his cradle. Isabel bent and picked him up, swaddling him in his blankets and bounc-ing him gently in her arms.

Mama sighed and reached out for the baby, placing him expertly in her own arms. "You must leave, Miss Freiberg. You have your students to consider. We will remain here with the baby until—Mrs. Montgomery, is it?—arrives."

Isabel looked torn. "Are you sure, Mrs. Woolson? I hate to leave you with Mr. Dunn. He's been in a terrible state since his wife died. It's true that he's not a patient man by nature, but I can't believe he means half of what he's been saying since Lucy passed away. It's true that she did everything for him. I honestly don't know how he's going to cope without her."

"Perhaps he'll be forced to do an honest day's work for a change," I said, still angry at the miserable varmint—one of Eddie's favorite vilifications, but most fitting, I thought, to describe this pitiful excuse for a human being. "I feel the need for some fresh air. If it's all right with you, Mama, I'll walk with Miss Freiberg to her home."

Although it was a relief to be out of Dunn's house, I did have another motive for wanting to accompany Isabel. I intended to interview as many inhabitants of Telegraph Hill today as possible. I was about to bring up the events of that evening at Remy's house when Miss Freiberg saved me the effort by inquiring how my brother was recovering from his ordeal.

"He was seriously injured," I replied. "But he's much improved. In fact, he was able to return home from the hospital two days ago."

"Oh, that is excellent news! Stephen—" She gave a little flush of embarrassment. "I mean, Mr. Parke and I have been very worried."

"I understand that you and Mr. Parke are close friends," I said, purposefully vague about where I might have acquired such knowledge.

She gave me a curious look, but after a small hesitation she answered, "Yes, we have discovered several interests in common, and have formed a fond friendship over the past year." She looked at me with frank eyes. "Why do you ask, Miss Woolson?"

"No particular reason. I noticed you speaking to him before

you and your father departed Mr. Remy's house the night Mr. Wilde spoke."

Her eyes fixed on me for another long moment, then she sighed. "I am too weary for games, Miss Woolson. The truth is that Stephen and I are in love. Unfortunately, my father heartily disapproves of the match. We are Jews, and Stephen is a gentile. Moreover, Papa has already chosen the man I am to marry." She smiled wryly. "Mr. Enoch Josephs is a gentleman from our synagogue, a most honorable man, I'm sure, but a widower nearly twenty years my senior. While it's true that I admire him, I cannot pretend to love a man when it is a lie."

"What will you do?" I asked her, truly interested in the answer. Stephen Parke had been a friend of my brother's for several years, and I did not want to see him hurt. And although I had known Isabel for only a short time, I was already coming to think highly of her. I should not care to see her hurt, either.

"I don't know," she answered softly. "My engagement is to be announced next week. Papa has already spoken to the man he has selected, and has assured me that Mr. Josephs is most agreeable to the match."

There was nothing I could think of to say. Isabel's was an all-too-familiar story, one that I abhorred. I was exceedingly thankful that my own parents were more modern in their thinking. Mama would have loved nothing better than to see me married and settled down with children—heaven knows she had done her best to introduce me to a number of "suitable" gentlemen—but if she had ever entertained ideas of forcing me into a loveless marriage, she had long given up on the notion. As I say, I was fortunate. Other young women were not so blessed.

"I am extremely sorry for your predicament," I told her, meaning every word.

"Thank you, Miss Woolson, I appreciate your concern." As if eager to change the subject, she asked, "Are the police any closer to locating the person who fired on your brother?"

"I'm afraid not. They've been unable to find a witness who might have seen something that night."

"Yes, they questioned me, as well as my father. But we noticed nothing unusual when we departed Mr. Remy's cottage. I believe we were among the first guests to leave, and we live only a short distance down the hill, so we were probably already home when your brother was shot."

It was my turn to sigh. "I gather your father saw nothing either?"

"I'm afraid not. But as I say, we were home in a matter of minutes. I truly believe that your brother was injured by accident. The residents on Telegraph Hill are far too ready to shoot their guns at squirrels or pesky possums and skunks. Several of us have begged them to be more careful, but of course no one heeds our concerns."

Just then, we spied Stephen Parke making his way up the hill. Seeing us, he removed his cap and smiled broadly.

"Miss Woolson, Miss Freiberg. How nice to see you both." He gave Isabel a particularly happy grin. "Miss Woolson, how is Samuel? I could hardly believe it when I heard he'd been shot. Some fool firing his gun without paying attention to where it was aimed. I'm so sorry I haven't been able to visit him in the hospital. I did try once, but some pitiless nurse declared he already had too many visitors and refused to allow me in."

"I'm afraid we weren't very popular with the matron," I answered, struck by the fact that he, too, seemed to consider the shooting an accident. "But as I was telling Miss Freiberg, Samuel was released from the hospital over the weekend, and is doing much better."

"I'm delighted to hear it," he said, looking genuinely relieved. "Would it be all right if I stopped by your house to see him, then?"

"By all means. I'm sure he would be delighted to have your company. Now that he's on the mend, I think he's finding his convalescence exceedingly boring."

"Uh-oh," he said, looking down the hill. "There's your father, Isabel. I had better part with you here." He donned his cap and made hurried good-byes. "It was nice to see you again, Miss Woolson. Please tell your brother that I'll be by to see him soon." And with that he was gone, walking up the hill with long strides.

When we reached Solomon Freiberg, he was standing outside a small, neat cottage, watching Stephen's departing back. "That man again," he said unhappily. "I thought I forbade you to see him anymore."

"I can hardly ignore Mr. Parke when I pass him on the path," she said, kissing him lightly on the cheek. "He's a good man, Papa, despite your prejudice."

"I am not prejudiced, Isabel," he protested. "He is just not the man for you. There are too many differences between you, and not just religion. The man makes his living as a writer, if you can actually call the few dollars he brings in now and again a living."

Isabel looked at me uneasily. "Papa, please. I'm sure we're making Miss Woolson uncomfortable discussing family matters in her presence. You remember Miss Woolson, don't you, Papa? She and her brother Samuel attended Oscar Wilde's lecture at Mr. Remy's house."

The man looked at me but did not, in fact, seem to remember. He took off his eyeglasses and polished them with a handkerchief, but even after he replaced them on his nose, he still did not appear to recognize my face. But then Samuel and I had been seated behind him and his daughter at Remy's house, so perhaps this was not surprising.

"I am pleased to make your acquaintance, Miss Woolson," he said in a rather high voice. "Please forgive my absentmindedness. I fear I am becoming a bit forgetful in my old age."

"Has Mary Kelley arrived for her lesson?" Isabel asked.

"Not yet," her father replied. "But it was getting late and I wondered where you were. How is the baby?" I noticed that he didn't inquire after the infant's father.

Isabel's face softened. "He's beautiful, Papa. But he needs a mother. Poor Lucy, she would have been so good to that child."

"Yes, she would have been," Mr. Freiberg agreed, shaking his head sadly. "Instead he is left with a useless father, and an uncertain future. That man has no one but himself to blame for his wife's death. The shameful way he treated her."

Once again, Isabel seemed embarrassed by her father's forthrightness. "We will have to wait and see, Papa. He hasn't had time to accept his loss." She smiled at me. "Please excuse me, Miss Woolson, but I must prepare for my students."

"Of course, Miss Freiberg, please do," I said, and watched as the young woman disappeared into the cottage.

"It is your brother who was wounded," the man said, as if suddenly remembering my connection to the gunshot victim. "Such a terrible accident. There are too many guns in this city, far too many for my peace of mind."

"You think Samuel was shot by mistake, Mr. Freiberg?"

He appeared surprised that I would question his statement. "But my dear young woman, why else would such an awful thing happen? Who would want to deliberately injure your brother?"

"That's what the police would like to know, and of course my family."

"Naturally, naturally," he said, bobbing his narrow face up and down in agreement. "Please tell me, how is your unfortunate brother doing?"

Once again, I explained that my brother had returned home from the hospital and was improving by the day. "You didn't notice anything out of the ordinary when you left Mr. Remy's house that evening?"

He shook his head. "That is what the police asked. So many questions they asked. I told them it was a dark night. How could I have seen anyone? Impossible, impossible."

"I believe the moon was out by then, Mr. Freiberg."

"Mmmm, yes, yes, that may be so," he said after giving the matter a moment's thought. He glanced down the hill, as if eager to be off. "You will please excuse me, Miss Woolson, I am meeting a friend at the synagogue. I pray your poor brother will make a speedy recovery."

Without further explanation, he gave me a stiff little bow and began hurrying down the hill. He had gone only a few yards when he met Tull O'Hara, Mortimer Remy's typesetter, who was coming the other way. Mr. Freiberg nodded to him, but the other man's head was down and I wasn't sure he had even seen him.

I was glad to see O'Hara approaching, as I hoped to speak to him as well. Squinting through round spectacles, he regarded me with a gruff expression, then deliberately increased his pace up the hill.

I was not to be put off by such a rude manner. "Mr. O'Hara," I called out, hurrying to catch up with him. "Mr. O'Hara, please wait, I would like to talk to you."

Not bothering to hide his irritation at this simple request, the man reluctantly stopped, his expression unwelcoming. Although I had seen him at Remy's cottage, I noticed for the first time that his bulbous nose was very red and crisscrossed with tiny purple veins, as if he were a heavy drinker.

I did not mince words. "Mr. O'Hara, my name is Sarah Woolson and I am the sister of the gentleman who was shot the night of Mr. Wilde's reading."

He stared at me, impertinently looking me over from head to boot. He did not say a word.

"Mr. O'Hara," I continued, deciding to ignore this insolent behavior, "did you see anything that night? Someone standing where he shouldn't be, perhaps? A man with a rifle? Perhaps someone aiming at a possum?"

He continued to stare mutely at me, as if I were speaking in a foreign language. What a frustrating man!

"Mr. O'Hara, please. My brother very nearly died that night. Did you see anything?"

He shook his shaggy head and grunted. "Didn't see nothin', lady. Mind my own business, I do, which is somethin' you might try."

I started to retort, but the surly man had already turned and was continuing his walk up the hill, mumbling fiercely beneath his breath about nosy women. I wondered where he was going in such a hurry. Perhaps he just wanted to get away from me.

"Not very sociable, is he?" I turned to find Emmett Gardiner watching O'Hara's retreating back. "I don't know how Mortimer puts up with him. But I understand he's one of the best typesetters in town."

"Mr. Gardiner, it's good to see you," I said, delighted as ever to meet the affable man.

"I thought I saw you and two other ladies entering Dunn's cottage on my way down the hill. What a terrible tragedy, losing his young wife like that."

"Indeed it was. Yes, my mother and sister-in-law and I were paying our respects to Mr. Dunn. Evidently, Miss Freiberg has been helping him care for the new baby. I just came from walking her home."

"So, you're on your way back up the hill?" He smiled when I nodded that I was. "Good. I'll walk with you, then, if that's agreeable."

"It would be most agreeable, Mr. Gardiner," I told him. "I'm happy for the company."

"Have you seen Mr. Dunn?" he asked, giving me a sidelong look as we walked. "I visited him earlier this morning, and he seemed to be taking poor Lucy's death very hard, which is understandable, of course. She was a sprightly, hardworking little thing."

"I only met her the one time at Mr. Remy's house the night Oscar Wilde spoke, but that was the impression I received. She looked extremely weary, and pale."

"As well she might," he said almost angrily. "She worked from sunrise to sunset, not only taking care of her own husband and home, but anyone else on the Hill who needed cleaning or laundry done. She did my washing and ironing, and also cleaned my cottage once or twice. She was a marvel, and is going to be sorely missed."

We continued in silence for a bit, then he said, "By the way, how is Samuel doing? I went by the hospital to see him yesterday afternoon, but I was told that he'd been discharged. That's very good news."

"Yes, it's wonderful to have him home." I looked at him, noticing how his blond hair appeared almost golden in the afternoon sunlight. "Please feel free to visit him there, if you'd like. I'm sure he would be happy to see you."

"I still can't believe that someone actually shot at him. It's absurd. He's one of the best-natured chaps I know."

"Several people I've spoken to believe it was an accident," I said, watching his face for a reaction. "Perhaps someone shooting at a fox, or a possum."

"That's possible, I suppose," he replied. "Almost everyone on Telegraph Hill owns a gun. But as far as I know, no one's ever been accidentally hit before."

"I wonder if you happened to see anything strange that night, Mr. Gardiner? After Samuel and I parted with you in front of Mr. Remy's house?"

He smiled. "In other words, did I see anyone slinking around behaving suspiciously? No, I'm sorry to say I didn't. After I left you and Samuel, I walked back to my house, which is one street over from Uncle Mortimer's. In fact, our properties share a common border in the rear. If someone were following your party down the hill, I wouldn't have passed them."

I sighed. "No one seems to have seen anything."

"The police have questioned me, Miss Woolson, as I'm sure they have the others who were at Wilde's reading. Eventually, they're bound to catch whoever did this."

"I pray you're right, Mr. Gardiner. It's all very frustrating. Not to mention frightening."

After Emmett Gardiner and I parted company, I wondered if Mortimer Remy might be home, then decided it was unlikely. I recalled Samuel telling me that Remy spent more time in his office than he did in his house; his newspaper, the *San Francisco*

Weekly, was his life's obsession. My thoughts went to Mrs. Montgomery. Confined as she was to a wheelchair, it was doubtful that she had seen anything, but you never knew. I would have to at least pay her a visit.

As I reached the Dunn house, I was pleasantly surprised to meet the very woman I wished to see being pushed up the path leading to the front door. Mrs. Montgomery gave me a regal nod of her head as I stepped up to meet her. She was dressed much the same as the first time I had met her: severely cut black day dress, a black silk hat, sheer black gloves, and neat, well-polished black boots. She was shielding herself from the sun with a lacy black parasol.

"Good afternoon, Mrs. Montgomery," I said. "I don't believe we were formally introduced at Mr. Remy's house the other night, but I am Miss Sarah Woolson."

She accepted my outstretched hand much as a queen might greet a subject. Even through the lacy gloves I could feel her brittle, cold fingers and their very slight tremor.

"Good afternoon, Miss Woolson." Her voice was high, but stronger than I expected, and she spoke with perfect diction, as did so many elderly women of my acquaintance. "It was your poor brother who was shot, was it not? A dreadful thing to happen. I pray he is on the road to recovery."

Once again I reported on Samuel's progress, then informed her why my mother, sister-in-law, and I happened to be on Telegraph Hill that afternoon.

"That is the purpose of my visit as well, Miss Woolson," she said, nodding to the box perched on her lap. The woman held up a lovely little yellow knit sweater, embroidered with tiny orange and blue flowers. Neatly folded beneath it was a matching knitted bonnet. "My sister, Mrs. Abigail Forester, was quite fond of Lucy, and spent a great deal of time making things for the new baby. Like myself, Abigail is a widow, and has lived with me since her husband passed away." She indicated the many handcrafted items

88

of infant clothing in the box. "She is very talented with her hands, is she not?"

Her pale, watery eyes closed and she shook her head, sadness clouding her lined old face. "Clothing and food, a poor comfort for losing a mother. But we must do what we can for that unfortunate little boy. Lucy Dunn did for Abigail and myself, you see, and was the most conscientious child." She lowered her voice. "I can't help but wonder if that is why she succumbed in childbirth. Wore herself to a frazzle, I daresay, and in her delicate condition."

While she was speaking, the front door was opened by my mother. Celia was standing behind her, rocking the baby gently in her arms. I could see no sign of Dunn.

I performed the introductions, then before Studds could maneuver his mistress inside, I said, "Mrs. Montgomery, I assume the police have spoken to you about the night of Mr. Remy's salon, but I would be in your debt if you could tell me what, if anything, you saw."

"But my dear child, I'm sorry to say that I saw nothing. As you know, my man Studds led your group down the hill. I was considerably fatigued after the long evening, and Mr. O'Hara wheeled me up to my own home. Perhaps you should speak to him. I daresay his eyes are a good deal sharper than mine."

"I have already spoken to Mr. O'Hara," I told her. "He claims that he, too, saw nothing."

She noticed me looking at the man behind her wheelchair and smiled. "Bruno, would you please tell Miss Woolson what, if anything, you saw the night Mr. Wilde spoke at Mr. Remy's house."

The man looked at me for an uncomfortable moment, then lowered his eyes and slowly shook his head.

His elderly mistress appeared a bit embarrassed. "I'm sorry, Miss Woolson, but Bruno is not a social man, and he rarely speaks. However, I fear he could have little to relate, since his back must have been turned to the shooter. I wish we might be of more help, but . . ." She spread her thin hands in regret.

"Thank you, Mrs. Montgomery," I told her, disappointed but not surprised that she could offer no information. I stood back so that Studds would be free to push his mistress into the cottage. "I think what you are doing for Mr. Dunn is most kind."

The woman made a deprecating sound, then looked up at me, her faded, intelligent eyes glistening with unshed tears. "I am not doing it for him, I assure you," she stated with surprising candor. "I am doing it for that poor motherless child. And for Lucy."

Mama, Celia, and I departed the Dunn house some few minutes later. I was disappointed to have learned so little about the shooting, although I wasn't sure what I had expected. But I simply could not believe that no one on Telegraph Hill had seen anything. Were they bound together in a circle of secrecy? I wondered. And if so, why? Or was it perhaps because they were afraid to speak?

As the three of us started the long trek down the hill, I caught a movement out of the corner of my eye. Glancing to my left, I saw Claude Dunn speaking to someone behind his house. At first I could not identify the other person, until he stepped out from the shelter of a tree and moved closer to Dunn. When he counted out some money and placed it in Dunn's hand, my breath caught in my throat.

The other man was none other than Samuel's newspaper archrival, Ozzie Foldger!

CHAPTER SEVEN

Instead of accompanying Mama and Celia back to our home, I took an omnibus and then a cable car to my Sutter Street office. The journey gave me time to consider the results of our visit to Telegraph Hill, if I could pretend that I had actually achieved any results. Which, unfortunately, I could not.

One by one, I went over the conversations I had had with Mortimer Remy's neighbors. Granted, several of them had been so brief that they could hardly be referred to as a conversation. However, I found it difficult to imagine any of them possessing a motive for wanting to harm Samuel. Not even the appalling Claude Dunn. He might be a miserable human being, but that was a far cry from being a murderer. And according to Samuel, he hardly knew the man, so unless there was more involved here than met the eye, I could not cast him as the shooter.

I considered Robert's fear that I might be the intended victim, but I dismissed this notion even more quickly. While it was true that I had alienated myself from San Francisco's more genteel society—and I was certainly resented by the male legal profession—surely I had antagonized neither of these groups sufficiently for them to wish me dead.

Assuming, as Sergeant Lewis pointed out, that no sane shooter would attempt to hit the men walking in front of us as we made our way down the hill, that left but one potential victim: Jonathan Aleric. This thought brought me little relief, as the only person I could think of who might want to rid himself of Aleric was Mortimer Remy. And I simply could not imagine the newspaper publisher as a murderer.

I was still mulling over the mystery when I arrived at Sutter Street. Walking up from Market, I was startled to see Mr. and Mrs. Dinwitty approaching the stairs leading to my office. I remembered Ricardo Ruiz's assertion that they would return to request my legal representation. Could he have been right? I wondered. Hastening my step, I was able to reach the couple as they were about to knock on my door.

"Mr. Dinwitty, Mrs. Dinwitty," I said politely. "This is a surprise. I did not expect you to pay me a second visit."

They moved aside to allow me to unlock the door. "Please, won't you come in and take a seat?"

It was clear from Celestia Dinwitty's expression that she was none too happy to be here again. The small dog she held cradled against her bosom somehow managed to mirror her distaste, giving me a little growl as its mistress swept past me into my office. Mr. Dinwitty removed his hat and regarded me with cautious optimism as he settled his wife and her pet into the same chair she had occupied upon the occasion of her first visit. That task attended to, he sank into the seat next to hers.

"How may I help you?" I inquired after hanging up my wrap. Seeing no benefit in beating about the bush, I came straight to the point. "Have you found an attorney to represent your case against Mr. Ruiz and his bullfighting ring?"

Mr. Dinwitty cleared his throat. "Actually, that is why we are here, Miss Woolson. Our search has proved to be unsuccessful."

He gave his wife a nervous glance, as if to make certain that she was still in agreement, before going on. She responded with the barest nod of her head.

"We have come to ask if you will take the case," he continued.

I studied my visitors for a long moment. Judging by his wife's derisive attitude toward me, it was clear that she had agreed to return to my office because there was no other choice. Evidently, no other law firm in town was willing to go up against Mr. Ruiz and his planned bullring. I had to ask myself why. I could not believe that their reluctance was due entirely to City Hall's curious support of the plan. Or perhaps not so curious, I decided. Money could be a powerful persuader, and Mayor Blake and his big bugs (as Papa referred to them) expected the arena to bring the city considerable income.

"Will you accept our case, Miss Woolson?" Mr. Dinwitty prompted when I did not immediately give him an answer.

Once again, I decided to be blunt. "I will have to look into the situation before I can give you a definitive answer, Mr. Dinwitty."

"Just what do you need to look into, Miss Woolson?" Celestia Dinwitty inquired acerbically. "Indeed, given the circumstances, you should be grateful to receive such an opportunity."

"And what circumstances might those be?" I asked, meeting the woman's haughty gaze. As if objecting to my tone, the little dog squirmed in its mistress's arms and uttered a series of angry yips.

"Miss Woolson!" the woman said sharply. "You are a brazen and foolish young woman to forsake the role God has ordained for the feminine gender. You eschew husband and children in order to push yourself into a man's world, where nature will never permit you to succeed. These are the circumstances to which I refer. You should be grateful that individuals of such high moral purpose as my husband and myself should seek your assistance."

"I see," I answered simply, refusing to be baited into yet another debate concerning my life's calling. I wholly accepted that the path I had chosen would not be easy to traverse, nor its goal speedily achieved. Inevitably, the prize would go to she who persevered.

"Be that as it may, Mrs. Dinwitty," I went on, "I shall have to give the matter some thought. As you have undoubtedly been told by other law firms you've visited, this is a highly unusual situation. And since city government appears all too ready to permit Mr. Ruiz to build his bullring, it will be a difficult case to win. I will have to examine San Francisco ordinances regarding the construction of such arenas within the city limits. That information, of course, will be vital in deciding how to construct the case."

Even Mrs. Dinwitty could hardly fault this plan of action and wisely said nothing. For his part, her husband seemed to take my strategy with hopeful optimism.

"Yes, yes," he said, rising from his chair. "I understand your reasoning. We can only hope that your inquiries prove encouraging for our cause."

I was somewhat surprised to find myself hoping the same thing. I found women like Celestia Dinwitty tiresome to deal with, given that they were so utterly immovable in their views. I also abhorred the notion that Ruiz might be denied his permit based on his Mexican heritage. But the thought of a bullfighting ring in the heart of San Francisco overrode these considerations.

"I will give you my answer by the day after tomorrow if that is acceptable, Mr. Dinwitty," I told the man.

He appeared disappointed that I would not immediately commit myself to the case, but finally he nodded his agreement to this plan.

"We look forward to hearing from you, then," he said, this time not bothering to consult his wife. "I pray you will have promising news."

I returned home that evening to find my mother appealing to Charles to do something about his younger brother. Evidently, Samuel had taken advantage of the time Mama, Celia, and I had been gone to move to the library and work on his book. I'm sure he'd intended to be back in bed before we returned from Telegraph Hill, but unfortunately he had fallen asleep, head lying on his arms atop the table. Which was where Mama discovered him upon her arrival home.

Charles was arguing that as no real harm had resulted from Samuel's time in the library, they should probably not make too much of the incident. In exasperation, Mama turned to me for help.

"Your brothers are hopeless! Even Charles, who should know better. I want you to talk to Samuel. Perhaps he'll listen to you. You must convince him that he needs to remain in bed until his wound is healed."

I agreed but doubted that anything I said would persuade him to follow our mother's rules. We were very alike in that respect, neither of us comfortable with the necessity of having to remain idle for any length of time. I knew that my brother's primary focus was to put the final touches to his book, and he most likely considered his convalescence an excellent opportunity to accomplish this. Still, I had given Mama my word, so talk to him I would.

My first opportunity to speak to him alone did not present itself until after dinner that night. As ordered, he was sitting up in his bed, surrounded by a sheaf of papers, magazines, and books.

"It was a battle to talk Mama into allowing me to have even these," he declared in frustration. "And I know full well that you're supposed to convince me to stay in this sodding room until I've healed. Well, I'm feeling better every day, and I'll go out of my mind if I'm forced to spend all of my time in bed!"

He grinned, obviously relieved to have vented his frustration. "So, enough of that. Tell me what you learned on Telegraph Hill. Did you come across any likely suspects?"

"Unfortunately, no," I said, displaying my own frustration. "I spoke to everyone on the Hill who was at Remy's house that night, except Remy himself, who I assume was at his newspaper office."

I went on to describe the substance of each conversation I'd had that afternoon, including my distasteful exchange with Claude Dunn.

"He is one of the most self-absorbed, insensitive men I have ever had the misfortune to meet," I said by way of conclusion. "He gives no indication that he cares one whit for that poor baby, but wails incessantly about how he is to survive without his wife to take care of him and pay the bills."

"He actually said that?"

"Oh, yes. He did indeed." I felt a rekindling of the rage I had experienced in Dunn's house. "The heartless man went so far as to say he hadn't wanted the child in the first place. He claimed it had all been Lucy's idea, and that she was supposed to take care of it. I think that was what annoyed me the most, how he referred to his son as an *it,* and the poor babe lying not five feet away in his cradle."

Samuel gave a soft whistle and shook his head. "I've never particularly liked Claude Dunn, not only because of the shabby way he treated his wife, but because he's so unprincipled when it comes to his work. I've personally known him to steal someone else's story, then lie through his teeth claiming that it was his to begin with. More than one reporter has accused him of distorting facts to make a piece more salable. All in all, he has a seedy reputation."

I was considering these revelations when our butler, Edis, knocked on the study door to announce that Mr. Campbell was here to see Mr. Samuel. My brother grinned, sat up straighter in his bed, and directed Edis to show his guest in.

As usual, Robert bounded into the room with a rush of energy, and I stifled a smile at the pained expression on Edis's well-mannered face.

"Shall I bring coffee, Mr. Samuel?" the butler inquired. "Or perhaps something stronger?"

"I would infinitely prefer something stronger, Edis," Samuel replied, looking regretful. "But I'd prefer not to do battle again tonight with my mother. So you had better make it just plain coffee, thank you."

Edis nodded his gray head and closed the door silently.

"So, Robert," my brother continued cheerfully, "to what do I owe this pleasure? Or have you come to check up on me, too?"

Robert pulled a chair closer to Samuel's bed and sat down. "Yes, I met your mother on my way in. I was instructed that under no circumstances were you to be troubled with anything more taxing than today's weather or the progress of the Golden Gate Park project. By the way, have you any interest in either of these topics?"

Samuel laughed, then winced and placed a hand on his injured shoulder. "Precisely none. I'm far more intrigued by Sarah's visit this afternoon to Telegraph Hill. I've been quizzing her about who might be responsible for this," he added, nodding to his wound.

Robert's face darkened and he glared at me. "Good Lord, Sarah, tell me you weren't foolish enough to return to that godforsaken Hill! What if someone had taken a shot at you this time?"

"Not that again!" I exclaimed, rolling my eyes. "Be sensible, Robert. There is no reason to believe that anyone, whether living on Telegraph Hill or not, would want to shoot me. I admit that I may have ruffled a few feathers since I began my law practice, but hardly to that extent."

"*May* have?" Samuel responded, chuckling softly as if mindful of not jarring his injury. "That's an understatement." He turned to my colleague. "She's right, though, Robert. I know most of the people who live on Telegraph Hill, at least the ones who belong to the writing community. Except for Mortimer Remy, Stephen Parke, and Emmett Gardiner, I doubt if any of them had even met her before Wilde's lecture. And I can think of no reason why any of them would want to see Sarah dead."

"I forgot to mention one of the strangest things I saw today," I said, suddenly remembering. "It was when we were leaving to come home. I spied Dunn talking to Ozzie Foldger behind his house."

"What?" Samuel asked in surprise. "Did you hear what they were saying?"

"No, I was too far away. But I'm almost certain I saw Foldger hand Dunn some money. It appeared to be a fairly substantial amount."

"Good heavens," Robert muttered. "Why would he do a thing like that?"

Samuel considered this startling news. "Even if Foldger's paper bought one of Dunn's stories, Ozzie wouldn't be the one to pay him." He looked at me. "Did you see Dunn hand over an article?"

"No, and they were behaving furtively," I said, "constantly looking around to make sure they were alone. As I say, it was all a bit bizarre."

We discussed the matter at some length, but when we could make no sense of the curious exchange, we eventually returned to what little I had learned on my trip to Telegraph Hill that afternoon.

"Everyone I spoke to either claims to have seen nothing untoward that night, or that the shooting was an accident," I said, concluding my report. "It seems as if a great many people living on that Hill own guns."

"A great many people in San Francisco own guns," Samuel commented dryly.

"Yes, but only one of them was used to shoot at you," Robert put in. He thought for a moment, then asked, "Do you suppose the people you talked to today are right, Sarah? Could it actually have been an accident?"

I sighed. "I would like to think so, but it seems improbable, not to mention careless. Who shoots their gun at night, marauding foxes or no?"

"Someone who's had too much to drink?" Robert opined.

Samuel thought a moment, then nodded slowly. "That's certainly a possibility."

"If that's the case, then the shooter could be anyone living there," said Robert, "not just one of the people who were present at Wilde's reading."

"If that's the situation, we may never find him," I said, feeling suddenly deflated.

Samuel read my expression correctly. "If it was an accident,

Sarah, we can only hope that the shooter has learned his lesson, and won't take any more potshots in the dark."

"Yes," I agreed without much enthusiasm. "That would be the most satisfactory ending to this awful business."

"It also means that you need not pay any more visits to Telegraph Hill," Robert said.

"If it was merely some fool shooting off his gun because he couldn't hold his liquor, or because there was a stray possum in his yard, then there's no reason why I should avoid the place," I told my colleague reasonably. "Especially in the daylight."

"Why must you be so all-fired stubborn?" Robert asked, rather too loudly.

"And why do you feel it necessary to meddle in my affairs?" I shot back more or less automatically. "May I remind you that where I go, or do not go, is none of your concern."

We both turned to find Samuel regarding us in amusement. "My dear little sister, for a woman of your intelligence you can be remarkably dense at times. The reason Robert meddles in your affairs is because he fears, and not without good reason, that one day you will poke your overinquisitive nose into a matter beyond your ability to control, resulting in it being lopped off."

I saw by Robert's sheepish expression that my brother had accurately described his concern. He started to say something, although whether it was to confirm or deny Samuel's assertion, I could not guess. In the end he remained silent.

"You have an exceptionally good friend here, Sarah," Samuel went on. The amusement on his face was gone, although I could not fathom the expression that had taken its place. Was I missing something? I wondered. Was there more to his words than I had discerned? If so, it was not like Samuel to speak in riddles. "A friend, I might add, whom you would do well not to take for granted."

Feeling strangely discomfited not only by my brother's words, but by the peculiar expression on Robert's face, I was about to change the direction of the conversation when Edis knocked softly on the door. With his usual care, he entered the room carrying a silver tray containing cups, saucers, and a fresh pot of coffee. After he had carefully set out the china on the side table, we thanked him, then waited until he had left the room to resume our discussion.

"Mr. and Mrs. Dinwitty visited my office this afternoon," I said, pouring out the coffee. "They've changed their minds and have asked me to take the case."

"What case?" Samuel asked, and I belatedly remembered that he'd been fighting for his life in the hospital on the occasion of the Dinwittys' initial visit.

I described Ricardo Ruiz's plan to build a bullfighting ring in the city and the San Francisco SPCA's opposition. When I finished, he regarded me in astonishment.

"A bullring in San Francisco? Is that possible? Will City Hall even sanction such a thing?"

"According to the Dinwittys, City Hall is very close to permitting the construction." I went on to tell him about the earlier bullring that stood across from Mission Dolores until the early 1850s.

My brother shook his head. "That's news to me. But I suppose things must have been different when the California territory was under Mexican rule."

"Not so different if City Hall is prepared to allow a second bullring in the city," Robert commented.

"So, are you going to take the case?" asked Samuel.

"I have yet to decide," I replied. "I told them I would have to look into the matter before I made a commitment."

Both men eyed me suspiciously. Robert spoke first.

"That attitude is out of character for you, Sarah. This is the sort of case you would ordinarily jump at. After all, they do kill the bulls in these places. It has always struck me as a rather barbarous sport, although I confess I've never actually attended a bullfight."

"Neither have I," Samuel admitted. "Nor have I felt an inclination to attend one." He sat thinking for a moment, then asked,

"I take it that this Ruiz fellow is a Mexican citizen? And a wealthy one at that?"

"Yes," I said. "According to the Dinwittys, the Ruizes are one of the most powerful families in Mexico. And Ricardo Ruiz seems familiar with San Francisco's city government. In fact, he implied that he enjoyed considerable influence with City Hall."

"What about this land he claims to own?" Robert asked. "What do you know about it?"

"Not much, yet," I said. "Ruiz maintains that his family has owned the property for years, and that he has a right to construct whatever he wishes there."

Samuel regarded me thoughtfully. "In what part of the city is the land located?"

"All the Dinwittys could tell me was that it was somewhere in the Mission District. I will have to look it up, along with any possible impediments I might be able to use to block the project."

"And what if you don't find any impediments?" my brother wanted to know.

I hesitated before answering. "I'm not sure."

"All right, Sarah, enough of this," Robert put in. "What's going on in that devious head of yours? You've never allowed a little matter like an absence of facts to stop you from taking a case. I can't imagine you passing up the opportunity to save the life of a single imperiled animal, much less an entire herd of the blasted beasts."

I looked from Robert to my brother, who was regarding me with an amused expression, then sighed and decided I might as well tell the truth. "I'm not well pleased with other factions who oppose the bullring. Despite my distaste for the project, I have no wish to align myself with them."

"What factions?" Samuel asked, looking interested. Then his face brightened. "Wait, don't tell me. I should have guessed it straight off. There are certain groups in the city who are opposed to the bullring based on Ruiz's nationality, am I correct?"

"Yes," I admitted. "Several groups, actually, the most prominent being Denis Kearney and his sandlotters."

"Oh," my brother said, drawing out the word. "That makes matters tricky, doesn't it?"

"Exactly," I said. "While I agree with their position on the issue, it's been arrived at for all the wrong reasons. I want nothing to do with them, or their racism."

"Surely turning the case down because of Kearney and his gang of rowdies is akin to cutting off your nose to spite your face," Robert ventured. "If you believe the case has merit, you should pursue it, no matter the reasons others give for their opposition."

"If only it were that simple," I told him. "Because of my work with the Chinese, Denis Kearney has openly declared himself to be my enemy. He will take great pleasure in denouncing me as a liar and every sort of hypocrite if I give the slightest indication of backing him in this cause."

When neither man seemed able to refute this logic, I continued, "As I told the Dinwittys, I have not yet made my decision. I'll be in a better position to do so after I've looked more closely into the matter. Until then, we'll just have to wait and see."

"Yes," Samuel agreed at length. "Moreover, if what you say is true about Ruiz holding the deed to that land, you may find it impossible to win the case in any event."

Robert was shaking his head. "Still, a bullring in San Francisco. It's outrageous."

"When I'm back on my feet, I'll see what I can find out about Ruiz and his family," Samuel promised. "Speaking of which . . ." He shot a hasty glance at the door and lowered his voice. "Oscar Wilde is making his second appearance at Platt's Hall tomorrow night and I plan to be there."

When Robert and I both drew breath to object, he hurried on, "Please, don't make a fuss about it. I'm sure that a fair number of the Telegraph Hill writing community will be there. It will provide the perfect opportunity to watch their reactions when they see me." He smiled, regarding Robert and me as if the matter were settled. "All right, all right, the two of you can accompany me if that will make you feel better."

"Have you taken leave of your senses?" I exclaimed. "You're but a few days out of the hospital, Samuel, and can barely sit in a chair without wincing in pain. You're not fit to go anywhere, much less to a crowded public hall. Furthermore, if you think Mama will ever agree to such an outrageous plan, whether Robert and I are with you or not, then that bullet damaged your brain as well as your shoulder."

My brother sat forward in his bed as if to offer a further argument, then almost immediately gasped and fell back onto his pillows. Looking at his pale, strained face, I was overcome with sympathy.

"I can understand why you'd want to attend Wilde's lecture, Samuel," I went on in a calmer tone, "but if you suffer a relapse, it will only prolong your recovery." I shot a quick glance at Robert, then came to a decision. "If you'd like, Robert and I will go to Platt's Hall in your stead tomorrow night. But you will remain here, in that bed, gracefully submitting to our mother's loving care."

Robert appeared taken aback by this offer. He started to speak, but after a moment he seemed to think better of it and merely nodded his agreement.

"And that is that, brother dear," I said, making it clear that I would brook no further argument on the subject.

CHAPTER EIGHT

To my surprise, Platt's Hall—a spacious music, theatrical, and public meeting facility located on the northeast corner of Bush and Montgomery Streets—was filled to near capacity the following night. The reason for my amazement was that the topic of Oscar Wilde's lecture that night had been widely publicized in newspapers and emblazoned on numerous playbills posted throughout the city: "Art Decoration! Being the Practical and Application of the Esthetic Theory to Everyday Home Life and Art Ornamentation!"

After the mixed reviews, and in several instances outright ridicule, Wilde had received upon his first visit to Platt's Hall shortly after his arrival in San Francisco, I would have expected the citizens of our fair city to be thoroughly weary of the poet and, to my mind, his overrated Aesthetic Movement. It baffled me that so many men in particular, a good number of them residing in boardinghouses and hotels, had actually paid good money to be told how to live their lives in accordance with some artists' and writers' ideas of the house beautiful!

If I looked forward to tonight's program with frank skepticism, my companion made not the slightest attempt to mask his annoyance, moaning ad infinitum that I had coerced him into listening to a blasted fool lecture him about how to decorate a house he didn't even own!

He sat beside me now making desultory comments as he scrutinized a pamphlet that had been handed out to attendees upon their arrival at the hall. The paper contained a brief description of Oscar Wilde and his recently published book of poems, his American tour, and information concerning the Aesthetic Movement.

"We are not here to listen to Wilde's lecture," I reminded him in a low but firm voice, weary of his grousing. If I hadn't required an escort tonight, I would have happily attended Wilde's lecture alone. But the unreasonable, not to mention cumbersome, dictates of society would not permit a woman—at least not a respectable woman—to venture out at night on her own. Ridiculous, of course, and a rule that I had successfully avoided on several past occasions—but there you have it. Even in San Francisco, some standards, however outdated, continued to be *une affaire réglée,* a matter that has been settled.

"I'll grant you that Samuel's idea to come here tonight was out of the question, but he had a good point," I went on. "It's a splendid opportunity to see who is in attendance from Telegraph Hill, and observe their behavior."

Robert did not appear convinced. "That makes no sense to me. If they've already heard the man speak, why bother to listen to him again? You can't really believe that if the shooter does make an appearance, he's going to be so overwhelmed with guilt that he'll jump up and make a public confession?"

"Don't be absurd. Wilde will be leaving town in a few days to continue his tour, so this is an opportunity not to be wasted. By the way, the reason writers from Telegraph Hill may come tonight is so that they can be seen by the right people, and perhaps contrive an introduction to an editor or a publisher." I glanced about the room, hoping to see a familiar face. "I realize you don't know any of these people, Robert, but at least try to look interested in the lecture while I do my job."

"Have you recognized any of your *suspects* yet?" he asked gloomily.

I nodded and inclined my head toward a young couple located a row or two to our right. "Do you see that man and woman sitting across the aisle? She's wearing a green gown with cream-colored lace framing her neck. He's dressed in a black long-coat and dark gray trousers."

Robert looked where I was gesturing. "Yes, I see them. Who are they?"

"He's Stephen Parke, a writer friend of my brother's who lives several houses down from Remy's cottage. The woman is Isabel Freiberg, who also lives on Telegraph Hill. The two claim to be in love, but the match is strongly opposed by her father, Solomon Freiberg."

"They were at Wilde's lecture the night Samuel was shot?"

"Yes; however, they paid more attention to each other than to the poet."

"Would Parke have any reason to shoot either Aleric or Samuel?" he asked, gawking so openly at the couple that I nudged him on the shoulder.

"Ouch," he said, rubbing his upper arm. "Why did you do that?"

"For heaven's sake, Robert, you were staring at them so hard, your eyes could have bored holes through their heads." My attention was suddenly caught by a middle-aged gentleman walking purposefully down the aisle from the back of the room. He had pale, washed-out blue eyes, a full head of graying hair, and a large salt-and-pepper mustache.

"Who is he?" Robert asked, following my gaze as the man swept past us on his way to the front of the hall.

"That's Jonathan Aleric, the author of *An Uncivil War*. It was extremely popular following the War Between the States. He's also the owner and publisher of the *Bay Area Express*. His newspaper and Remy's *San Francisco Weekly* are bitter rivals. They had a heated argument that night at Remy's cottage."

Memory sparked on Robert's suntanned face. "I remember now. At the hospital, you and Sergeant Lewis wondered whether Remy might have been shooting at Aleric and accidentally hit Samuel instead."

"It's true that there's no love lost between the two men," I admitted reluctantly. "Yet I cannot imagine Mortimer Remy as a killer, regardless of the animosity he might feel toward someone."

"Your faith in the man is admirable, yet it may be misplaced. If not Remy, who else had a motive for shooting Aleric?"

"For all we know, he may have dozens of enemies. And just because George and I discussed the possibility that he was the target doesn't mean it's true."

Robert gave a sigh of frustration. "Then who else could have been the intended victim? Samuel insists that he can think of no one who might want to see him dead. So, if the intended victim wasn't your brother, then it had to be either you or Jonathan Aleric. Since you adamantly deny it could be you, that leaves only Aleric. And from what you've told me about their newspaper rivalry, not to mention the scandal involving Remy's late wife, he has more than enough reason to want to see Aleric dead." With a small grunt of satisfaction, he sat back in his chair, apparently pleased that he had proved his case.

I started to rebut this argument, then sat quietly for a moment, giving serious thought to what he had said. Why, I asked myself, was I so certain that Mortimer Remy was incapable of taking someone's life? I was aware that Samuel held the publisher in high esteem; after all, he had been the first person to purchase one of my brother's crime articles. In truth, however, I knew very little about the man. Had I allowed his ready smile and smooth southern charm to influence my opinion? I calculated how many times I had actually been in Remy's company and realized that it numbered no more than two or three occasions, hardly enough to form an unbiased judgment of any individual. And as Robert pointed out, Remy had valid reasons for hating his rival. Good Lord! What if Jonathan Aleric *had* been the intended victim?

"What is it, Sarah?" my companion asked, breaking into my thoughts. "I can just about see smoke coming out of that over-worked brain of yours."

I was spared the need to answer him as the object of my deliberations walked to center stage and faced the audience. He was dressed nattily in evening clothes and a bright blue-and-gold cravat. I was pleased to note that he no longer seemed afflicted with a toothache.

Before my companion could ask, I said, "That's Mortimer Remy."

A tightly corseted woman seated to my left whispered for me to be quiet, and I shook my head slightly as Robert started to ask another question.

"I'll explain more later," I told him in a hushed tone, which nonetheless earned me another admonishing glare from my neighbor. I responded with an innocent smile and friendly nod.

The room gradually grew quiet as Mortimer Remy announced Oscar Wilde's second appearance at Pratt's Hall, his introduction including a great many overblown adjectives to describe the Irishman's North American tour as well as his recently published volume of poems.

"And now, ladies and gentlemen," he finished with a broad flourish of his hand, "I present to you the young author of *Poems,* and one of the leading advocates of the Aesthetic Movement, Mr. Oscar Wilde."

There was a smattering of applause as Wilde took the stage. Robert gave a grunt of disapproval as he scrutinized the poet's clothing. This evening he was attired in a purple coat that had been left open to reveal a lining of lavender satin. As before, he wore knee breeches, black silk hose, and shoes with polished silver buckles. Over one shoulder he carried a bright yellow velvet cloak, adding a jarring flash of color to an already gaudy ensemble.

Although Robert had met the poet when he visited Samuel in the hospital, he still stared at him in disbelief as the Irishman strode with an air of majestic nonchalance to the center of the stage.

"Good God!" he exclaimed. "The man looks like a full-plumed peacock. Has he no idea how ludicrous he appears?"

"I think he cares very much about his appearance, and is generally well pleased with the effect it achieves. Its very absurdity has brought him priceless publicity, and has served the goals of the Aesthetic Movement he champions."

"Shh," shushed the woman to my left.

Once again I favored her with an innocent smile, saying quietly, "I'm sorry. My friend and I were just commenting on Mr. Wilde's, er, unusual apparel."

To my surprise, the woman responded with a fawning smile. "Yes, it is unique, is it not? If only more gentlemen were inspired to dress with such distinction and flair."

As the applause died, it was replaced by a few hisses from the audience. The woman immediately turned her aristocratic face to glare at several nearby offenders, then turned to voice her indignation to the amused-looking man seated to her left. I received the impression that he and other men in the auditorium had been dragged there against their wishes by wives eager to behold Wilde in person. I felt a stab of guilt as I realized that by insisting Robert escort me to Platt's Hall that evening, I could be regarded as having behaved like one of them.

Before Wilde could commence his lecture, there was a thunder of footsteps coming from the rear of the hall. Looking around, I saw a number of late arrivals marching noisily down the center aisle. They were attired in velvet coats, knee breeches, satin shirts, and black hose, presenting a jarring array of pink, blue, violet, yellow, and purple in an obvious parody of Wilde's costume. As they took seats in the front rows of the auditorium, the audience instantly erupted in laughter, whistles, and cheers. Demonstrating their appreciation of this reception, the men—whom I assumed by their age and demeanor to be students of the nearby University of

California—gave low bows and raised their arms to wave on their admirers.

"I have a feeling this is going to turn ugly," I said to Robert, only to find that he had risen halfway out of his seat and was smiling at the rowdy young men. "Robert!" I admonished, tugging him down by the coattail. "Do not encourage the scoundrels."

"Come now, Sarah, you must admit that they've perfectly taken the man's measure. Wilde is nothing but an overdressed coxcomb, strutting about and speaking a lot of twaddle." He gave a derisive snort. "How can any intelligent person take the popinjay seriously?"

As if agreeing with this pronouncement, a young man in the front row stood up and screamed, "Nancy boy!"

"Fop!" yelled out one of his companions.

"Disgrace to the Irish," called yet another.

An abashed and red-faced Mortimer Remy hurried out onto the stage from the wings, glowering at the troublemakers and trying rather ineffectively to put a stop to the heckling, which by now had been taken up by a number of other men in the audience.

"Please! Please!" Remy said, shouting in order to be heard over the din. "Remember that Mr. Wilde is our guest. I insist that you treat him with respect."

Out of the corner of my eye, I noticed that three or four police officers had slipped into the auditorium and stood quietly watching and holding billy clubs in their hands. I was surprised to see Sergeant Lewis among their company. He did not brandish a club, but his sharp brown eyes were carefully taking in the members of the audience. As heads turned toward the uniformed men, the commotion gradually subsided.

On the stage, Wilde gave every appearance of not being in the least put out by the jeering. He had, in fact, seated himself comfortably in the chair that had been provided for him, casually lighting a cigarette and then taking a sip from a glass of what appeared to be absinthe. He viewed the more outspoken members of the audience with amused disregard, as if *they* were the objects of derision and not himself.

When all was quiet, Wilde put down his glass and walked to the lectern, facing his audience as if he had been greeted with cheers of enthusiasm rather than catcalls of derision. A moment later, he was forced to duck when one of the young men stood to chuck an overripe tomato at him.

Although the tomato had missed its mark, the poet took a long sip of his drink before once again taking his place behind the podium. With an air of outward calm, he executed a little bow and faced his hecklers.

"Thank you, gentlemen," he drawled with a self-aggrandizing smile. "Your behavior has proven my observation that America is the only country that went from barbarism to decadence without civilization in between."

This, of course, aroused more taunts, and several more pieces of rotten produce flew onto the stage. Before he could drop behind the lectern, a decaying orange splattered onto his purple coat. With a disdainful curl of his full lips, Wilde nonchalantly swept out a graceful hand and brushed the offending fruit onto the floor.

"Clearly you propose to intimidate me with overripe projectiles," he said, rather bravely squaring off once again to face the young offenders. "However, I think you will find that these efforts are doomed to failure. It is a simple fact, you see, that a poet can survive everything but a misprint."

This comment was met by more taunts, and several students stood up with arms pulled back, ready to pummel the poet with another rash of verbal and physical abuse. As if suddenly jolted out of their shock at this crude demonstration, a number of women in the audience rose from their seats to voice their disapproval at the university men. This was instantly rebutted by several dozen men. Robert shot me a quick glance, as if eager to add his own voice to the din, but at my disapproving expression he thankfully remained silent in his chair.

Before pandemonium could break out, the police in attendance made their way down the aisles, nightsticks raised as if to reinforce their shouts for everyone to settle down and stay in their seats. A few insults were directed at the advancing men in blue, but finally the auditorium fell silent, and Wilde was able to commence his lecture.

"Dear people," he began, "some of you no doubt would like to put me to death. You would send me to the gallows on clearly proven charges of having written poems entirely composed of three wonderful things: romance, music, and sorrow."

These words elicited a fresh explosion of whistles and jeers, which were instantly silenced by the angry police and the more outspoken women in the audience, many of whom were now brandishing umbrellas and canes at the students, and in some instances at their male companions.

Wilde's voice cut through the ruckus. "And to those of you who are so loud, let me say that you're wonderfully tolerant. You forgive everything except genius."

To my relief, this comment, delivered in a dry, mockingly humble tone, elicited a wave of laughter, even from a few of the young men seated in the front rows. Now that the police had taken up positions throughout the auditorium—and the students were evidently satisfied that they had made their point—Wilde went on with his talk.

Which, unfortunately, was every bit as boring as it had been at Mortimer Remy's house. The evening—which had, however distastefully, begun with some excitement—rapidly deteriorated into monotony.

Catching a movement to my left, I saw Eddie slip into a row across the aisle from our own. Robert and I had not reserved a seat for the lad, since we were not sure if he would be able to secure a parking place where he might leave the brougham unattended. Never one to miss a spectacle, he had apparently found a suitable spot and was now here to see for himself the man satirically touted only days earlier in the *San Francisco Wasp* as being "the Modern Messiah."

I nudged Robert, and together we watched the lad lean forward in his seat and stare wide-eyed at the tall, slightly overweight man on the stage.

I was smiling at his reaction when I noticed another familiar figure hurry down the center hall to take a seat almost directly behind Eddie. It was Samuel's writer friend Emmett Gardiner, looking as amused as Eddie by the spectacle taking place on the stage. Evidently feeling my gaze on him, Gardiner met my eyes, smiled, and gave me a little wave of his hand.

I was acknowledging his greeting when I caught Eddie's eye. He was grinning from ear to ear as he pointed to the stage and mouthed, "Is that him?" I inclined my head, thinking it was just as well that he had arrived after the earlier demonstrations. I feared the students' behavior would have had a negative influence on the polite civility I was attempting to instill in the boy.

I could sense that Robert was growing restless. "How long is he going to babble on about furnishing houses that will live in 'song and tradition'?" he grumbled, gazing wistfully at several men who had risen and were departing the hall.

"Hopefully not much longer," I answered, sharing his sentiments.

I studied Stephen Parke and his lovely young neighbor Isabel Freiberg. From the way their heads bent toward each other, I suspected that they were no more enamored with Wilde's lecture than were Robert and I. If either was guilty of trying to kill Samuel, Jonathan Aleric, or me, neither one appeared to be suffering any pangs of conscience.

My gaze went to Aleric, who was absently stroking his bristly mustache as he listened to Wilde from his front-row seat. How could he appear so absorbed in such a tedious discourse? I wondered. However much I had been put off by the man's poetry, I found his current topic to be infinitely worse. If Wilde was the personification of the Aesthetic Movement, I for one wanted nothing to do with it! Frankly, I found it disappointing that so few Telegraph Hill residents had come to Platt's Hall tonight. Given her age and physical health I was not surprised that Mrs. Mont-gomery was not in attendance. And her man, Bruno Studds, was surely at her hilltop home attending to her needs. Remy's typeset-ter, Tull O'Hara, had demonstrated little enough interest in Wilde at his employer's home; I should have guessed that he would not be in attendance. Claude Dunn, of course, had just lost his wife and was left with a newborn son to care for, and Isabel's father, Solomon, hadn't displayed much interest in the Irishman, either. I smiled, thinking this was probably why Stephen and Isabel had taken the opportunity to come here tonight. They appeared so deeply in love, they would undoubtedly jump at any chance to be alone and away from her disapproving father.

When the long evening finally came to a close, Wilde bowed to very modest applause, lit yet another cigarette, and picked up his drink, which had been refilled during his lecture. Mortimer Remy started to step out from the wings, but Jonathan Aleric was quicker, racing up the stairs located on either side of the stage. Pushing Remy aside, he grabbed hold of Wilde's arm and faced the audience.

"A stirring talk, Mr. Wilde," he exclaimed. "I'm sure everyone present here in Platt's Hall has learned a great deal about the ex-hilarating Aesthetic Movement, as well as how to best incorporate it into their own lives."

A visibly angry Mortimer Remy pulled Aleric's hand off Wil-de's shoulder. "Yes, yes, we are all very grateful to Mr. Wilde for visiting our fair city. Now if you will please—"

"In honor of the occasion," Aleric interrupted, "I have planned a reception for Mr. Wilde at the Baldwin Hotel. You need only present your ticket for tonight's lecture to gain admission. Food and drinks are compliments of my newspaper, the *Bay Area Ex-press*. Copies of my record-selling book, *An Uncivil War,* will also be available at the hotel for purchase."

This was received with enthusiastic shouts from the audience. The Baldwin was one of San Francisco's premier hotels, designed in the style of the French Renaissance, with a mansard roof and

Corinthian columns. Few of San Francisco's working class had ever stepped a foot inside the grand edifice, much less been wined and dined there. Shouts of approval filled the hall as everyone present, whether a fan or a heckler, raced to join the party. Jonathan Aleric had suddenly become one of the most popular men in town.

"Wait! Please . . ." Remy's words were lost in the cacophony of noise as the auditorium quickly emptied of people. "I've arranged for refreshments to be served here in the hall. There is no need to rush off."

Even as he spoke, I could see waiters entering the auditorium bearing trays laden with food. Departing members of the audience snatched at slices of bread and meat from the platters, barely pausing before continuing their exodus out of the hall.

I tried to make my way through the crowd toward Stephen Parke and Isabel Freiberg, but the mass departure was going against me. By the time I reached the row where they had been sitting, I was disappointed to see that they were no longer in sight. I did catch a glimpse of Emmett Gardiner making his way out of the hall, but there was obviously no way I could reach him through the throng.

"Now what?" Robert asked, elbowing his way between two protesting men to my side. "Don't tell me you plan to go to the Baldwin."

I shook my head. "No, I'm not hungry. Besides, I've had enough of Mr. Wilde for one evening."

"Praise God," he said, looking relieved. "I can't remember the last time I was forced to listen to so much pure hokum."

I took a hasty step back from the center aisle as the last party of students rushed past us. "I had hoped to speak to Mr. Parke and Miss Freiberg before we left, but I was too late to catch them."

"And even if you had, what did you expect to learn?"

"I don't know," I answered truthfully. "Probably not much. It's so frustrating, Robert. We are no closer to uncovering the identity of the scoundrel who shot Samuel now than we were last week."

"Surely you don't suspect Parke or the Freiberg woman to be the culprit, do you?" he asked, taking my arm and leading me toward the doors.

"That's the problem, I can't imagine why any of the people present at Mortimer Remy's house would want to harm Samuel. Yet someone did shoot that gun, and I will enjoy no peace of mind until I have identified the villain."

We exited the hall to find that it had started to rain. Pulling up my collar, I looked around for Eddie and was surprised to find him standing on the curb, watching Sergeant Lewis speak to a constable who had pulled up in a police wagon. It required but a brief glance at George's grave face to realize that something was wrong.

I hastened forward, but George had already climbed inside the wagon, which was hitched to a pair of sturdy brown horses.

"Did Sergeant Lewis say where he was going in such a hurry?" I asked Eddie, reaching him as the police wagon, bells clanging, took off at a rapid clip up Montgomery Street.

"I didn't talk to him, Miss Sarah," the boy replied, eyes fixed excitedly on the departing wagon. "But I heard the roundsman tell him that a bloke had gone and hung himself on Telegraph Hill."

I knew Eddie was referring to the young patrolman who had been speaking to George. My heart skipped a beat, however, at the mention of Telegraph Hill. "Did the constable say who the victim was?"

The lad thought for a moment. "He was in a hell of a—" He stopped, realizing what he'd said. "Sorry, Miss Sarah, I mean the leatherhead was in a powerful hurry, so I ain't sure I got the name right. But I think he said it was a feller called Down or Dunn, or somethin' like that."

CHAPTER NINE

This was one time I could not fault Eddie for pressing his horse to breakneck speed in order to keep up with the police wagon we were following. It was a weeknight and just after ten o'clock. Theaters and many restaurants had not yet let out their late-evening trade, consequently the lighter traffic enabled us to reach Telegraph Hill in good time.

We had gone but part of the way up Sansome Street, however, when Eddie's dappled-gray began to struggle under the weight of the brougham. His head went down as he strained against his harness, and I could hear his breathing grow labored. Ahead of us, the police wagon was experiencing far less difficulty climbing the hill, since it was being pulled by a span of horses rather than just the one. When Eddie's poor dappled-gray lowered his head even farther and began to snort in protest, I could no longer bear to see the animal pushed beyond his endurance. I pounded my umbrella on the roof of the carriage, then poked my head out the window and shouted for the boy to immediately cease this inhumane treatment. Reluctantly, he pulled the brougham to the side of the road, set the brake, and with a series of mumbled complaints about "ole Joe bein' a good deal tougher than he looked!" jumped down from his perch.

By the time the lad reached the cab door, Robert had already exited the brougham and was helping me to do the same. I paused only long enough to tell Eddie to hand Robert one of the carriage lanterns to light our way, then extended my umbrella and headed off through the rain in the direction of the Filbert Street Steps. Thankfully, tonight's temperature was more moderate than it had been on the night of Remy's literary gathering, and although it was a bit slippery because of the moisture, at least the wind was nearly nonexistent.

"Do you know where you're going?" Robert called out from behind me as we reached the steps and commenced our ascent.

I did not waste my breath attempting an answer but, holding fast to my skirts with one hand and my umbrella with the other, continued to forge my way upward. There was just enough spill of light from the lantern to guide my way.

Honesty compels me to admit that I was a bit short of breath by the time I reached the top of the stairs, and I was pleased to have a moment or two to recover as I waited for Robert to conclude his own climb. I was hardly surprised to see Eddie following hot on my friend's heels, then passing him as he practically flew up the steps; he would never willingly allow himself to be excluded from such an adventure.

"Where do we go now, Miss Sarah?" he asked, seeming not in the least winded by his rapid hike. "Do you think they've gone and cut down the bloke what hung himself yet?"

"I doubt they'll do that until Sergeant Lewis has viewed the body," I replied, straightening my hat as well as my disordered coat and skirts. The boy was now close enough that even through the rain I could make out his bright eyes and eager face. I was struck by a sudden, disturbing thought. "Eddie, you must promise that you'll contain your enthusiasm and stay out of Sergeant Lewis's way. The police may not be well pleased to realize that we have followed them."

As soon as Robert joined us, I turned and led the way up the now familiar path to Claude Dunn's cottage. As I did, I wondered what was to become of little Billy Dunn. Not yet a week old and already an orphan, I thought bleakly. The poor little tyke. Who would take him in? Thinking of the well-intentioned but grim orphanages the city had to offer for such unfortunate children, I prayed that would not become his fate.

We approached Dunn's house to see the police wagon reined up in front and two men whom I knew to be "regular" patrolmen, or officers appointed by the police commissioners and receiving pay from the city. There was no sign of Sergeant Lewis. However, I did spy Lieutenant Leonard Curtis, a glum-looking, thickset man in his late thirties, sheltering beneath an umbrella as he hurried through the rain toward a smaller police carriage parked in front of the newly arrived wagon. With a sharp word to the junior officer driving the vehicle, Curtis climbed inside and was driven off.

Preferring not to deal with the uniformed regular standing guard at the front door of the cottage, I waited until he was distracted, then led my little band around the side of the property. Lantern light illuminated a rear window, and approaching it, I saw George standing inside a back room, a handkerchief held over his nose and mouth. He did not see me, as his attention seemed riveted on something across the room, just out of my view. A second officer—I could not recall his name, although I remembered meeting him several months earlier beneath Rincon Hill's Harrison Street Bridge—was standing just behind Lewis. Using a pencil and an artist's pad, he was executing what appeared to be a quick sketch of the room. Although this practice was not officially sanctioned by the San Francisco police department, George had explained that it was growing increasingly common on the East Coast. He claimed that the drawings had proven valuable on more than one occasion when attempting to reconstruct the crime scene days, or even weeks, after the fact.

I walked to the back door and started to go inside, then halted abruptly. I felt rather than saw Eddie as he started to push past me with his usual youthful abandon, and I swept out an arm to stop him. His eagerness vanished when he looked up and, eyes bulging in horror, spied the gently swaying body of a man hanging from a thick rope across the room. An overturned chair lay behind the victim, making it look as if he had used it to stand on, then had kicked it aside, where it had fallen against the wall.

I daresay my face must have reflected every bit as much shock as the lad's; certainly I will never forget the dreadful vision that assaulted my sensibilities. If I hadn't known the figure dangling before me was Claude Dunn, I doubt I would have recognized the man who had so recently been a living, breathing human being. His face was a ghastly purple color, and his swollen tongue protruded from his mouth. The noose had dug so deeply into his muscular neck that it nearly disappeared into the folds of bloody flesh.

I stood, frozen in place, trying to take it all in. As I did, I suddenly became aware of the pungent odor permeating the room. Sweet Jesus, I thought, clapping a hand over my nose. Now I understood why George had half his face buried inside a handkerchief and why, I belatedly realized, the police artist looked to be a sickly shade of green. For an awful moment, I feared I might gag. Then I saw Lewis staring at me in alarm and swallowed hard to contain my nausea. I had come here of my own free will, I thought sternly. I would not disgrace myself by being sick!

As if he'd been caught behaving less than professionally, George dropped the handkerchief from his face, stuffed it into his uniform pocket, and said in dismay, "Miss Sarah, what are you doing here? This is no place for a lady." He took in Eddie's ashen face and added, "Nor a boy, for that matter."

For once I did not pretend that his words were anything less than the truth. "You're right, George," I admitted, trying to infuse my stupefied voice with at least some good grace. "We followed you on an impulse, and we have paid the price of our misguided curiosity." I glanced at the man hanging above our heads, then quickly looked away. "No one should have to view the consequences of such a tragic act. Mr. Dunn's life was too precious to be so carelessly thrown away, no matter how profound his despair."

George's sudden look of interest let me know that he had not yet heard of the writer's recent loss. "His wife, Lucy, passed away in childbirth just days ago," I told him. "I personally witnessed his bereavement. Yet giving in to his misery has now deprived his pitiful new son of both a father and a mother."

George did not immediately comment on this. After turning back to the body, he regarded it thoughtfully for several moments, then seemed to reach a decision.

"If you've finished with the sketch, you can leave now, Fuller," he told the police artist. Without a word, the man gratefully closed his sketchbook, pocketed his pencil, and hastily departed the room. George gave a long sigh. "Here's the thing, Miss Sarah. I'm not convinced the poor sod *did* take his own life. Lieutenant Curtis seems satisfied that it's a suicide, but, well, I'm not sure that I agree."

"Good God!" Robert exclaimed from behind me. "You think the man was murdered?"

Eddie gave a little cry of excitement. "Well, dog-gone it! If that don't beat all."

I stared at George, not bothering to mask my own surprise. "What leads you to that conclusion? It certainly appears as if the poor man did himself in."

George ran fingers through his mop of brown hair, a familiar gesture when he was concentrating on a case. As usual, it caused an errant lock of hair to fall over his eyes, once again giving him a youthful look. His expression, however, was anything but boyish.

"I've seen my fair share of suicides since I've been on the force, Miss Sarah," he said solemnly, "and this one just doesn't add up quite right. You see, when a bloke decides to end it all, he usually makes some mistakes, starting with not allowing himself room enough to drop."

"I don't understand," said Robert. "What possible difference does that make?"

"It makes all the difference in the world to the victim," George explained patiently. "If a person is determined to kill himself and falls far enough, he'll break his neck. That means his death will be fairly quick and more or less painless. To be sure that happens, he needs to fall at least six feet. On the other hand, if he stands on a chair like that one"—He pointed to the overturned chair lying against the wall—"he'll have only a foot or two to drop when he kicks it over. That's rarely enough of a fall to break his neck, especially a man of Dunn's size, and the poor sod ends up choking to death. That's when he usually decides he doesn't want to die after all, and tries everything he can to untie the rope, or pull the noose off his neck."

"Yes, I can see that," Robert agreed, still looking puzzled. "But what makes you think this fellow didn't panic after the chair went over, and behave exactly as you described?"

George unhooked one of the lanterns off the wall and carried it closer to the body. He took hold of one of Dunn's arms and held up the hand. "Look at this."

To better see the hand, it was necessary to approach the hanging body. Eddie and I did so after a brief hesitation, but Robert hung back, studying the appendage from over my shoulder.

Attempting to breathe through my mouth rather than my nose, I examined Dunn's hand. I could see nothing strange about it; as far as I could tell, the palm and fingers seemed typical enough for a writer—that is, the hand looked as if it had engaged in little manual labor. There were no calluses, unusual marks, or even a single broken fingernail.

"I see nothing wrong with the fellow's hand," Robert said, his ruddy face having gone a shade or two paler as he stared at the body. I noticed that he, too, seemed to be trying to breathe through his mouth. The smell in the room was really quite awful. Swallowing hard, he took another step or two back from the corpse. "Spit it out, Lewis. What are you getting at?"

I nodded in agreement, for a moment as baffled as my companion. Then it hit me, and I felt a little thrill of excitement, suddenly understanding what Lewis was trying to tell us.

"That's it, isn't it, George? It's the very fact that there's nothing wrong with his hands. When he found himself choking to death, he would have done everything possible to free himself of the rope, just as you described. But his hands are normal. They show no sign of rope burns or even broken or cracked nails."

George gave me a gratified smile. "Exactly, Miss Sarah. Because of that, I suspect that Dunn was already unconscious when he was strung up. Poor gent never had a chance of saving himself."

"Son of a—" Eddie stopped abruptly as I nudged him none too gently in the ribs.

"If you're right and it's murder," Robert said, "it would have been difficult to string up a man of his size."

"Yes, it certainly rules out a woman," said George.

"But why go to all this effort?" I wondered. "Someone went to a great deal of trouble to make it appear a suicide."

"That's the question, isn't it?" George replied. "Although I doubt I'll be given an opportunity to ask it. The lieutenant's convinced Dunn did himself in, and that's that."

Through the sound of rain pounding on the roof of the house, we heard the loud clang of police bells and the sound of another carriage pulling up in front of the house. Without bothering with an umbrella, George went outside to meet the new arrivals. A moment later he returned, leading two policemen who were carrying a stretcher and several blankets; the Black Maria was here to collect the body. George, his head and coat dripping water onto the wood floor, nodded grimly toward Claude Dunn, then stood back to allow the men to do their work. Taking up the same lantern he had used to examine the body, he indicated that we should follow him into the front room of the cottage.

"I'd like to talk to you for a few minutes, if that's all right," he said, indicating that Robert and I should seat ourselves in the two chairs the room offered. Eddie sat cross-legged on the floor, while the sergeant remained standing. "Even though I expect the lieutenant to close the case, I'd still like to find out everything I can about Dunn, including where his new child might be. I've already searched the house, and the baby isn't anywhere to be found."

"I have no idea where he is," I admitted, abashed and beginning to worry. "Isabel Freiberg, who lives farther down the hill, was helping to take care of him, but she was at Platt's Hall tonight with Stephen Parke, another neighbor." Suddenly I remembered Mrs. Sullivan, the woman who was wet-nursing the baby. I told George what I could about her, including the area where I had been told she and her large family lived, and he immediately sent one of the patrolmen to see if the baby was there.

"All right, then," he said when the constable had hurried off. "Now, tell me everything you can about Claude Dunn and his late wife."

Sympathy for the man's appalling fate, and reticence to speak ill of the dead, caused me to hesitate.

"Please, Miss Sarah," George prompted, obviously guessing at my thoughts. "This is no time for social niceties. I'd appreciate it if you'd be as plainspoken as possible about the man."

He was right, of course. If there was any possibility that Dunn's death had not been a suicide, we would have to start by examining the character of the victim himself.

I cast back in my mind, trying to remember everything I could about the night of Wilde's talk in Remy's cottage, as well as yesterday afternoon when Mama, Celia, and I visited Dunn's cottage bearing gifts for the new baby.

"I only met him twice, George," I said at last. "But honesty forces me to admit that on those two occasions I was not favorably impressed by the man. He struck me as being a selfish and ambitious individual, a man who put his own welfare above those of his wife and child. He kept going on about how was he going to continue writing without the income she earned cleaning houses, and how could he manage raising a son he hadn't even wanted."

"My God, Sarah!" Robert cried, looking scandalized. "The man must have been a cad."

"Be that as it may," George said, bringing us back to the subject at hand, "we need to concentrate on who would want to kill the bounder. The fact that he was a poor husband and father hardly provides us with a motive for murder."

"Unless his late wife, Lucy, has family in the city," I speculated. "Say a father, or a brother who sought revenge for the way Dunn treated his wife. He did allow—more likely encouraged—the unfortunate woman to engage in heavy physical labor right up to the time of her delivery. Perhaps one of her relatives felt Dunn's behavior contributed to her early death."

Once again, George withdrew his notebook and pencil and began to write. "I'll check on that, without Curtis knowing, of course." At that moment, with hair falling across his forehead and the tip of his tongue showing between his lips as he concentrated on his notes, I thought he resembled a mischievous boy rather than a seasoned policeman. I could not help feeling a deep fondness for my brother's friend. "Any other ideas, Miss Sarah? Anything at all that might help?"

"Well," I said, struck by another thought, although one unlikely to have had anything to do with the writer's death. "I saw Dunn speaking to Ozzie Foldger yesterday afternoon when my mother, sister-in-law, and I visited the Hill to pay a condolence call on Mr. Dunn."

"Foldger? You mean the newspaper reporter?" George asked in surprise.

"Yes," I replied. "They were talking together behind the house, as if they didn't want to be seen by anyone. I'm almost certain that Foldger gave Mr. Dunn quite a bit of money."

"I remember you mentioning that last night," Robert put in. "I thought you must have been mistaken. I mean, why would that grubby reporter give Dunn money?"

"I have no idea," I answered. "I thought it very peculiar at the time."

Robert was shaking his head doubtfully. "Even if you're right, it doesn't mean Foldger had any reason to murder Dunn."

"No, it doesn't," George put in, looking from one of us to the other. "We must be missing something."

Eddie suddenly popped up from his place on the floor, saying excitedly, "Maybe that Dunn gent had somethin' on Foldger and was rookin' him. After a while, it might have put the reporter in enough of a pucker to string the sharper up."

Both Robert and I stared at the lad blankly, not understanding a word he had spoken.

Despite the severity of the circumstances, Lewis had to work to repress a smile. "The lad is suggesting that Dunn might have been blackmailing Mr. Foldger, eventually making the reporter angry enough to commit murder."

"Good heavens," I said.

Robert rolled his eyes, giving me an accusing look. "I thought you said you'd been working on the boy's vocabulary."

"I have," I said, my tone rather more defensive than I'd intended. "It has proven to be a formidable task." I turned to George. "Who discovered the body?"

"Evidently, the death was reported by one of Dunn's neighbors." He consulted a page in his notebook. "A Mrs. Annabelle Carr, who lives next door. She says she brought him his dinner a little after seven o'clock. When he didn't answer her knock, she came inside to leave the plate in his kitchen. That's when she found him. Since I was at Platt's Hall, Lieutenant Curtis responded to the boy she sent to the station to report the death. You know the rest."

"Yes," I said thoughtfully. "So, all we know is that he died sometime before seven this evening."

"I'm afraid so," George agreed.

"Is there no way of telling how long he's been—that is, when he died—by examining the body?" Robert asked.

"Not really," answered George. "At least not by me. Despite Lieutenant Curtis being so sure it's suicide, I intend to ask the coroner to have a look for himself. It's nigh on to impossible to establish the exact time of death, but it won't hurt for him to try. And I'd particularly like to hear his views on whether it was suicide or murder. The coroner owes me a favor, and I trust him to keep the examination to himself."

"What a mess," Robert said with a frown. "It would be a good deal easier if Dunn really did kill himself, rather than having to deal with all these niggling doubts."

"I agree," said George. "But I can't ignore the evidence of my own eyes just for the sake of expediency."

"Of course you cannot," I put in heartily. True, I had not cared for the dead man, but that did not lessen my determination to see a possible murderer brought to justice. "It is a conundrum, though, and as you say, Robert, it makes little sense. First my brother is shot, then Claude Dunn is very probably murdered in such a way as to make it appear a suicide."

"You think this man's death has something to do with Samuel's shooting?" Robert asked.

"I have no idea," I admitted, feeling a cold shiver run down my spine. "But the two events seem an unlikely coincidence."

CHAPTER TEN

The policeman George sent to Mrs. Sullivan's house returned in considerable agitation, informing George that the wet nurse refused to speak to him or indeed even to open her door.

"When I tried to tell her about Mr. Dunn's death," he reported, "she started crying and saying she'd have no truck with the police, and to go away."

"Does she have a husband?" George asked the man. "Did you try talking to him?"

"She claims her husband works nights and that she won't open her door to no man, especially not a copper."

"Do you know if she has the Dunn baby?" I asked the constable, hoping he had been able to obtain at least that information.

"Couldn't even get her to tell me that much," he answered, looking frustrated. "I could hear all kinds of kids running around and crying inside the house, but she wouldn't say if one of them was the dead man's baby."

George looked at me in silent appeal. There was no need for him to request my assistance. I was as anxious as he was to locate little Billy Dunn and assure myself of his safety.

"Let us see Mrs. Sullivan posthaste," I said, donning my wrap.

As the three men, Eddie, and I stepped outside, I was relieved to see that the rain had become little more than a drizzle, too light to bother with umbrellas, which would only have impeded our progress. It took us little more than five minutes to reach the wet nurse's house, which was located almost directly across the road from Bruno Studds's shack. Despite the late hour, the residence resonated with the sounds of children laughing and squabbling. Above the din, it was possible to hear a woman's voice pleading for quiet.

Standing on the disorderly porch, which was littered with toys, scruffy shoes, and a child's battered wagon, I knocked smartly on the door. The same woman's voice ordered me to go away. When I called out to her by name, however, she finally opened the door a crack.

"Yer a woman," she said, looking surprised to see me standing on her porch. "You ain't with them coppers, are you?"

"No, Mrs. Sullivan," I told her in soothing tones. "My name is Sarah Woolson, and I was acquainted with the Dunns. I'm sorry to disturb you, but I have come to inquire if little Billy is here in your care."

The woman glanced fearfully at the group of men standing behind me, then opened the door a bit wider. "You ken come in, Miss Woolson. But I won't have them men in me house. 'Specially not the leatherheads."

"Go on, Miss Sarah," I heard George say quietly. "We'll wait outside."

Without looking back, I slipped into Mrs. Sullivan's house, and she hastily shut the door behind me. There seemed to be children everywhere, the eldest appearing to be no more than seven or eight years old. I remembered Isabel Freiberg telling me that the Sullivans had recently welcomed their fifth child. Sure enough, I spied a cradle in a corner of the room and a basket nearby that I recognized as coming from the Dunns' house.

"There he be, Miss Woolson," Mrs. Sullivan said, pointing to the basket. "Little Billy, safe as houses. I dunno how he ken sleep through all this racket, but he seems to take to it right enough."

I peered into the basket to find the infant sleeping peacefully, just as Mrs. Sullivan claimed, his blankets neat and tidy and tucked snugly about him to keep out the night chill.

"You have taken good care of him, Mrs. Sullivan," I told the woman with a smile.

"I'm happy enough to do what I ken for the poor tyke," she said, regarding him sadly. "Got a real bad beginnin' in life, didn't he? Such a wee bit of a thing, too."

Ensuring that none of the older children were listening, I informed Mrs. Sullivan of Claude Dunn's death.

"That's what that copper kept sayin'," she said, her tired blue eyes regarding me anxiously. "Didn't believe him at first, but seein' all the fuss goin' on out on the road, I reckoned it had to be true." She looked toward little Billy's basket. "What's gonna happen to him, Miss Woolson? That's what I wanna know."

"I truly wish I could tell you, Mrs. Sullivan," I replied. "We shall have to hope for the best."

We talked for several more minutes. I was relieved when Mrs. Sullivan agreed to keep the Dunn baby for the night, and I promised to leave word for Miss Freiberg to collect him in the morning.

Departing the Sullivan cottage, our little group walked back to Dunn's house in time to see the officers carrying Claude Dunn's body out to the Black Maria. The solemn procession was illuminated by the men's lanterns, as well as the lamps of several passing carriages traveling down the hill. The light also revealed Emmett Gardiner, Mortimer Remy's nephew, standing in front of the house, watching the men place the stretcher into the back of the closed wagon.

"Miss Woolson," he said, regarding me with surprise. He tipped his hat politely. "I didn't expect to see you here. I heard all the noise and decided to walk down to see what was happening. Was that Claude Dunn they just carried out on the stretcher? Is he ill?"

"I fear it's rather worse than that, Mr. Gardiner," I answered. "I'm sorry to have to tell you that Mr. Dunn died tonight."

He looked at me, thoroughly shocked. "Good Lord! But how?"

Since I had no idea how much information I should impart to Remy's neighbor, I was grateful when George came over to inspect the new arrival, Robert and Eddie following in his wake. After I had performed the introductions, George took the notebook out of his pocket. Thumbing through it, he apparently found what he was looking for.

"Yes, here you are, Mr. Gardiner," he said. "You were one of Mr. Remy's guests at that reading he held at his house last week. My men questioned you in regards to Mr. Woolson's gunshot injury."

Gardiner nodded. "Yes, they did. Unfortunately, I wasn't able to give them any information, since I didn't walk down the hill." He returned his gaze to the Black Maria, looking as if he still could not take it all in. "I was just telling Miss Woolson that I heard all the commotion from my house and came to see what was wrong. I never expected to find that Claude Dunn—I mean, that he had died."

"Yes, I imagine it came as quite a shock," George commented, not without sympathy. "You live in the house behind Mortimer Remy, do you not, Mr. Gardiner?"

I missed Emmett Gardiner's response, as my eye was caught by something shiny reflected in the spill of lights. It took a moment for me to realize that a figure was standing motionless beneath a tree to the side of the yard. Peering closer, I thought I recognized the short, squat form of Tull O'Hara, Mortimer Remy's crotchety typesetter. I guessed that his spectacles had briefly caught the light of one of the lanterns. George also spied the man and called out, demanding to know who was there. Instead of answering, O'Hara—if it truly was the unfriendly little man—abruptly turned and bolted down the street.

George took off after him, then lost sight of the fleeing figure as he darted across a field. After a few minutes, he came back looking frustrated and annoyed.

"Who in tarnation was that?" he asked of no one in particular. "Did anyone get a look at that fellow's face?"

"I only saw his back as he ran down the hill," Gardiner said. "He was very fast."

"I think it was Tull O'Hara," I put in, "although I can't be absolutely sure. O'Hara works as a typesetter for Mortimer Remy's newspaper."

George looked at me, pleased, and I think a little surprised, that I had recognized the figure. "He was another fellow my men questioned after Samuel was shot. He lives somewhere down the hill, doesn't he?"

I nodded. "It's the first cottage you come to at the top of the Filbert Street Steps, almost directly opposite the Sullivans' house. Actually, it's more of a shack, very small and not in good repair."

"Good. Then I'll know where to find him." He waved a hand at the Black Maria. "You can go now. I'll contact the coroner tomorrow about what is to be done with the body."

I knew he was referring to the autopsy he planned to request, despite Lieutenant Curtis's insistence on ruling Dunn's death a suicide. I only hoped the coroner would be able to prove which of the men was right.

Once the black transport van had started down the hill carrying its gruesome cargo, Lewis bade us good night and stepped into the police wagon.

Emmett Gardiner watched as it drove off. "This is usually a quiet neighborhood," he said, "but in just a week your brother was shot, and now Claude Dunn has died. That poor baby of his."

"We are all concerned about the child," I replied.

He started to say something, then caught sight of an elderly woman walking, rather quickly for her age, toward us.

"Unless I'm mistaken, that's Abigail Forester, Mrs. Montgomery's sister," Gardiner said. "If you don't mind, I'll bid you all good night. She's a sweet old soul, but, er, a bit verbose."

I barely had time to return his farewell before he had turned to walk rapidly up the hill. The woman started to speak to him as he passed her, but he merely tipped his hat and continued on. By now she had seen Robert, Eddie, and me and hurried toward us in a flurry of sweeping skirts. I was taken aback to see that she was wearing a formal gown, although from the casual knit of her shawl it appeared to be a garment she had hastily thrown over her shoulders to ward off the cool night air.

"I heard the police wagons as our guests were leaving," she went on. "Has there been an accident?"

The woman paused to catch her breath, affording me a few moments to examine her more closely. I guessed her to be in her late sixties or early seventies. She was of medium height and possessed the rather substantial figure that society preferred to describe as "pleasantly plump." She was, as I had noted, wearing a purple evening dress several seasons out of date. Her head of thinning white hair was in disarray, undoubtedly due to her hurried pace down the hill, and the oddly assorted jeweled and beaded combs that had been scattered about her head as if at random appeared in danger of falling out altogether. She wore a colorfully beaded necklace, which unfortunately did not match the beads decorating her hair, while her gaudy earrings were so heavy, they seemed to be pulling down her delicate earlobes. I felt a pang of sympathy that her obvious attempt to dress fashionably had fallen so far short of its goal.

"I am Mrs. Abigail Forester," she said, regaining her power of speech. "Mrs. Katherine Montgomery is my sister. We live in the house at the top of the hill. But what has happened here? Please tell me the poor little Dunn baby hasn't taken ill."

"I am pleased to meet you, Mrs. Forester," I said, smiling. "I am Miss Sarah Woolson, and these are my companions, Mr. Robert Campbell and Eddie Cooper." I hesitated, not sure how to explain Claude Dunn's sudden, and violent, demise. "I assure you that the baby is fine, Mrs. Forester. His father, however—I fear there is no tactful way to say this. Mr. Dunn passed away earlier this evening."

Even in the dim light, I could see the woman's face pale. She clapped a small hand to her mouth, and I feared for a moment that I might have need of the smelling salts I carried in my reticule as a precautionary measure. Owing to the unfortunate frequency with which some women yielded to the vapors, they had proven useful on more than one occasion.

Robert must have had the same thought, for he positioned himself behind the woman in case she should swoon. Fortunately, she seemed to be made of sterner stuff.

"I am profoundly sorry to hear that," she said softly. "How did it happen? Was it an accident?"

Again, I was unsure how to answer. Whether Dunn had met his death by his own hand or by someone else's, there was no possibility of categorizing the hanging as an accident.

I heard a quick intake of breath, and Eddie suddenly appeared beside me, eager to provide all the gruesome details. "Why, we found him hangin' in his house, his face all swollen like an' purple—"

The boy broke off as I prodded him with my reticule. "That will be for the police to announce when they see fit," I said, giving the boy a look that plainly charged him to hold his tongue. "You say you were entertaining guests?" I asked, remembering the carriages that had passed the Dunn house as the police were carrying out Dunn's body.

"Yes, it is my dear sister's seventy-fifth birthday, and I insisted that we celebrate with a dinner party." She smiled and her face lit up, becoming quite pretty. She must have been a real beauty in her youth, I thought. "I believe Katherine mentioned meeting you, Miss Woolson, when you visited Mr. Dunn yesterday? I fear she is a most stubborn woman, and dislikes having anyone fuss over her. In the end, however, I am persuaded that she quite enjoyed her party." Her face once again clouded. "Until, of course, we heard the police bells. Oh, dear, I hardly know how I am going to tell her such distressful news. She was not unduly fond of Mr. Dunn, it is true, yet he was that poor child's only surviving relative. And it is all so sudden, less than a week since poor Lucy died!" Her small hand once again flew to her mouth.

I took advantage of this pause to ask, "There is no family in the area?"

"To the best of my knowledge, no," the woman answered sadly. "Lucy did for my sister and I, you know, and more than once I heard the poor girl say how sad it was that her new child would have no grandparents, or indeed even aunts and uncles, to fuss over it." She seemed to suddenly become aware of the child's precarious future. "Oh, dear, what is to become of that darling little boy? We cannot allow him to be taken into an orphanage. Mrs. Montgomery would never hear of such a thing. Oh, dear, no, she will never allow it. I must return home immediately and inform her of what has happened. And on her birthday, too. Oh, my, I am sure she will be devastated. Completely devastated."

She took up her skirts to hurry off, then asked in alarm, "But where is the infant now? The police didn't take him, did they? Oh, dear, I hope I am not too late."

"No," I assured her. "He's with Mrs. Sullivan, the wet nurse. She's keeping him with her family for the night."

Mrs. Forester sighed in relief. "Oh, thank heavens. Mrs. Sullivan is a fine woman. A great many children, of course, but he will be quite safe with her." She had another thought. "My sister and I shall have to do something about the situation in the morning. Yes, that is what we must do." She seemed once again about to take her leave, then went on, "Thank you again, Miss Woolson, Mr., er, Camden, was it?" She looked doubtfully at Eddie, then back to me. "You have been most helpful. My sister told me I was foolish to come down here so late at night, but, yes, yes, I am glad that I did. We will have to do something for little Billy. First thing in the morning. Yes indeed, that is what we shall do." With that, she bustled back up the hill.

"I'm exhausted just listening to that woman," Robert said,

taking me firmly by the arm and starting down the narrow road. "Hurry, we must leave before she thinks of something else to say and comes back."

We had made it perhaps a hundred yards when we saw the figure of a man walking up the hill toward us. His head was down, and he was obviously lost in thought, because he didn't appear to see us until we had pulled abreast of him.

"Why, it's Mr. Parke, is it not?" I said, recognizing the full head of curly brown hair escaping from beneath a dark bowler hat.

The man started and stopped walking, looking as if my greeting had caught him by surprise. He raised his face, and I saw that it was indeed Stephen Parke, although I fear it took him a moment or two longer to as easily place the identity of the woman addressing him.

At length, his somewhat dazed expression cleared, and he removed his hat, looking embarrassed. "Miss Woolson! Please forgive me for not recognizing you at once. I fear I was lost in my thoughts."

I took a moment to introduce Robert and Eddie, then inquired if he had enjoyed Mr. Wilde's discourse on art decoration that evening at Platt's Hall.

"Damn waste of time, if you ask me," Robert grumbled.

I shot him a look, then said to Stephen, "I noticed you seated in the audience tonight with Miss Freiberg. I attempted to speak to you after the lecture, but was prevented by the push of people leaving to attend the party at the Baldwin Hotel. Since you are only now returning home, I gather that you and Miss Freiberg attended the dinner?"

"As a matter of fact, we did," he said, still sounding a bit unfocused. "It was generous of Mr. Aleric, although in truth it turned out to be little more than cold meat slices and punch. Still, it was a nice gesture."

I regarded him more closely. His usually friendly eyes appeared drawn and worried, and I noticed that he kept clenching and unclenching his hands as we spoke.

"Is something bothering you, Mr. Parke?" I asked. My question was undeniably blunt, but I was worried about the man. I have found that the surest way to obtain an answer is to ask the question. "You look distracted."

"Good Lord, Sarah," Robert exclaimed, darting me a reproachful look of his own. "If there is something bothering Mr. Parke, then it is patently none of our business."

"That's all right, Mr. Campbell," Stephen told him. He eyed me silently for a moment, then sighed. "Isabel told me that she had spoken to you about us . . . that is, the fact that we have fallen in love and would like to marry. Unfortunately, Mr. Freiberg has chosen another man for his daughter, a man from their synagogue."

"Yes, she did tell me," I replied. His face appeared so crestfallen that my heart truly went out to him.

"Please don't misunderstand me, Miss Woolson. I don't blame the man. He loves Isabel very much, and feels that it would be best if she married someone of her own faith."

Robert started to say something, then seemed to think better of it. He covered this change of heart by clearing his throat.

"I think I know what you were about to say, Mr. Campbell," Parke told him. "You believe Isabel's father is right, and that she should marry another Jew."

"No, Mr. Parke," Robert stammered. "I'm sorry. I assure you—"

Stephen held up a hand, forestalling further apologies. "Actually, you are probably correct. In most cases, I believe it is prudent to marry someone of your own faith." He regarded us through miserable eyes. "But you see, we love each other. And I care very little about religion. I'd be more than willing to convert to Judaism, if that would solve the problem. But Mr. Freiberg will have none of it. He maintains that I would be changing my religion for the wrong reasons. He informed me not five minutes ago that he has made his decision, and that is an end to it."

"You have just left him, then?" I asked.

He nodded. "He attended a meeting at his synagogue tonight.

We, that is, Isabel and I, believed he would be out until late this evening, which is why she dared to slip out to attend the lecture at Platt's Hall with me. Neither of us cared a whit to hear Wilde go on about that aesthetic nonsense, but it was an opportunity to be alone. And we took it. Our mistake was going on to the Baldwin Hotel afterwards. Mr. Freiberg arrived home earlier than planned and was waiting for us. He was furious, and has forbidden us to see or speak to each other again."

"Oh, Mr. Parke, I'm so sorry," I said, realizing that my words were less than useless.

He attempted a smile, but it failed utterly. "Her engagement to this Josephs fellow is to be formally announced this Saturday at the synagogue. And that will be that." He paused, looking suddenly embarrassed that he had shared so much personal information with near total strangers.

Robert shifted his tall body uneasily. We looked at each other, searching for something to say that might console the unfortunate man. But of course we could find no suitable words; what could one possibly say in the face of such unhappiness? It was a Shakespearean tragedy, in every sense of the word. One, moreover, just as unlikely to result in a happy ending.

Perhaps to cover the awkward moment, Stephen cleared his throat. He started to don his hat when he appeared struck by a thought.

"Excuse me, but may I inquire what brought you to the Hill at this late hour? Since you were at Platt's Hall, I assume you did not attend Mrs. Montgomery's birthday dinner."

"No, we didn't," I answered, then hesitated. Given his wretched frame of mind, I hated to burden him with more bad news. Still, word of Claude Dunn's death would be all over town tomorrow, and certainly the residents here on Telegraph Hill would be among the first to know. "I'm afraid Claude Dunn died earlier this evening."

"Died?" He looked at us uncomprehendingly. "But that's impossible. I saw him earlier tonight on my way down to Isabel's house."

"You saw him?" I asked, feeling a rush of excitement. "What time was that, Mr. Parke?"

"Let me see, it must have been shortly after six thirty," he answered. "Why do you ask?"

"You may have been the last person to see him alive," I told him. "What was Mr. Dunn's manner? I know he's been behaving, er, rather moodily since his wife's death, but did he appear different this evening? Perhaps more morose, or unusually bleak about his future?"

Stephen thought for a moment. "No, I don't think so. But then we only talked for a minute or two. He seemed excited about an article he was submitting to the *Overland Monthly* tomorrow, and another he planned to write for the *Daily Alta California*."

"Did he really?" I gave Robert a significant look.

"Mr. Parke," I said, "it's extremely important that you inform Sergeant Lewis about meeting Mr. Dunn earlier this evening, especially the exact time you saw him, and your discussion concerning his newspaper articles." I gave him the address of George's station, then instructed him to give the information to George Lewis and no one else.

He looked confused but nodded. "All right, Miss Woolson, I'll see this Sergeant Lewis first thing tomorrow morning, if you feel it's that urgent. But what is this all about? And how did Claude die? He was so young, and I assumed he was in good health."

I sighed. "I'm afraid he hanged himself, Mr. Parke. A neighbor discovered his body shortly after seven o'clock."

Stephen opened his mouth as if to speak, but apparently he found words impossible.

Eddie, who had been blessedly quiet for most of our conversation, pushed toward Stephen, his eyes bright with eagerness. "Dash it all if Sergeant Lewis don't think—"

Before the boy could blurt out anything else, I cut him off.

"The police have ruled it a suicide, Mr. Parke. Brought on, of course, by grief over his wife's sudden death in childbirth. Sadly, his despair has rendered his poor infant son an orphan."

If nothing else, it appeared we had given Stephen Parke something else to think about than his misery over Isabel Freiberg. He was still shaking his head over Dunn's inexplicable death as he turned to continue his walk up the hill.

"How fortunate that we chanced upon Mr. Parke," I said, energized by this new information. "Now George will know within half an hour when Dunn died. And if he was about to have an article published, and was planning more in the future, it hardly sounds like he said good-bye to Stephen, marched into the house, took out a rope, and hanged himself."

Eddie slapped his leg and guffawed. "By gum, I reckon you got the grist of it, Miss Sarah. Sure as thunder that feller was done in, like Sergeant Lewis said."

"Do you think he'll keep his promise to see Lewis in the morning?" Robert said, ignoring the boy's comment.

"I think so, but I don't plan to take any chances." I turned to Eddie. "I'd like you to take us to Sergeant Lewis's police station as soon as we get down the hill. I doubt he'll be there, but I can at least leave him a note. That way we can be certain he'll receive the information the minute he arrives in the morning."

Robert and I spoke little during the carriage ride to my home on Rincon Hill. As I expected, George had not been at his station, but I had written a note explaining that Stephen Parke claimed to have seen Dunn alive at six thirty that evening, placed it in a sealed envelope, and signed it to him personally. The lone officer on night duty promised to leave it on Sergeant Lewis's desk.

After that, I requested that Eddie take me home, after which he could deliver Robert to his boardinghouse. It had been a long, eventful evening, and both of us were wearily immersed in our own thoughts. The only sounds at that late hour were the carriage wheels rolling over the poorly paved streets and the clap-clap of the dappled-gray's hooves. It was one o'clock, and San Francisco was as quiet and peaceful as it ever became. Even the ever-present smells of coal smoke and uncollected horse paddies seemed less objectionable at this early hour of the morning. A gentle breeze swirled fog in and out of doorways and floated it in ghostly tentacles past gas lamps and street signs. The city seemed determined to snatch all the sleep it could before awakening to yet another bustling day.

Eddie reined up in front of my house, but before he could spring down from his perch, Robert had opened the carriage door and stepped onto the pavement. He signaled for the boy to stay where he was and helped me to descend.

After walking me up the stairs to my home, he paused when we reached the front door. "I know I'm probably wasting my breath, but I beg you to please let the police do their job. Whether Dunn's death was a suicide or murder, it does not concern you."

"Whatever makes you think I plan to involve myself in this affair?" I asked him with understandable pique. It never failed to annoy me when Robert took it upon himself to read my mind.

He harrumphed. "Sarah Woolson, your thoughts pass across your face like words printed on a page. I definitely do not like what I am reading there at this moment. Your brother was shot while on that blasted Hill, and now Claude Dunn has been found dead there. I realize that it is not in your nature to heed any sort of practical advice, but whatever is going on there, you need to stay well out of it, whatever your devious plans."

"You are mistaken, Robert," I told him, fumbling inside my reticule for my house key. "I am fatigued, as I daresay you are as well. Right now I have no plan other than to retire to the comfort of my bed and get some sleep."

"For tonight, yes. But what about tomorrow? Damn it all, Sarah, why must you be so pigheaded?"

"And why must you continue to fuss over me like a—like an overwrought mother hen? Really, it's exasperating." Having located my house key, I attempted to insert it into the lock, but it was too dark to see the latch. "Robert, you are blocking what little light is issuing from that gas lamp."

Instead of moving, he exclaimed, "I insist that you give me your word to stay away from that cursed Telegraph Hill until this grisly matter is settled."

I turned and looked up at him in surprised anger. If the heat I felt flooding my cheeks was any indication, my eyes must have been blazing. "You *insist*? Is that really what you just said?"

"Well, I . . . that is . . . ," he stammered. Then, meeting my direct stare, he drew himself up to his full, considerable height. "Yes, Sarah, that is exactly what I said. You must not become any further involved in this damnable matter."

"Insist? Must?" Despite my anger, I attempted to keep my voice low so as not to awaken the entire household, or the entire street, for that matter. "You overstep yourself, Robert."

"How, by trying to keep you safe?"

"May I remind you that my safety is not your concern."

"It most certainly *is* my concern," he snapped, his voice so loud that lights began to go on in a neighboring house. He clamped large hands on my shoulders and pulled me against his chest so hard that the air was expelled from my lungs in a rush. "Damn it all, woman, I lo— That is, I am extremely fond of you. Can't you see that? Your foolhardiness is driving me beyond the boundaries of human endurance."

Before I could prevent what happened next—indeed, before I even realized it was coming—his lips were pressing on mine with fierce insistence. After my initial surprise, reason told me that I should be resisting his embrace. But my body didn't appear to be listening. Indeed, it seemed to have developed a will of its own, and the unexpected and, if I am to be entirely candid, exhilarating heat coursing through me had nothing whatsoever to do with reason.

He had kissed me once or twice before, but never with such hunger. (I am, of course, aware of the dramatic connotations this word inspires, yet I cannot think of one which more accurately describes the fervor he demonstrated upon this occasion.)

As suddenly as the kiss had begun, it ended. He continued to hold me fast in his arms for a long moment, staring down at my upraised face. Since the feeble light spilling from the gas lamp was behind him, I could not read his expression. Even in the gloomy recesses of the front stoop, however, I could not fail to recognize the intense gleam in his eyes.

"Blast it all, Sarah, this can't go on," he said, his mouth still so close that I could feel his warm breath on my lips. "When I am with you I am driven to— Oh, hell and damnation!"

He jumped a good foot off the ground as a neighbor's tabby cat brushed between his trouser legs, giving a loud yowl of indignation, and surely pain, when Robert's foot landed on its tail.

With another curse, this one thankfully beneath his breath, he released me so abruptly that I nearly lost my balance and fell. By the time I had righted myself, he was disappearing into the brougham and slamming the door behind him.

With a series of clicks, Eddie urged the dappled-gray into the street and pulled away from my house.

CHAPTER ELEVEN

Rising shortly after dawn the next morning was scarcely a hardship. In truth, I had hardly slept all night. I would like to claim that the tragedy of Claude Dunn's death was responsible for my restlessness, but while it was a contributing factor, Robert was the primary cause of my distress. His actions mere hours ago had been so utterly unexpected that I hardly knew what to think.

The kiss we had shared played over and over in my head, long after I should have been asleep—especially the surprisingly enthusiastic way my body had reacted to the embrace. All this fitful ruminating despite my best intentions, for I truly did try to divest myself of these unsettling thoughts. I have always scoffed at the nonsensical idea of counting sheep as a means of lulling oneself to sleep, but I gave even that a try. Without success, I need hardly add. Robert's words could not be banished from my mind. Had he really been about to proclaim his love for me? Surely I must be mistaken. It was true that despite our occasional disagreements we had become fast friends. But love? *Romantic* love? I could not bring myself to credit it.

I finally gave up my futile attempts at sleep as the first signs of daylight began to peek out from behind my bedroom drapes. I rose and dressed in one of the suits I had specially ordered for my law practice. Although differing in color, they were cut along similar lines, each designed to achieve a delicate balance between contemporary feminine fashion and office practicality. In truth, any woman attempting to succeed in what was universally considered to be a man's profession was forced to stoop to any number of these ridiculous contrivances.

The delicious smell of fresh bread wafting up from the kitchen told me that our cook, Mrs. Polin, was busy with her day's baking. It would still be nearly an hour, however, before our Irish maid, Ina Corks, had prepared the dining room for the family's first meal of the day. Ample time for me to visit Samuel's room before the others made their way downstairs. I had to smile as I slipped out of my room and moved quietly down the hall toward the rear of the house. Yesterday he had moved back upstairs and into his own bedroom, which made it a great deal more convenient to keep my visit free from prying ears.

To my surprise, my brother was already up when I knocked softly on his door. I entered the room to find it in some disarray. Several shirts had been tossed untidily atop the unmade bed, and my brother's handsome face was drawn tight in pain. It appeared that he had been struggling unsuccessfully to ease one of the shirts over his injured shoulder, but it kept catching on the bandages binding his wound.

"Good," he exclaimed, eyeing me with relief. "You're just in time to help me into this blasted shirt."

I regarded him in surprise. "What are you doing up so early?"

He gave me a guilty look. "I have to go out for perhaps an hour or two this morning. John Frisk, a gentleman from my club, is picking me up in his carriage."

"Picking you up to go where?" I pressed, moving closer to help him on with his shirt.

I caught his quick glance at the writing desk. A thick brown paper package bound in string lay on top of the blotter.

"Is that your manuscript?" He did not answer, but I knew him

145

too well not to guess his secret. "I see that it is. You've worked on it since you returned from the hospital, haven't you? Even after Mama expressly forbade it."

Somehow he was able to look sheepish and defiant at the same time. "It was either that or go crazy. Our mother missed her calling, little sister. She should have been a nurse—or even a jailer. All day long she fusses over me as if I'm a child, incapable of doing anything for myself. My left arm may be incapacitated, but there's nothing wrong with my right hand, and I certainly don't need her help to do everything from eating to using the—" His face reddened and he looked away. "Well, you get the idea."

I stifled a laugh. "Yes, I'm afraid I do." I crossed to the desk and picked up his manuscript. It had grown heavier since the last time I had seen it. "Good heavens, Samuel. You've finished it! Although how you managed it with Mama hovering over you, I can't imagine."

"I've become adept at hiding parts of it under pillows, bedcovers, newspapers, magazines, even my dirty clothes. Ina's been a wonderful partner in crime," he added. "She seems to find it all a splendid adventure."

This time I couldn't repress my laughter. "Yes, she would. So, where are you submitting the book?"

"To Moure and Atkins Publishing House on Market Street. I thought I might as well start with the most prestigious house in town, then work my way down if need be." His expression said that he hoped working his way down would not prove necessary. He eyed me curiously. "Speaking of being up early, what brought you to my room before breakfast? Considering how late you got in last night, I'm surprised you didn't sleep in this morning."

"How do you know what time I returned home?" I asked suspiciously, wondering if he'd been spying on me.

He gave a little laugh. "Oh, you were quiet enough, but at one point Campbell bellowed loud enough to wake the dead. I'm surprised Papa didn't descend on you both like an avenging angel. Their room is at the front of the house, remember."

"Oh," I said rather feebly, remembering the neighbor's lights going on as Robert and I stood arguing on the front stoop.

"So, I repeat, what got you up at this ungodly hour?"

"I, ah, passed a restless night." I could not tell even my favorite brother the principal cause of my sleeplessness. "In fact, that's why I'm here. George was at Platt's Hall last night. After the lecture, a constable called him out to Telegraph Hill. Robert and I followed in Eddie's brougham."

I had captured his attention. He sank onto his bed, watching me with keen interest. "Why? What happened?"

"It was Claude Dunn," I said, observing his face closely. Dunn hadn't been a particularly close friend of Samuel's, but I worried that any shock so soon after the shooting might impede his recovery.

"Go on, what about him?"

"He was dead. Presumably by his own hand."

"Good Lord!" He thought about this for a moment, then studied my face. "Wait a minute, you said 'presumably.' Is there reason to believe it might not have been suicide?"

I recounted George's rather lurid description of how a victim would appear if it had been a self-inflicted hanging as opposed to a homicide. "George is requesting an autopsy, although he doubts the coroner will be able to substantiate this theory."

"I take it Lieutenant Curtis disagreed with these observations?"

"I doubt that George was afforded an opportunity to voice them," I said dryly. "But I daresay you know Curtis better than I do."

"Yes, I do. The man is headstrong and not always willing to listen to the opinions of his subordinates. Which can be unfortunate."

"Which can be stupid," I said. "If Lieutenant Curtis has his way, I fear the case will be closed without any further investigation."

"Leaving a possible killer on the loose."

"Exactly," I agreed.

"That's a chilling thought."

He paused again, perhaps thinking the same thing that was going through my own mind—namely, that this might well be the same person who had shot at him. Out in the hall, I heard the sound of our parents' footsteps as they descended the stairs for breakfast. A few moments later, Charles, Celia, and their two eldest children, Tom and Mandy, went down as well.

"Samuel, listen," I said, hoping to change his mind about going out this morning. "Why don't you let me deliver your book to Moure and Atkins? I'm going downtown anyway, and it won't be out of my way. It will spare you from facing Mama's wrath later. Her *well-deserved* wrath, I might add. You haven't been out of the hospital a full week yet."

"Thanks for your offer, Sarah, but I'd prefer to do it myself." He tilted his handsome chin up in that attitude of determination I knew all too well. "Our dear mother is going to have to realize that her youngest son is healing nicely, and is well able to run his own errands."

I sighed. "You're a fool, Samuel. But clearly nothing I say is going to change your mind."

He gave me a jaunty wink. "Don't worry, little sister, I'll be back before anyone even knows I'm gone." Smiling, he reached for his coat and the package containing his manuscript. "I'm going to wait until everyone is in the dining room, and then slip out of the house. Frisk should be here at any moment." He knew there was no need to ask me to keep his secret. We had been conspiring with each other since childhood, even when it wasn't always in our own best interests.

I helped him on with his coat, sucking in my breath as he winced when I gently guided his left arm into the sleeve.

"You realize that this is imprudent in the extreme. I can't believe I'm actually helping you do such a stupid thing."

"I'm not giving you much choice, am I?" He gave me a quick kiss on the cheek. "I promise to treat you to a lovely dinner as soon as I'm allowed out of the house. Legally, that is. Now, go and see if the coast is clear."

With a sigh of resignation, I went to the door and checked the hallway. It was deserted.

"I'll go down first and make sure no one is about," I told him without enthusiasm. At his smiling nod, I added, "Good luck at Moure and Atkins. And for heaven's sake take care of your shoulder!"

After breakfast I went downtown, but not to my office. I had set aside the morning to examine San Francisco guidelines regarding the construction of a bullring in the city. It did not take me long to discover that under current rules and regulations, City Hall had the right to approve or disapprove any new buildings in town. It also seemed clear, as the Dinwittys had informed me, that this body was about to issue just such a permit to Ricardo Ruiz, allowing him to build his appalling arena.

Determined not to give up so easily, I spent the next several hours making my way through a mountain of files and state law tomes, attempting to locate any city ordinances, no matter how long ago they had been issued, that might contain some clause or phrase prohibiting the construction of such a monstrosity. There were none to be found. Moreover, the fact that a bullring had previously existed in the city did not bode well for the SPCA's case. If that earlier arena had not resulted in a law prohibiting the construction of a similar stadium, a lawyer could well argue the doctrine of precedent.

By the end of the morning, I stretched my weary back and gave a long sigh of frustration. After four hours of searching, I had found nothing that would help our case. *Our* case? Good heavens. The use of this pronoun implied that I had already made up my mind to take on the society's cause. True, I sympathized with their position, but I could ill afford to ignore the consequences should I choose to become involved. First of all, it was a litigation that very likely could not be won. Clearly, money had changed hands; City Hall had been bribed—unfortunately not for the first time—and they were committed to allowing Ruiz to build his ring. Since neither the SPCA nor I would consider paying these corrupt officials to change their minds, even if we had the funds to do so, our cause would probably be lost before it even began.

I was ashamed of the second reason I was reluctant to accept the Dinwittys' case: pride. According to Ricardo Ruiz, Denis Kearney and his sandlotters were trying to defeat the bullring. If I joined their ranks, many of my critics would accuse me of racial prejudice. The fact that I had previously defended members of the Chinese community would be heralded across numerous San Francisco newspapers as my "hypocrisy."

I continued to consider the situation as I ate a light lunch at a nearby café. Common sense dictated that I decline the Dinwittys' case. On the other hand, could I allow my professional choices to be influenced by fear or the threat of coercion? Robert had advised me to do what I felt was right, without regard for public opinion or possible censure. In the end, of course, I was forced to admit that he was right. This was the only criterion that need guide me in reaching my decision.

I spent a fruitful hour at the downtown library, and then, since I was not far from the office of San Francisco's Society for the Prevention of Cruelty to Animals, I decided to deliver my decision to them in person. I boarded a horsecar and disembarked at an unassuming brick building at 614 Merchant Street. The society's second-floor offices consisted of three not overly large rooms, simply but functionally furnished.

To my happy surprise, the first person I saw upon entering was Mrs. Jane Hardy, the kindly woman I had met while representing her neighbor Alexandra Sechrest, who had been suing her abusive husband for divorce the previous year.

Mrs. Hardy was a tall, handsome widow in her early fifties whom I knew to be intelligent, hardworking, and ever ready to give of her time to charitable causes. Having experienced my own difficulty selecting practical yet fashionable attire for work, I quite approved of the gray cotton day dress she wore. Although the cut was out of date by several seasons, it complemented her slim figure, possessing a cuirasse bodice, a simple pleated skirt, and gray and red frills along the hem to lend a touch of color. Her brown hair, showing rather more signs of gray than it had the last time I had seen her, had been gathered into a neat bun at the crown of her head. The overall effect was feminine yet professional.

"Miss Woolson," she cried. "How very good to see you again. I have been praying that you will take our case. As have Mr. and Mrs. Dinwitty."

Although I frankly doubted that Mrs. Dinwitty was beseeching a deity on my behalf, I decided to hold my tongue on that issue. Instead, I replied, "That's why I'm here, Mrs. Hardy. Is Mr. Dinwitty in?"

"I'm sorry, my dear, but he has gone to the post office on Battery Street." She consulted a timepiece pinned to her shirtwaist. "If you don't mind waiting, he should return shortly. Please, take a seat." She pulled out a chair situated at a desk where she had been working. "I do hope that you have decided to help us. We must find some way to prevent Mr. Ruiz from erecting his dreadful bullfighting ring."

"I agree, Mrs. Hardy, and yes, I have decided to represent the society. Of course, I cannot promise we will succeed, but I believe I've developed a strategy which may help us to delay, if not defeat, Mr. Ruiz's project."

Despite this deliberate note of caution, the woman was so pleased by my acceptance of the case that she actually clapped her hands. "But that is wonderful, Miss Woolson!"

"Please, it's far too early to celebrate. As I say, we may only succeed in making the bullring more challenging to construct. Defeating it will not be easy."

"Oh, but I have great faith in you, Miss Woolson," she replied, refusing to be discouraged. "What you did for poor Alexandra far exceeded our expectations. And in the end, we can but do our best, can we not? That is our motto here at the society."

We spent a pleasant few minutes discussing the valuable work the SPCA had achieved since opening its San Francisco office in 1868. The ill-treatment of horses alone justified the existence of the organization, not to mention the thousands of homeless and starving dogs and cats who roamed the city's streets. Of course, it was still a relatively small group of no more than two hundred members, and it continued to encounter resistance of one sort or another throughout town. However, as Mrs. Hardy pointed out, the organization did what it could, which was a good deal better, in my opinion, than doing nothing at all.

"We are fortunate to have a dedicated group of directors, including Mr. Dinwitty. Mrs. Dinwitty and I volunteer our time, as do a number of other concerned individuals. I'm pleased to say that every year we add more members to our group, and thank heavens the contributions continue to grow as well."

From talk of the SPCA, our conversation went to our mutual friend, Mrs. Sechrest, and her two small boys. "Are they still residing with you?" I inquired.

I had not seen Alexandra since we had gone to court and obtained a divorce from her drunken and abusive husband. Mrs. Hardy had not only taken in the young woman and her two small boys, but also braved public censure by going to court and testifying on Alexandra's behalf during the custody hearing.

"I'm delighted to tell you that she recently purchased a home in Noe Valley," she reported with a wide smile. "Alexandra is so grateful to you, Miss Woolson. Her ability to buy the house was only possible thanks to the generous divorce settlement you were able to obtain."

Our agreeable discussion was interrupted when Mr. Dinwitty returned to the office, carrying several parcels and an assortment of mail. He smiled with obvious delight to find me seated at Mrs. Hardy's desk.

"Miss Woolson," he exclaimed, dropping his mail onto a table piled high with papers and hurrying over to shake my hand. "I cannot tell you how pleased I am to see you. Does your visit mean that you have decided to accept our case?"

"It does, Mr. Dinwitty," I answered. "Although as I was just telling Mrs. Hardy, I cannot guarantee that we shall succeed in preventing Mr. Ruiz's bullring. But we can certainly place a number of obstacles in his path."

"Excellent, excellent!" He pulled over a chair and joined us at Mrs. Hardy's desk. "Mrs. Dinwitty will be so delighted that you are going to lead our campaign to save innocent animal lives."

I nodded with good grace, once again deciding not to debate Mrs. Dinwitty's gratification at having me as their attorney.

"It will be a difficult battle," I told them. "And it will require a great deal of time and effort. Mrs. Hardy informed me that you have a number of individuals who might be willing to offer their services. I must be honest with you, Mr. Dinwitty. In order to achieve our objective in the limited time at our disposal, we shall require every able volunteer we can muster."

"And you shall have them, Miss Woolson," he declared. "We may be a small organization, but we are determined to do everything within our power to protect God's innocent creatures." He reached for a pencil and some blank paper lying on the desk. "Mrs. Hardy, if you will kindly bring us coffee—or tea, if you would prefer, Miss Woolson—we shall begin preparing our battle strategy here and now."

Unfortunately, there was little strategy to prepare. We would first appeal to the city department in charge of construction approvals, in an attempt to persuade them to reverse their decision to allow the bullring. Frankly, I doubted that this request would prove successful, but it was a logical place to begin.

Second, SPCA volunteers would be sent throughout the city armed with petitions opposing the construction. Once we had collected as many signatures as time and circumstances allowed, they would then be submitted to the city council, along with a list of arguments explaining why the signatories were contesting the project.

Our third, and least likely, tack would be to argue that the bullring posed a threat to public safety. I held little hope that this argument would succeed, but it could be tried if all else failed.

"We must start collecting names tomorrow morning," Din-witty proclaimed. "I will draft a letter to be delivered to all our volunteers this very afternoon. It will be short notice, but I believe we will be able to muster at least twenty to thirty individuals." He took a clean sheet of paper and, after consulting a map of the city, began to draw a quick chart, indicating the areas each volunteer would canvas.

After some minutes of this, he put down his pencil and regarded me seriously. "You have been straightforward with us, Miss Wool-son, and I have taken your misgivings concerning this affair to heart. However, I would like you to give me an honest assessment of our chances of actually preventing the construction of Mr. Ruiz's bullring."

I gave a inward sigh. He was correct; I had gone out of my way to present the situation candidly. Since opening my law office, however, I had learned that people often preferred to be given false assurances than the naked truth. The reality was that money ruled the city of San Francisco, and we possessed precious little of this valuable commodity to level the battlefield.

"I wish I knew," I replied honestly, as he had requested. "At the moment I can think of no better course of action than the one we are about to employ. On the other hand, I intend to continue exploring other possibilities."

As I departed the society office, I fervently hoped that my exploration would unearth bigger and better guns for our arsenal. I was certain that we would need them!

CHAPTER TWELVE

I had one more errand to see to before returning home. I boarded yet another horse carriage, this time exiting on Sansome Street. I felt a twinge of guilt as I walked toward the interminable wooden steps leading up Telegraph Hill. Just last night, Robert had urged me to stay away from what he had termed "that cursed Telegraph Hill," although surely he was allowing his imagination to ride roughshod over his common sense. I truly wished that he would cease his incessant worrying. I must be free to lead my life the way I saw fit.

I felt my pulse race and uttered an unladylike curse. Thinking of Robert reminded me of what else had happened last night. I had reached the Filbert Street Steps, but I paused, closing my eyes and forcing thoughts of his kiss out of my mind. Why could I not forget it? I asked myself for what seemed like the hundredth time. This was exactly why I had vowed never to marry, or even to fall in love. It was too disturbing, too all-consuming.

I gave myself a mental shake, picked up my skirts, and ascended the stairs, determined to turn my mind to the business at hand. This afternoon I wished to interview Claude Dunn's neighbors and anyone else who might have seen something out of the ordinary the night before, particularly now that we had narrowed the time of his death to just half an hour. Presumably, the police had already sent out officers to question the inhabitants on Dunn's street, but I wished to hear their accounts firsthand. With the exception of George, I held few illusions concerning our regrettably corrupt police department, especially its leaders. A city the size of San Francisco should have a force led by men of intelligence, integrity, and a well-developed sense of justice for all. It was deplorable to think that our safety and welfare were under the control of such a greedy, self-serving city government.

The first house I came to after leaving the steps belonged to Tull O'Hara, but I did not expect to see him at home during the afternoon. Just to be certain, though, I knocked on the front door. It went unanswered. His tiny cottage appeared deserted and as untidy as ever.

Several blocks farther up the hill, I came to the Freibergs' residence. The front door was open, and I could hear the sounds of women's voices coming from inside. Mrs. Montgomery's man, Bruno Studds, sat on the front porch, smoking a cigarette. He followed me with his dark eyes as I approached, then nodded silently toward the door, as if giving me permission to enter.

Tapping lightly, I peered inside to find three women seated amicably in the front parlor. It was not a large room, but it was uncluttered and furnished simply. My eyes were drawn to the upright piano placed across from the front window. This, of course, must be where Isabel taught her students. It was an older piano, but it gleamed in well-polished elegance where it was touched by the late-afternoon sun streaming through the west-facing window.

I had walked in upon a homey scene. Isabel Freiberg was sitting in an armchair, cradling little Billy Dunn on her lap. Mrs. Montgomery, her wheelchair pushed close to the two, sat placidly cooing and fussing over the baby. Her sister, Abigail Forester, was ensconced in a second chair set closer to the window, a straw basket containing blue yarn at her feet. She was busily knitting a garment that I assumed from its tiny size was for the infant.

The three women looked up at my arrival. Isabel and Mrs.

Montgomery smiled, appearing surprised but pleased to see me. It was several moments before Abigail Forester recognized me. She lowered her spectacles to the end of her nose, studied me carefully from over the rim, then at last appeared to remember.

"Why, it's the woman from last night, is it not?" she said, her round, friendly face breaking into a smile.

"It is, Mrs. Forester," I said, returning her smile. "It's good to meet you again under less unpleasant circumstances."

Isabel Freiberg was rising from her chair. She handed the baby into Mrs. Montgomery's outstretched arms and came to greet me.

"Miss Woolson, I am delighted to see you."

She took my hand, and I was surprised to find her skin cold to the touch. Her face was as lovely as ever, but she appeared tired and her eyes were ringed faintly with red, as if she had been crying. I remembered our conversation with Stephen Parke the night before and suspected the young woman had passed an unhappy night. Anyone could see how much she loved Stephen and how wholeheartedly he returned these feelings. I could not deny that a common religion was important in a marriage, but surely love must be accorded equal significance.

"Yes, yes, Miss Woolson, that is the name," Mrs. Forester said, breaking into my thoughts. She carefully placed the piece she was knitting in the basket and stared up at me with bright blue eyes. "I'm afraid I did not immediately know you. It was very dark last night, and of course, as you say, we met under dreadful circumstances. I was just telling my sister of our discussion regarding little Billy, and how we must find a good home for him as soon as—"

"Not now, Abigail dear," said Mrs. Montgomery, cutting off what well might have been another of her sister's rambling dialogues. "It is a pleasure to see you again, Miss Woolson. I understand you were present when the police were called to Mr. Dunn's house last night."

"Yes, Mrs. Montgomery, I was there," I said, noticing again that despite her infirmity, she seemed to possess a strong, determined character.

Her sister looked at me curiously. "I confess that I was considerably upset last night, but now that Katherine mentions it, how did you happen to be here on the Hill at such a dreadful time?"

I would have preferred not to answer this question, but I realized that it was bound to be asked sooner or later.

"It's a long story, Mrs. Forester," I answered, determined to keep my explanation as simple as possible. "My brother is acquainted with one of the policemen who received the call last night, which is how I came to hear the sad news."

"And this policeman asked you to accompany him to Mr. Dunn's house?" Mrs. Forester asked, her eyes wide in amazement.

"No," I told her. "Actually, my friend and I followed the police wagon." I adopted a look of chagrin. "Foolish of us, of course. I'm ashamed to admit to succumbing to such vulgar curiosity."

The expression on Mrs. Montgomery's face clearly indicated her disapproval. "Are we to understand that you actually went *inside* the house?" She gave a censorious little sniff. "Really, Miss Woolson, what can you have been thinking?"

"Oh, my, it must have been quite horrible," Mrs. Forester said in a small voice. Despite this display of revulsion, her round, pink face was lit with more than a hint of morbid excitement. "Seeing the poor man hanging like that, I mean. Good gracious! I'm surprised that you didn't faint straightaway."

"Abigail, please," her sister admonished. "Can you not see how this talk is affecting poor Miss Freiberg?"

Sure enough, Isabel's pale face was now almost stark white, and she had sunk back onto the chair she had vacated upon my arrival. I went to kneel by her side, fearing that she was about to be ill. From inside my reticule I took out my bottle of smelling salts, kept there for just such a situation.

"Here, my dear." I raised the little bottle to her nose. "This may help."

Isabel shook her head and held up a protesting hand. "No, thank you, Miss Woolson. I'm so sorry. I don't know what came over me.

I didn't sleep well last night. Perhaps fatigue caused me to feel a bit light-headed."

As I stood, I noticed Abigail was once again about to speak, and since I feared it might well be more talk about Claude Dunn's death, I hastened to say, "That piece is lovely, Mrs. Forester." I crossed to her yarn basket and fingered the tiny garment she had been knitting. The workmanship was exquisite. "Is it a sweater for the baby?"

"It is indeed," she said with obvious pride. "I began knitting it after I returned home last night. I found it difficult to sleep after the excitement of Katherine's party and, of course, poor Mr. Dunn's death."

Once again, I attempted to head off a return to Claude Dunn's recent demise. Turning to Mrs. Montgomery, I said, "Yes, I remember now. Your sister mentioned that you celebrated your birthday yesterday evening."

The older woman gave a short laugh. "Yes indeed, my seventy-fifth birthday. Abigail insisted on giving me a dinner party to mark the occasion, although spending three-quarters of a century on this planet hardly seems cause for a celebration. It's all rather tedious, actually." She smiled fondly at Abigail. "But my dear sister is thoughtful to a fault."

"Of course we could not allow your birthday to pass without having a party," Abigail exclaimed, clucking her tongue disparagingly at such a thought. Suddenly she gave a little shudder, and her bright eyes grew solemn. "Just think, poor Mr. Dunn might have been taking his life at the very time we sat down to dinner. It is quite terrible to contemplate. I keep asking myself if there was something we might have done to forestall such a dreadful act." She regarded her sister unhappily. "We should have insisted that he come to the dinner party, Katherine. If he had, he might still be alive. Oh, dear, I shall never forgive myself."

Mrs. Montgomery shook her head wearily. "Abigail, please, stop distressing yourself. Claude Dunn was a grown man, capable of making his own decisions. Of course the action he chose was a tragedy, but we must each take responsibility for our own lives."

Sensibly spoken, I thought, although I did not say so aloud. I had no desire to cause her sister further distress. As it was, the tears forming in her faded eyes looked as if they might escalate into a downpour at any moment.

"Of course it was not your fault, Mrs. Forester," Isabel assured her neighbor. "We all reached out to the unfortunate man, but it seems his grief was too overwhelming. He must have felt that he could not go on without Lucy."

Mrs. Montgomery's chin jutted out, and her eyes grew dark. "It was a selfish act, Isabel, plain and simple. I do not doubt for one moment that the man missed his wife—after all, she spent her short married life seeing to his every need." She bent down to kiss the top of the infant's head. "However, by making such a self-serving choice, he has deprived this unfortunate little boy of the only parent he had left. I am sorry if I appear cruel or hard-hearted, but that action was irresponsible in the extreme!"

"My poor sister has a soft spot in her heart for little boys," said Mrs. Forester, regarding Mrs. Montgomery fondly. "Her only son, Lawrence, by her late first husband, Mr. Giraud Tilson, was killed in the march on Vicksburg. What a handsome and clever lad he was. And so talented. We had such high hopes for him. The poetry he would write. Why, when he was only a slip of a boy—"

"Abigail!" A look of sadness shadowed Mrs. Montgomery's lined face, although I could see she was trying to hide it from the rest of us. "You will tire these poor ladies with your stories."

Mrs. Forester drew out a handkerchief to wipe at a tear. "I do tend to ramble on, I'm afraid. And my poor sister has never entirely recovered from losing her only child, have you, dear?"

Katherine Montgomery's face had paled, and her own eyes appeared suspiciously moist. "Nonsense, that was a long time ago. Miss Woolson is not interested in our family's dreary history."

"But, Katherine, it is because of Lawrence that you established a literary foundation," Abigail said, looking a bit hurt by her sister's harsh words. "Some nights I hear you crying when you think I am asleep. You do grieve, my dear. It is nothing to be ashamed of. In fact, I consider such undying love to be—"

"Sister, I beg you," Mrs. Montgomery said, growing increasingly distressed. Two bright spots of red had appeared on her cheeks, contrasting with her pallid skin. "Please, my dear, that is enough."

"Yes, of course. I, that is . . . ," the woman stammered unhappily, aware that she had upset her sister but looking as if she were not entirely sure why.

There was an awkward silence, and I regarded the infant sleeping peacefully on Mrs. Montgomery's ample bosom. His tiny eyes were closed, but his mouth was making little sucking sounds, and I wondered when he had last been fed.

"Have any decisions been made about the baby?" I asked, once again attempting to channel the conversation onto smoother waters.

"As I promised last night, Miss Woolson, we are already searching for a suitable home for the tyke," Mrs. Forester replied, regaining some of her previous animation. "In the meantime, we have worked out what I am certain will be a satisfactory arrangement. Katherine and I have hired a live-in wet nurse, who will reside with us until we are able to find a permanent home for the baby. Mrs. Sullivan has done a fine job feeding the baby, but it is awkward when she has so many children of her own. And of course the family will soon be leaving for Los Angeles, although I cannot think why they would wish to move to such a hot, dreary place. Personally, I hope to remain in San Francisco until the day I—"

"That is very welcome news," I said, speaking quickly as Mrs. Montgomery cleared her throat, fearful she was about to reproach her sister yet again for rambling. And I truly was relieved to learn that little Billy was not to be sent to an orphanage.

"Because of your kindness," I went on, "the baby is sure to receive excellent care. Please do not hesitate to let me know if there is anything I can do to help."

I departed the Freiberg house a few minutes later, to find Bruno Studds standing with Tull O'Hara under an acacia tree, its branches ablaze in a dazzle of golden blooms. From the ink spatters covering the typesetter's shirt and rough trousers, I guessed that he had just returned from work. Considering O'Hara's aloof nature, I was taken aback to see him actually speaking to someone, although judging by his unsteady appearance, I suspected he might have been drinking. Even more surprising, since I'd yet to hear the man utter a single word, was that Bruno Studds was actually participating in the unlikely conversation. I wondered if O'Hara had been on his way to visit Studds the afternoon Mama, Celia, and I visited Telegraph Hill?

I started toward the men, hoping to ask the typesetter a few questions about Dunn's death, but the moment he caught sight of me, he turned and scurried down the hill. Before I could reach Studds, he too had hastened away. Watching Mrs. Montgomery's handyman's departing back, I wondered why both men were so reluctant to speak to me. Was it because I was a woman? If so, this would not be the first time I had encountered such prejudice. Or did they consider me an outsider because I didn't reside on Telegraph Hill? Surely they couldn't believe I posed a threat to either one of them, could they? That thought was so absurd, I nearly laughed.

I continued to ponder this as I walked farther up the road, which was a muddy mess. The dirt lane was filled with a great many puddles left over from last night's rain, and I was forced to pull up my skirts in order to keep them dry. I did not bother to stop and interview the few people I passed along the way, most of them women working in their gardens, beating rugs, or calling in children for dinner. Glancing at the gold timepiece on my shirtwaist, I was surprised to see that it was after five o'clock, a good deal later than I had realized. I picked up my pace and hurried to reach Claude Dunn's street, where I planned to commence my interviews.

I had progressed another block when I spied three men walking toward me down the hill. As they drew closer, I recognized Stephen Parke, Emmett Gardiner, and Mortimer Remy.

"Good afternoon, Miss Woolson," Parke and Gardiner said almost in unison, doffing their hats politely.

"What brings you to the Hill, Miss Woolson?" Remy inquired. "I thought you would have had more than enough of us by now."

"I came to see how little Billy Dunn was faring," I answered, truthful enough as far as it went. I saw no reason to share the primary reason for my visit.

"That is precisely what we are doing," said Remy in his pleasant southern drawl. As always, the editor was perfectly attired in a vest and day coat, trousers pressed, his cravat neatly tied. "I understand that Miss Freiberg is caring for the child today, and we wished to see if there was anything we could do to help the dear young lady."

"I must say that I'm surprised to see you here at this time of day, Mr. Remy," I said. "Samuel tells me that you often work at your office late into the night."

Remy gave a rueful smile. "Ah, you've caught me out, Miss Woolson. It is true that I am a slave to my newspaper. Ever since my wife passed away, I'm afraid it has become my passion in life." The smile vanished, and he grew serious. "After last night's tragic events, however, I found it difficult to concentrate on my work, so I left early. Mr. Dunn's death was a dreadful shock to us all. And of course a tragedy."

Stephen shook his head in sad agreement. "As I said when you delivered the terrible news last night, Miss Woolson, it is difficult to take in. I knew Claude was devastated by Lucy's death, but I never expected that in his sorrow he might resort to such desperate measures." He stole a glance over my shoulder. "Did you happen to see Mr. Freiberg as you were walking up the hill?"

The young man kept his face carefully bland, but I knew exactly what he was asking me: Was Solomon Freiberg at home, or was Isabel there alone with the baby?

I sought to repress the smile that twitched on my lips. "Actually I just left the Freiberg house. Mr. Freiberg was not there, but Mrs. Montgomery and her sister, Mrs. Forester, were visiting."

"Well, I don't imagine they will object if we drop in and have a peek at the little one."

"No, I'm sure your visit will be most welcome, Mr. Gardiner," I agreed. "It is reassuring to see all the support that poor child is receiving." Aware that it was growing late, I smiled and said, "If you will excuse me, gentlemen, I have another friend I wish to see before I return home."

"Of course," said Emmett Gardiner, placing his hat back on his head. "We mustn't detain you any longer. Please give Samuel my best wishes."

"I hear that his recovery is progressing so speedily that it is difficult to keep him in check," Stephen Parke put in. "I have been meaning to stop by and see him."

"I'm sure he would enjoy that, Mr. Parke," I answered with a laugh. "It's impossible to keep him down. I promise to give him your regards."

The three men wished me good day, then continued their journey down the hill. I turned and resumed my walk in the opposite direction.

When I reached Mrs. Annabelle Carr's residence, I tapped lightly on the door. This was the neighbor who had discovered Dunn's body the previous evening, and I was uncertain if she would be willing to speak to me after such a shock. However, the door was opened by a plump woman whom I took to be in her late thirties.

"Whatcha want?" she asked a bit curtly.

I smiled in an attempt to put the woman at ease. "I'm sorry to disturb you, Mrs. Carr, especially after your dreadful experience last night."

This seemed to surprise the woman, and she regarded me with more interest. "How do you know about that?"

"My name is Sarah Woolson, Mrs. Carr, and I was a friend of

Mr. and Mrs. Dunn." This last statement was greatly exaggerated, of course, but I felt the white lie was necessary if I was to gain admittance. "I will understand if you don't feel up to it, but I wonder if you might spare me just a moment or two of your time?"

The woman regarded me without speaking, then seemed to make up her mind and held the door open, indicating that I should come in. I nodded my thanks and entered, following my hostess into a small front room.

Mrs. Carr was dressed in a faded yellow day dress, and her feet were shod in rather scuffed brown boots. As I feared, her full, round face was pale, and dark circles were plainly visible beneath her light green eyes. She indicated that I should take a seat in one of the upholstered chairs, while she sank into one opposite me.

"I am feeling poorly today," she said, not bothering to offer me any of the usual libations. "Why don't you just tell me straightaway why you want to talk to me."

Her words bordered on rudeness, but I could not blame the poor woman. She really did appear fatigued, and I did not doubt that she had slept poorly the previous night. Since my own lack of sleep had begun to weigh upon me as well, it was easy enough to sympathize.

"I agree that is the best course," I said. "Actually, I wondered if we might discuss how you happened to discover Mr. Dunn's bod— That is, how you happened to be at his house last night?"

She gave an involuntary shudder at the memory this evoked, but her voice remained steady. In fact, I received the impression that she did not mind discussing her alarming experience nearly as much as I had expected. Perhaps she had no one else with whom to share the ordeal and was relieved at the opportunity to unburden herself.

"It was horrible," she said, wiping her hands vigorously on a towel she must have carried in with her from the kitchen. "I'd been bringing Mr. Dunn dinner from time to time since poor Lucy died, you see, but I was late yesterday because my husband was sick and had been pestering me something awful. It was just after seven when I finally had time to take him the tray. I knocked on the front door, but there was no answer. Thinking he might be in his yard, I went around to the back." She licked her lips and swallowed, then continued in a small voice, "I thought I'd just put the food in his kitchen, but I—I saw him as soon as I went in the back door. He was—"

I held up a hand. "There is no need to describe the scene, Mrs. Carr. I was there later in the evening and witnessed it for myself. It will not be a memory easily erased from my mind."

She closed her eyes and took in a deep breath of air, then released it in a rush. "I'm sure I screamed when I saw him, but I can't remember much of anything, to tell the truth. I know I ran home and sent our son, Donny, down the hill to fetch the coppers. They got there later—I don't know what time. After that, it seemed like the police were coming and going for hours. I went to bed, but I hardly slept a wink all night."

"That is certainly understandable. With such a terrible shock, I don't suppose you noticed anything out of the ordinary at Mr. Dunn's house. Was he alone? Did you straighten or move anything that might have been in disarray?"

This last inquiry caused her to regard me suspiciously, as if only now speculating about the nature of my questions.

"Why do you want to know?" she asked, her voice sharper now. "Who did you say you were?"

"Miss Sarah Woolson, Mrs. Carr. I'm an attorney involved with the case." I felt a twinge of conscience at offering yet another misrepresentation of the truth, but I steadfastly ignored it. "I would truly appreciate anything you could remember about what you saw last night."

"You're a lawyer?" she asked in surprise, subjecting me to a long, appraising look. "If that don't beat all!"

My vocation, however, seemed to overcome her misgivings, and she sat for several moments considering my question. Finally, she shook her head.

"No, I don't think anyone else was there, leastways I didn't see no one. And sure as you're sitting there, I didn't touch nothing." She gave a little shiver. "To tell the truth, I was too flummoxed to move. I suppose I must have dropped the tray, but it's mostly a blur."

"That's perfectly all right, Mrs. Carr," I told her reassuringly. "You have been most helpful."

I heard a male voice call out something from another room and assumed it was Mr. Carr requesting his wife's attention. Rising from my chair, I thanked my hostess and then took my leave of the house.

The sun was beginning to set as I started down the hill. I passed Claude Dunn's cottage, pausing for a moment as I recalled the dreadful events of the night before. Had it been just over a week since Samuel was shot? It seemed more like an eternity. No wonder I was tired; the past seven days had been some of the most taxing I had ever experienced. Wearily, I decided to pay a quick visit to the neighbors who resided on the other side of Dunn's house, then make my way home.

The sounds of boisterous children reached me as I approached the neighbor's front door. The young girl with black hair who answered my knock informed me that her parents, Mr. and Mrs. Flattery, were not at home. In a single rush of breath she told me that her name was Clara, that she was sixteen, that she was minding her little brothers, and that moreover she was in the middle of cooking dinner and if she didn't get right back to the kitchen, her chops would burn.

I thanked her and was about to leave when I thought to ask if she or her parents had seen or heard anything unusual around seven o'clock the previous evening. Her reaction to this simple question took me by surprise.

The girl's dark eyes grew large and frightened, and she commenced wringing her small hands in front of her food-smeared apron.

"I'm sorry, miss, but I can't," she blurted out. "Mama said I was imagining things and that we shouldn't get involved with the police anyways, as it was none of our business."

With that, she started to close the door. I'm ashamed to admit that I used my boot to hold it open.

"It's all right, Clara," I said with what I hoped was a soothing tone. "You can tell me. I'm not with the police, and I won't inform your mother. What did you hear last night?"

The poor child looked conflicted, and I feared she would end up rubbing all the skin off her hands. Then she put her head out and looked carefully in either direction. There was no one in view.

"I did hear something last night, miss. It was a kind of cry, or maybe more like a yell. I don't exactly remember now, but it was loud 'cause I could hear it over the rain."

"Where did the cry come from?" I asked, holding my breath as I awaited her response.

"It was from next door, you know, where that man Mr. Dunn lives. I mean, who *used* to live there. It sounded like he was really scared, or maybe fightin' with someone, I'm not sure. Mama said I couldn't hear nothing like that because of the rain bein' so loud and all. But I know what I heard, miss, no matter how loud the storm was."

"I believe you, Clara," I told the girl, "and you did the right thing by telling me. And you think you heard Mr. Dunn cry out at about seven o'clock?"

She nodded. "It had to be about then, 'cause I'd just finished washin' up the dinner dishes, and was puttin' the bread away in the pantry—that's the room closest to Mr. Dunn's house, you see."

There was a loud noise from inside the house, and the sound of the boys grew louder again, as if they were fighting over some toy or other.

"Sorry, miss, but I gotta go," the girl said. "My brothers go at it something awful, and I'm sure my chops will be burned black by now."

With a quick look that might have been of regret, she slammed the door closed, and I could hear her yelling at her little brothers to behave themselves. I stood on the front porch for a few more moments, thinking. I would have to pass this information on to

Sergeant Lewis immediately, I decided. If Clara really did hear Dunn cry out, then it made George's murder theory a great deal more plausible.

The afternoon sun was fading rapidly by now. Anxious to take my leave of Telegraph Hill, I walked a block or two down the muddy road, then took what I thought would be a shortcut through a small grove of trees. Suddenly, the quiet around me was shattered by a loud bang. My brain barely had time to register it as the same noise I'd heard the night Samuel was shot when the trunk of a nearby tree exploded. Shards of bark flew in all directions, scaring off a trio of goats that were grazing in a neighboring field and striking me painfully in my face and neck.

I cried out and fell to the ground. Then, following some innate sense of self-preservation, I half crawled around the tree until it stood between me and whoever had taken the shot. I am not ashamed to admit that I was badly shaken; my body had begun to tremble, and I was suddenly very cold. Despite the chill, I realized that beads of perspiration were forming on my forehead and that the vision in my right eye was blurring.

"Dear God!" I croaked, barely recognizing my own voice. I sucked in several deep breaths of air, trying to bring my quivering body under control. Had someone really fired a gun at me? And in nearly the same place where Samuel had been hit?

Attempting to stop the flow of moisture into my eyes, I wiped a hand over my brow. I stared incredulously at the red, sticky mess on my fingers.

It was not perspiration running down my face, but blood!

CHAPTER THIRTEEN

I cannot say how long I remained huddled behind the tree, my body shivering in shock. Perhaps because of this overriding fear, my senses were on full alert: I was keenly aware of every sound, every stir of the leaves, every breath of wind, even the smell of fresh dung emitted by a team of horses laboring up a nearby street. The onset of dusk made it difficult to see who, or what, lay behind me, which merely served to increase my terror. Was the shooter still there, waiting for me to move so that he could discharge another bullet? Or had my cry and sudden collapse convinced him that he had hit his mark?

As if reciting a mantra, I kept reminding myself to breathe. It was imperative that I bring myself under control and make my way down the hill before the encroaching darkness became even more pervasive. Then again, perhaps the cover of darkness would be my friend, I thought uncertainly. It might serve to hide me from the madman lying in wait somewhere behind me—*if* he was still there. Again I raised a hand to wipe at my forehead as more blood dripped down my face. Why were my thoughts in such turmoil? This unaccustomed confusion was nearly as frightening as the knowledge that someone was trying to kill me!

Condemning myself for such a sad display of cowardice, I took in a final deep breath, counted to three, then leapt up from behind the tree trunk. In an effort to make myself as small a target as possible, I darted this way and that behind the remaining trees. My skirts caught and tore on brambles, and more than once I tripped over protruding roots, but I dared not stop. Blood continued to trickle into my eyes from the cuts on my forehead until I could barely see where I was going, and my heart beat wildly as I waited for another shot to ring out. Still, I did not slow down until I had nearly reached the wooden steps that led down the hill.

To my relief, I saw no one at Tull O'Hara's cottage and slipped behind part of an old rotting fence that at one time must have enclosed the small property. I stood there for several moments, fighting to catch my breath, constantly peering around the sagging wood to see if I had been followed. Reassured that no one was in pursuit, I forced myself to take stock of my situation. For the first time, I noticed my torn and filthy skirts. Even worse was the blood that had trickled down my face to stain my bodice. I must have presented a terrible sight. How could I make my way down the stairs without attracting unwelcome attention? Even when I reached the street, would a conductor allow me to board his omnibus in such a disreputable condition?

Then there was the question of where I should go. I had intended to go directly to George Lewis's police station to report what young Clara Flattery had heard the night before. Now, of course, I had even more reason to see him. But my timepiece indicated that it was nearing seven o'clock. Would he even be at the station this late? I wondered. In light of my past experiences with the police, I think I may be forgiven my stubborn determination to confide this afternoon's alarming events solely to my friend George.

After much thought, I decided that I did not care to walk into the station looking as if I'd made my way there through a battle zone, especially as there was a possibility George had already left for the day. What if I happened upon Lieutenant Curtis? I already had enough people warning me away from Telegraph Hill without Curtis actually forbidding me to go there.

In the end, I decided that it would not matter if I notified George tonight or in the morning. Moreover, I shrank at the thought of spending more time in public than was absolutely necessary. After tearing off strips from my petticoat, I wiped at the blood on my face as best I could, then went to work on my shirtwaist. To my dismay, these efforts merely smeared the blood, making the matter worse. Without a mirror, I had no way of knowing what my face looked like. Well, I thought, it would have to do. I could not remain concealed behind Tull O'Hara's shack all night.

I brushed the dirt and leaves off my skirts and then did my best to arrange the torn remains in some semblance of order. Hoping that the rents and stains were not too noticeable, I stiffened my spine and set off down the steps. Once I reached Sansome Street, I searched for a cab, deciding it would be faster and considerably more private than public transportation. How I wished Eddie were waiting for me with his faithful dappled-gray instead of having to endure the curious, and in some cases distasteful, stares of people who passed by me on the street. I must look even worse than I imagined, I thought in dismay when one woman stopped and offered to help me reach a hospital.

Thankfully, I did not have to wait overlong for a cab. Doing my utmost to ignore the coachman's questioning eyes as they traveled over my disordered and blood-smeared clothing, I allowed myself to be handed into the vehicle, and we set off for Rincon Hill.

My next challenge, of course, would be sneaking into my home unobserved. It was nearly dinnertime, so I would have to speedily wash and change my clothes or plead a headache and avoid joining my family altogether.

To my relief, slipping into the house unnoticed proved easier than I had anticipated. I could hear our butler, Edis, speaking to Papa in his study, and Mama had evidently not yet come downstairs. Cook and our maid, Ina, were occupied in the kitchen preparing for dinner. Delighted to find the coast clear, I hurried up the stairs and into my bedroom. I had just begun to remove my boots when there was a soft knock on the door. For a moment,

I froze and thought to ignore it. Then better sense prevailed, and I realized that this would merely create more problems than I already faced. Opening the door a crack, I was relieved to see that it was Samuel. Before I could invite him in, he pushed past me, closing the door gently behind him.

He started to speak and then stopped, mouth open, as he stared at me in alarm. "Good God, Sarah, what happened to you? Are you all right?"

"Shh, please," I said, placing a finger over my lips. "I'm fine, but I don't want to alarm Mama or Papa."

"Never mind them, you've already alarmed me." He reached into a pocket with his good hand and drew out a hip flask. "Here, take a good long sip of this. You're as white as that bed covering."

Shaking my head, I pushed the flask away. "You don't look particularly hale and hearty yourself," I told him, thinking that he appeared a bit peaked. Then I remembered that he had snuck out of the house that morning to visit the book publisher. So much had happened since then, it seemed that whole days had passed rather than mere hours. "How did you fare at Moure and Atkins?"

"Not now. First I want to know what happened to you." He pushed the flask firmly into my hand. "Drink some of this, Sarah. Now! Trust me, it will help."

I started to refuse it again, then decided that perhaps the whiskey might be just what I needed. It burned going down my throat, but I felt almost instantly revived.

"Thank you," I said, handing it back to him. "Now you really must leave. I have to change before Edis rings the dinner bell."

"Not so fast," he said, practically pushing me down onto the edge of the bed. "I'm not going anywhere until you tell me what happened. You look as if you've been in a street brawl—and lost!"

Once more, he pressed his flask on me. "Take another sip, Sarah. You still look far too pale."

I took another mouthful of the strong drink, then, resisting his insistence that I remain seated, rose from the bed. "If I don't change now, I'll be late for dinner."

Using my washbasin, I splashed water onto my face and neck, this time with the aid of a mirror. No wonder people had been regarding me peculiarly. My brother was right, I looked as if I had just fought my way through the Battle of Bull Run. I had no idea how I would be able to explain away the scratches and cuts.

"There's no point in not showing yourself, if that's what you're thinking," he said, as usual reading my mind. "Those scratches are going to appear even more brutal tomorrow, so you might as well face the music tonight."

"But what am I going to tell everyone?" I groaned, realizing he was right. Even if I tried to skip dinner, Mama would be sure to visit my room afterward to see what was wrong. I wasn't sure if I was experiencing some residual shock, but my limbs felt unsteady and I feared that the whiskey had gone straight to my head. I decided that sitting down for a few minutes might not be a bad idea after all.

"Sarah, that's enough prevaricating," he said as I sank beside him on the bed. His voice was serious, and his blue eyes regarded me with concern. "Tell me exactly how you received those cuts and bruises and tore your gown to pieces. And I want the truth!"

With a sigh, I briefly related my trip that afternoon to Telegraph Hill. When I told him about the gunshot, he uttered a curse and stared at me in disbelief.

"Good Lord, Sarah! Somebody actually tried to kill you? Did you go to the police?"

I shook my head wearily. "No. It was late, and I feared that George might have left the station for the day. And I was such a mess. I just wanted to come home."

"But you have to tell him. The sooner the better." He stood and began pacing the room. "This is deadly serious."

I gave a little shudder. "An apt choice of words, Samuel. Don't worry, I intend to see George first thing in the morning. Although I don't know what good it will do. The police have done little enough to catch this shooter."

Too restless to sit any longer, I rose, pulled a clean gown from my wardrobe, and retired behind my dress screen. I could hear my brother continue to stride back and forth across the floorboards as I changed. After listening to one or two more mumbled curses, I stole a peek at him from behind the partition. He was staring out the window into the front garden, his handsome face set in lines of angry determination.

"Samuel?" He appeared not to hear me speak. "Come now," I prompted, "you must have some thoughts on the subject."

"Oh, I have thoughts all right," he replied, his voice grim as he turned away from the window. "I don't like this one bit, little sister. Shooting at me was bad enough, but shooting at you? What in hell is happening on that Hill?"

I sighed. "I wish I knew."

He regarded my face thoughtfully. "I'm beginning to believe that you were the actual target the night of Wilde's reading after all. Else why would the shooter attempt it again?"

I stopped in the act of fastening up my dress and stepped out from behind the screen. Motioning for him to finish the task, I said, "I still say that makes no sense. Who would want to kill me?"

"I don't know. But the fact is that someone tried. What about this Ricardo Ruiz?" he said, then stopped. "No, it can't be him. I was shot before the SPCA first approached you to represent them. He would have had no reason to harm you—at least not then."

He had finished fastening my buttons, and I turned around to face him. "You think he'd want to hurt me now, just because I've taken the society's case? I don't believe that for one minute!"

After a brief hesitation, he said, "To tell the truth, nor do I. It was just a thought." He studied me for a moment. "I suppose it could be someone you bested in court. An old case—perhaps someone from Chinatown? You can't deny that you've tread on a lot of toes while representing Li Ying's people."

"I'm sure I have. But if one of them decided to seek revenge, do you really believe they would lie in wait—*twice,* moreover—on Telegraph Hill, of all places? Why not just take up a position outside our house, or at my office? That seems a great deal more likely."

He sighed as the dinner bell rang. "The fact is that none of this makes any sense, Sarah. It was much easier to suppose that Jonathan Aleric was the intended victim, rather than either one of us. After this afternoon, that theory has flown out the window, and I don't know what to think. The very idea of someone taking a potshot at you makes my blood boil."

"I don't care much for it myself," I said, then went to the looking glass to arrange my gown. I did not like the visage staring back at me but saw no way out of my predicament. Once again, Samuel was right: tonight was as good a time as any to face my parents' inevitable inquisition.

He took hold of my arm before I could open the door. "Wait, we have to talk more about this after dinner. And I have something to show you."

This caught my attention. "What is it?"

"There's no time to get into it now. If the library is available after we finish eating, I'll meet you there for coffee."

Dinnertime was as uncomfortable as I feared. The rest of the family were already seated at the table when Samuel and I arrived, and not surprisingly, all eyes turned to stare at my battered appearance.

"Good God, Sarah!" Papa exclaimed. "What in blazes did you do to your face?"

Mama was so alarmed by my appearance that she gaped at me in openmouthed horror, too upset, it seemed, to speak. My sister-in-law Celia obviously shared her reaction, while my brother Charles's gaze made me feel as if I were a specimen under a microscope.

"You look as if you waged war with a cactus bush," Papa continued when no one else spoke.

"Actually, I scraped my face on some tree branches while walking to the omnibus line," I said without looking up, not for the first time that day assuring my conscience that at least a portion of this story was true.

The explanation provoked more pointed silence, broken when Charles said, "Let me take a look at those scratches after dinner, Sarah. I can still see smudges of dirt on your face."

My brother firmly believed in cleanliness when it came to fighting disease and infection. He was a devoted follower of Louis Pasteur and the British physician Joseph Lister, who had performed lengthy experiments to test the germ-killing abilities of carbolic acid. Although I was not fully conversant with "germ theory," as it was called, the liberal utilization of soap and water, particularly on an open wound, struck me as a sensible precaution.

While it caused Samuel considerable discomfort, I must admit I was relieved when the conversation turned to his morning's excursion. Although he had hoped to slip back into the house unnoticed after his trip downtown, he had been caught red-handed by our worried mother. Apparently she had noticed his absence not half an hour after his furtive departure, and was lying in wait for him when he returned. The fact that he looked tired and was obviously experiencing shoulder pain did nothing to support his reasons for visiting Moure and Atkins Publishing House.

On the whole, it was an awkward dinner, and I think everyone was relieved when it finally came to an end. Although my mother rose from the table still fussing over her youngest son's foolhardiness, she did appear somewhat mollified by my less than convincing tale about how I had come to resemble a pincushion. Papa clearly had not bought a single word of it. The sharp look he gave me as he followed Mama out of the room left me in no doubt that I had not heard the last of the matter.

My father and Charles retired to the library after leaving the dining room, making it necessary for Samuel and me to continue our pre-dinner conversation back upstairs in his bedroom.

Edis thoughtfully delivered a tray containing coffee and an assortment of cookies, then left quietly, closing the door behind him. The moment he was gone, Samuel crossed to his desk and extracted a newspaper from the top drawer. I saw that it was a copy of the *San Francisco Tattler*.

"Take a look at this," he said, pointing to one of the lead articles on the front page.

The first thing I noted was that it carried Ozzie Foldger's by-line, and I automatically steeled myself before reading the piece.

"He hints that Claude Dunn's death might not have been a suicide," I said, looking up incredulously. "How could he possibly make such a statement? As far as I know, George is the only one who thinks it might be a homicide, and I'm certain he would never share this with a reporter, especially Ozzie Foldger."

"Of course he wouldn't," said Samuel. "I have no idea how he came up with this story. Even more inexplicable, he promises to reveal more information in a future column."

"What information?" I wondered out loud as I continued to scan the article. "Do you suppose this is simply an attempt to raise newspaper circulation, or do you think he really does possess information which has eluded the police?"

"Knowing Ozzie, it's most likely a ploy to sell newspapers. But who knows?"

We were silent for a moment, lost in our own thoughts. I sipped my coffee, wishing we had thought to have Edis add some brandy to the tray. Truthfully, I was still a bit shaken by the day's events, and my pre-dinner sips from Samuel's flask had long since worn off. More than anything, I longed for the quiet comfort of my bed.

But Samuel wasn't yet ready to let the matter rest. Taking a seat in the room's solitary chair, he indicated I should sit on the bed, then reached for a notebook and pencil on his desk.

"Before you go to the police station in the morning," he said, "let's think through what happened to you this afternoon, starting

178

with a list of everyone you met on Telegraph Hill. At least that might help us form some basis for who shot at you."

"If we include everyone I spoke to today, Samuel, we're going to end up with a great number of suspects. Nearly as many people were there this afternoon as on the night you were shot."

He did not appear put off by my reservations. "That's all right. As you're always saying, it's a place to start. Now, when you reached the Hill, did you go directly to Dunn's house?"

"No, I spied Bruno Studds sitting on the Freibergs' front porch and stopped there first."

He jotted this down. "Good. Who was there, besides the Freibergs, I mean?"

"Mr. Freiberg was at work, and Isabel was minding the Dunn baby. Mrs. Montgomery and her sister, Abigail Forester, were visiting. They seem quite concerned about little Billy's future, and are trying to find him a home."

He looked up from his notebook. "Really. I wondered what was going to happen to the child. I was afraid he'd be placed in an orphanage."

"The sisters appear determined to keep him out of an institution. Fortunately, Mrs. Montgomery seems to have the financial resources to find a suitable family to take him in."

"That's a relief. After such a terrible beginning in life, that little boy is lucky to have a pair of guardian angels looking out for him." He smiled, then returned to his notes. "Now then, who did you meet after you left the Freiberg home?"

Briefly, I went on to list everyone I had encountered that afternoon, including Annabelle Carr and, finally, young Clara Flattery, who lived on the other side of the Dunn house.

"The girl claims she heard Dunn cry out at around seven o'clock last night, either out of fear or pain," I told him.

My brother looked up, startled. "Did she tell this to the police?"

"Evidently not. Her mother didn't want her to get involved,

and kept saying she must have been mistaken. However, the girl appears very certain of what she heard."

"This could be really important, Sarah. I assume you're going to tell George about this when you see him in the morning?"

"Of course," I answered, a bit annoyed that he thought I might neglect to pass on such a vital piece of information. "The girl's testimony certainly seems to indicate that Dunn wasn't alone in his house that evening. Hopefully it will convince Lieutenant Curtis to reexamine the evidence."

"'Hopefully' being the operative word," he commented a bit skeptically. "I'm not sure that her story will be enough to change Curtis's mind. He tends to jump to conclusions, then digs in his heels and refuses to admit that he might be wrong."

"He's a proud man," I said.

"He's a stubborn man, Sarah. And not a particularly bright one from what I've observed. Still, he needs to know what the Flattery girl said."

He closed the notebook, then passed his good right hand over his brow. As he did so, he winced in pain and rubbed at his left shoulder. My brother could offer Mama all the excuses in the world as to why he had felt compelled to call upon the publishing house in person this morning, but it was obvious that the excursion had wearied him a good deal more than he was willing to admit.

"All right, Samuel, I've given you my report. Now tell me what Moure and Atkins had to say about your manuscript."

He shrugged, then again tried to hide a sudden stab of pain. "I gave it to Atkins, who promised to look it over as soon as his busy schedule permitted."

"That was all he said?"

"I hardly expected him to jump up and down with excitement," he said dryly. "But I'm still glad I went, despite the disapproval I can see written on your face. I felt it was important to meet with the man in person—to put a face to the name. Someone told me once that that was good business."

"That someone was Papa," I reminded him. Studying his wan

face, I added, "You need to go to bed, Samuel. You look exhausted. I understand why you wanted to deliver the manuscript yourself, but I agree with Mama that it was too soon for you to be out and about."

"I knew you were going to say that," he said gloomily. "What is it about women that they can't resist treating men like helpless children?"

"Because all too many men behave like foolish children," I told him with a smile as I rose from the bed. I started for the door, then turned to face him. "Please promise me that you'll rest in bed tomorrow."

"Only if you promise me not to go back to Telegraph Hill alone—night *or* day." His smile had turned to a look of frustration. "I'd love to go with you to see George tomorrow. You don't know how damn irritating it is to be locked up in this house day after boring day. And you know Mama will be watching me even more closely after this morning. Good Lord! Enough is enough!"

"You're not going to help your cause by overdoing it. You've delivered your book to the publisher. Now all you can do is await their verdict, which I'm certain will be favorable. You've been blessed with more than your fair share of talent, and this book is going to prove it."

I went over to the chair and kissed him on the cheek. "I promise to tell you what George has to say about Clara Flattery's story. As well as his reaction to my being shot at today. And don't worry, I have no plans to visit Telegraph Hill tomorrow, or anytime soon. That you can believe!"

CHAPTER FOURTEEN

I was delighted to find Sergeant Lewis present at the police station early the following morning. As soon as the desk officer announced my arrival, George came out and personally escorted me into his small, overcrowded office.

"Miss Sarah, you'll be happy to learn that Mr. Parke has already come to the station and made a statement about seeing Claude Dunn the night—" He broke off, apparently only then noticing the sad state of my face. He stared in alarm at the scratches and bruises which, true to Samuel's prediction, were even more visible today than they had been the night before. "Good Lord! What happened to you?"

"That's one of the reasons I have come to see you, George." Without waiting to be asked, I took a seat on the other side of his untidy desk. "Someone shot at me late yesterday afternoon as I was making my way down Telegraph Hill."

He stared at me in shock, then stammered, "Are you—are you telling me that you were actually fired upon? Just like Samuel was only last week?"

"That is exactly what I'm saying. Fortunately, the bullet struck a nearby tree and I was merely scratched by flying bark. I received the rest of my bruises when I stumbled in my rush down the hill."

He continued to look at me, thunderstruck. "I don't understand. Why would anyone want to harm you?"

"I have no idea," I replied. Thankfully, I seemed to have recovered from the shock that had afflicted me the day before and was able to discuss the event calmly. "Suffice it to say that had the bullet's trajectory been twelve inches closer to my head, I would not be sitting here now relating my story."

"But—Miss Sarah, what were you doing on Telegraph Hill in the first place?" He continued to stare at me with wide, incredulous eyes, hardly the demeanor, I thought, of a trained and seasoned investigator. According to Samuel, George Lewis had long suffered a rather juvenile crush on me, although I considered this to be a fanciful idea. I had to concede, however, that he frequently became awkward, occasionally even tongue-tied, when in my presence.

"I visited Telegraph Hill to reassure myself that the Dunn baby was being properly cared for," I explained. For obvious reasons, I decided not to mention that my real motive had been to interview Dunn's neighbors. Even a good friend like George might frown upon my demonstrating such barefaced initiative. It was up to someone, however, to do exactly that. The police seemed dismally incapable of conducting a proper investigation on their own.

"And you say you were shot while going down the hill?" he asked. He had sufficiently marshaled his astonishment to begin scribbling notes on a pad of paper. "Did you see anyone? No one called out to you?"

"Unfortunately I saw no one, George. I wish I had."

He jotted this down, then raised his head and studied me. "Excuse me for being blunt, Miss Sarah, but something tells me you're not being completely honest about your reasons for visiting Telegraph Hill yesterday."

I felt my cheeks flush with unwelcome heat. "I don't know why you would think that, George," I countered, attempting to look innocent.

His expression made it clear that he was having no truck with this subterfuge. "Miss Sarah," he admonished, "if I am to resolve this case, I must have the truth. While I do not doubt your concern for the Dunn baby, I cannot believe that was your sole reason for being there."

He watched me with disconcerting directness as I considered how best to answer him. In the end, of course, I was forced to admit that he deserved the truth, even if it made it more difficult for me to continue my investigation.

"All right, George. I went there hoping to question some of Mr. Dunn's neighbors concerning the night of his death."

His reaction surprised me. Instead of the show of anger I expected, a gleam of curiosity crossed his handsome face. Leaning forward in his chair, he asked, "Who did you visit? Did you learn anything new?"

In for a penny, in for a pound, I told myself, and went on to recount everything that had happened the previous day, including whom I had spoken to, as well as their responses to my questions. As I had foreseen, he expressed interest in my talk with young Clara Flattery. When I repeated her insistence that she had heard Claude Dunn cry out at the approximate time of his death, he gave a grunt of satisfaction and pulled a sheaf of papers from a desk drawer. Thumbing through them, he chose one and then held it out for me to inspect.

"I had one of my men speak to the girl's mother yesterday morning," he explained. "In fact, they questioned most of Mr. Dunn's neighbors." He tapped a finger on the report in question. "Officer Miller clearly states that Mrs. Flattery denied hearing anything amiss next door the previous evening."

"According to Clara, her mother forbade her to tell the police what she heard for fear of getting the family involved."

"It happens all the time," he said in exasperation. "People expect the police to protect them, then hold back important facts, even when it concerns a man's death. It's enough to make you lose faith in human nature."

"It's fortunate that I was able to talk to the girl without her mother in the house."

He harrumphed. "Yes, although given the same circumstances she very likely wouldn't have spoken so freely to any of my officers."

He put down his pencil and regarded me levelly. "Visiting Telegraph Hill on your own was extremely foolhardy, Miss Sarah. There can no longer be any doubt that a very dangerous individual is determined to do you or your brother an injury. I cannot deny that you managed to provide me with valuable information. However, you must promise me that—"

"What did your men discover when they questioned Dunn's neighbors, George?" I broke in, anxious to avoid the promise he was about to ask of me. "I had time to visit only a few of the houses."

I released my breath when he answered, "Most of the people we've talked to claim never to have heard of Samuel, or you, for that matter."

"What about Jonathan Aleric?"

"Well, yes, of course they've heard of him," he said, misunderstanding my question. "Most of the country knows Aleric. After all, he did write one of the most famous books to come out of the Civil War."

"I agree," I said. "However, I wasn't referring to his reputation as an author. What about the animosity, both personal and professional, that exists between Aleric and Mortimer Remy?"

He looked at me, confused. "You seemed to feel strongly that Remy would never harm anyone."

"That's right," I agreed. "Nor have I changed my mind. But that wouldn't rule out someone taking it upon himself to do it for him. Say, one of Remy's friends or associates? An individual who objected to Aleric's attempts to put the *San Francisco Weekly* out of business, perhaps."

"I hadn't thought of that," he admitted. "Can you think of anyone who might do such a thing?" He paused, then said with some excitement, "Wait a minute! What about Tull O'Hara? He was skulking around outside Dunn's house the night he was killed. And if I remember correctly, he works for Remy's newspaper."

185

"Yes, he's employed there as a typesetter. And you're right, George, he was certainly behaving strangely that night."

"And he ran away when I tried to speak to him. I was too busy to follow up on him yesterday, but I think I'll pay him a visit at the newspaper." He thought for a moment. "Didn't you say that O'Hara lives in the first house at the top of the Filbert Steps?"

He hardly waited for me to nod my head in agreement before rushing on, "By gum, he just may be our shooter. Samuel was fired upon not more than thirty yards from that shack. And so were you."

"That's right, but don't forget that O'Hara wheeled Mrs. Montgomery to her home, while her man Studds led our group down the hill."

"Dang it all! I forgot about that. Sorry, Miss Sarah, but I thought I was on to something." Still, he seemed reluctant to let go of this theory. "How long do you suppose it would have taken O'Hara to see Mrs. Montgomery home?"

I thought back to my hike up the hill the day before. I had not gone all the way to Mrs. Montgomery's mansion, but I judged the distance from Remy's house to hers to be the equivalent of two or three city blocks. Of course the narrow road was unpaved, but it had been a clear, cold night, and I doubted that O'Hara would have tarried along the way. We already knew, of course, how fast he could run.

"I think he might have reached her house in less than five minutes," I estimated.

"And he could have hightailed it back down the hill much faster." He considered this. "Give him a minute to grab his rifle, and he just might have been able to ambush your group as you reached the Filbert Steps."

"Perhaps," I said uncertainly.

He stared at me, an abashed look appearing on his handsome face. "Miss Sarah, you're the one who brought up this O'Hara fellow. Now you're pouring ice water on my theories."

"I agree, George, you present a feasible case against the type-setter."

"Then why are you shaking your head like that? I'm just ashamed I didn't put it together sooner. As you yourself pointed out, O'Hara is a cold, even hostile, individual. He might well have decided that the only way to save his employer's newspaper—and his own job—was to kill Remy's major competitor."

"That would all be well and good, but why would he turn around a week later and shoot at me? I pose no threat to the *San Francisco Weekly*."

He opened his mouth to answer, then closed it without uttering a word.

"It just seems illogical," I continued. "And I didn't mean to single out Tull O'Hara as a probable suspect. I merely offered the suggestion that one of Mortimer Remy's friends or associates might have decided to champion his cause."

"Without his knowledge."

I nodded. "I truly do not believe that Remy has a violent bone in his body. And I consider myself to be an excellent judge of character."

Did his lips twitch as I said this? I could not be certain, for he quickly cleared his throat. "Well, you have certainly given me a great deal to consider, and I appreciate it. I'm glad you came in to report yesterday's attack, Miss Sarah, as well as your conversation with the Flattery girl."

I leaned forward in my chair. "Yes, of all the people I spoke to, what young Clara told me seems the most promising. You know, George, her testimony supports your theory that Claude Dunn was murdered."

He held up his hands in a gesture of helplessness, then placed them palms down on his desk. "I only wish that it did. The truth is, in the end it doesn't matter what the girl told you, Miss Sarah. Lieutenant Curtis has closed the Dunn case. He insists he committed suicide and that's all there is to it. It'll take a good deal more than the word of a young girl to change his mind."

"But you must at least try," I persisted. "Surely he'll want to be informed of this latest development."

He shook his head dolefully, and there was a strong note of frustration in his voice. "Lieutenant Curtis is an obstinate man. Once he makes up his mind on a case, he'll hear no more about it. It would be worth my job to even bring up Dunn's death again. I promise you I've tried."

"I believe you, George. But it's a deplorable state of affairs. I look forward to the day when you are promoted to lieutenant. This city needs more clear, honest heads in positions of authority."

He laughed, but his face held no humor. "You'll be waiting a long time for that, Miss Sarah. There are some people in the department who still object to my having been promoted to sergeant last year."

"My point exactly," I exclaimed, angered as ever by the corruption, present to one degree or another at every level of city government. "Advancement on the force should not be dependent on politics or whom one knows, but solely on ability and experience. When was the last time Lieutenant Curtis personally investigated a case—other than walking into a crime scene, jumping to a hasty and frequently erroneous conclusion, then turning and walking out again?"

"You know that I cannot comment on my superior officers." He glanced at his open office door and lowered his voice. "Particularly not here in the station."

I gave him a rueful smile, then sighed and rose from my chair. "It is a shameful situation. With men like Curtis in charge, I hold out little hope that the villain who shot at Samuel and me will ever be apprehended."

At least not apprehended by the police," I added beneath my breath as I boarded a cable car that would convey me to within a block or two of Sutter Street.

It was ten thirty when I reached my office. After removing my wrap, I used my small brazier to brew coffee in my back room, then set to work on the arguments I would present when I delivered the SPCA petitions to City Hall. I had barely commenced work when my office door flew open and Ricardo Ruiz stormed inside. He was followed by the two heavily muscled men who had accompanied him on his previous visit. Not bothering with a greeting, he marched across the room and slammed a paper on my desk.

"What is the meaning of this?" he demanded, his dark eyes flashing.

Ignoring his rude tone, I picked up the paper and saw at once that it was one of the society's petitions. Mr. Dinwitty was as good as his word; he had wasted no time in sending out his volunteers. The sheet I held bore about half a dozen signatures.

"Well?" Ruiz pressed when I did not immediately reply.

"Well what, Señor Ruiz?" I inquired, keeping my own voice civil. "The purpose of this petition seems to be perfectly clear. I cannot understand why you would require an explanation from me."

His finely sculpted face darkened, and an unwelcomed part of my mind registered that he was even more handsome than I remembered. Perhaps anger enhanced the appearance of some individuals.

"I do not need you to explain this *ridículo* document, Señorita Woolson," he thundered. "I want to know why it was handed to me this morning at the restaurant where I was eating my breakfast?"

I smiled up at him. "Since I was not present to observe the incident you describe, Señor Ruiz, I cannot be expected to answer that question." I ran my eyes down the list of names entered on the page. "It appears that some of your fellow diners considered the petition worthy of signing. Perhaps your proposed bullring will not be as popular in the city as you seem to think."

I looked up to find him staring at my face, as if noticing it for the first time since barging into my office.

"What have you done to your face, señorita?" He leaned across my desk to peer closer. "It does not appear as it did before."

"I scratched myself on some bushes yesterday, Señor Ruiz," I said, wishing he would stop gaping at me as if I were a circus oddity. "It is nothing, I assure you."

To my alarm, he reached out as if to touch my face. I sat back in my chair and out of his reach. Appearing a bit flustered, he jerked his arm away. In doing so, he caught sight of the petition lying on the desk and picked it up, his expression once again irate.

"You know nothing about the *corrida de toros,*" he declared, waving the document around as if it were a flag. One of the men standing behind him took a hasty step backward to avoid being hit by his employer's flying hand. "Neither do the *imbéciles* who signed this—this worthless paper. You cannot understand the spectacle, the bravery, the magnificence of the *fiesta brava!*"

Ah, but I could understand, I thought with an inward smile of satisfaction. I had done my homework the previous day during my productive time at the library.

"The *corrida de toros* is performed with strict ritual," I told him as if instructing a neophyte. "After the opening parade, the matador studies the bull while an assistant uses his cape to test its ferocity and how it moves. Then two picadors enter the arena mounted on horses. They use lances to stab the bull's neck, weakening the animal and causing it to lower its head and horns when it eventually faces the matador."

I stared hard at Ruiz. "The bull often injures or kills one or both of the horses during this stage."

He had stopped pacing and was regarding me disdainfully. Before he could launch the diatribe I saw forming on his lips, I pressed on.

"Next, more assistants plant barbed sticks into the bull's shoulders, further damaging the animal's neck and shoulder muscles. Finally comes the *tercio de muerte.* Alone now, the matador reenters the ring and engages the bull in a series of passes. When the bull is so weak he can barely charge, he attempts to thrust a sword through the animal's heart. If the matador fails in this *estocada,* the bull will be stabbed with a dagger. Either way, the creature will be killed."

I waited for Ruiz to respond to my portrayal of his magnificent *corrida.* I could not deny a feeling of satisfaction as I watched him sputter in an effort to locate the right words.

"Well?" I asked.

"You describe the *fiesta brava* in scientific terms, señorita, not in the language of legend and tradition." His black eyes flashed with a passion I could not doubt was genuine. "You mock a proud spectacle with hundreds of years of history. It is one man's dance with death. It is the arena where the matador's courage and artistry are tested. It runs through our veins like the blood of life."

"What about the blood of the bull, señor?" I countered. "While your matador's courage and artistry are being tested, the bull suffers a slow, torturous death. I cannot comprehend how people can consider killing an animal in this way to be sport."

He threw up his hands in exasperation, mumbling a string of words I couldn't understand. Their general meaning, however, was all too clear.

"This is *imposible!*" he declared, pointing an accusing finger in my face. "You are a woman, how can you understand? You cannot know what it is like to be caught up in a moment of such exhilaration and raw fear."

I shivered, remembering the bullet that had narrowly missed hitting my head the previous afternoon. Actually, I thought I *did* know what it was like to experience raw fear.

"Señor Ruiz," I said, growing weary of the man and his arguments, "if you have come here hoping that I will stop the SPCA from circulating these petitions, you have wasted your time. I have agreed to represent the society, and I intend to honor this commitment to the best of my ability. Now if you will please—"

"But you are a woman!" he protested, once again pointing out the obvious and waving the petition in my face. "I will not allow my plans to be thwarted by a woman who pretends to be an attorney. Where is your father? I need to speak to him at once. He must do his duty and return you to your home." He leaned across my desk. "If necessary, he must lock you in your room until you forget all this nonsense and behave like a proper young lady."

Heat rushed to my cheeks. I rose from my chair and faced this insulting man with a fury I could no longer control.

"You will leave my office at once, Señor Ruiz," I demanded. "You will take your two henchmen with you, and you will never return. Do I make myself clear?"

He drew himself up to his full height, forcing me to look up into those dark, fuming eyes. "You cannot order me from this room. We have business to discuss, and I am not yet finished."

"Oh, but you are finished. There is nothing left for us to discuss." I rounded my desk and, pushing past the two men standing guard behind my unwanted guest, I threw open my office door, then stood there waiting for the trio to depart.

Ruiz stared at me in outrage, as if no one had ever dared treat him in this manner. Then he grabbed his hat and stormed across the room until he stood face-to-face with me in the doorway.

"You will regret this, Señorita Woolson," he said, his voice dark and threatening. "I will make it my business that you do. I have powerful friends in San Francisco. They will ensure that you can no longer practice law in this, or any other, city."

He drew so close that his baleful eyes filled my vision. "Moreover, I will instruct the first matador who steps into my new arena to dedicate his kill to you!"

The men stormed down the stairs, practically knocking aside my neighbor as she was ascending to my office. Fanny clutched at a covered plate she was carrying, barely preventing it from crashing to the ground. I heard Ruiz cry out an apology as he passed, *"Dispénseme, señora."* Then, thankfully, they were gone.

I hurried down to her. "Are you all right, Fanny? It's a wonder you weren't sent flying down the stairs!" After taking the plate from her hands, I led the way into my office.

"Good heavens, Sarah, who were those men?" she asked a bit breathlessly, following me inside. "I began to worry when I heard shouting up here. They didn't hurt—" She stopped and stared in horror at my face. "Sarah, what did they do to you? Those scratches!"

"It's all right, Fanny," I said quickly. "These scratches aren't new. I fell into some bushes yesterday, that's all."

She peered more closely at my abrasions. "Yes, I see now that they're not fresh. But however did it happen? Were you pushed?"

"I, ah, was just careless, I'm afraid," I told her, doing my best not to embellish the lie. If she knew what had really happened, it would merely cause her unnecessary worry. "It's nothing, Fanny, really."

She subjected me to one last, penetrating look, then ticked her tongue that I had allowed such a thing to happen. Obviously not satisfied with my answer, she nonetheless seemed disinclined to press me further and uncovered the plate, which was filled with her delicious ginger cookies.

"It's almost lunchtime, but I thought a few of these would do no harm. More often than not, you don't take time for your mid-day meal anyway. At least this way you'll have something in your stomach."

She continued speaking as I went into the back room to pour her a cup of coffee and refresh my own.

"Who were those men, Sarah?" she pressed as I reentered the room.

I carried a tray containing the cups of coffee, sugar, and a pitcher of cream that I kept fresh in a small icebox. "That was Ricardo Ruiz, the man who is planning to build a bullring here in town."

She very nearly dropped the cookie platter for the second time. "Did you say a *bullring*? Dear Lord! You mean like the ones they have in Spain?"

Belatedly, I realized that I had been so preoccupied with Samuel's recovery, and the frightening events which had occurred on Telegraph Hill, that I had not spoken to her in several days. She evidently had not heard of Ruiz's planned construction, but then it had not yet been featured in the newspapers.

"Unfortunately, yes, Fanny," I answered. "Just like they have in Spain. And in Mexico as well. Mr. and Mrs. Dinwitty asked me to represent their group, the Society for the Prevention of Cruelty to Animals, in fighting the arena. And I agreed." I picked up the petition Ruiz had dropped on the floor after waving it in my face. "Their office has already started circulating a petition opposing the construction."

"I see. And that is why he was ranting at you as I came upstairs," she said, taking the paper and reading through the names. Without a word, she crossed to my desk, dipped my pen into the inkwell, and signed her name to the document. "There. One more person opposed to such an atrocity. I expect you to let me know if there is anything else I can do to help in this fight."

"And what fight is that?"

The familiar voice came from the door, which my neighbor had left open behind her. We both looked up as Robert entered the room. He was studying us curiously, obviously awaiting an answer to his question.

"Fanny and I were discussing Ricardo Ruiz's bullring, Robert," I told him, lowering my head in the hope that he would not observe my battered face. Naturally, that was the first thing he noticed.

"What happened to your face?" he asked, walking close enough to lift my chin with his fingers. His turquoise eyes studied every one of my cuts and abrasions.

Clinging to my previous lie, I explained, "I fell into some bushes yesterday. Don't make a fuss, Robert. They aren't serious."

He glanced at Fanny and then back to me, saying, "I came to see if you wanted to have lunch with me, Sarah. We haven't talked since Sunday night, and I wondered if there was anything new on Claude Dunn's death."

"I read about that in the newspaper," Fanny put in, unable to mask her excitement. "Do you know what happened to the poor man? The article mentioned that he has a newborn son, and that his wife died in childbirth."

"As a matter of fact," I began, "Robert and I were at Platt's Hall the night it happened, and we—"

"I'm sorry, Mrs. Goodman, but Sarah will have to tell you the rest of the story another time," Robert broke in. He grabbed my wrap, which was hanging on a peg, then took hold of my arm. "I have to return to the office in less than an hour, so we had best be on our way if we're to have time for lunch."

Before I could object, or indeed even offer Fanny an apology, he swept me out of the room, closing the door behind him.

CHAPTER FIFTEEN

That was extremely rude," I protested when we reached the bottom of the stairs. "Fanny and I were about to have a cup of coffee. What has gotten into you, hurrying me out of my own office like that?"

"I was trying to avoid a scene in front of your neighbor," he said. "You were lying to me. I thought you might prefer telling me the truth in a more private setting."

He guided me across the street to a small restaurant we frequented from time to time. I was forced to hold my tongue until we were escorted to a small table toward the back of the room. The moment the waiter handed us menus and departed, I looked at my companion, not bothering to mask my anger.

"Why are you making such a fuss over a few scratches?" I demanded. "I told you, it's nothing serious."

"Nothing serious indeed. Do you take me for a complete fool?"

I feigned a look of innocence, or at least I tried to. Judging by his expression, I was not successful. "I don't know what you mean by that."

"Humph!" he replied. "If you've taken time to examine yourself in the mirror, which I'm sure you have, then you know why it's impossible to swallow such a preposterous tale. You cannot have suffered all those scratches and cuts by simply falling into a bush. For God's sake, Sarah, they're on your neck and hands, even on your arms. Your right ear looks as if someone chewed on it." His blue-green eyes bored into mine. "Now, tell me what really happened to you."

How could I avoid telling him the truth? There must be some way. Yet even as I sought to find some explanation that might be remotely plausible, I knew it was hopeless. He was right; simply falling into a bush could not have caused so many lacerations.

"All right, I'll tell you," I agreed at length. "But only if you promise not to fuss that I go about naïvely stumbling into harm's way."

"I fuss because you attract danger to you like a magnet," he declared. "Whether it's through naïveté or out-and-out pighead-edness, you constantly place yourself in harm's way. Anyone would worry."

"Do you agree to my terms or not?" I challenged.

"All right, all right," he said, giving me a cantankerous look. "Have it your way. Just tell me the truth."

Knowing I would probably live to regret it, I took a deep breath and then described my visit to Telegraph Hill the previous afternoon. He seemed to forget his irritation when I related what young Clara Flattery told me about hearing Claude Dunn cry out at about the time he supposedly died.

"Good heavens, Sarah," he exclaimed. "Have you told Sergeant Lewis about this? It lends credence to his theory that Dunn was murdered."

"I saw him this morning, but Lieutenant Curtis has already closed the case. George claims that what Clara heard will not be enough to change the obstinate man's mind."

"Of all the foolish, egotistical bast— The man is an idiot!" The waiter returned to take our orders, but Robert waved him away. "Do you mean to say that Curtis does not even mean to look into the girl's story?"

I shook my head. "As far as he's concerned, Claude Dunn committed suicide and that's an end to it."

"The man should be removed from the police department." He sat stewing over our city's less than effective law enforcement officers, then turned his attention back to me. "You haven't finished telling me what else happened to you yesterday on that godforsaken Hill. Go ahead, let's hear it."

Sighing inwardly, I told him about leaving the Flattery house, walking toward the Filbert Street Steps, and then, finally, being shot at as I walked through the copse of trees.

"Someone shot at you?" He rose out of his chair, his ruggedly handsome face suffused with rage. Several patrons seated about the room looked our way, obviously startled by my friend's booming voice.

"Shh, Robert," I said, leaning toward him and lowering my own voice. "You promised to listen to me calmly."

"Dammit all, I did listen to you calmly. Until you told me someone shot at you. That I refuse to take calmly." He picked up his hat and coat. When he spoke again, his voice was still far too loud. "I'm going to that blasted Hill right now and rout out that villain." He clamped his mouth shut as a woman at the next table gasped and stared at him indignantly. "Come, Sarah, I'll see you back to your office. I want you to stay there until I come back to escort you home after work."

I didn't budge from my seat, but took hold of his arm and refused to allow him to take another step. "You will do no such thing, Robert Campbell. Sit down this instant. You're creating the very scene you claimed you wished to avoid."

Seeming to realize for the first time that nearly every eye in the restaurant was on us, he reluctantly sank back onto his chair, his face still red with fury.

"I don't care what promise you managed to wheedle out of me," he said tightly. "I intend to find whoever took that shot at you. It's obvious the police are too incompetent to find the shoes on their own feet, much less a would-be murderer."

"And what if he shoots at you, Robert? What good will that do me, or Samuel? No, that isn't the way to handle this."

"Then what is? Are we going to allow this—this madman to continue shooting willy-nilly at people?" Some of the color drained from his face, and his eyes grew very large. "He could have killed you, Sarah. My God! Another few inches and that bullet might have hit your head instead of the tree."

"That thought had occurred to me as well," I said wryly.

"You must have been terrified."

I started to refute this, then remembered being unable to control my trembling and dashing pell-mell down the hill like a frightened rabbit, unmindful of the scrapes and bruises I sustained along the way.

"Yes," I agreed in a small voice. "I admit that it was not one of my finest moments."

"I presume you reported this to George when you saw him this morning? What does he plan to do about it?"

Before I could answer, the waiter returned to our table yet again to take our orders. I spied several people waiting to be seated and almost at random chose an item off the menu. Robert didn't bother consulting his own menu but simply told the waiter he would have the same.

When the man left, I said, "George assured me that the department is doing everything possible to catch the shooter."

He did not look impressed. "Which probably amounts to bloody little."

I nodded unhappily. "I suspect you're right. Everyone George or his men have spoken to denies seeing anyone with a gun that night. Or even behaving strangely."

"That does it, then," Robert exclaimed, slapping the table so hard that our utensils went flying. Once again several diners regarded us with disapproval. "You must not return to Telegraph Hill alone, Sarah, even in broad daylight. It is far too dangerous. If there's a new development and you feel you must go there, I'll accompany you."

I started to object that I would make no such promise, then realized that what happened yesterday could easily happen again. If someone really was out to kill me . . .

"All right. I don't like it, but I agree to inform you if it becomes necessary to visit Telegraph Hill again."

He looked relieved and a little surprised that I had given in so readily. His eyes narrowed. "Do you mean that, or are you just agreeing with me so I'll drop the subject?"

"No, I'm serious. I feel the same way about Samuel returning to the Hill. One near miss might have been an accident, or someone shooting at a possum or fox. Two incidents in practically the same place defies coincidence. Then there's Claude Dunn's death to consider. No, I agree that something very dangerous is going on there. We must take all necessary precautions."

We ate our lunch—or perhaps I should say we picked at our lunch—mostly in silence, as we were both taken up with our own thoughts. When at last it was time for Robert to return to his office, he suddenly took hold of my hand from across the table.

"Sarah, please promise me you will exercise caution whenever you're away from your home. Especially when you're on the street, or even in your office. God knows anyone could walk in and out of those rooms without being seen."

I thought of Ricardo Ruiz and his men doing just that, last week and then this afternoon. I had intended to tell him of Ruiz's anger and threats while we ate our lunch, but I changed my mind. He was already anxious enough about my safety.

"I told you I'd be careful, and I will." I started to pull my hand away, but when he squeezed it a bit harder, I let it stay where it was. His skin was warm, if a bit rough, his fingers dwarfing mine. It surprised me to realize how comforting his touch felt.

"I—" He was obviously experiencing difficulty finding the right words. Swallowing hard, he proved my suspicions when he continued, "I've tried, but I have a hard time saying how I feel . . . that is, how much you mean—" He expelled a frustrated sigh. "Dash it all, Sarah, you must know by now that I love you. If anything were to happen to you, I just, well, I don't know what I would do."

The moment the words were out of his mouth, I knew they were true. In all honesty, I'd known it for some time, even before our last kiss. I just hadn't wanted to admit it. I did not want our friendship to change; and if romantic love came into the picture, it surely would. My determination never to marry had not changed. I had chosen the law over having a husband and children. I could see no way to have both.

He was watching my face apprehensively. "Sarah, did you hear what I said?"

I nodded my head slowly, not certain how to respond. "I have taken you by surprise," he said, starting to pull back his hand. I held fast, refusing to let it go.

"I care for you very much, Robert," I told him softly. "But love—"

"Yes, yes," he broke in, looking miserably self-conscious. "I didn't mean to go sentimental on you. Just concerned for your welfare, you know. Got carried away, sorry."

This time when he pulled his hand away from mine, I allowed it to go. He signaled the waiter for the bill. When I reached into my reticule to help pay, he uttered a curse about that being a damn insult and burst out of his chair, nearly knocking it over in his haste to reach the cash register.

As we left the restaurant, I asked him if he would care to accompany me on Saturday afternoon to see Oscar Wilde off on the train. Following a busy two weeks in San Francisco, the poet seemed ready to complete the remainder of his American tour.

Robert hesitated, still looking embarrassed by his recent declaration.

"Come now, my dear, you have given me a great compliment, and I am honored," I said, smiling up at him in the hope that we might move beyond this awkward moment. "I would greatly enjoy your company."

He studied me as if trying to decide if I were serious or just attempting to soothe his injured feelings. My expression must have convinced him of the former, for after a moment or two he accepted my invitation, said good-bye, and hurried back toward Joseph Shepard's law firm.

When he had disappeared down the street, I removed a folded map from one of the pockets I had had sewn into all of my business suits. It was a grid layout of the Mission District, copied from the documents department at City Hall. On it, I had marked Ricardo Ruiz's property, a large rectangle of land roughly bordered by South Van Ness Avenue to the east, Twenty-second Street to the north, Harrison Street to the west, and Twenty-fourth Street to the south.

This district was named after Mission Dolores, which had been standing in San Francisco for nearly a hundred years. I was aware that at one time it featured outdoor markets and lively fiestas, as well as horse racing and the bull and bear fights of the late 1840s and early 1850s. Before the Gold Rush, the area around Mission Dolores had been largely populated by ranchos and adobe homes, chosen because of its good soil and the fact that morning fog burned off there earlier than in other parts of the growing city. Since then, the neighborhood had changed significantly. Instead of the rancheros, it was now home to a few Mexicans, but mainly Irish, Italian, German, and other European immigrants who found the area hospitable. I was unhappy to see that according to the map, Ruiz's rectangular-shaped property was more than large enough to contain a bullring, with a good deal of land left over.

Half an hour later, I exited an omnibus at South Van Ness and Twenty-second Street, then stood on the corner to get my bearings and to unfold a copy of the SPCA petition I had brought with me. Deciding that the most logical course would be to walk the perimeter of Ruiz's property, then the inner streets, I started off down Twenty-second Street.

In contrast with a number of fashionable homes located on the higher elevations of Dolores and Guerrero Streets, the land east of South Van Ness was generally flat, well suited, I realized with a sinking heart, to Ruiz's planned bullring. How many of these hardworking families had any inkling how drastically their lives were going to change if one wealthy man had his way? Even when they learned of his grand scheme to bring bullfighting to San Francisco, what could they do to prevent it? For that matter, what could I do to forestall what would surely forever change the character of this neighborhood—nay, of the entire city?

I spent the next few hours knocking upon the doors of the small houses and shacks situated on the eight square blocks Ricardo Ruiz claimed to own. I entered several restaurants, two laundries, a leather store, a candy store, and a surprising number of grog shops and saloons. Those residents who would speak to me appeared universally shocked to learn of the Mexican's planned bullring— indeed, that he even owned the land upon which they lived or earned their livelihood. They were especially distressed when they realized that their homes were more than likely going to be torn down to accommodate the new construction.

The owner of the butcher shop on the corner of Folsom and Twenty-third Streets was so outraged that he demanded to meet with this Ricardo Ruiz so that he could "settle his hash good and proper!" Several saloons expressed much the same sentiments, albeit in language no lady could repeat. Nearly every individual I encountered was more than willing to sign my petition, including those who could sign only with an "x." (I noted these entries with the signers' names and addresses.)

I was particularly delighted to meet several Mexican families, who were not only surprised to be told of the bullring, but greatly displeased to learn that it was to be built in their neighborhood. One mother of two small children claimed that she had lived near a bullfighting arena in her native Mexico. She considered it a cruel sport that often attracted a rowdy crowd and had no desire to see one erected here in her adopted city. A middle-aged man who had moved to San Francisco from Durango a decade earlier told me that the Ruiz family patriarch, Javier Ruiz, was well-known and generally disliked in Mexico as a bully and a corrupt businessman.

The man was furious to learn that one of Javier's sons claimed to own the land he had lived on for the past ten years. He vowed not only to sign my petition, but to go out and circulate them himself.

I had reached the final block of my walk through Ruiz's property when a familiar, and frankly unwelcome, man hurried across the street to intercept me.

"Fancy meeting you here, Miss Woolson," said my brother Samuel's nemesis, Ozzie Foldger. Before I could catch my breath, he had pulled a notebook and pencil from one of his pockets, obviously prepared to commit to paper any information I might be foolish enough to impart. He noticed the petition I was carrying. "This must be my lucky day. Why don't you tell me all about this SPCA business. I hear they plan to oppose the new bullring."

"Please be kind enough to get out of my way, Mr. Foldger," I told him, attempting to move past the annoying little reporter. "I have nothing to say to you."

"Come on, Miss Woolson," he cajoled, blocking my path. "You could at least tell me if you're having any luck getting people to sign your paper."

"That is patently none of your business," I told him, losing my patience. "Now allow me to pass."

"Seems like that petition is showing up all over town," he went on, ignoring my protestations. He looked around the neighborhood. "So, this is where that Mexican fellow plans to build his bullfighting arena. Poor folks around here must be knocked for six, not that I blame them."

I suddenly remembered the article Samuel had shown me the night before. With everything that had happened over the past two days, it had completely slipped my mind.

"As long as you insist on pestering me, Mr. Foldger, perhaps you'd care to explain that story you wrote in last evening's newspaper concerning Claude Dunn's death. You implied that it might not be a suicide. I'd like to know what led you to such a startling conclusion."

He gave me a sly smile, and I had the feeling that he was mentally rubbing his hands in glee. "Read it, did you, Miss Woolson? What about that know-it-all brother of yours? Did he see it, too? Bet it's giving him a conniption fit."

"Never mind about Samuel," I retorted. "Tell me why you think Dunn might not have killed himself."

"Well now, that's for me to know and for you to find out, isn't it?" He gave me a wink and tapped the side of his nose with a finger. "I have my sources. *Inside* sources, if you know what I mean."

"And what sources are those?" I challenged. "You made some very serious allegations in that article, Mr. Foldger. The police have ruled Mr. Dunn's death a suicide. What evidence do you possess to prove them wrong?"

"That's the big question, isn't it?" he said, the expression on his face crafty. "But you haven't seen anything yet. If you think last night's story was a jaw buster, just you wait until you read Saturday's article. I promise you the next installment is going to knock this city on its ear, just see if it doesn't."

There was a feverish gleam in Foldger's eyes that frightened me. While it was true that I heartily disliked the irksome man, I did not wish to see him burned, an outcome I very much feared given his determination to play with fire.

"If you have information concerning Mr. Dunn's death, you should tell the police, not publish what you think you know in the newspaper."

"Oh, I don't just think I know, Miss Woolson," he said, giving me yet another mysterious wink. "Like I said, I've got a damn good source for this story. It's the real goods, I promise you that." He wagged his head in mock regret. "Poor Samuel. Too bad he missed out on the biggest scoop of the year. I'm real sorry about that." He slapped his knee with his notepad as if he had just made a wonderful joke. "You be sure to tell him I said so!"

Doubling over in laughter, he finally moved out of my path, allowing me to continue my walk toward South Van Ness Avenue.

My thoughts as I waited to board the next horsecar were, I fear, not fit to print.

Stephen Parke and Emmett Gardiner visited Samuel at our home that evening. As we sat in the study enjoying coffee and Cook's excellent cake, our conversation went to Claude Dunn. I had had no opportunity to tell Samuel about my unexpected encounter with Ozzie Foldger that afternoon, but when Stephen mentioned the reporter's article about Dunn's death, I took a moment to describe meeting him on Twenty-fourth Street.

"He actually told you he had proof Dunn didn't commit suicide?" asked my brother in amazement.

"Not in so many words," I said, "but that's what he implied. He claims to have an inside source."

"An inside source?" said Emmett. "Who might that be?"

I shook my head. "He said that was for him to know and for me to find out. He promises that his next column will be even more explosive."

"The idiot," exclaimed Stephen. "If he really knows something about Dunn's death, why in Sam Hill doesn't he tell the police?"

"Come now, Stephen," my brother said with a wry smile. "You know Foldger. How many newspapers would he sell if he shared whatever he *thinks* he knows about Dunn to the police?"

"True," Stephen agreed, sipping his coffee thoughtfully. "He hasn't had this much attention in ages."

Samuel gave a little laugh, then winced slightly and rubbed his shoulder. Although he never complained, I knew he was still experiencing a good deal more pain than he would admit. I think our brother Charles had largely given up trying to convince him to rest his wound. Mama, of course, continued to fuss over her youngest son.

"I'll wager the little weasel is bluffing," Samuel said. "If you ask me, he's made the story up out of whole cloth. Since when was reporting the truth any part of Ozzie Foldger's work ethics?"

I wished I could be as sure of this as Samuel. That gleam in Foldger's eyes seemed to indicate more than mere bravado.

As I refilled our coffee cups, Emmett speculated, "Still, I wonder what he'll write in his column on Saturday?"

"Whatever it is," proclaimed my brother, "you can be sure that sleazy newspaper of his will sell out the entire edition, whether or not Foldger has anything of substance to say."

"How is Miss Freiberg faring with the Dunn baby?" I asked, deciding a change of subject was in order. "Is she still caring for little Billy?"

I was surprised when Stephen's soft hazel eyes saddened at my mention of the young woman. "Not anymore. Her father made her give the baby to Mrs. Montgomery and her sister last night. Mr. Freiberg has ordered Isabel to prepare for her wedding. Under the circumstances, he doesn't consider it suitable for her to be caring for another man's child."

He stumbled to a halt, looking thoroughly miserable. I wished I could find something comforting to say, but no words came to me. Couldn't Solomon Freiberg see the rare and beautiful affection Stephen and his daughter shared? With such a solid foundation, surely any religious differences could be surmounted.

Neither Samuel, Emmett, nor I spoke, our friend's pain all the more terrible since we could think of no way to assuage it. Before the silence became too uncomfortable, the study door opened and my father entered.

"Well, here you are," he said, eyeing the coffeepot appraisingly. "We'll need another cup, won't we? That is, if you young people don't mind my joining you." Naturally, we all nodded our assent.

"Of course, Father," Samuel said, making room for him on the sofa. Before joining his youngest son, Papa crossed to the pull cord to summon Edis to bring an extra coffee cup. "We were just discussing Ozzie Foldger and his recent newspaper articles."

I gave an inward sigh of relief that Samuel had chosen not to mention the real topic of our conversation. If we could not help Stephen, we could at least try to divert his attention. Briefly, I told my father about my chance meeting with the reporter that afternoon, including his prediction that his next article would "knock this city on its ear."

"He's a gal-darn blunderbuss," Papa proclaimed heatedly. "And a reckless one to boot. That man is a prime example of everything that's wrong with journalism today. I've said it before, and I'll say it again. The whole bunch of them are social scavengers, making money at the expense of public awareness and debate."

His gaze faltered a bit as it fell on Samuel, who he had only recently discovered was a member of this offensive company. I could see paternal loyalty and pride waging war with years of conviction. "At least you're writing a book, son," he went on, obviously as much to convince himself as the rest of us. "That puts a different complexion on the matter."

Not so fast, my girl," Papa said as I started to climb wearily up the stairs to my room. Stephen Parke and Emmett Gardiner had just departed for home, and I looked forward to settling into my comfortable bed for a well-deserved night's sleep. "I think you owe me an explanation."

My heart sank. The promised moment of reckoning had at last arrived. "I suppose you mean my scratches," I said, too tired to keep up the pretense.

"Those and the cuts and bruises you think you're hiding beneath your sleeves. That cock-and-bull story that you fell into some bushes may convince your mother, but it won't wash with me." He nodded toward the study, which we had vacated not five minutes earlier. "Shall we?"

With a resigned sigh, I followed him into the room, took a seat, but declined yet another cup of coffee. "All right, Sarah, what really happened to you yesterday?"

Steeling myself for his reaction, I told him of my visit to Telegraph Hill and finally, most reluctantly, of the unknown person who had taken a shot at me.

His response was everything I feared it would be. He fairly

leapt out of his chair, staring down at me with a horrified expression.

"Someone shot at you, and you didn't tell me so at once? Have you no sense at all?"

He began to pace agitatedly in front of the sofa, for him a most unusual behavior, far more indicative of his distress than mere words. His face was so suffused with color that I feared he might suffer some sort of fit. "Your brother Frederick may be right after all. I've been far too lenient with you. And now you've very nearly gotten yourself killed!"

"Papa, please, how could I have possibly foreseen that someone would shoot at me? I merely checked to see if Claude Dunn's poor baby was all right. It should have been perfectly safe."

"Should have been?" He stared down at me as if he truly did think I had lost my senses. "After your brother was shot there only a week ago? As far as I can see, there's nothing safe about that damn Hill."

"I agree, but the police don't seem to be getting anywhere. Lieutenant Curtis has declared Dunn's death a suicide, and they've made no progress whatsoever in catching the shooter. Surely I can't be blamed for paying my respects to a friend."

Papa stopped pacing again to look at me incredulously. "Pay your respects to a friend? That's pure bunkum and you know it! You went to that blasted place to poke around and see what you could dig up about Claude Dunn's death. Obviously someone didn't like it."

I wished he would sit down; his color darkened with every word he spoke. I was growing seriously concerned for his health.

Attempting to keep my voice calm, I said, "I've been to see George Lewis, and he's redoubling his efforts to find whoever is doing this. As much as I hate having to make such a promise, I have no intentions of visiting Telegraph Hill again without an escort."

"My dear girl," he said, clipping off each word for emphasis, "you will not be visiting that Hill again, with or without an escort. And that includes the entire San Francisco police force."

I started to argue, but he cut me off. "No, Sarah. Not one more word on this subject. Especially not to your mother. If she found out that someone tried to kill you, as well as Samuel, I'm not sure what it would do to her. You are to remain silent. And you are to stay off that damn Telegraph Hill!"

Rarely had I seen Papa so angry. No, I thought, it wasn't anger. It was fear. My father was terrified of losing me!

CHAPTER SIXTEEN

Robert and I said little as we sat in Eddie's brougham on Saturday morning. The atmosphere between us was strained; neither of us wished to speak of our conversation at lunch two days ago. Were my worst fears being realized? I wondered with a sinking heart. Was Robert's declaration of love to come between our friendship? For the first time, perhaps, I found myself fully appreciating the depth of the bond we had forged since we had first met at Joseph Shepard's law firm a year and a half ago. Was I to suddenly to lose him because his feelings had changed to something more than friendship?

It was a relief to finally reach the train station, where Oscar Wilde was departing San Francisco. Eddie did his best to park the carriage as close to the building as possible, but it was unusually crowded. During his brief stay in town, Wilde had been mocked and criticized in a blizzard of newspaper editorials, all of which had succeeded in making him the subject of enormous interest and speculation. It certainly seemed as if half the city had turned out this morning to bid farewell to one of their most talked about visitors since President Rutherford Hayes came to town in September of 1880.

In addition to the merely curious, a number of mostly young

men mocked the poet by dressing in knee breeches, flowing cravats, silk stockings, and enormous hats with wide brims. Women as well as men waved large yellow sunflowers, which had become the symbol of the Aesthetic Movement. Unfortunately, more than a few spectators had commenced drinking earlier than usual in honor of the occasion, and they were now rowdy and ill-mannered. Members of the uniformed police force patrolled the streets in a mostly vain attempt to keep the order, but they were hardly a match for the exuberant throng.

"This will do," I called up to Eddie, who was seated in his perch above the brougham. He had just finished circling the block for the second time and had found no space to park the carriage. "We'll get out here and walk to the terminal. You can meet us there after you've found a suitable place to leave the brougham."

Robert, who had been staring out the window at the milling crowd, already showed signs of regretting his decision to accompany me this morning. If he hadn't agreed, however, I fear my father might have barred the doors to our house and stationed Edis to watch my every move. Even with the formidable Scot by my side, Papa had been reluctant to let me out of his sight until the Telegraph Hill shooter was apprehended. While I understood his concerns for my safety, I did not appreciate being treated like a child. Not for the first time, I longed for the day when the income from my law practice would be enough to allow me to rent my own rooms.

"Tell me again why it was necessary for us to see Wilde off this morning?" Robert asked as we exited the carriage and made our way toward the train depot. He stepped aside quickly to avoid several young men who came by, wearing outlandish attire and waving sunflowers in our faces. "This is like a three-ring circus."

"It was the only way I could prevent Samuel from coming here himself. He's bored to death being confined to the house, and can't wait to be back to work, especially now that his book is finished." I didn't want to admit that without Robert acting as my escort, Papa would have forbidden me to leave the house.

212

"That is very foolish of Samuel. It's obvious that he's still in considerable pain."

"Yes," I agreed, dodging a man who weaved toward me, tilting a bottle of whiskey to his mouth. "But he'll never admit it." I gave him a sidelong look. "You're a good one to criticize. I have no doubt that if you were treated like an invalid and forced to remain at home for over a week, you'd be just as unhappy as he is."

He started to retort, then stopped and offered me a contrite smile. "I daresay you're right, Sarah. I hadn't thought to put myself in his place. The poor man must be desperate to be out and about."

"Just as desperate as my mother is to keep him at home. In the meantime, I've volunteered to become his eyes and ears." Looking up and down the bustling street, I had to smile. San Francisco was once again taking advantage of any reason to celebrate. "Aside from all the spectacle, however, I doubt if I'll have much to tell him. Just see all the reporters. Wilde's departure will be covered in every newspaper in town tomorrow."

"I'm sure it will," he agreed. "Although why that peculiar young man should warrant such attention remains a mystery to me."

We had reached the station and were making our way inside when I spied Ozzie Foldger. He was standing on the base of a pillar inside the lobby, not many feet away from a group of dignitaries surrounding the man of the hour. Clever of the reporter, I thought, giving the little weasel his due. Taking up a stance some three or four feet above the floor of the station afforded him a much clearer view of Wilde and the various city personages who had come to see him off.

Foldger's sharp-featured face bore its usual look of determination, and he was calling out questions to the poet along with other reporters on the scene. I wondered if he had already filed the sensational article he had promised me would be in tonight's paper. Several hours remained until his deadline, so perhaps he had yet to turn it in. If that was the case, perhaps it would be possible for me to inveigle some information out of him.

Deciding this would make a much more meaningful tidbit to

pass on to my brother than all the nonsense going on downtown this morning, I started to make my way toward Foldger. It was not easy. The train station was a madhouse, and Robert balked at walking any farther into the fray. But when I started to push forward without him, he moved quickly to catch up.

"Why must we get any closer than this?" he demanded, grunting as a long feather decorating a woman's hat poked him in the eye. "Surely you've seen enough of this debacle to satisfy Samuel's curiosity."

"Then leave, by all means," I called to him over my shoulder. "I wish to speak to Foldger."

"You mean that disreputable little reptile who calls himself a reporter? I thought that by now you would have had more than your fill of him."

I did not waste breath answering him as I squeezed past the gawkers and hecklers. I knew he would never abandon me in such a hubbub.

Once I was inside, the first people I spied were Stephen Parke and Isabel Freiberg. In fact, I nearly collided with Stephen when an unsteady gentleman pushed me from behind.

"Miss Woolson," he said, looking startled. "I did not expect to see you here."

"Nor did I expect to see you, Mr. Parke, Miss Freiberg," I answered. I was not surprised to see her flush in embarrassment that she had once again been caught with Stephen.

The young man had observed me studying Isabel. "Miss Freiberg and I . . ."

"Thought you might steal one last opportunity to be together before her engagement was announced," I said, stating the obvious.

He looked for a moment as if he meant to deny this, then gave a little nod. "You're right, of course. Mr. Freiberg would be most upset if he knew we were meeting like this. But we have so little time left."

"You need not fear that I will betray your confidence, Mr. Parke," I assured him. "In truth, I do not hold with arranged marriages. Perhaps I am a romantic, but I believe that love is a necessary component in any such union."

Isabel had been listening intently to this exchange. "You state my feelings perfectly, Miss Woolson. I am devoted to my father, but as I said before I cannot pretend to have feelings for the man he has chosen to be my husband."

My heart went out to the poor girl. "You are in a very difficult position, Miss Freiberg. You have my sincere sympathy."

Before she could reply, Robert joined us, looking red-faced and out of breath. "This is absurd," he declared after greeting Stephen and Isabel without much enthusiasm. "It's so crowded, we'll be lucky if we can even catch a glimpse of Wilde."

Realizing that Stephen and Isabel preferred to be alone, we politely excused ourselves and moved farther into the room until we were able to make out the tall figure of Oscar Wilde. Mortimer Remy and Jonathan Aleric were standing on either side of the poet, carrying on a heated argument. Behind Remy, I spied his contrary typesetter, Tull O'Hara, who was regarding Aleric with obvious dislike. Next to him stood Remy's nephew, Emmett Gardiner, who was watching the two arguing men with concern.

Suddenly Remy's face suffused with anger as Aleric held a book high over his head, circling slowly so that the volume was visible to everyone present in the station. When he turned in our direction, I saw that the book he was holding was a copy of his best-selling novel, *An Uncivil War.*

"Take that down, you pompous fool!" Remy shouted. "We are here to make our farewells to Mr. Wilde, not to show off that frivolous gibberish you call a novel."

If Mortimer Remy hadn't appeared so distraught, the scene before us would have been comical. The generally good-natured publisher was jumping up and down, arms outstretched in an attempt to grab the book out of the other man's hand. Aleric, who was smiling broadly, managed to keep the tome just out of the shorter man's reach. The appreciative crowd was cheering on the combatants as if they were engaged in a boxing match.

"You're making a fool of yourself," Remy shouted.

"On the contrary, dear Remy," Aleric said, laughing mockingly at his rival. "You are the one behaving like a fool." He pulled back the arm that held the book, as if he were about to throw it into the crowd. "There's a good boy, fetch!"

Although he did not, of course, throw the book, Remy actually started to dart in that direction, causing Aleric, Wilde, and most of the mob to laugh uproariously.

Realizing he was the butt of the joke, Remy's face flushed dark red with fury. "You bastard!" he cried, raising a hand as if to strike the other man.

Smiling acidly, Aleric moved forward, jutting out his pointed chin for Mortimer to punch. "Go ahead, Remy, strike me. I'll sue you until you won't have a single printing press left to publish that worthless rag sheet of yours."

He looked almost disappointed when Remy hesitated, then slowly dropped his fist. "What? Too chicken to go the whole hog? I always knew you were nothing but a lily-livered coward."

Remy was so furious, he actually started to shake. The crowd hooted and hurled jeers at the mortified publisher. "I'll kill you for this, Aleric!" Remy threatened. "I should have done it when you first came to town. You took my wife, and now you want to take my newspaper. Well, you're not going to get it. I'll see you dead first!"

"Come, old fellow," Aleric said, amicable enough now that he had achieved his goal of stirring up his rival. "Don't tell me you can't take a joke?" Smiling, he threw his arm around Remy, giving him a friendly pat on the shoulder.

Reporters were scribbling madly in their notepads. During the argument, Oscar Wilde had stepped back a few paces to a safe distance, where he had observed the row with an amused expression. No doubt he regarded the vulgar display as yet more evidence to support the stories accusing California of still being part of the Wild West.

Before the fracas could develop into a riot, Emmett Gardiner stepped between the combatants. Over the din I could just hear him chastising Aleric while attempting to soothe his uncle. Remy's face was still as red as a beet, but now I suspected it was due more to embarrassment than to anger. Aleric displayed an expression of smug satisfaction, and I noticed that Wilde was now holding the man's book. He was thumbing through it with interest, and I remembered him mentioning that he had enjoyed reading the volume as a boy.

Remy took a deep breath and pointedly turned his back on his adversary, directing some workers to erect a simple wooden platform for Wilde. It was only a few feet tall, but high enough for most of the people in the station to see him. Leisurely, as if he had all the time in the world, instead of only minutes before catching a train for Salt Lake City, the poet stepped onto the makeshift podium and smiled out at the crowd. This morning he was dressed in more modest attire, stylish trousers and a day coat instead of his usual knee breeches and black silk stockings.

"It is kind of all of you to see me off this morning," he began, eyeing several women who were regarding him with fawning adoration. "Especially the beautiful women who abound in this fair city. Ah, ladies, you begin by resisting a man's advances, and end by blocking his retreat. We are completely at your mercy."

There was a burst of laughter, and a few catcalls that once again questioned Wilde's romantic proclivities.

"You have proven to me that America is the noisiest country that ever existed." Wilde shook his head, appearing almost sorrowful. "All art depends upon exquisite and delicate sensibility, and such continual turmoil must ultimately be destructive of the musical faculty."

There was another roar from the crowd, and I saw Mortimer Remy grab the sleeve of the police constable, obviously imploring him to quiet the noisy throng so that Mr. Wilde could be heard. The patrolman took a firm hold of his baton and set off to calm the fray, but it was like trying to stop crashing waves at the beach armed with nothing but an umbrella.

"That's Mortimer Remy from Platt's Hall, isn't it?" Robert asked, leaning close to my ear. "What possessed him to lash out at Aleric like that? He's made a spectacle of himself."

"Unfortunately, Aleric has a way of infuriating him. He deliberately antagonizes poor Mortimer until he does something foolish. It will be in all the papers, I fear, and he'll be humiliated."

I felt a tug on my sleeve and, looking around, found that Eddie Cooper had joined us. "What's happenin', Miss Sarah?" he asked, taking in the crowd with huge eyes. "Have I missed somethin'?"

"No," I told him dryly. "Only grown men behaving like street hooligans. Mr. Wilde is attempting to make a speech."

"He looks different today," Eddie commented, studying the Irish poet with interest. "Not barmy like the other night at Platt's Hall."

"Yet he still stands there laughing at us," Robert put in, his tone disapproving. "If he's an example of the Aesthetic Movement, I want nothing to do with it."

"Yes, but that's no excuse to treat the man so shamefully," I said. "I shudder to think of what he's going to tell people about us when he returns to London." I was about to say more, but Wilde was finally able to continue with his farewell speech.

"But, friends, I have found San Francisco to be a beautiful city. Indeed, perhaps the most beautiful part of America is the West. Unfortunately, to reach it involves a journey by rail of six days, racing along tied to an ugly tin kettle of a steam engine."

Mortimer Remy caught the poet's attention. Pointing to his pocket watch, he indicated the time.

"Mr. Remy informs me that I must leave you now to catch my train." He held up Aleric's book. "Before I depart, however, I want to recommend that those of you who have not already done so purchase this amazing narration of your calamitous Civil War. I read it as a young boy, when such tragedies as war held a certain fascination for me. It is a gruesome tale and it is cruel, but it relates a story that mankind would do well to remember." He smiled down at Aleric, who was beaming up at him. "And his mastery of the English language . . . ah, Mr. Jonathan Aleric is, in his own way, a poet."

Despite Emmett Gardiner's efforts to calm his uncle, Mortimer Remy looked so furious that I feared he might burst a blood vessel. Since there was clearly nothing he could do to silence Wilde without causing another commotion, he put a good face on it and helped the poet down from his perch.

Instead of following the publisher in the direction of the train tracks, however, Wilde turned to Aleric, opened the copy of *An Uncivil War,* and held it out to be signed. The smiling author produced a pencil and wrote his name on the proffered page with a flourish. To the delight of the reporters, the two men posed together in front of the noisy throng, then proceeded side by side to the waiting train.

Emmett Gardiner took his mortified uncle by the arm and gently led him behind Wilde and Aleric as they exited the lobby.

"Good God!" Robert exclaimed, watching their departing backs. "I admit I enjoyed reading Aleric's book when it first came out. But now that I've met him, I have to say there's something about the man that curdles my blood. The way he harassed Remy in front of Wilde and all these spectators is enough to set my teeth on edge. I begin to see why your friend Remy dislikes him so thoroughly."

"Their animosity is escalating," I said, experiencing a shiver of fear. "Remy seems to be alarmingly close to his breaking point. I wonder how far Aleric will push him?"

"Not much further, if he has any sense," said my companion.

"Can we go now, Miss Sarah?" Eddie asked. "I don't want to leave the brougham for too long in this crowd."

"Just a minute, Eddie," I told the boy. "I want to have a quick word with someone before we leave."

Ignoring Robert's protesting groan, I made my way with some difficulty through the departing crowd, toward where I had last seen Ozzie Foldger. He was no longer standing on the base of the pillar but was speaking to some of the women who had been ogling

Wilde earlier. He was so occupied jotting down notes in his messy-looking pad that he did not notice my approach.

"May I have a quick word with you?" I asked, forcing myself to be polite. Throughout our childhood, Papa had often preached the old adage that you could catch more flies with honey than with vinegar paper. I hoped he was right.

Foldger's pale gray eyes regarded me warily. Nonetheless, he appeared interested enough to close his notebook and bid good-bye to the young women.

"All right, then, Miss Woolson, what's this about?" he asked, following me to a relatively quiet corner of the station. "You didn't seem all that eager to speak to me the other day when you were taking around those SPCA petitions."

I gave him my best imitation of a winning smile. It was not my custom to mask my opinion about an individual I disliked as thoroughly as Ozzie Foldger, but I doubted that candor would elicit any meaningful information about this evening's issue of the *San Francisco Tattler*.

"I was curious as to what we might expect to read next in your series about Claude Dunn," I said, holding the false smile on my face as if it were glued there. "You indicated that it would appear in tonight's edition."

The reporter's sly sneer let me know that he had not been taken in by my sprightly performance. "That toffee-nosed brother of yours sent you to find out, didn't he?" He laughed unpleasantly. "Well, you can run back home and tell him that he can read all about it in tonight's edition."

"I still say you're playing a dangerous game, Mr. Foldger," I said. "Especially if you're right about Claude Dunn's death not being a suicide. You should go straight to the police."

"That'd make your brother happy, wouldn't it? Well, you can tell him not by a jugful. This is my story and it's gonna stay that way." He gave another caustic laugh. "Tell you what, I'll have a copy of the *Tattler* personally delivered to your house tonight. Look for my article on the front page, above the fold."

He was still chuckling when he left the station. I watched him go but could think of nothing further to say that might change his mind. I found Robert and Eddie waiting for me out on the street. They were looking after Ozzie Foldger's retreating back.

"What did you say to him?" Robert asked. We were following Eddie, who indicated the carriage was parked in the same general direction the reporter had taken. "He had some uncomplimentary things to say about you as he left the terminal."

I sighed. "The man is a fool. He promises to reveal new information about Claude Dunn's death in tonight's *Tattler*."

He gave a dismissive grunt. "I don't know why you're letting that worry you. Foldger is a reporter. You can bet that this is just another wild story he's made up to sell copies of that disreputable paper."

"I hope you're right," I said, quickening my pace to keep up with Eddie. "There was something about the way he described the article, though. As if he really had come across some kind of evidence."

"If he has, then he surely is irresponsible not to take it to the police. But that's his business; it need not concern us."

"I can't shake the feeling that it may concern us a great deal," I said more to myself than to my friend. "How far away did Eddie park the brougham?"

Before he could answer, there was the sound of a woman screaming, and we both came to a startled halt. More shrieks followed. They seemed to be coming from nearby, but it was difficult to tell from which direction. Ahead of us, Eddie had also stopped in his tracks; then, after looking around, he charged after a group of people who were rushing toward the corner.

"What the devil?" Protectively, Robert took hold of my arm.

I watched Eddie round the corner. "Let me go, Robert. We must see what's happened."

Before he could stop me, I wrenched free and rushed after Eddie. I could hear Robert hard on my heels as I stumbled on my skirts. Muttering an unladylike expletive, I picked them up and ran full out around the block toward what appeared to be a small alley behind a warehouse. It was a narrow passageway, and a group of spectators were clustered around the filthy entrance. There was a strong smell of garbage and other, even fouler, odors made by vagrants. Most of the women were standing well back.

Pushing my way through the crowd, I saw what appeared to be a pile of rags thrown carelessly in the narrow space between the warehouse and another building. I drew closer, and my heart caught in my throat as I realized that these were not rags at all. It was the body of a man, blood slowly forming in a pool by his side. Through the alley's deep shadows, I could just make out the blade of a knife sticking out of his chest.

As I took in the scene, I caught sight of a small notebook lying several feet inside the alley opening. I gave a little gasp as I recognized that all-too-familiar pad. I had, in fact, seen it only moments before. It belonged to Ozzie Foldger!

Brushing aside a faint stir of conscience, I looked around to make sure no one was watching, then snatched up the notebook and placed it in my pocket. I knew it was evidence and that it would have to be turned over to the police. But I was determined to have a quick look at it for myself first. After that, I would make certain that it was handed over directly to George Lewis and to no one else.

CHAPTER SEVENTEEN

At my request, Papa purchased a copy of that evening's *Tattler*. I did not expect to find Foldger's much-touted story on the front page, or anywhere else in the paper, but I had to be certain.

To my mother's consternation, talk of the reporter's death dominated our dinner conversation. Several times she attempted to shift us onto more suitable subjects, but under the circumstances it was difficult to feign enthusiasm over mundane topics.

Shortly after we left the dining room, Robert and George Lewis arrived at the house. Samuel and I had invited the men over to discuss Ozzie Foldger's death, which weighed heavily on both our minds. Papa was obviously determined not to be left out of the conversation and indicated we should all join him in the library. There, we made a forlorn little assembly, drinking coffee—at my father's insistence, heavily laced with brandy—and trying to absorb the latest in this growing string of tragedies. Although it was early April, the night was chilly and Edis had lit a hearty fire, which was as restorative as the liquor.

"The man was a fool."

Robert was the first to speak after our elderly butler left the library, closing the door silently behind him. I wondered if he realized he was repeating the very words I had spoken outside the train station not five minutes before Foldger was killed.

"I tried to convince him to tell us what he was planning to write in that second article," George said pensively, and took a sip of his coffee. "He just laughed at me. In fact, he called our entire police department a farce."

Papa reached for his pipe. "I've said this before, but it bears repeating. The press today is out of control. They print gossip and innuendo, even lies when it suits their purposes. Never mind sticking to the truth. The only thing that matters to them is selling newspapers." He eyed Samuel, as if again remembering that his own son was a part of this much reviled industry. "Sorry, my boy, but it's no more than the truth."

My brother merely nodded. His handsome face appeared pale and drawn. It frightened me to see him looking more tired than he had in several days. Ozzie Foldger had been the bane of his professional life for five years, but the reporter's brutal murder had shocked him. I worried that it might even set back his recovery.

"Sarah talked to him not ten minutes before he was stabbed," Robert put in. "He accused her of spying. He claimed she was trying to get him to divulge details of his article so that she could turn them over to Samuel."

"Foldger was always afraid I was going to steal one of his absurd stories," said Samuel, speaking for the first time. "He was obsessed with making a name for himself."

"Well, he's succeeded," I said quietly. "His death will be on page one of every newspaper in town tomorrow. George, have the police any idea who stabbed him?"

"I'm afraid not," he answered. "The knife the killer used was so common as to be untraceable. Although there were a number of people leaving the train depot, none of them used that alley, which is hardly surprising since it's so squalid. Evidently, a passerby heard a man cry out, but by the time he got there, the lane was deserted. Well, except for the body, of course. And precious little to go on."

Uneasily, I cleared my throat. It was time to admit that I had removed a potentially vital piece of evidence from the crime scene. Suddenly, four sets of male eyes were focused on me, and I was disconcerted to feel my face flush.

"I have a confession to make, George," I began, and reached into my pocket for Foldger's notebook. "I found this lying on the ground near the body, and I took it away with me."

There was a dumbfounded expression on George's boyish face. "You took it? But it's evidence."

"Yes, I know, and I'm sorry. I'm afraid I couldn't resist the temptation." Even as I spoke, I recognized this was a poor excuse. "I was hoping it might contain information about Foldger's next article."

"And does it?" my father asked.

I shook my head, unable to hide my disappointment. "Very little," I admitted. "It's written in some kind of a code, or a style Foldger invented to jot down his notes." I handed the book to George. "The proper names are easy to make out, but the rest of it looks like so much gibberish."

"I do that, as well," put in Samuel. "When you're on a story, there's often little time to write words out properly. George, let me see that pad, will you?"

His friend handed it over, and Samuel thumbed through the pages. "Here are his notes on the Stockton Street bank robbery last week," he said. "And on this page he mentions Claude Dunn. Ha! And the fact that he gave him twenty-five dollars." He looked at me. "That must be the money you saw him hand Dunn when you were on Telegraph Hill." He continued turning pages. "He's written Dunn's name several more times, but I can't make out the details. You're right, Sarah, a lot of this is all but impossible to make out." He handed the notebook back to George. "Maybe someone at the station can make sense of it."

George didn't look hopeful. "I'll try, but I doubt that any of my men will have better luck than you."

"Well," Papa said after a short silence. "Whatever that notebook reveals, if anything, one thing seems clear. Someone was worried about what Foldger was going to write in his article this evening." He regarded George with approval. "Looks like you were right all along about Dunn's hanging not being a suicide." At the policeman's surprised expression, Papa explained, "Sarah mentioned your suspicions about his death being staged to look as if he killed himself. Don't worry, I haven't mentioned it to anyone else."

George gave my father a rueful smile. "I informed Lieutenant Curtis, but he had already made up his mind."

"To tell the truth, I've never been overly impressed with your lieutenant, George." Papa once again took up his pipe, reached for his tobacco pouch, and began filling the bowl. "He was only promoted because he has relatives at City Hall. As far as I'm concerned, a good leader is a man who has proven his mettle in the field. Curtis lacks experience and sound judgment."

When George regarded him in silent discomfort, Papa went on, "I realize that you can't afford to speak ill of your superior, George, but I'm free to speak my mind. Two or three of Curtis's cases have ended up in my courtroom, and I can attest firsthand to his incompetence. I don't envy you your job, my boy. Not one jot."

"Even if Curtis was a first-rate officer, I doubt he could have done anything to prevent Foldger's murder," I said. "For once, I think Foldger was telling the truth when he claimed to have evidence that Dunn was murdered. That leaves us with only one course of action. If Lieutenant Curtis refuses to listen to reason, it's up to us to discover the nature of that evidence."

I'm not certain who protested loudest at this perfectly reasonable statement.

"There is no *us,* my girl," exclaimed my father.

"Are you insane?" Robert shouted at the same time.

Lewis seemed taken aback by the fervor of these cries. To my annoyance, Samuel regarded me in amusement.

"That seems to settle that," he said. "It appears that you are to stay out of the affair, little sister. And for once, I must say that I concur."

"Not you, too, Samuel," I objected.

"Sarah, two men are dead, and you have been shot at, as have I," my brother said reasonably. "Robert is right. It would be reckless of you to involve yourself any further in this matter."

"Then we are in agreement," Robert said with finality. "We must leave this to the police. At least to Lewis here," he added. "And hope to heaven that Lieutenant Curtis keeps his nose out of this business before someone else is killed."

"Amen to that," agreed Samuel.

Papa gave his son a skeptical look. He had lit his pipe and was puffing at it thoughtfully. "Foldger's death is certain to be a high-profile case. You can bet tomorrow night's dinner that Curtis will be drawn to the publicity like a moth to a flame." He looked at George. "You'll have to do some fancy dancing to get anything worthwhile accomplished with that scalawag in charge."

Lewis nodded unhappily. "You're right, I'm afraid. It won't be easy."

My father gave an abrupt laugh. "That's a considerable understatement. You're going to be on your own hook, my lad. One way or the other, this murdering scoundrel must be brought to justice before he strikes again."

"I'd give a good deal to know why Foldger gave Dunn twenty-five dollars," said Samuel. "That's a lot of money for a story."

"Perhaps Dunn had information to sell," Papa speculated. He drew on his pipe, producing a great puff of smoke. "As you've said more than once, son, Foldger was not above buying, stealing, or even making up a story if it would sell newspapers. Either he suspected Dunn of being privy to valuable information, or he was buying the man's silence."

George Lewis started, almost spilling his coffee. "Buying his silence? You think Foldger committed a crime of some sort, and he feared Dunn would expose him?"

"Maybe. Maybe not." Papa smiled benevolently at the eager policeman. "I'm just trying to allow for all the possibilities. I can't see Ozzie Foldger handing over a packet of money because he was feeling generous."

Samuel gave a sarcastic little grunt. "Hardly. Not to speak ill of the dead, but Foldger was as tight as a tick."

"Even if those speculations are correct, what do they have to do with Samuel and Sarah being shot at?" Robert regarded each of us in turn. "As far as I know, they had nothing to do with either Claude Dunn or Ozzie Foldger."

"Samuel and Foldger were rivals, of course," I said. "And Samuel, you knew Dunn because he was a member of the writers colony on Telegraph Hill, didn't you?"

"That's how I initially met the man, yes, but we were hardly friends," my brother said.

"Didn't he work as a reporter?" asked Lewis.

Samuel smiled. "It's true that he was forced by financial circumstances to sell an occasional newspaper article, but Dunn generally looked down his nose at reporters. He considered us inferior to more serious writers. Meaning purists like himself, with little money but a lot of hope."

"Did he have any talent?" Robert asked. "I never heard of Dunn until he died."

"I believe he was working on a novel of some sort," Samuel answered. "But then a number of us are. I have no idea what it was about, though, or if it was any good. His newspaper articles were all right, but not first-rate enough to allow him to make his living in journalism."

"Be that as it may," Lewis interjected, "I still don't see how those murders can have had anything to do with Miss Sarah or you, Samuel. If only we had some idea of what Foldger planned to put in tonight's article."

"Yes, all roads lead back to that question, don't they?" Samuel said, sounding as frustrated as we all felt. "He bragged to Sarah that the story would result in a scandal. He was determined that it would make his name famous."

"And so it has," Papa said dryly. "For the next week or two, at any rate."

Since there seemed to be nothing more to say, we were forced to let the matter rest, at least for that evening.

Despite the events of the day, or perhaps because they had left me exhausted, I slept well that night, awakening refreshed and ready to take on whatever the new day might bring. As my father had so succinctly put it, there was a mystery to be solved. And no matter what anyone said, I had no intention of playing spectator while others set out to unravel it.

Not surprisingly, Papa had different ideas. After breakfast on Monday morning, I was not happy to learn that I was expected to share a cab with him on his way to the courthouse. He promised to drop me off at my office, claiming with an admirably straight face that this was an *invitation*. However, I believe I know a command when I hear one.

As we rode downtown, my father took the opportunity to re-iterate his warnings of Saturday night. He had discussed the situation with Robert after I had bade the men good night and retired to my bedroom, and my friend had promised to escort me home this evening. In the meantime, according to Papa I was to remain in my office all day. There were to be no outside excursions, and under no circumstances was I to set foot on Telegraph Hill.

"In fact, I'd feel infinitely better if you would remain at home until the shooter is apprehended," he added. "I don't believe for one moment that you were mistaken for a fox or a raccoon. Nor do I think you were shot at by accident. If someone wants to see you dead, they're not going to stop at just one attempt."

This was too much! I was twenty-eight years old and a licensed California attorney with my own law practice. True, I continued to live with my parents—as did many unmarried women of my station—but the vast majority of them did not work outside the home. I deeply appreciated my parents and understood that they loved me and were concerned for my safety, but not for the first time I chafed at still being under their roof and, consequently, under their control. Although I feared it might break my mother's heart, I did not waver in my determination to find a modest flat of my own as soon as my financial situation improved.

"I assure you there is no need for a man to escort me home from work," I informed him calmly. "I've already promised to be careful. And I must go to my office today. I'm working on a case."

"Yes, defeating the bullring," he commented dryly. "A case that will be all but impossible to win. When City Hall smells money, my girl, they can be dashed ornery."

"Which is all the more reason why I cannot remain idly at home."

My father sighed. "You're as obstinate as a mule, Sarah, have been since you were knee-high to a mosquito. More than once I've thought of taking your brother Frederick's advice and locking you in your room." He gave me a sidelong glance. "But I suppose you'd just climb out the window."

Or Samuel's window, I thought, deciding not to mention this aloud. My brother's room, located at the rear of our home, overlooked a large old oak tree that was very handy for leaving the house unnoticed. He had employed this method of silent escape since childhood. I must confess that I had accompanied him on more than one occasion, shinnying down those sturdy, thick limbs, all the while fearful that my mother would catch me in this extremely unladylike exercise.

As our coach turned onto Sutter Street, Papa patted my hand. "The Lord knows I'm not a sentimental man, Sarah, but I have grown extraordinarily fond of you. For my sake, if for no other reason, do be careful."

"I will, Papa," I assured him. "Please don't worry."

My father reluctantly deposited me in front of the building I shared with Fanny Goodman. I alighted to find her standing outside her shop, scrubbing her windows clean with a large pail of soapy water.

"Sarah, you're just the person I've been waiting to see," she greeted me, dropping her washing rag into the pail. "Have you heard the news about that reporter, Ozzie Foldger? He was stabbed to death Saturday morning in broad daylight. Can you imagine such a thing?"

"I fear I can, Fanny. In fact, I was there when it happened."

She looked at me in astonishment, and I watched thoughts of clean windows vanish from her mind.

"You need a hot cup of coffee," she declared. Before I had time to respond, she had picked up her pail and was motioning me inside her shop. "I want to hear every detail of what happened."

Several minutes later we were settled in her kitchen, hot coffee and a selection of fresh doughnuts placed on the table before us. The pastries looked and smelled delicious, but since I had partaken of breakfast not an hour earlier, I limited myself to coffee.

Once she was seated in the chair across from me, I briefly described the scene at the train station on Saturday morning. I recounted my discussion with Ozzie Foldger, along with his newspaper article that was to appear in Saturday evening's *Tattler*. Finally, I told her of finding the reporter dead in an alley hardly more than a block from the depot.

"Heaven help us!" she declared when I finished the story. She gave a little shiver. "Did his article appear in the *Tattler?*"

"No. Either he hadn't turned it in yet, or for some reason the editor decided to hold it back for a day or two."

She took a sip of coffee, then regarded me over the rim of her cup. "Seems to me that newspaper of his would want to capitalize on Foldger's death and print the story as soon as possible."

"I agree. But since we have no idea what the article contained, it's impossible to speculate."

"Surely someone must have witnessed the murder," she said, looking bemused. "You said Wilde's departure attracted a large crowd."

"That's true, but Foldger was stabbed in a filthy little alley behind a warehouse. I don't think many people used it. It would have been easy enough for the murderer to slip away unnoticed."

231

"And the police have no idea who did it?"

"Apparently there's little to go on." Even I could hear the note of discouragement in my voice. "Sergeant Lewis is doing his best, but I'm not sure how much help he's getting from his lieutenant."

"Is it possible . . ." She hesitated, seemingly fearful of expressing a sudden thought. "Do they believe that the man who murdered Mr. Foldger could be the same person who shot at you and Samuel?"

"It's certainly occurred to George, as well as to Samuel and me. Unfortunately, there are a great many pieces to this puzzle which don't seem to fit together."

"Your parents must be beside themselves with worry," she said, rising to refill our cups. "I'm surprised you even came into your office today. If someone was brazen enough to stab Mr. Foldger on a public street, what would stop him from trying to harm you here?"

"Not you, too, Fanny," I said with a soft groan. "I cannot live my life in the constant fear that some madman will attack me if I step a foot outside my house."

Her face was more serious than I had ever seen it. "I've grown to love you and Samuel like the children I was never blessed with, Sarah. If I could, I would sit you both down in this kitchen and watch over you until that predator was caught."

I couldn't stop the smile that curled on my lips. "You sound just like my father, dear Fanny. He would like to lock me away in my room. But we dwell in a world filled with risks. We can't allow them to rule our lives." After drinking the last of my coffee, I stood. "I must get upstairs if I'm to accomplish any work today."

"You haven't had any more bother from that Mr. Ruiz, have you?" she asked. "Have you told the police about him and his thugs? What if he comes back here to badger you?"

"There's little the police can do, Fanny." There was no sense adding Ricardo Ruiz to her list of concerns. "He blusters a good deal, but I'm certain he's more of a nuisance than an actual threat."

She did not look convinced. "I hope you're right, dear. I'm not ashamed to admit that the man frightens me. He acts like he owns City Hall and that they'll do anything he asks them to."

"That may be true, but I have more important things to worry about right now than Señor Ruiz's foul temper." I picked up my briefcase and walked to the door. "Perhaps I'll see you again before I leave. Papa has asked Robert to escort me home. I cannot imagine why he agreed to such a silly request."

Fanny's expression appeared to be a strange mixture of amusement and pity. "Despite that quick mind of yours, Sarah, you are remarkably naïve about men and the ways of the heart, Mr. Campbell is in love with you, silly girl. He'd do anything to ensure your safety."

Upstairs, I settled down to work at my lovely cherrywood desk, but I found it impossible to concentrate. Only then did I realize that I had been trying for several days to put Robert's declaration of love out of my mind. Now, Fanny's words unleashed a flood of emotions, feelings I hardly understood, much less knew how to deal with.

Was it possible that Robert had misread his feelings for me? I wondered. We had been through so much since we'd first met. Together, we had faced danger—indeed, life-and-death situations. Could he have mistaken the thrills and excitement of those experiences for love? Did being devoted friends necessarily equate with being in love, romantically in love? I was forced to admit that I did not know.

Restlessly, I stood and walked to the window. Sutter Street was crowded as usual at this time of day. Carriages of various sizes and designs, drays, a horsecar, and even a somber black-and-silver hearse passed below my second-floor rooms.

Standing there, I became conscious of the nearly constant clamor and congestion of downtown San Francisco, noise that I was ordinarily able to ignore: the man driving the dray was cursing at a hansom cab, a drummer's wagon had stalled in front of the butcher shop across the street, causing a landau, his brass horn blasting loudly away, to swerve in an effort to avoid a collision.

Two young boys appeared to be fistfighting over a dog, while their mothers screamed at each other as they attempted to separate their offspring. I could not help but smile, thinking that perhaps Oscar Wilde was correct in calling America the noisiest country in the world. In some strange way, it reminded me of the conflict going on in my mind, and in my heart. I wished I could come up with one of the Irishman's easy platitudes to put everything in perspective. But then I was not a poet.

I had finally settled down to working on the written argument I would present to City Hall, outlining the SPCA's objections to Ruiz's bullring, when I heard someone hurrying up the stairs to my office. There was a quick knock, then the door opened to reveal a somewhat disheveled-looking Jane Hardy standing in the doorway. She was breathless and clearly upset.

"Please, Miss Woolson, we need your help," she managed to say after taking in a gulp of air. "Señor Ruiz is at our office with a police constable. He is demanding that we turn over all of our signed petitions to him, or he will have us arrested and taken to jail!"

CHAPTER EIGHTEEN

Mrs. Hardy and I were fortunate to find an unoccupied cab and made our way speedily to the SPCA's Merchant Street headquarters. We were halfway there when I suddenly remembered Papa charging me to remain in my office all day until Robert came to escort me home. Had I agreed to this command? I wondered, searching my memory. No, I decided, I had not actually promised him that I would not go out, but rather had given him my assurance that I would be careful. And I certainly was being cautious. Sharing a cab with a proper, middle-aged matron must be considered conscientious behavior by anyone's standards.

While Mrs. Hardy paid the cabman, I hurried inside the building housing the SPCA. Upon entering the second-floor office, I found Ricardo Ruiz shouting at Mr. Dinwitty, who, although cowed by this tongue-lashing, appeared to be doing his best to stand up to the fiery Mexican aristocrat. Behind Ruiz stood a uniformed policeman, along with the same two brawny men who seemed to accompany their employer everywhere.

Mr. Dinwitty's wife, Celestia, was seated at a nearby desk, her dark green ensemble once again styled more formally than the

235

circumstances would seem to warrant. Her oversize hat was an unbecoming shade of olive green and looked as if someone had tossed an assortment of flowers, feathers, and one or two stuffed birds onto it in no particular order for decoration. Her round, fleshy face peered out from beneath this garish chapeau, bearing its usual expression of arrogant disapproval. As usual, she held her small brown dog tightly to her bosom, where it regarded us all with distrustful, beady black eyes. About half a dozen society workers and volunteers were clustered around the back of the room, as if trying to get as far away from Señor Ruiz and his thugs as possible.

When Mr. Dinwitty caught sight of me, his expression became one of profound relief. "Miss Woolson, I am so grateful to see you. Will you please explain to—"

Before he could finish speaking, the police constable stepped in front of me. "I'm sorry, miss, but this office is temporarily closed. If you'll please return later, I'm sure they will be able to help you at that time."

"Officer, this is Miss Sarah Woolson," Dinwitty protested. "She is the society's attorney."

The young police officer looked from the tall, nervous man, to Señor Ruiz, and finally back to me. "An attorney?" he asked in considerable surprise. "But she's a woman."

"How astute of you, Officer," I replied, unable to mask my sarcasm. I was growing infinitely weary of having to justify my legal credentials. "Despite my gender, I am a licensed attorney in the state of California. As Mr. Dinwitty stated, I am representing this society in their efforts to prevent a bullring from being constructed in San Francisco."

Mrs. Dinwitty snorted with indignation. "On that score, at least, Miss Woolson is correct," she proclaimed. Her agitation caused the small dog in her lap to commence barking. "This man plans to debase our city by constructing a vile arena dedicated to violence and the slaughter of innocent animals."

"My dear, please," her husband said, moving to where his wife was sitting. Placing a tentative hand on her shoulder, he attempted to quiet both her and the dog. "Miss Woolson will take this situation in hand, I am sure."

"Don't be ridiculous, Bernard," his wife snapped, trying unsuccessfully to quiet her dog. "The police do not even recognize her as a legitimate attorney. I warned you that hiring this woman to represent us was a mistake, but you would insist—"

"Please, ma'am," the policeman said, eyeing the dog with distaste. "Can you make him stop barking?"

While Mrs. Dinwitty murmured soothing words to her pet, I noticed that Ricardo Ruiz did not look pleased to see me here. For a moment intense anger showed on his handsome face, only to be squelched almost instantly. Assuming a smile so insincere that it would not have fooled a five-year-old child, he removed his hat and bowed respectfully.

"Ah, the beautiful Señorita Woolson, what a delightful surprise to see you again. Unfortunately, as you can see, I am presently occupied on a matter of business which need not concern you."

"I beg to differ with you, Señor Ruiz," I said coolly. "Your business with this society is of considerable concern to me, as I'm the legal representative of the SPCA." I turned my attention to the policeman, who continued to glare at the dog in Mrs. Dinwitty's lap. "Would you kindly give me your name, Officer, as well as why you have accompanied Señor Ruiz to this office?"

The young man shot Ruiz a perplexed look, as if not sure whether or not to respond to my questions. At Ruiz's curt nod, he said, "I'm Rodney Kimball, miss. Mr. Ruiz has accused this group of bullying people to sign the petitions they've been taking all over town."

"Bullying people?" I asked incredulously.

I stared at Mr. Dinwitty, who was anxiously wringing his hands. His wife uttered a cry of outrage, causing the dog she was holding to once again begin its dreadful yapping.

"No, no, absolutely not!" Mr. Dinwitty proclaimed. "I assure you, Miss Woolson, that we have done no such thing. Each and every name on our petitions has been lawfully obtained, without any coercion on our part." He motioned to the people standing in the back of the room. "Please, ask our volunteers. They will tell you they have followed my instructions to the letter."

I studied the one man and eight women standing at the back of the room and had to repress a smile. Accusing any of these well-dressed, middle-aged matrons of coercion was ludicrous in the extreme. As for the gentleman, he was slightly built, gray-haired, and well into his sixties. He looked as if he would have a difficult time taking a cookie away from a baby.

"These are the people who have been circulating the petitions?" I asked.

Mr. Dinwitty nodded, undoubtedly guessing the direction of my thoughts. "Indeed they are. I am proud to say that these fine volunteers have worked tirelessly to collect the signatures of individuals opposed to the bullring." He picked up a pile of papers from his desk. "So far, we have exceeded our goal."

Ricardo Ruiz grabbed for the petitions, but Mr. Dinwitty was too quick for him, hastily returning them to his desk.

"If you refuse to turn those worthless papers over to me immediately, you will leave me with no choice but to have you arrested," Ruiz threatened. He nodded to the policeman, who took a step forward.

"One moment please, Officer Kimball," I said, blocking his path to my clients. "Before you do anything rash, I would like to speak to the people who are bringing these charges against the society. Are they here with you, Señor Ruiz?"

He hesitated only a moment, then indicated that the complainants were waiting downstairs. At my request, he ordered one of his burly guards to bring them up to the office. Despite his bluster, he did not appear happy to do so, which gave me hope that the matter might be more readily settled than he had let on.

It was a sad little group that straggled upstairs some minutes later. Ricardo Ruiz must have been truly desperate to attempt such an outrageous ploy, I thought. The accusers consisted of three frightened older women and a wide-eyed boy of about sixteen. They were all poorly dressed in clothes that were little better than rags. The soles of the boy's shoes were held together with strings, and his mop of tangled hair hadn't been washed in heaven knew how long. The women ranged in age from early forties to perhaps sixty or older; they were so thin and bedraggled that it was difficult to venture an accurate guess. All four appeared frightened and confused, as if they weren't sure why they were standing here in a room full of strangers.

"This is patently ridiculous," Mrs. Dinwitty proclaimed. Her pale eyes roamed disdainfully over the motley band. Once again, her dreadful little dog punctuated her words with another outburst of barking. "These are people you have taken off the street, Señor Ruiz. You cannot expect us to believe a word they utter."

"My dear," her husband said, trying to calm his wife. "Let us allow Miss Woolson to handle this."

"Bah!" the woman declared, subjecting me to a withering look and ignoring her noisy pet. "She is not qualified to handle a—"

Officer Kimball appeared to have had enough. "Ma'am, if you cannot keep that dog quiet, I will have to ask you to leave the room." Although his back was to me as he faced Mrs. Dinwitty, there must have been something in his face that, for once, cut the woman's words off short. She began shushing her dog, rocking it in her arms as if it were a small child. I silently applauded Officer Kimball and made a mental note to mention him to George Lewis.

"Tell the policeman your stories," Ruiz tersely instructed the shabby assortment of litigants once the incessant yapping had stopped. He nodded toward one of the women, indicating that she was to begin first.

The unfortunate soul looked from Ruiz to the policeman, then to the rest of the people in the room, her expression so anxious that I was afraid she might dissolve into tears.

"Go on," Ruiz prompted when she lowered her eyes to stare at the floor. "You *can* speak, can you not, woman?"

"Señor Ruiz, the poor soul is terrified," I chastised him. "Perhaps we should begin with the boy."

The youngster started at this. "I, ah," he began, staring uncertainly at Officer Kimball as if he had never been this close to a policeman before. Or if he had, that it had not been a pleasant encounter.

"Take your time, young man," I told the lad. "The officer will not harm you. Just tell us your story truthfully and all will be well."

He looked at me as if he wanted to believe my reassurances but was too hardened by a lifetime of brutal survival to accept the word of a stranger.

"Come on, boy," Ruiz said, losing what little remained of his patience. "Spit it out. What did these people do to you?"

"They brung me that paper to sign," the lad said, pointing a dirty finger at the petitions lying on Dinwitty's desk. His voice was so soft that even though I stood not three feet away, I had difficulty catching the words.

"And did you put your name to it?" Ruiz persisted.

"I dunno how to write," the boy admitted, lowering his face to the floor.

"*¡Madre de Dios!*" said Ruiz. "So what happened then?"

The boy shuffled from one foot to the other. "The gent said if I didn't make my mark, he'd settle my hash good an' proper."

In obvious frustration, Ruiz picked up the boy's right hand and, pushing back his torn and filthy sleeve, revealed a jagged cut that ran from his wrist halfway up to his elbow. The wound appeared fresh and was still oozing a small amount of blood. It also looked very dirty and likely to fester if not cleaned immediately.

"Did he do this to you?" Ruiz demanded. "Did this 'gent' cut your arm?"

The boy nodded without raising his face. Señor Ruiz jerked him forward until his arm was practically beneath Officer Kimball's nose. The policeman bent over and examined the wound.

"You say someone from this office used a knife to force you to sign the petition?" he asked.

Once again the lad nodded, keeping his eyes lowered.

240

"Could you identify this man if you saw him again?" Kimball asked.

The boy hesitated a moment before answering. "I, ah, guess so."

Kimball turned the lad around so that he had a clear view of the entire room. "Do you see him here? Raise your face, boy. We haven't got all day."

The frightened lad looked as if he might burst into tears, but he dutifully looked around the room. At last, he raised a hand and pointed at the elderly man standing with the women at the back of the office.

"That there's the gent what cut me," he said softly, instantly dropping his eyes back to the floor.

The accused man gasped and took a step forward. "I have never seen this boy," he cried. "I didn't injure him. I don't even carry a knife."

"Officer," Ruiz said, "you've heard the boy's story. Either make these people turn over their so-called petitions, or arrest them all for assault."

"Wait a moment, Officer," I said, placing a restraining hand on his arm. I turned to the boy. "Young man, you have made a very serious accusation, and we must make certain that you aren't mistaken. Now, what is your name?"

"Henry, ma'am," he answered in a small voice, still unable to meet my eyes.

"All right, Henry," I said, trying to make my tone reassuring. The boy glanced quickly at the door, as if wanting nothing more than to be out of this room. "You say that Mr. . . . ." I looked questioningly at the gray-haired gentleman at the back of the room.

"Alfred Jenson," the man replied, eyeing the boy in considerable distress. "I assure you that I have never injured another person in my entire life. Most particularly not that boy!"

"Yes, Mr. Jenson, I'm sure you haven't," I told the man calmly. Turning back to the boy, I said, "Now, Henry, please tell me where you were when you encountered Mr. Jenson."

The lad looked at me in confusion. "Huh?"

"Where did you meet Mr. Jenson, Henry?" I said, rephrasing my question.

He still looked confused. Darting a panicked look at Ruiz, he finally mumbled, "I dunno. I was on the street."

"Which street, Henry?" I persisted. "Surely you can remember where you met the person who made that terrible cut on your arm. It must have been quite painful."

"I swarn it hurt like a son of a—"

"Yes, I'm sure it did," I interjected hastily. "If you can't remember exactly where it happened, Henry, perhaps you can tell us when you received that terrible cut?"

Henry rubbed at his wound, wincing a bit and causing it to start bleeding afresh. "It were yesterday morning," he said, looking again at Ruiz as if seeking approval for having the answer to this question, at least.

"Yesterday morning, you say. Hmmm." I picked up his arm and studied the wound, turning it this way and that, watching the blood bubble out of the cut to run down his hand and onto the floor. I reached into my reticule and withdrew my handkerchief, which I used to cover the wound. "That's interesting, Henry. This cut appears remarkably fresh to have been inflicted twenty-four hours ago. Wouldn't you agree, Officer Kimball?"

He leaned over Henry's arm, nodded thoughtfully, then stood up and looked the boy in the eye. "Look here, son, lying to the police is a serious matter. You don't want to land in jail, do you? Now let's have the truth. When did you get this cut? And who gave it to you?"

The boy's face had turned pale, and beads of perspiration had appeared on his forehead. "I, ah . . ." He looked in panic from Officer Kimball to Señor Ruiz, then stammered, "I g-gotta go." Before anyone could stop him, he turned and ran out the door and down the stairs.

Ruiz said something in Spanish beneath his breath, but when

one of his henchmen started after the boy, he told him not to bother.

"Obviously, the guttersnipe lied to me as well," he told Kimball, putting on a show of righteous indignation. "But these ladies will bear witness to the devious methods this society has used to obtain their fraudulent signatures."

"Will you, ladies?" I asked, regarding each of the women in turn. "Are you prepared to tell the truth? Please remember that this is a society dedicated to protecting the homeless and stray animals of this city. The reason that they are protesting Señor Ruiz's bull-ring is that it will result in the deaths of many innocent animals. And as Officer Kimball told the boy, it is against the law to lie to the police."

I waited a moment to allow my words to sink in, then let my gaze rest on the first woman, the oldest of the group. "What is your name, madam?"

The woman fidgeted, stole a look at the woman next to her, then opened her thin mouth to reveal a row of missing teeth. "I'm Mrs. Lila Murphy, an' I ain't no liar."

"I am very pleased to hear that, Mrs. Murphy," I said. "Now, would you please tell us why you are accusing a member of the SPCA of bullying you into signing their petition?"

"I, ah, don't know how to read, or write, neither," she said haltingly. "Told 'em so, too."

"You said this to the person who asked you to sign the petition?" I asked. "Was it a man or a woman?"

"It, ah, were a woman."

"Do you see that woman here in this office?"

She didn't even bother to look around. "No. She ain't here."

"Well, then, can you describe her?"

"No. Don't remember."

"Was she young or old?"

"Don't remember."

"I see," I said, regarding the woman thoughtfully. "Well, then, what did this woman do to you when you refused to sign her petition?" I asked.

"She got all huffy, she did. Pushed me right down onto my bum. Then she made me put an 'x' on the paper."

"Did anyone see this woman push you?" I persisted.

"Nobody weren't around," she said, her weak eyes darting nervously from me to Ruiz and then to Officer Kimball.

"I see. Did you sustain any bumps, or bruises, when you fell to the ground?"

"If I did, I sure as hell ain't showin' 'em to you," she replied in a huff.

"Mrs. Murphy," I said coolly, "you have told us a story about an attack that no one witnessed, perpetrated by a woman you can neither name nor describe, in a location you cannot remember, resulting in wounds you refuse to display." I eyed her steadily. "Are you certain you want to swear to this story? In a court of law? Please remember that the penalty for perjury is prison."

She blanched. "I don't want no trouble." She moved away from Ricardo Ruiz. "He didn't say nothin' about goin' to prison."

Officer Kimball's face darkened. "Are you saying that this man put you up to telling that story?"

The elderly woman, tiny to begin with, seemed to shrink even farther into herself. "I don't want no trouble," she said again. "It don't matter what happened. No, no, don't matter at all."

Ruiz was regarding the woman with ill-disguised fury, but he said nothing. Kimball was looking at the three remaining women, all of whom bore the expressions of frightened rabbits.

"And what do you ladies have to say for yourselves?" he asked tersely.

All of them shrank away, not saying a word as they quietly filed out of the office.

"I believe you have your answer, Officer Kimball," I said, then turned to Ruiz. "And you, señor, should be ashamed of yourself for attempting such a despicable ruse. Bribing those poor souls straight off the street to lie for you. On behalf of my clients, I request that you vacate these premises immediately. And do not return, or we shall be obliged to have you forcibly removed."

Ruiz's handsome face suffused with fury. "You have not heard the last of this, Señorita Woolson! Those petitions of yours will not stop me from building my bullring. Nothing will prevent me from bringing the glorious spectacle of the *corrida de torros* to this city."

He stormed to the door, then turned back to me. "You may do your best, señorita, but you do not know who you are dealing with. Ricardo Ruiz will not be defeated by *una mujer*!"

I t was mid-afternoon when I returned to my office. My parting advice to Mr. and Mrs. Dinwitty was to place the petitions that had already been signed in a safe place, outside the society office. Although I hoped that Señor Ruiz would not stoop to burglary or some other dire scheme, the fact that he had bribed those unfortunate individuals proved that he was not above such chicanery.

Back on Sutter Street, I envisioned a quiet afternoon where I might at last work on the brief I intended to present to City Hall on behalf of the SPCA. Unfortunately, that was not to be.

I had barely reached the stairs leading up to my office when Robert stormed down to grab me unceremoniously by the arm.

"Where have you been?" he demanded, disregarding any form of polite greeting. "I was about to call the police."

"I cannot imagine why you would do such a thing," I told him, pulling free of his grasp and starting up to my rooms. "In any case, it would have been a wasted effort, since I have spent the past two hours sequestered with the police."

"What?"

"Calm down, Robert. I have just returned from settling a charade concocted by Señor Ricardo Ruiz in an effort to defeat the SPCA's opposition to his bullring. The entire affair was vastly encouraging. We must be causing the man sleepless nights for him to go to such ludicrous lengths to stop us."

"You're making no sense," he bellowed, ascending the stairs

behind me. "You were supposed to remain in your office today until I came to take you home."

I spun around so quickly, he nearly crashed into me. "You've been conspiring with my father behind my back," I accused him angrily.

"I wouldn't call it conspiring," he said somewhat defensively.

"Oh, really? What would you call it, then?"

While he fumbled to find words that might justify such a collusion, I pulled out my office key and opened the door. Before I could close it, he barged inside after me.

"We are concerned for your safety, Sarah. Even you must admit that we have valid reasons." He threw his arms in the air as if to punctuate his words. "Since we first met, you have been held against your will in a sex, er, in a vile men's club, you have been poisoned, you have been kidnapped by an infamous Chinese tong lord, and now you have been shot at. For heaven's sake, Sarah, an army would have trouble protecting you."

"Don't exaggerate, Robert," I told him, hanging up my cloak. "I was never in any risk in Chinatown. Li Ying has been one of my staunchest supporters."

"Yes, when it serves his purposes. The fact that he controls a major share of the vice in Chinatown is neither here nor there, I suppose."

I was in no mood for a lecture. Especially one from him. It was enough that I had my father watching over me as if I were still the sweet little girl who loved to crawl into his lap.

"By the way, why are you here so early?" I consulted my lapel watch. "It's barely three o'clock. I didn't expect you until six."

"I spent all morning at the courthouse. On my way back to the office, I purchased this." He removed a newspaper from inside his coat and spread it open on my desk. "I thought you'd want to see it."

He pointed a finger at a column that appeared on page four of the *Daily Alta California*. I started to read the article, then sucked in my breath.

"Good Lord!"

"Exactly," he said. "That plug-ugly Denis Kearney is claiming that you and he are working together to defeat Ricardo Ruiz's bullring. I must admit the article surprised me. I thought Kearney and his Workingmen's Party lost power a year or two ago."

"Evidently, he's not a man to give up easily." I stared at the story, then suddenly stiffened. I felt the short hairs along the back of my neck rise in fury. "Good heavens, Kearney refers to Ruiz as an ignorant wetback. And he insinuates that I approve of such racial invectives! How dare he make such a vile accusation?"

"Have you even met the man?"

"No. And I hope I never do. I've followed his sick rhetoric, mainly in regard to his prejudice against the Chinese. Now he seems intent on bullying the Mexicans as well."

Robert sank into one of my office chairs. "Kearney's made no secret of his opposition to the bullfighting arena, at least since it came to his attention. You knew there was a possibility you might be linked with his cause when you took the SPCA's case."

"Indeed I did," I agreed with a rueful shake of my head. "And now my fears have been realized. The *Daily Alta* is all but accusing me of being a hypocrite, championing the Chinese while defiling the Mexicans, who were here long before California was accepted into statehood."

He was staring at me, his blue-green eyes uneasy. "Tell me what you're thinking, Sarah?"

Despite the circumstances, I had to resist an urge to smile. "Don't look so worried, Robert. I'm not going to dash out and confront Kearney on a street corner. That would draw even more attention to the situation."

He watched warily while I pondered my best course of action. I had understood and weighed the risks of representing the SPCA, knowing that it could be construed in some quarters as a personal prejudice against our city's Mexican population. But decisions were always open to misinterpretation. I could not falter now out of fear that my actions might be regarded as racially offensive.

"Well," he said at last, "what do you plan to do about this?"

"I think I shall ignore Denis Kearney altogether," I said at last. "He can say what he will about my motives, I cannot control that. I have taken a position to oppose Ruiz's bullring, and I intend to see the affair through to the end."

CHAPTER NINETEEN

The next few days were uneventful, for which I was grateful. There had been no new violence over the weekend, nor had anyone attempted to shoot at me or otherwise cause me harm. Samuel continued to improve, albeit at a slower pace than his impatience to be out of the house and back to work as a crime reporter. Adding to his frustration, he had as yet heard nothing from the publishing house where he had submitted his book manuscript. His mood at any given time of the day or evening vacillated between burgeoning hope and deep gloom.

Robert fulfilled his promise to my father and dutifully escorted me home from Sutter Street that entire week. Each time he arrived, I was to be found working quietly in my office, not off gallivanting about the city, as I am certain he expected me to be. To my quiet amusement, I received the impression that this somehow disappointed him. Other than eyeing me with suspicion, though, he did not press me for details of my day.

I received frequent notes from Mr. Dinwitty and Mrs. Hardy, informing me of how well the petition drive was proceeding. I had heard nothing more from Ricardo Ruiz or his thugs but was too realistic to assume they had given up their fight. On the contrary,

I feared they were merely gathering their forces before launching another offensive.

For my part, I continued to prepare the written brief I would deliver to City Hall along with the petition signatures. It would contain every point and authority I could uncover which might argue against the bullfighting arena. Naturally, this made it impossible for me to remain inside my office all day, despite the fact that both my father and Robert seemed determined to keep me there. I spent little time fretting over the necessary subterfuges I was forced to employ, and I certainly experienced no pangs of guilt. Contrary to society's outdated paradigm, I was a grown woman capable of making my own decisions and accepting my own risks. Moreover, I had given my word to a client; I owed the SPCA no less than my best efforts.

Fanny Goodman was a co-conspirator in the plan, helping me to come and go freely as I prepared my case. She seemed to look upon the deception as some kind of game and would have carried the ruse to rather comical lengths had I not set practical limits to her active imagination. Eddie, too, was happily drafted into the scheme, providing me with transportation to and from the courthouse, the SPCA office, and any other destination I felt called upon to visit. He, too, found the "caper," as he put it, great fun.

Other newspapers in town had taken a cue from the *Daily Alta* and run their own stories concerning my implied complicity with Denis Kearney to oppress the city's Mexican population. I continued to ignore them all, hopeful that in time the true motivation for my opposition to the bullring would be understood.

By the end of the week, Mr. Dinwitty and I decided that we had obtained nearly enough signatures to present to City Hall. It was agreed that the SPCA volunteers would finish collecting petitions over the weekend and I would turn them in to the city council the following Monday, along with my prepared brief.

I wish I could say that I felt confident about our success in this endeavor. Unfortunately, I was not at all sure that a list of names, no matter how extensive, would be enough to challenge a project that had the potential to bring so much money into the city coffers. My arguments, too, were weakened by the fact that they were based on nuisance factors, public safety, and general community disdain for the arena, rather than established city laws regarding property use. The fact that a bullring had previously existed in San Francisco provided Ruiz with a precedent that was going to be difficult to defeat.

Although I had honored my promise to Mr. Dinwitty and continued to search for other, more powerful ammunition to fight Ruiz, I had so far been unsuccessful. With only two days remaining before we would turn in the petitions, however, I decided to make one last trip to the courthouse. Once there, I spent dreary hours poring over pages of recorded material, evidentiary briefs, writs, and ordinances, until I began to develop a dull headache. When I finally came upon a promising lead, my eyes were so weary that I nearly missed it.

I read the section through twice, my heart beating faster each time as I digested the words. It described a commission that had been established by Congress in 1851 to unsnarl land titles granted by the Mexican government during the years it had controlled California. I was avidly engaged in reading and taking notes when I heard my name called out in an all-too-familiar voice.

Robert Campbell!

"I knew it! You have played false with me from the first. Here you are out in public with nary a care for your safety. Yet had I not discovered your subterfuge, you would have sworn that you had remained innocently inside your office all day."

"I have never lied to you, Robert," I responded with a clear conscience. "You did not once ask me directly if I'd gone out. If you had, I would naturally have told you—"

"A fabricated story." He regarded me in frustration. "Please, Sarah, show some respect for my intelligence. I know you far too well to expect honest disclosure when the matter involves your freedom. I told your father so, but he preferred to cling to the fanciful belief that he held some sort of control over you."

"I'm delighted to hear that you appreciate my predicament, Robert. Naturally I could not sit by idly in my office when I have a legal case to prepare." I was struck by a sudden idea. "Why are you here, by the way?"

"Shepard is out of town for the day," he said, referring to the senior partner of the firm where he was employed as associate attorney. He nodded to the briefcase he carried. "He left me with a great deal of tedious research to accomplish in his absence." His expression grew suspicious. "Why do you ask?"

"As long as he is out of the office, there is no pressing need for you to rush back to your desk." I pushed across the book I was reading, and he sank into a chair opposite me to scan its contents.

"Adverse land possession?" he said, appearing confused. "What's this all about?"

Briefly, I filled him in on what I had discovered, then explained why I required his assistance.

"But that could take all day," he exclaimed, his sharp tone assuaged by a curiosity he could not entirely conceal.

"Yes, it undoubtedly would if I were to attempt it alone. Dividing the list between us will take but half the time."

"You're serious, aren't you? No, don't bother to answer, you're wearing that expression which means you are determined to have your way, no matter the inconvenience to others."

"Come, Robert, you're being overdramatic. Naturally I'll help you with your research once we have finished with mine." I passed several more large volumes of public records across the table to him, then handed him one of the sheets of paper upon which I had jotted my notes. "Now, you begin with these, while I complete the preliminary research."

His eyes traveled unhappily down the paper. "There are a great many names."

"Yes, isn't it wonderful? If I am correct, and I believe I am, this information should greatly increase the likelihood of our success."

He gave a soft groan but wisely chose to keep any further complaints to himself. Thus we worked in companionable silence for the next two hours, speaking only when one of us uncovered an unexpected point or to avoid duplication. As I predicted, the job was completed in far less time than if I had been forced to perform it on my own.

After we had returned the law tomes to the stacks, Robert seemed to believe that he could now deliver me to my office. I quickly set him straight, informing him that although we had completed our task here, a good deal more work remained to be done. Ignoring his protests, I led the way to the tax office, where I informed the clerk which books we would need to examine. Despite my companion's continued grousing, I found a quiet table situated in a corner of the office library and instructed him on what we must accomplish.

"My absence at the firm is bound to be noticed," he grumbled. "What am I supposed to tell them?"

"You're there every day," I said, not looking up from the book I had just opened. Glancing over the numerous entries, I realized I would once again be forced to compile a lengthy list of names and dates. "Perhaps you could plead a headache, or a touch of catarrh."

"Humph! Now you are suggesting that I resort to lies." He thought for a moment. "Although it would not be entirely untruthful to plead a headache. You often cause me to suffer from that particular malady. Today being no exception."

"Excellent. You may begin by checking these names against the list I provided you, while I examine the documents in this volume."

"You could at least spare me that supercilious look on your face," he said, regarding me in annoyance. "If I had not been reluctant to leave you here on your own, I could have pretended not to see you and gotten on with my own research."

Regarding this as an opportunity to turn the tables on this annoying rash of overprotectiveness, I said with a touch of sarcasm, "Ah, yes, you wouldn't want to abandon me to the cutthroats and desperadoes who threaten the corridors of City Hall."

This comment had the desired effect, and we once again worked in amiable silence until it was at last time to end our labors for the day.

"I need to stop by my office and collect some paperwork before returning home," I said as we exited the building. "I trust that will not inconvenience you?"

"Of course not," he replied, raising his eyes to the heavens. "You have already disrupted the better part of my afternoon. What is another hour or two?"

"It will not take that long," I told him, paying no heed to his acerbic tone. "Shall we take the omnibus at the next corner?"

"We had better find a cab," he said, regarding the late-afternoon traffic with dismay. "That should prove a good deal easier and faster than public transportation."

Naturally, it did not. I have never understood Robert's reluctance to take advantage of the city's numerous horsecars and omnibuses. If we had had the foresight to engage Eddie and his brougham, he would be correct in supposing the ride to Sutter Street would be faster. Given Eddie's proclivity for speed, however, it would be unlikely to prove more comfortable. At this time of day, it was nigh on to impossible to locate an unoccupied cab. Consequently, it took us roughly twice as long to reach my office as it would have if we had relied on the nearby omnibus. Ironically, as we were dropped off in front of Fanny's shop, we spied Eddie's carriage parked outside.

"Oh, dear!" I exclaimed, filled with guilt. "I forgot I was supposed to give Eddie a reading lesson this afternoon. I wonder how long the poor lad has been waiting?"

As it turned out, the "poor" lad was seated comfortably in Fanny's cozy kitchen, happily partaking of a slice of warm apple pie and a glass of milk. To my considerable surprise, my brother Samuel was sitting with him at the table, enjoying his own piece of pastry. His left arm was in a sling, but he didn't appear to be in pain, although he had become remarkably adept at masking his discomfort.

"Samuel, what on earth are you doing here?" I exclaimed. "You're supposed to be at home recuperating."

"Mama and Celia left to pay house calls this afternoon, and I took the opportunity to slip out." He grinned. "Even Edis didn't see me. Besides, as it happens, I *am* recuperating. In fact, I'll wager I'm doing far better here than if I'd remained at home. Fanny's pie is just the medicine to expedite a quick recovery. Right, Eddie?"

"Yes, sir, Mr. Samuel," the boy answered, beaming at the plump woman bustling about with cups and saucers, cream and sugar, and large slices of pastry. "No one can beat Mrs. Goodman's apple pie, and that's God's honest truth."

I started to correct the lad's misuse of the Lord's name, but when I saw the pleasure in Fanny's warm gray eyes, I decided to let it rest.

"Sit down, sit down," she said, fairly beaming with delight to have so much company in her small kitchen. "I have just brewed fresh coffee, and there is a second pie to cut into." She gazed fondly at Samuel. "What a surprise it was to see this dear boy walk into my shop. And about time, too. He looks far too thin and pale."

Having not been blessed with children of her own, my grandmotherly neighbor had all but adopted the young cabbie, taking him under her wing as if he were a long-lost grandson. The friendship had done wonders for the lad. Since meeting Fanny, he had grown at least two inches taller, and his painfully thin body had started to fill out. Even his pallid skin had taken on a healthier glow and was less marked with outbreaks of unsightly spots.

I feared Robert might decline her invitation to sit down and join them, but he smiled and relaxed his tall, muscular body into a chair. Although he was loath to admit it, Robert was fond of Fanny, and even Eddie. For my part, I was so pleased to be sitting here with my friends, and especially my brother after he had given us all such a terrible scare, that a cup of coffee struck me as just the thing before returning home.

"You look a good deal better than the last time I saw you, Samuel," Robert said, eyeing his immobilized arm. "How is your shoulder healing?"

"Much better than anyone expected, I'm happy to say," my brother answered, gently moving his left arm as if to demonstrate the improvement. "At least that's what Charles told me. Incidentally, he said last night that I could start back to work as long as I didn't overdo it. Which was the best news I've heard in over two weeks."

"Samuel, that's wonderful," I exclaimed, sharing his excitement.

"Which brings me to some disturbing news," he said, his smile fading. "Jonathan Aleric has mysteriously disappeared. I dropped by to see George at his station on my way here, and he told me Aleric hasn't been seen for two days."

"Good Lord," Robert said. "Is it possible he was called out of town unexpectedly, and failed to tell anyone?"

"That's unlikely," said Samuel. "Don't forget, he owns and runs a newspaper. Believe me, if he'd had to leave the city, he would have informed his editors and made plans to ensure that the *Bay Area Express* came out on schedule."

"Does George have any reason to suspect foul play?" I asked, feeling a stab of fear.

"I don't think so," he replied. "At least he didn't mention any strange circumstances. Aleric was in his office most of the day on Wednesday, then that evening he attended the theater with friends, after which they had a late supper. Evidently, he hasn't been seen or heard from since."

Dear Lord, I thought in growing alarm. I did not particularly care for Aleric and normally would pay little attention to his whereabouts. After what had been happening over the past two weeks, however, it was too much to suppose that his disappearance was simply a coincidence.

"What are the police doing about it?" asked Robert. He, too, was looking concerned.

"They're making inquiries, as George put it. Naturally they've questioned his employees at the newspaper, and spoken to the friends he went out with that night. He has a manservant to see to his personal needs, a cook, and a maid. They claim not to have seen him since he left to join his friends at the theater."

"Oh, my," said Fanny. "Sarah, didn't you say he was with you on Telegraph Hill the night Samuel was shot?"

I nodded. "Aleric, Samuel, and I were walking down the hill with Oscar Wilde when the gun was fired."

"If I recall correctly, there was even talk that he was the intended victim, and not Samuel," she said somberly. "Then Mr. Dunn died and you were shot, so I just assumed that wasn't the case after all."

"I don't mean this as a reflection on your friend Mortimer Remy," said Robert, "but after that fracas at the train depot the day Wilde left town, everyone knows that there's no love lost between the two men."

I didn't care for the look on his face. "You aren't suggesting that Mortimer had something to do with Aleric's disappearance, are you, Robert?"

"I'm not suggesting anything," he answered. "I'm simply pointing out that Aleric was Remy's archenemy. The police may not be overly bright, but even they can't fail to put two and two together. And come up with your friend's name."

"There's always the chance that Mr. Aleric really did leave town for a day or two," Fanny pointed out, trying to find a less drastic explanation. "Perhaps there was a family emergency, and he didn't have time to tell anyone."

We all nodded, but clearly no one actually believed this explanation, not even Fanny, judging by the troubled look on her face. Samuel was right. Aleric would not suddenly disappear without informing at least one of his editors at the newspaper. The *Bay Area Express* was too important to him.

"Have the police inquired to see if any clothes are missing from his room?" I asked Samuel.

"That was one of the first things George asked Aleric's man-servant," he told us. "Apparently everything is accounted for."

The bell above Fanny's door rang, and she rose from her chair and hurried into the shop. A moment later she returned, leading a uniformed George Lewis into the kitchen. There was a somber expression on his normally boyish face.

"I thought I might find you here, Samuel," he said, appearing a bit taken aback to see so many of us gathered around Fanny's table. "You mentioned you might stop by to see Miss Sarah when you left the station."

"Has something happened, George?" my brother asked, rising from the table. "Do you have news about Aleric?"

Lewis looked from Samuel to Fanny and then to me, uncertain whether or not he should speak frankly in front of ladies.

"Out with it, man," Robert prompted impatiently. "What's wrong?"

George combed his fingers through the lock of light brown hair that habitually fell across his brow. "We, ah, found Mr. Aleric. Dead, I'm afraid, and buried in a shallow grave on the east side of Telegraph Hill. Not too far from the Filbert Street Steps."

Robert gasped, staring at George in disbelief. "Good heavens! How did you ever find him there?"

Once again George shuffled unhappily, continuing to regard Mrs. Goodman as if still unsure how she would react to such lurid news. "After all that's happened on that Hill, I had my men out searching, more to be thorough than in any real hope of finding him. It turns out a fox happened upon the body while it was, er, scavenging for food."

Fanny blanched and sat down heavily in her chair. She looked so pale, I feared she might be ill. Instinctively, I reached for my reticule, but she forestalled me by raising a hand.

"No, dear, I'm quite all right," she said weakly, then looked at the men in embarrassment. "Forgive me, please. It was just the mental image of that fox digging up— Oh, my, I'm afraid it rather unsettled me for a moment."

"There is no need to apologize, ma'am," Lewis said. Guiltily, he studied the woman to ensure that she truly was recovered. "It gave my men a turn, I can tell you. As well as me, if I'm to be honest. I'm sorry to have distressed you, though, Mrs. Goodman."

"Were you able to determine how he died?" I asked.

"He'd been shot," said Lewis. "We won't be able to tell the approximate time until the coroner's examination is completed. From the condition of the remains, though—" His eyes again flew to my neighbor. "That is, if I were to hazard a guess, I'd say he was killed sometime Wednesday night or yesterday morning."

"In other words, shortly after he was last seen with his friends having a late dinner on Wednesday night," I observed.

"I suppose it's too much to hope that someone witnessed the attack," said Robert, "or that you and your men found some evidence. For a change."

George's face flushed and he lowered his eyes, obviously chagrined by this not wholly undeserved indictment.

Noticing his friend's discomfort, Samuel asked, "Perhaps someone happened to see whoever disposed of the body? People going up or down the stairs, or a neighbor?"

Lewis shook his head. "We've questioned nearby houses, but so far we've found no one who saw anything out of the ordinary."

"No one ever seems to see anything out of the ordinary on that blasted Hill," Robert grumbled. "Yet people keep dropping like flies. It wouldn't surprise me if half the neighborhood was acting in collusion. Lying through their teeth, the lot of them."

I shot Robert a look, indicating that he was not helping matters. "You said that you'd questioned Aleric's friends, George. Did any of them notice where he went after leaving the restaurant?"

"It seems that they said good night outside, then went their separate ways," George told us. "That was the last time he was seen. By anyone."

"So there are no suspects," I mused aloud.

George hesitated, regarded me awkwardly, then said, "I wouldn't go so far as to say that, Miss Sarah."

Samuel looked at his friend, then at me. I think we both had a good idea to whom he was alluding. "Go on, George. Who do you believe did this?"

Again, Lewis shifted his weight uncomfortably. "Lieutenant Curtis is convinced that only one person could have killed Jonathan Aleric." He looked at Samuel and then at me, as if wishing he did not have to be the one to deliver such distressing news.

"He's planning on obtaining a warrant for Mortimer Remy's arrest."

CHAPTER TWENTY

Lieutenant Curtis was as good as his word. Mortimer Remy was arrested the next morning as he worked at his desk in the offices of the *San Francisco Weekly*. According to George, the publisher vehemently proclaimed his innocence, insisting he knew nothing about Aleric's death. Unfortunately, he could provide them with no alibi for the previous Wednesday night. Moreover, several dozen people—including Robert and me—had heard him threatening Jonathan Aleric's life less than a week before the publisher disappeared. The final disastrous blow was the fact that he owned a revolver of the same caliber as the one that had killed Aleric.

"I could name any number of people who own that same revolver," Samuel said as we rode in Eddie's brougham to visit Mortimer at the jail later that afternoon. "It's a Colt forty-five-caliber, one of the most common guns in the city, probably in the entire West."

"Do they have any way of proving that Mortimer's revolver was the one that shot Aleric, though?" I asked, anxious to find some way to demonstrate the newspaper man's innocence.

"Not really. They can identify the caliber of the bullet, along with the type and model of revolver it was fired from. Some methods are even being used to establish when a gun was last discharged, but it's nearly impossible to tell with any certainty if a bullet came from any particular revolver."

"Perhaps that will work to Mortimer's advantage," I said hopefully.

He did not appear to share my optimism. "The police may not be able to prove the bullet came from his gun, but his defense attorney won't be able to prove that it didn't. Of course, right now his public threat on Aleric's life is weighing most heavily against him. And of course his lack of an alibi. Remy claims he was at his home alone last Wednesday night. Since he has no live-in household staff, there's no one to confirm his story."

I sighed, then held on to my seat as Eddie took a corner too fast. A horse whinnied in protest, and several men shouted out curses. All of which Eddie blithely ignored as he continued on at full tilt.

"That boy is going to be the death of me yet," I protested, straightening my hat, which had tilted to the side of my head during the turn.

"What amazes me is that he never seems to get into an accident," Samuel said in obvious admiration. "In this city, that's quite an accomplishment."

"Don't you dare think to compliment him on his driving skills," I warned my brother. "There is always a first time for everything. Eddie's luck cannot last forever." After a brief silence, I said, "That threat Mortimer made at the train depot angers me. It was spoken in the heat of the moment. I'm sure he didn't mean a word of it."

"You said that Aleric deliberately set out to provoke him. If that's true, what did he have to gain?"

"He mentioned something about suing Mortimer if he resorted to violence. He seemed almost disappointed when Mortimer backed down."

When afternoon traffic along the street caused Eddie to come to a near halt, I looked out the window to see a newsboy hawking

newspapers. The huge black headlines caused me to cringe: FA-
MOUS AUTHOR KILLED BY NEWSPAPER PUBLISHER!

"Oh, dear Lord, Samuel," I said, nudging my brother as we
once again began to move. "Look."

He leaned across me to peer out the window. After uttering a
low (and unrepeatable) curse, he said, "I hate to admit it, but I
sometimes think Papa isn't that far off the mark when he denigrates
today's journalism. Every newspaper in town—excluding the *San
Francisco Weekly,* of course—is vilifying Remy and naming him as
Aleric's murderer. Whatever happened to innocent until proven
guilty?"

I was outraged. "How can he receive a fair trial with all this
adverse publicity? The poor man was only arrested this morning.
They haven't yet heard his side of the story."

"No," he said, taking up his hat. "But we soon will."

Looking out, I saw that Eddie had turned onto Broadway and
was reining up in front of the two-story brick structure that housed
the city jail, a building I had grown to know and abhor over the
past year. Exiting the carriage, we instructed Eddie to wait, then
passed through the huge iron gate and up the stone steps leading
to the entrance. Inside, we found a uniformed officer on duty at
his usual station. Owing entirely to my gender, I was commonly
required to argue my credentials when visiting a prisoner; consequently I allowed my brother to provide the necessary explana-
tions concerning who we were and whom we wished to see. Not
surprisingly, he was allowed to pass inside with no difficulty.

A taciturn jailer led us down the all-too-familiar corridor containing cells to either side. He finally halted in front of a door mid-
way down the hall. After turning a large key in the lock, he pulled
it open, then stepped back to allow us to enter. As soon as we were
inside, he slammed the iron door shut behind us.

Mortimer Remy's cell had brick walls and was the standard
size of twelve feet long by five feet wide. It contained a single cot
for a bed, a chamber bucket covered with an old rag, and a small
grated window located high up one of the walls. The window

allowed in little light and even less air. As usual, the smell in the claustrophobic room was foul beyond description.

Mortimer sat upon the cot, looking miserable. His usual steady brown eyes appeared dull and glazed. I had never seen the man looking anything but meticulously dressed and groomed. Today, his full head of white hair was more untidy than usual, his brown trousers and day coat wrinkled. He appeared as if he had been languishing in this terrible place for days rather than just a few hours.

The smile that lit Remy's face when he saw Samuel quickly faded as I followed my brother inside the cell.

"Miss Woolson!" he exclaimed, leaping to his feet in obvious distress. "You should not have come. This is no place for a lady."

"In my opinion, it isn't a fit place for anyone," I said, covering my nose with a handkerchief. "Man or woman."

"Then why . . . ?"

"Do not distress yourself, Mr. Remy," I said, lowering the cloth to attempt what I hoped was a reassuring smile. "I have visited city jail more times than I care to remember."

"That's right, I remember now," he said, still looking ill at ease. "You have represented several people who have been imprisoned here, have you not? One of them a woman?"

"Unfortunately, two of my clients who have been incarcerated in this miserable place were women—with no more amenities than you have been afforded," I told him. Resisting the urge to once again employ my handkerchief, I returned it to the pocket from whence I had removed it upon entering the cell. If he and Samuel could stand the ghastly odor, then so could I. Moreover, it was difficult to carry on a sensible conversation with one's mouth covered.

Looking embarrassed, Remy moved away from the cot, indicating that I should take his place. I eyed the straw mattress with instinctive aversion, then quickly masked my distaste so as not to offend the poor man. Despite its shabby appearance, it was the only available seat in the room. Smiling my thanks, I accepted his offer.

"You just missed seeing my nephew, Emmett," Remy told us. "He was understandably upset to see me like this."

"I'm sure he was," I said, regarding the poor man with sympathy.

"When is your arraignment?" Samuel asked. Both he and Remy had moved to stand beneath the window in a mostly futile attempt to take advantage of what little fresh air circulated in the tiny cell.

"I believe it will be on Monday," said Remy, his present circumstances seeming to accentuate his southern drawl. "My attorney is visiting me again tomorrow morning. He promised to give me the details at that time."

"Who is representing you?" asked Samuel.

"Mr. Arthur Sanderson," he said, his tone sounding doubtful. "Actually, he's the attorney who represents the newspaper. I'm not certain how much experience he's had in criminal law."

"Then you must find a lawyer who is qualified," Samuel declared. "You've been accused of murder, man. You must mount the best possible defense."

Remy nodded gloomily. "That's what Sanderson told me. But it's all happened so quickly, I've hardly had time to think. Can you suggest anyone?"

Samuel thought for a moment, then said, "You might try Gilbert Reese, of Reese and Markham."

"Aren't they the lawyers who handled the defense for William Peters, the lumber tycoon?"

"That's right, last year," said Samuel. "I've heard they're very good."

"Yes, I'm sure they are."

He lowered his eyes, and I guessed what he was thinking. Reese and Markham were one of the most prestigious criminal law firms in the city. Judging by his humble cottage on Telegraph Hill, and the recent decline in subscribers due to Aleric's efforts to put his newspaper out of business, I doubted he could afford such costly representation, even when it might mean his life.

"Sanderson thinks I killed Aleric," Remy blurted out. "He didn't accuse me in so many words, but it was written clearly enough on his face. He said that the evidence against me was compelling."

I was filled with indignation that Sanderson would make such a statement, and on the very day his client was arrested and thrown into this pesthole. Whatever the man's true feelings, his client was facing one of the most arduous ordeals of his life. He deserved loyalty and an open mind, not an automatic assumption of guilt.

"Perhaps he doesn't know you as well as we do," I said. "My brother and I believe in your innocence. The evidence may appear compelling, but for the most part it's circumstantial." As I recalled my conversation with Samuel in the carriage, an idea occurred to me. "When was the last time you fired your revolver?"

"What?" Remy looked confused.

"Have you fired your Colt revolver lately?" I repeated. "If you haven't discharged it recently," I explained, "then you may be able to prove that the bullet that killed Aleric didn't come from your gun."

Remy brightened at this possibility, then just as quickly deflated. "I shot at a skunk a day or two ago. Couldn't get it out from under my porch. The damn thing stunk to high heaven." He looked at us with renewed despair. "So it appears that won't help me."

"I'm afraid not," Samuel answered. "Although your revolver is a common enough weapon."

"Very common," Remy said. "In fact, I know half a dozen residents on the Hill who have one. But that isn't going to help me either, is it?"

"No," I said truthfully, "I'm afraid not. There must be something, though. Where were you last Wednesday evening, by the way?" George had already explained that he had no verifiable alibi, but I wanted Remy to tell us himself.

"Well, I left the newspaper about eight o'clock," he said, "and dined at a restaurant not far from my office. After that I went directly home, arriving there at about nine thirty or ten, as I recall."

"Did anyone see you? A neighbor, or a passerby?"

He thought this over. "I don't think so, at least I didn't see anyone. Someone might have observed me walking up the hill, but if they did, they didn't bother speaking to me."

I considered this. Even if someone had seen him making his way home, it would only prove that he had been there earlier in the evening. He could easily have left his house later, returning to town to attack Aleric after he left his friends. No, that wouldn't help his case.

"What time did you retire that night?" I asked.

"Why, I'm not sure," he said, looking puzzled. "Eleven o'clock, or perhaps as late as midnight. I honestly don't recall. But what does it matter when I went to bed?"

"It's a matter of establishing a time frame," I explained. "According to the police, Aleric's friends last saw him leaving a restaurant sometime after midnight. And, of course, he didn't return home. If your attorney could locate someone who saw your lamp being extinguished at that hour, it might at least lend some credence to your alibi."

"Yes, I see where you're leading," he said, another glimmer of hope lighting his eyes. "But how would one go about locating such a person? That is, if one exists."

I sighed. "I'm afraid the only way to do it properly is to inquire door-to-door."

"Good heavens," he burst out. "That could take days."

"Yes, it could," I answered honestly. "However, anything less than a complete survey of the neighborhood is apt to miss the very witness you hope to find."

Samuel gave a short laugh. "Don't look so surprised, Mortimer. My sister has amazing perseverance, although some would call it pigheadedness. She will go to any lengths to sniff out a clue."

I ignored this. "Another tactic would be to question the employees of restaurants and clubs in the vicinity of the one Aleric and his friends frequented. He might have been seen hailing a cab, or perhaps talking to someone. He cannot have simply become invisible as he left the restaurant. It would be a great help to at least learn the direction in which he walked."

267

"But won't the police be doing that?" he said.

"Ha!" Samuel interjected. "You have a good deal more faith in that august force than do I. Of course, there are a number of good men in the department, but they haven't the time or the resources to be in every place they're needed."

"And I fear the department is already convinced of your guilt, Mr. Remy," I added in a soft voice. Much as I hated to speak so bluntly to the unfortunate man, this was no time for glib, and false, reassurances. "They'll not be readily motivated to launch such a search, when they're confident they already have the killer in custody."

Whatever small hope had flickered to life on his face was just as quickly extinguished, and he buried his head in his hands. "Then it is truly useless."

"Nonsense," I said, silently berating myself for perhaps being too forthright. "Granted, defending these charges will not be easy. But nothing is ever hopeless."

He regarded me with infinitely sad eyes. "Thank you for trying to bolster my resolve, Miss Woolson, but you haven't yet heard the most damaging evidence the police have against me. I said some foolish things to Aleric the day Mr. Wilde left San Francisco. I—" He stopped, as if the words were too dreadful to be acknowledged or spoken aloud. "I'm afraid that I actually threatened his life. I was very angry, you see, and now those hastily spoken words will certainly be used against me."

"As it happens, I was at the train depot that morning and overheard what you said, Mr. Remy," I confessed. "It was my impression that Mr. Aleric was deliberately trying to provoke you into doing or saying something rash."

He looked at me in surprise. "You were there, Miss Woolson? I apologize, but in all the commotion I didn't see you. I'm mortified that you witnessed such a childish demonstration. Mr. Aleric has, er, *had*, a way of bringing out the worst in me, I fear. I do not offer that as an excuse for my appalling behavior. No, no, I should have learned by now to control my temper where he was concerned. The good Lord knows I have had ample opportunity since the day he set foot in San Francisco."

I recalled the rumor that Jonathan Aleric had persuaded Remy's wife to leave him, only to pass away several months later. As far as I was concerned, it was a wonder he was able to bear the sight of the author at all, much less attempt to be civil toward him. Remy was right, of course: the prosecution would certainly use those hastily spoken words in their case against him.

"There is no need to apologize," I told him sincerely. "As I say, I was there and saw the altercation for myself. Mr. Aleric's conduct was inexcusable."

"That is good of you to say, Miss Woolson. But every man must take responsibility for his actions, and the fact remains that I did not behave well that morning." He lowered his head, then looked up at us, this time not bothering to disguise the trepidation on his face. "But never would I have actually harmed the man. Perhaps in the heat of the moment I might have struck him. But murder?" He gave a small shudder. "No, never murder."

"Which brings us to the question of who else might have wished to see him dead," I said. "Have you any thoughts to offer, Mr. Remy? Surely such a provocative man must have made enemies in the city."

"Yes, I'm sure he did. He was undeniably ambitious, especially when it came to his newspaper. Mine were not the only toes he stomped on in his attempts to obliterate the competition." He paused. "I think he missed the wildly popular acclaim he enjoyed after the publication of his Civil War book. I asked him once if he had ever tried writing a second novel, but he insisted that such a great story came only once in a writer's life. Perhaps he thought to recapture his lost fame in the field of journalism."

"Then that is yet another possibility your lawyer should explore," I offered. "Every life has secrets, Mr. Remy, as I'm sure you know. It is up to a good defense attorney not only to unearth them, but to follow them to their logical conclusions."

"I admit I hadn't thought of that," he said. "Do you really

269

think that looking into Aleric's past might shed light on his death?"

"It might," I told him. "The more one understands the victim, the more likely one is to find his killer."

"You say you weren't even aware that Aleric was dead when you were arrested?" asked Samuel.

Remy shook his head. "No, I wasn't. I couldn't imagine what the police were doing in my office. Then, before I realized what was happening, they had put me under arrest."

"That must have come as quite a shock," said Samuel.

"Indeed it did. I hadn't seen him in a week, not since the morning Mr. Wilde left San Francisco. In truth, after that dreadful episode at the train depot, I hoped never to see him again."

"I wouldn't be surprised that whoever shot him was taking advantage of that altercation," I said, then was struck by another thought. "Mr. Remy, who might have known that you had no plans for Wednesday evening?"

"Why, I don't know." Suddenly my meaning seemed to dawn on him. "You think someone deliberately conspired to make it appear that I shot Aleric?"

"You must admit the circumstances may have presented the killer with an opportunity too good to be ignored," Samuel said.

"Precisely," I concurred. "However, if this is what actually happened, the murderer had to know beforehand that you would have no alibi."

There was a loud bang at the door, and the jailer's voice called out that our time with the prisoner would be up in five minutes.

Remy stepped to the cot and held out his hand to help me rise. "You have brought me more comfort than I can say, Miss Woolson," he said in his soft southern drawl, and I detected a suspicious moisture in his brown eyes. "It was kind of you and your brother to visit me here in this—in this deplorable place."

"We are delighted if we have been of some small assistance," I replied. "Please, do let us know if there's anything we can bring you. Perhaps food of some kind, or reading material?"

He didn't answer. In fact, he was staring at me with a peculiar expression on his face.

"Actually, I rather think there is something you can do for me, Miss Woolson," he said at last. "Would you . . . would you consider representing me in this matter? As my attorney?"

I stared at him, dumbfounded.

"You're asking Sarah to be your lawyer?" Samuel said in surprise.

"Yes, that is exactly what I am asking her to do," Remy replied, looking more animated than he had since we had entered his cell. "In the short time you have been here, your sister has not only declared her belief in my innocence, but she has asked far more pertinent questions about the case than Sanderson did in an entire hour. Not only that, but she's suggested several steps we can immediately initiate in my defense."

"But what about Reese and Markham?" asked my brother.

"They are undoubtedly a fine firm," Remy declared. "But I am committed to placing my faith in your sister." He looked at me intensely, as if I held the fate of his life in my hands. Which, if I agreed to take his case, I surely would. "What do you say, Miss Woolson? Will you agree to represent me?"

I hesitated for only a minute, but during that brief time a dozen reasons for not taking the case flashed through my mind. Despite my words of reassurance, the evidence against Remy was daunting, if largely circumstantial. There was nothing to tie the man directly to the crime scene, mainly because no one knew for certain when the murder had taken place, or even where. On the other hand, he had threatened Aleric just days prior to his death, and he had undeniably good reasons for wanting to see the man dead. He also lived just a few blocks from where the body had been buried, and the fatal bullet had been fired from the same caliber revolver as one in his possession.

It would have required a woman with a far more callous heart than I possessed, however, to refuse the man standing before me, his kind face silently, desperately, awaiting my decision.

"Yes, Mr. Remy, I will act as your attorney," I told him, extending my hand so that we might formally seal the agreement. "I give you my word that I will do everything in my power to clear your name, and see you released from this dreadful place."

Have you any idea what you've gotten yourself into?" Samuel asked the instant we were back in Eddie's brougham. "It's all well and good to promise to go door-to-door looking for witnesses, but you have about as much chance of finding one as you would locating the proverbial needle in a haystack."

"You know as well as I do that we must at least try. Oh, and thank you very much for your support back at the jail. You sounded as if you couldn't believe Mortimer had actually asked me to represent him instead of Gilbert Reese."

He smiled sheepishly. "Well, I was a bit taken aback. As were you, for that matter. Don't deny it."

"Yes, actually I was. But no one seems to be on the poor man's side. Even his present attorney thinks he's guilty. We have to do something to help him."

"Well, it's not going to be—" He stopped suddenly, turning to look at me. "Wait a minute, you've used the word *we* twice, Sarah. You mean to drag me into this mess, don't you?" He gave a dry little laugh. "Although I can't imagine why that surprises me."

"Questioning Mortimer's neighbors means returning to Telegraph Hill," I told him, belatedly remembering my father's thoughts on that subject. "Papa would have a fit if I went there alone."

"He'll have a fit if either of us steps foot on Telegraph Hill again," he reminded me. "Not to mention what Robert will say."

"Hmmm. If he's so worried, perhaps he can help. And Eddie as well."

"Good Lord, Sarah, you're serious, aren't you?"

I regarded him in surprise. Surely he of all my family knew me well enough that such a question was superfluous.

"Naturally I'm serious," I told him. "There'll be a number of other avenues to explore in planning Mortimer's defense, but we shall have to begin by canvassing the neighborhood."

"If Father gets word of your plan, he's going to explode," he said, his mouth twitching as he attempted to repress a smile. "And whether you like it or not, so will Robert."

"Robert has no business caring one way or the other where I go, or why I go there," I said firmly. "He is not my father."

"True, nevertheless he's concerned for your safety." Out of the corner of my eye, I saw him studying my profile. "You may pretend to disdain any sort of romantic entanglement, but you must know that poor man is besotted with you."

"Don't be ridiculous," I said, refusing to discuss the subject with him. "Besides, I don't merely *pretend* to scorn romantic entanglements, as you put it. You know it's impossible for a woman to have marriage as well as a career. I have made my choice and I am living with it, very contentedly, as it happens."

"Yes, you've been telling me that since we were children. But what if you come to regret your decision one day, and it's too late to have a home and a family?"

"Please don't start lecturing me on the blessings of hearth and home, Samuel," I told him shortly. "I hear more than enough of that from Mama, sometimes even from Celia and Charles." I sought for a way to make him understand. "My current situation is a good example of why marriage and a career could never succeed. Papa, and even Robert, who is merely a friend, after all, have decided that it is too dangerous for me to leave my home, or my office, unescorted by a man. Do you honestly believe it's possible to marry a man who would not impose the same restrictions upon me under similar circumstances?"

Samuel started to respond, then seemed to think better of it. "When you put it that way, I begin to appreciate the difficulties involved. Still, I—" He stopped in midsentence, looking out the carriage window. "Why are we stopping here?"

"I instructed Eddie to take me to City Hall," I said. "I must find out exactly when Mortimer's arraignment is to take place, so that I will be prepared."

"What about Ricardo Ruiz's bullring? How are you and the SPCA coming along on your petitions?"

"Mr. Dinwitty and I have decided to submit the signatures and the brief Monday morning. However, I've been working on a new approach, which I'm hoping may make the petitions unnecessary."

This sparked my brother's interest. "Really? And how do you propose to accomplish that small miracle?"

I smiled. "If you'd like to come inside and lend me your assistance, I'll be happy to explain."

CHAPTER TWENTY-ONE

I submitted the SPCA petitions and my brief to City Hall on Monday morning. Once I had completed this piece of business, I requested a formal hearing with the city council as soon as possible, in order to present the new evidence I had unearthed. I was pleased when it was scheduled to take place in two days' time. The clerk informed me that Mr. Ruiz would be duly notified of the proceeding.

Mortimer Remy's arraignment was held later that morning. I'd had little time to prepare for the proceeding, but it would not have made much difference if I had. The charges against my client were read, at which point we submitted a plea of not guilty. Owing to the severity of the crime and fear that Mr. Remy might be a flight risk, our request for bail was denied by the judge. The entire procedure was over in less than ten minutes. I was allowed a brief consultation with my client in a guarded area outside the courtroom, after which he was returned to his jail cell.

So far, Samuel and I had been able to keep the knowledge that I was representing Remy a secret from my father. Because of Papa's position as superior court judge for the county of San Francisco, however, we knew this could not last for much longer. Any reprieve from the outburst we would face when he eventually found out, however, was appreciated.

I was pleased when Samuel offered to accompany me to the courthouse for the arraignment. Not that I required his help, but I feared that Papa's ire would be that much more volatile if he discovered I had attended on my own.

Because I required Robert's help, I reluctantly informed him that I had agreed to represent Mr. Remy. After he'd ranted on for a full five minutes, pointing out the folly of my taking on such a hopeless case, I was able to calmly catalog the tasks I wished him to perform. Naturally, this elicited another five minutes of thunderous objections. As he was a fair-minded man, however, and one who believed as firmly as did I in the principles of justice, he eventually relented. Getting him to agree to keep the stratagem from reaching my father's ears was more difficult.

After a good deal of calm persuasion (not threats about my safety in the event that he refused to help, as he continued to insist!), he realized the efficacy of keeping the plan to ourselves—the others consisting of Samuel, Fanny, and George Lewis.

"It's something that should have been ordered as soon as we discovered Aleric's body," George said when the five of us met in my office early that afternoon. "That's proper police procedure. But since Lieutenant Curtis was convinced Remy was the killer, no further investigation was even considered."

We were discussing how best to go about questioning Remy's neighbors, in the hope that someone might have seen him the previous Wednesday night. Robert had carried up two chairs from Fanny's kitchen, and he, Samuel, George, and Fanny were comfortably seated about the room, partaking of the generous lunch my neighbor had provided.

I was sitting behind my desk, taking notes of our meeting, when my office door flew open and Eddie charged into the room. As if drawn by a magnet, his eyes went instantly to the generous array of lunch food Fanny had laid out on my desk.

"I saw Sergeant Lewis's wagon reined up out front," he declared by way of explanation. "When I saw Mrs. Goodman weren't in her shop, I figured somethin' must be goin' on up here."

"Take a sandwich and sit down, Eddie," Fanny told the boy with a smile. Hastening to do as he was told, he assumed his favorite perch on the windowsill and began to eat with his usual hearty appetite.

"Whatcha talkin' about?" he asked, his mouth full of bread. "Are we investigatin' another killin'?" he added hopefully.

"Don't talk with your mouth full," I corrected him. "And yes, we're discussing how to prove where Mr. Remy was on the night of Mr. Aleric's murder."

"I heard he got tumbled for the job," the boy said seriously, this time being careful to swallow his food before he spoke.

"He was arrested, yes," I told him. "I have agreed to act as his attorney."

"Well, then, he's as good as out of the cooler, ain't he?" said Eddie, displaying his customary, if somewhat idealistic, confidence in my abilities.

"I appreciate your faith in me, Eddie," I told him. "Actually, I'm glad you dropped by this afternoon. We would like you to assist us in our investigation."

His brown eyes lit up with excitement. "I reckon I'm yer man, Miss Sarah. What do you want me to do?"

Samuel was trying hard to stifle a smile. He had grown fond of the boy over the past year and was assisting me in the lad's education. Although I did not always approve of the reading material he passed Eddie behind my back—namely, lurid copies of the *Police Gazette*—I could not fault the boy's progress. He had, in fact, used his newly acquired reading skills to help us solve a series of murders resulting from a séance Robert and I attended last year at San Francisco's Cliff House.

"We would like to hire you as our driver for the next few days, perhaps a week," my brother told him. "Would that be possible?"

"You betcha!" the lad exclaimed, in his enthusiasm very nearly choking on a slice of beef. Robert, who was seated closest to the boy, patted him hard on the back until the bite dislodged from his throat and he regained his breath. "Just tell me where you want to go, and I'll get you there. Quick as greased lightning, too."

I had to repress a little shudder at this promise, since riding in Eddie's brougham all too often meant risking life and limb.

"You can start by driving Miss Sarah on an errand this afternoon," Samuel told the boy, then looked to me. "That's agreeable to you, is it not?"

"It is indeed," I said. The day after tomorrow, I was scheduled to speak before the city council. I held a trump card up my sleeve, or at least I prayed I did. My work with Samuel at City Hall the previous day had provided me with the final documentation I required. Now, all that remained was for me to pay one last visit to Ricardo Ruiz's property, which I planned to do that afternoon.

Once that issue was settled to our mutual satisfaction, we moved on to how we would go about interviewing businesses near the restaurant where Aleric and his friends dined late Wednesday evening. As Remy had pointed out, it was going to be a long and tedious search, but one that must be undertaken.

"I've got one or two friends on the force who might agree to help," George added thoughtfully. "Off the record, of course. We can't afford to be caught investigating the case behind Curtis's back. We'll have to do it on our own time, too."

"Of course, George, we understand," I said. "It will be difficult for Robert as well."

"It's possible I may be able to join you on Thursday afternoon," Robert said, looking as if he still harbored a few misgivings about the operation. "Shepard and his wife are spending an extended weekend in the country, so I may be free on Friday as well."

"Since I haven't gone back to working full-time yet, you can count on my help," said Samuel.

"Only if you're feeling up to it," I put in, determined not to endanger my brother's recovery.

He gave me a sidelong glance. "You're a fine one to set conditions."

"The bullet that was fired at me missed," I reminded him. "Yours didn't. You'll bring the wrath of our parents down upon both our heads if you suffer a relapse."

"Sarah is right, Samuel," said Fanny, once again passing around the platter of sandwiches. "You must take care of yourself. Your health comes first."

"It was kind of you to prepare all this food, Fanny," my brother said in an obvious ploy to change the subject.

"That's right, Mrs. Goodman," Eddie chimed in, claiming his second sandwich from the platter. "Ain't nobody makes beef fixings like you do."

I cringed. Although the boy's progress in reading was truly remarkable, I could not seem to improve his language skills. How could he read so beautifully yet speak so appallingly?

"Don't forget that I'm free whenever you need me," Fanny said, sitting down to eat her own sandwich. She was beaming almost as broadly as Eddie, obviously excited to be included in the plan.

"You're a good friend, Fanny," I told her, blessing the day I had taken the rooms above her shop. "This is going to be a formidable undertaking."

"Do you believe we have a realistic chance of finding anyone who saw Mortimer Remy last Wednesday night, Lewis?" Robert asked, looking frankly skeptical.

"I honestly don't know," George told him. "There's always a bit of luck involved in an inquiry of this sort. But Miss Sarah is correct when she says it's the only way to go about it. Very tedious it is, though, no doubt about it."

"Quite honestly, I find this entire affair baffling," said Robert, shaking his head. "First Samuel is shot, Claude Dunn is apparently hanged, and someone tries to shoot Sarah. Next, Ozzie Foldger is killed, and now Jonathan Aleric has been murdered. What do any

279

of these crimes have to do with one another? They appear to be completely arbitrary."

"Obviously there must be some connection," said George. "We just haven't been able to find it."

"What does your Lieutenant Curtis make of the puzzle? Particularly the part where Sarah and I were shot?" asked Samuel.

George couldn't mask his vexation. "He continues to believe that you and Miss Sarah were accidentally fired upon by someone aiming at a fox or a skunk, or some other kind of small animal. He's convinced that Claude Dunn committed suicide, and that Ozzie Foldger was killed because of a story he was writing, or by a person he might have maligned in the past. And of course he's sure that Mr. Remy followed through with his threat to kill Jonathan Aleric. Curtis doesn't see the crimes as being linked in any way, which certainly makes it all a great deal less complicated."

"Remarkable." Samuel shook his head. "I know Curtis has relatives at City Hall, but how he ever attained the rank of lieutenant is unfathomable. If you ask me, that's the real mystery here."

The third item on my agenda was to examine Jonathan Aleric's life before he came to San Francisco two years earlier. As I had mentioned to Remy, it was necessary to know as much about the murder victim's life as possible if we were to find his killer. And hopefully make sense of this puzzle.

In the end, we decided on a plan that assigned people to various neighborhoods and streets, at times they could manage given their work schedules. Samuel would help George question the residents of Telegraph Hill, but first he promised to take advantage of some of his journalistic connections to find out everything he could about Jonathan Aleric's life before he arrived in San Francisco.

When everyone but Eddie had left my office, I double-checked the list of people I hoped to speak to for the remainder of the day. Upon ascertaining that everything was in order, I donned my coat and the lad and I departed in the brougham for South Van Ness and Twenty-second Street.

After the first hour spent on Ruiz's Mission District property, I began to suspect that either Robert or Samuel had taken the boy aside and instructed him to guard me as if I wore the crown jewels of England. Observing Eddie's furtive behavior as I made my way through the blocks, speaking to as many people as would open their doors, I found it difficult not to laugh. He looked for all the world as if he had stepped out of the pages of one of Samuel's *Police Gazette* magazines. As he clicked his dappled-gray along, careful to keep the carriage parallel to me, his squinty eyes continually swept up and down the street, suspiciously following every man, woman, and child as if he'd seen their faces featured in a rogues picture gallery.

Ironically, a brougham cab crawling along the street, sans a passenger, attracted far more attention than if I'd been walking the block on my own. I would have to tell Samuel that his young watchdog was nothing if not resolute in carrying out his responsibilities.

Only one or two of the houses I visited yielded fruitful results. I was more successful at several of the corner stores in the area. These general stores sold a large variety of goods, including salt, spices, sugar, tea, coffee, and pickles, as well as beer, whiskey, and the canned goods that had become widely available after the Civil War. I quickly realized that these owners were far more threatened than most of their neighbors and began to concentrate my efforts on the other shops and restaurants in the area.

It was after six o'clock when I finally completed my trek through the neighborhood, climbed wearily back in the brougham, and instructed Eddie to take me to the law offices of Shepard, Shepard, McNaughton and Hall. As arranged, Robert was waiting for us in front of the building. Once he had joined me inside the carriage, we began the trek toward my home on Rincon Hill.

"What a lot of bother just so your father will believe you spent the entire day in your office," Robert commented as we made our tedious way through heavy evening traffic.

"Do you want him to think that you have broken your word?"

I responded shortly. I assuaged my guilt by reminding myself that if Papa had not taken it upon himself to rule my life in this overbearing manner, I would not be forced to resort to such machinations. "This way you can state with absolute honesty that you escorted me to my front door every day for a week."

"Yes, I suppose that's true enough." He held on to his briefcase as Eddie took a corner rather faster than safety dictated. "Tell me, did you meet with any success in the Mission District?"

"Not as much as I hoped, but enough to convince the court, I believe. This evening I'll draw a map of the blocks I covered. Then I shall know if I've located enough tenants. I fear I still have a great deal of work to do before Mr. Dinwitty and I visit City Hall."

"Yes, I can well imagine." He was silent for a moment, then blurted rather abruptly, "Can I be of help? Perhaps tonight, when you have to correlate and write the new brief? I know you plan to spend most of tomorrow with Mrs. Goodman, visiting businesses near the restaurant Aleric frequented the night he was killed. You'll have to complete the SPCA work tonight if you're to be ready to submit the material the day after tomorrow."

I stared at him in surprise. "You're offering to help me, Robert?"

He fidgeted in his seat, arranging and then rearranging his briefcase in his lap. "Of course I am. You're going to wear yourself to a frazzle if you keep this up. Dealing with Ruiz's bullring was demanding enough, without taking on a first-degree murder case. I don't know what you were thinking."

"I was thinking that as far as the police are concerned, they have Jonathan Aleric's killer safely locked up in city jail," I told him with fervor. "The evidence against him is circumstantial, but extremely damaging. If someone doesn't take immediate action, the authorities will have him put on trial, found guilty, and hanged before he knows what has befallen him. I cannot stand by and allow that to happen."

"No, of course you cannot." He sighed, sounding weary but resigned. "But you don't have to do it alone. If it's agreeable with your parents, I'll help you tonight. That way you can concentrate your attention on Remy's case tomorrow."

He gave me a sidelong smile. "And perhaps you won't faint away from exhaustion."

My mother was taken aback, but not in the least dismayed, that I had invited Robert to dinner without arranging it with her first. Cook always prepared more than enough food for one or two extra guests, and Mama was fond of Robert. I'm certain she was secretly delighted that I had invited an eligible man to the house—at this point in my spinsterhood, she would probably have been thrilled if I'd shown interest in a chimney sweep!

Since my father found my colleague far more interesting than other guests we had entertained over the years, the conversation at dinner that evening was lively, covering subjects that my brother Frederick and his wife would have considered gauche had they been there, which, fortunately, they were not.

When Samuel quietly asked me how we would deal with questions having to do with Remy's arrest, I had to admit that we had come up with no real plan. My colleague and I would be forced to improvise if the subject was broached.

Which, of course, it was. To my dismay, it became the primary focus of our dinner conversation. Thankfully, Papa still appeared not to have heard that I was representing the defendant, yet Robert and I were forced to skirt the issue uncomfortably, attempting to answer his questions without telling an outright lie. Through it all, my brother looked on in ill-disguised amusement. If only he had been sitting next to me, I thought, I would have given his shins a solid kick beneath the table.

Professing, honestly enough, that we had a great deal of work to accomplish on the bullring case, we retired to the library. I can't say that I was overly surprised when my father and a grinning Samuel joined us a few minutes later, followed by Edis, who was bearing a tray laden with coffee and Papa's beloved brandy. I was relieved that we actually were working on the SPCA case and not Remy's defense. At least my father could not accuse either of us of lying when he inevitably learned the truth.

Since my brother was privy to my newly hatched strategy to defeat the bullring, he lounged languidly back in his chair, feet propped up on a hassock, drinking his brandy-laced coffee, and apparently enjoying himself immensely. If he thought either Robert or I would slip and drop a careless word about what I was really up to these days, he was disappointed. Robert impressed me by being discretion itself, never telling an outright falsehood but subtly veering away from topics that threatened to cross into dangerous territory.

As it turned out, Papa was keenly interested in what I planned to present to the city council. It came as a pleasant surprise to learn that he had presided over a number of cases of adverse possession, which were evidently common, especially in the West. He even offered several suggestions to augment, and at the same time simplify, my legal arguments. The evening flew by as we sat in companionable discussion, happily poring over papers, documents, and maps I had drawn of Ruiz's landholding.

"I wish I could be there with you and Dinwitty on Wednesday," Papa said as I placed our completed documents in neat folders. "Will you be going with her, Robert?"

I cursed silently. The agreeable evening had caused me to temporarily forget that as far as my father was concerned, I was obeying his stricture not to leave my office without an escort, a *male* escort.

"Robert has to work, Papa," I answered, finishing the last of far too many cups of coffee. This beverage rarely interfered with my ability to sleep, but tomorrow would be a full day, and I needed to get a good night's rest. "Samuel has promised to accompany me."

"Yes," my brother said. Despite his relaxed posture, he appeared weary, and I said a silent prayer that our plans for the next several days would not exhaust him. "I wouldn't miss it for the world."

"You'll take a cab, of course," Papa said, making this a statement and not a question. I knew that for the time being, public transportation was out of the question as far as my father was concerned, and I nodded.

"We've arranged for Eddie to take us," I told him.

"Excellent." He eyed his youngest son warily. "Just make sure this brother of yours doesn't overdo it." He gave Robert a friendly wink. "I swear, these two have always been two peas in a pod. Can't keep them down for love or money. I could tell you stories of the shenanigans they got up to as children that would—"

"I'm sure you could, Papa," I said, rising from my chair before my father could expound on this embarrassing subject. "But it's late and Robert must be getting back to his rooms."

My father consulted his pocket watch, looking surprised to realize that it was nearly eleven o'clock. "My goodness, I had no idea it was so late. It's high time we called it a night."

Samuel clapped Robert on the back, bade us good night, and headed up the stairs, giving us one last smile over his shoulder as he ascended.

My father put a companionable hand on Robert's shoulder and led him out of the library, then down the hall toward the front door. Robert threw me an entreating glance over his shoulder, indicating that he wished to speak to me privately before he departed. I nodded my agreement, but Papa had already opened the door and was ushering him out onto the steps and into the cold night air.

Left with little choice but to take his leave, Robert shook my father's hand and wished me a pleasant good night. Since Papa was standing beside me, I could do no more than thank him again for his help that evening. He nodded to me, then turned and walked down the street to the corner, where it would be easier to find a cab at that late hour.

CHAPTER TWENTY-TWO

I awoke the next morning to hear a bustle of activity going on outside my bedroom. A glance at my bedside clock told me that it was barely seven o'clock, yet I heard the lusty cries of Celia and Charles's baby, people calling out to one another, and footsteps treading up and down the stairs.

After pulling on a robe, I opened my door to find Celia standing there, hand poised to knock. She held her squirming seven-month-old son in her arms.

"Sarah, I'm so glad you're awake," she said, sounding a bit breathless. "Can you please take Charlie for me? He's been fed, but seems reluctant to settle down. I'm trying to help Mama prepare to leave, and Mary is busy with Tom and Mandy," she added, referring to the children's nanny.

I happily reached out for my nephew, then looked questioningly at Celia. "Leave? Leave for where? They said nothing about going away last night."

"That's because they just found out," she explained, chucking a finger beneath her son's chubby chin, causing him to stop crying long enough to laugh. "A telegram arrived about half an hour ago. Papa's sister Flora has taken ill. Your parents hope to board the nine o'clock train this morning for Williamsport."

"Oh, dear," I said rather inadequately, bouncing little Charlie in my arms as he appeared to be gearing up for another wail. I had met my aunt Flora only twice, once when we made a trip to Pennsylvania when I was a child of eight, the second time when she traveled to San Francisco shortly after her husband's death ten years ago. I hardly knew the woman, but she had seemed nice, and I understood that she was my father's favorite sister. "How seriously ill is she?"

"According to the telegram, her condition is dire." My sweet, caring sister-in-law looked near tears herself. "I pray they will reach her in time. She and Papa are very close." She brushed moisture from her cheeks and kissed her tiny son's cheek. "I must help them, Sarah. Thank you for minding little Charlie."

I started to speak, but she had already hurried back to my parents' room. I saw my father carrying bags down the stairs, assisted by my brother Charles. As I stood watching, thinking there must be more I could do than just hold the baby, Samuel poked a sleepy head out of his bedroom door.

"What in the name of all that's holy is going on out here?" he asked, rubbing the heel of his hand over his eyes. "It sounds like a herd of elephants is tramping through the house."

I walked over to him and explained the telegram that had arrived describing Aunt Flora's illness.

"I hope they reach her in time," he said, looking worried and fully awake now. "Poor Aunt Flora. She used to tell me really spooky ghost stories, then give me cookies, although sometimes I was so unnerved by her scary monsters I'd be too frightened to eat them."

"I remember now," I said, thinking back to the time we had visited Flora at Williamsport. "She thought I was too little to hear her tales, so I'd hide under your bed and listen to them without her knowing."

He smiled at the memory. "Then you'd insist on sleeping with me, because you'd be too scared to go back to your own room."

Papa came up the stairs and saw us. "I suppose you've heard

287

about Flora," he said, running a hand over the baby's fair head. Immediately, Charlie held out dimpled arms, leaning toward his grandpa and demanding to be taken from me. It made me feel a bit jealous and at the same time touched that the child had grown so fond of my father.

"That baby is besotted with you," Samuel said, laughing.

"So were you at his age, son," said my father, giving him a sad smile. "Then you grew up, far too fast."

"Children have a tendency to do that," Samuel said. "Fortunate that you have three grandchildren. Well, four if you count Freddy Jr."

"It's difficult to forget Freddy, son." He regarded us seriously. "Now listen to me, you two. I know you're going to present your case to the city council tomorrow, Sarah. You've prepared well, and with any luck they'll rule in your favor. But I want you both to promise me that you'll stay out of trouble while I'm gone." His gaze went from Samuel to me. "Do I have your word on it?"

My brother and I both nodded. Papa continued to regard us thoughtfully for a long moment, then sighed and shook his head. "I don't like the way you've both been behaving for the past few days. I know you're up to something, but I don't suppose you'd tell me what it is if I asked?"

He made it a question, looking so hopeful that one of us might give him an honest answer that I felt a stab of guilt. But if I revealed that I had agreed to defend Mortimer Remy—and would therefore be forced to revisit Telegraph Hill—it would only exacerbate a journey already fraught with apprehension.

Samuel started to blurt out an excuse, but Papa stopped him with a raised hand and a rueful look. "Don't bother, son. I have no time now to listen to a litany of clever half-truths. I'll find out soon enough. I just hope the two of you can steer clear of any serious danger while I'm gone."

He heard Mama calling his name from downstairs and picked up the last bag. "We had better be off if we're to catch that train."

"Give Aunt Flora my love, Papa," I told him.

"As well as mine," my brother added.

"I only hope that will be possible," Papa said. He stooped to kiss little Charlie's rosy cheek and then mine. His brown eyes twinkled for a moment. "Mind you, don't burn down the house while we're gone." He turned and hurried down the stairs, where Mama waited with their cabbie.

E ddie collected Fanny and me at my office three hours later. Samuel had left the house to interview a "source," who might have information about Jonathan Aleric's past. George Lewis and his men hoped to commence a house-to-house search on Telegraph Hill that day, looking for witnesses who might have seen Remy at his house Wednesday night. For our part, Fanny, Eddie, and I would start our own investigation by questioning the staff at the restaurant where Aleric and his friends dined the night of his death.

Our intrepid young driver once again assumed his detective persona, this morning wearing dark clothing and pulling his cap so far down on his forehead that it nearly covered his eyes. As he helped us into the carriage, he looked covertly up and down the street, then proudly displayed a worn pocketknife that he had polished to a fine sheen. He also carried his trusty cosh, which consisted of various coins and rocks stuffed into an old sock and tied off at the ankle. Fondly, I remembered this as the same weapon he had used to save the day during the Cliff House investigation. I fervently hoped that these weapons would not prove necessary but informed the lad I was pleased that he had come prepared.

The restaurant where Aleric was last seen alive was located on Bush Street, not far from the California Theatre, where they had attended a play that evening. We arrived as the establishment was preparing to serve its luncheon trade. I had brought with me a picture of Aleric that had appeared in one of the newspapers. It was a fair likeness, and I hoped it might help jar people's recollections of seeing him on that fateful night.

I started by showing the picture to the restaurant manager, while Fanny set off to question the waiters. He was a stocky Italian man, with a bald head and busy eyes that kept darting about the dining room as we spoke.

"Yes, yes, what can I do for you, signorina?" he asked with a slight Italian accent. He seemed to be paying more attention to his employees than to Aleric's picture, I thought, but I pressed on with my inquiries.

"I wonder if you remember seeing this gentleman in your restaurant late last Wednesday night," I asked, holding the photograph a bit higher. "He would have been dining with friends."

For the first time he looked down at the picture, tilting his head to one side as if considering. "The man with the big mustache, the one who was murdered? The police were already here." He gave me a suspicious look. "Who are you? Why do you ask me these questions?"

I was prepared for this inevitable question and handed the man my card, which he read with obvious skepticism.

"I am an attorney, signore," I told him, "and I'm attempting to learn where Mr. Aleric might have gone after he left your restaurant that night."

He spread out his arms in a gesture of futility, and I heard him mutter the word *stupido*. "How can I know where he went? I do not follow my diners outside." After saying something in rapid Italian to one of his staff, he turned away. "I am busy. You go now."

Realizing there was nothing more I would get from him, I gazed around the restaurant, looking for Fanny. I finally spied her by one of the front windows, speaking to a short young man dressed in a waiter's uniform. I was encouraged to see him nodding his head as if in agreement, then pointing a finger out toward the street. Catching the manager's baleful eye on me from across the dining room, I decided it would be best if I waited for her outside the restaurant.

She soon joined me, appearing excited. "That young man saw Mr. Aleric last Wednesday night," she told me, nodding at the waiter, who seemed to be receiving a heated reprimand from the manager, probably for speaking to my neighbor.

"What did he say?" I asked eagerly.

"As it happens, Mr. Aleric forgot his hat when he left the restaurant. The waiter hurried outside to return it to him." She turned in the direction of Kearny Street. "He says he finally caught up with him at the corner over there. Mr. Aleric was apparently trying to hail a cab."

"Did he actually see him get into a taxi?" I asked.

"No, he just handed him the hat, and ran back into the restaurant. He says Mr. Aleric gave him a nice tip for his efforts."

"All right," I said, starting to walk toward Kearny and Bush Streets. "Let's question the shops and cafés on that corner."

Upon reaching the intersection where the waiter had seen Aleric, we took a moment to decide which businesses to try first. I was startled when Fanny took hold of my arm.

"Look," she said, motioning up the street.

Following her gaze, I spied Eddie's brougham parked halfway up the block on Kearny Street. Parked, I might add, so that it was blocking traffic. Seemingly oblivious to the clanging carriage bells and cries of disgruntled drivers, Eddie stood talking to a group of young roughs who were laughing and slapping one another on the back. When he saw that Fanny and I were watching him, he shook his head slightly, the gesture clearly indicating that we should stay away from the group.

"I don't like the look of those boys," Fanny said, sounding worried.

"Nor do I, but he's playing the great detective today. I suppose we must leave him to conduct his investigation the way he sees fit." I nodded toward a grocery store on the west side of the corner. "Let's start there. Hopefully, some of these stores stay open late on Wednesday night to take advantage of the theater trade and saw Aleric."

No one had. Not in the café, the bookstore, the laundry, or the dry goods store. Fanny and I made our way down one side of

Kearny Street, then up the other. What few people we found who had been present at that late hour worked in either saloons or restaurants and had been too preoccupied with the late-night crowd to notice a lone man attempting to hail a cab.

By two o'clock, Fanny and I had visited every shop, store, restaurant, café, grog shop, and saloon along Bush, Kearny, and Dupont Streets. Weary and hungry, I suggested that we take our lunch in one of the cafés we had visited. We were searching for Eddie so that he might join us when he pulled up in the brougham, appearing excited and very pleased with himself.

"I found some buggers what seen him," he called out. He practically flew off his perch atop the carriage, words tumbling out of his mouth like rows of falling dominoes. "The poor bloke dang near got hisself sandbagged by some knucks I met who are out on hocus-pocus and were lookin' for a mark in order to pull a swartwout and—"

"Eddie, please. Stop," Fanny cried, holding out a pleading hand. "Sarah, dear, have you any idea what the boy is prattling on about?"

"Only vaguely," I said, feeling nearly as befuddled as she looked. "Let's go inside and order lunch, then Eddie can tell us all about this remarkable piece of detective work. Preferably in English!"

This was the first time since I had met the boy that he seemed more interested in talking than eating. He gave the waiter his order after barely consulting the menu, then squirmed impatiently in his chair while Fanny and I took rather more time making our own selections.

"All right, Eddie," I said when we were once again alone at the table, "please start at the beginning and tell us what you discovered, only this time use words that Mrs. Goodman and I can understand."

"It's clear enough, Miss Sarah," he insisted, looking a bit offended. "I come across some fellers I knew, is all. Last I heard they was in jail, but now they're out 'cause of some shyster lawyer. The buggers, er, pickpockets, said they'd seen that Aleric feller lookin' to find a cab."

"Excuse me, Eddie," I said, breaking into his account. "How do you know that the man they saw was actually Jonathan Aleric?"

"They said he had an almighty big mustache, and was dressed like a dandy," he explained. "When I showed 'em the picture you gave me, they said that were him no doubt about it. Right off they pegged him as an easy mark, and were gonna hit him over the head with a sandbag."

At Fanny's bewildered expression, he pulled the cosh from his pocket. "They was gonna hit him with a sandbag, Mrs. Goodman, kind of like this only filled with sand, then nip his watch and wallet, and whatever else they could find."

He paused in his narrative to look meaningfully from one of us to the other. Lowering his chin, he peered up at us through squinted eyes for added effect. "Afore they could get to him, though, a carriage came barrelin' down the street and pulled up right beside the bloke. Bud—that's the feller I've known since we was no bigger'n gallnippers—told me the driver hopped down from his box, hit the mark over the head with somethin'—Bud weren't sure what he used—then picked him up and threw him inside the rig. He said they was off and runnin' faster'n you could swat a fly."

Fanny and I stared at him in astonishment.

"Eddie, you clever boy!" I exclaimed. "You managed to learn more in one conversation than either of us did in four hours. I'm extremely proud of you."

Fanny reached a hand across the table to pat his arm. "I always knew you had a fine head on your shoulders, Eddie dear. What a fine policeman you'd make."

The lad seemed a bit embarrassed, but it was easy to see from the gleam in his bright brown eyes that he was basking in this praise.

"Did your friend recognize the type of carriage the man was driving?" I asked.

"He said it were a Dearborn, you know, one of them real light buggies," Eddie answered. "Black, with some kind of fancy design on the sides. It was dark, but Bud said it carried two oil-burning lamps, which was why he could see it pretty good."

"A Dearborn carriage," Fanny repeated. "Sarah, you can find those all over the city."

"I know," I said thoughtfully. "Did Bud mention what the design looked like?"

"He said it was two long, wavy lines, purple and gold, that ran back and forth through each other. Bud said the buggy looked really old, but that it had been kept up good."

"What about the driver?" I asked. "Was your friend able to describe him?"

Eddie started to speak but stopped as the waiter delivered our meals. As soon as the man left, he looked around cautiously, then rested his arms on the table and leaned forward.

"Bud said the feller was dressed in black, even his hat, and didn't seem to be real tall, but not real short, neither. Says he couldn't see the bloke's face all that good, 'cause he mostly kept it down."

I tried not to show my disappointment. Without some sort of description, almost any man in town could have been driving the Dearborn, which, as Fanny pointed out, was a common enough vehicle in San Francisco. The man could even have been Remy, I thought despondently. He did not own a Dearborn that I knew of, but he could have borrowed or rented one from any number of carriage dealers in town.

Fanny and I asked the boy more questions, but it was clear that he had told us everything he had learned from his friends. When I inquired where I might find Bud, he looked horrified.

"He ain't gonna talk to you, Miss Sarah," he said in alarm. "Only told me 'cause I promised not to rat him out to the leatherheads. I reckon he was feelin' pretty wrathy about the whole job, you know, his mark bein' took off right from under his nose and all."

Once again, I thanked the boy. He had, after all, provided us with the first real information concerning Aleric's movements after he left the restaurant. Unfortunately, we were left with a great number of unanswered questions. As we departed the restaurant and drove back to Sutter Street, I wondered how, and where, we were going to find the answers.

When I arrived home that evening, I was informed by Edis that Samuel would not be present for dinner. He had sent a note explaining that he had spent the day making inquiries about Jonathan Aleric. He was following a hot lead, as he put it, and would have dinner with his source. He promised that he would be home later that evening and expected that George Lewis would also be joining us.

I had already invited Robert to dine with us that night, and he, Charles, Celia, and myself enjoyed a quiet meal. The house seemed oddly empty without my parents, and I found my thoughts going to them and their long journey to Pennsylvania. I prayed that they would reach Aunt Flora in time. It would be a sad reunion, but at least they would have an opportunity to say their farewells.

Since Eddie had made the most significant discovery that day, at least as far as Fanny and I were concerned, I had asked him to be present for our meeting that evening.

Once Samuel, George, and Eddie arrived, Robert and I joined them in the library. I had instructed Edis to serve our usual coffee and pastries and was touched to see that, unasked, he had added Papa's favorite brandy to the tray.

George seemed surprised to see that Eddie had been included in our company, but when the boy gave his report—carefully leaving out the names of his friends—he regarded him with newfound respect.

"Bully for you, Eddie!" he declared with a wide smile. "That was very fine work. I'll have my boys start checking tomorrow for the carriage you described. There are a lot of Dearborns in town, but I don't recall seeing many with that particular design. Thanks to you, we finally have something concrete to go on."

Lewis went on to explain that he had been unable to make it to Telegraph Hill that day. There had been two stabbing deaths at a saloon on the Barbary Coast, which had required his attention.

"I'll try to start our inquiries there tomorrow," he promised. "And it won't hurt to ask the residents if they've ever seen a Dearborn carriage on the Hill with that particular design."

"Samuel, you're going with Sarah to City Hall in the morning, aren't you?" Robert asked my brother.

"Oh?" George looked interested. "Does it have to do with that bullring the Ruiz fellow wants to construct?"

"Yes," I answered. "We're presenting new evidence which we hope will force the city council to prohibit the arena."

"I'm drivin' you there, ain't I, Miss Sarah?" asked Eddie, eager to be back on the job.

"*Aren't* you, Eddie," I corrected automatically.

He looked confused. "That's what I'm askin' you, Miss Sarah. I don't rightly know if you want me to take you there or not."

I sighed. "Yes, Eddie, we would appreciate it if you would bring the carriage around to the house at nine thirty tomorrow morning. You won't be able to accompany us inside the council chamber, but we'd like you to wait for us in the brougham. We plan to visit city jail after the hearing is concluded."

"To see that Remy feller? The one we're tryin' to prove didn't do in Aleric?"

Before I could confirm this, George said, "I hate to point this out, Miss Sarah, but judging from Eddie's description of that driver, he could be anyone, including Remy."

"I realize that, George," I said. "It's far too general to be of any practical use to us. But the make, and the decorative design on the side of the carriage, may help narrow the search."

"That's what I'm hoping," he said. "I just don't want you to get your hopes up that this information is necessarily going to help your client."

"I know that all too well," I told him. "That's why I'm determined to conduct a thorough search of Telegraph Hill. We must do everything possible to locate anyone who might have seen Mr. Remy in his home Wednesday night. At this point, it appears to be his best hope of confirming his alibi."

We discussed the case for another hour, after which George left, grateful for Eddie's offer to drive him to his boardinghouse. When they had gone, Samuel declared that he needed a good night's sleep if he was going to face City Hall the next morning, and he ascended the stairs to his room.

"You will be careful tomorrow, Sarah," Robert said as I showed him to the door.

"Samuel and Mr. Dinwitty will be with me, as well as our stalwart hero, Eddie Cooper," I said, smiling. "Moreover, we'll be at City Hall most of the morning, then at the jail. Surely we should be safe enough."

"Hah! As far as you're concerned, no place is safe. Trouble follows you around like your own shadow."

"Oh, for goodness' sake, don't be so dramatic."

"Only if you promise not to be so headstrong," he retorted. Before I could answer, he went on, "I doubt that I'll be able to leave the office tomorrow, but I should be free on Thursday afternoon. I want you to give me your word that you won't venture onto Telegraph Hill unless I am with you."

"I just told you that Samuel will be with me most of the day," I protested.

"Do I really need to remind you that someone tried to kill you and your brother on that blasted Hill?" He regarded me in frustration. "Sarah, listen to me. George and his men plan to commence their inquiries there tomorrow. You already have a full schedule, and going to City Hall and the jail will be more than enough for Samuel. You don't want him to suffer a relapse."

"No, of course not." Much as I hated being told where I could go and what I could do, there was an element of truth in his words, especially about Samuel's health. "All right, Robert. We'll visit the Hill on Thursday. And I'll insist that Samuel take a rest when we return home tomorrow afternoon."

He looked so relieved that only then did I realize how truly worried he had been. Taking me off guard, he pulled me into his arms. This time he didn't hesitate but lowered his head to kiss me full on the lips.

The embrace rattled my senses so thoroughly that he had been gone for several minutes before I realized that I had kissed him back. Rather enthusiastically, I feared.

I was surprised to see the light on under Samuel's door as I walked to my bedroom. Since there had been no opportunity to speak to him earlier about his research on Jonathan Aleric, I knocked softly. At his response to come in, I slipped quietly into his room. He was sitting at his desk, busily writing in a notepad.

"I thought you were going straight to bed," I said, taking a seat on his bed.

"Nonsense," he said, giving me a sly wink. "Surely you've heard the old saying about three being a crowd? I wanted to give you and Robert a little privacy, some time to discuss, well, whatever you and he discuss when you're alone."

"Oh, for the love of—" Suddenly restless, I rose from the bed. "I'll tell you what we discuss when we're alone, dear meddling brother. He orders me to be careful crossing streets, not to speak to strangers, to get enough sleep, not accept hopeless legal cases, and generally keep my nose out of trouble. He fusses at me until I want to scream." I stared down at him, furious to see amusement twinkling in his eyes. "There! Is that romantic enough for you?"

He placed his right hand over his chest, fluttering his eyelids.

"Be still, my racing heart. I cannot bear this frenzied display of passion."

"Samuel Woolson," I declared, placing my hands on my hips, "did you or did you not find out anything about Aleric today?"

"Patience, little sister. First things first. Remember I said I had a source who might have information regarding Aleric? Well, I spent the better part of the afternoon with him."

"Is this the man you had dinner with tonight?"

"No, that was another friend. Well, more of an acquaintance, actually. But it turns out he was an even better source than the first one."

"Samuel, please!" I said in exasperation. "All these sources. You're beginning to sound like Ozzie Foldger." I stopped, chagrined to remember that Foldger had just been violently murdered. "Just tell me what you learned."

He turned back to his desk and picked up his notepad. "Sit down and I'll tell all."

With a little sigh of impatience, I resumed my seat on the bed. "All right, I'm sitting. Now, what did you find out?"

Glancing over his notes, he said, "Russell Druitt, a fellow Bohemian Club member, went to school in New York with Aleric some twenty years ago. I remembered him mentioning that when Aleric moved to San Francisco a couple of years ago. It seems that the famous author was a real hell-raiser in his youth, eventually getting himself expelled from at least two schools. After that, he pretty much continued going downhill. Druitt says he was arrested for petty theft when he was twenty, and was sent to jail."

"Good heavens," I exclaimed. "How long did he remain incarcerated?"

"A year or two, Russell thinks. By the time he was released, the Civil War had broken out, and he enlisted as a Union soldier. The war must have seemed like a stroke of luck to him at the time. He possessed no practical skills, had no money, and probably didn't care to end up back in jail."

"Actually, it did turn out to be fortunate for him, didn't it? Because of the war, he was inspired to write one of the most acclaimed books to come out of that horrible conflict."

"Yes, I suppose it did," my brother said, obviously thinking about his own manuscript and looking just a tad envious. "Druitt lost track of Aleric after he deployed to Mississippi to serve under General Grant, which is where my second source comes in."

"The source you dined with tonight."

"None other. Jeffery Markham is also a member of my club, and happened to serve with Aleric during the war. Druitt overheard him discussing this after Aleric was killed and put me on to him."

"What did he tell you?" I asked, eager to know where this was leading.

"It seems that Mr. Aleric was a mediocre soldier at best. According to Markham, he invariably remained as far back in the ranks as possible when faced with enemy fire, never volunteered for a dangerous detail, and constantly complained about the food, the climate, the mosquitoes, and anything else that didn't suit him."

"That last fault being one which apparently never changed," I commented, remembering Aleric's behavior at Oscar Wilde's reading, as well as at the train depot.

"If it hadn't been for Markham and a couple of his buddies," Samuel went on, "Aleric might well have deserted his unit during their march on Vicksburg. As far as his regiment was concerned, he was a bully, a coward, and a blowhard."

"What amazes me is that such a poor soldier managed to pen such a brilliant book about a war he wanted to run away from."

Samuel sighed and placed the notebook back on his desk. "So, was any of this helpful?"

I did not immediately answer, lost in my own thoughts. Something Samuel said bothered me, but I couldn't put my finger on what it was or what it meant.

"I honestly don't know," I said at last. Suddenly, I was very tired; the long day was catching up with me at last. And my brother looked exhausted.

"Get to bed, Samuel," I told him. "It's late and we have a busy day tomorrow. You need your sleep."

"So do you, little sister. In the morning we take on City Hall. And for that, we're going to need all the energy we can muster."

CHAPTER TWENTY-THREE

Samuel and I entered City Hall shortly before the hearing was due to begin. We found Mr. and Mrs. Dinwitty waiting for us, along with Mrs. Hardy.

"I just couldn't stay away," Jane explained, doing her best to ignore Celestia Dinwitty's look of disapproval. "I promise not to say anything, or get in the way."

"She has worked so diligently on the petitions, I felt it only fair that she attend," said Bernard Dinwitty, also trying to disregard his wife's displeasure. "Miss Woolson, please tell me truthfully, what do you think our chances are of winning the case?"

I felt a flicker of guilt that I had not fully explained the true purpose of this morning's hearing to the Dinwittys. As far as they were concerned, we were here for the sole purpose of outlining our objections to the bullring. I had not felt comfortable sharing my new stratagem with them until I had completed my research. Now, there seemed insufficient time to explain it in detail. I simply told them that I had unearthed new information, which I hoped might improve our chances of success. Mr. Dinwitty started to question this; then, realizing the hearing was about to start, he simply nodded and told me to do whatever I felt was best for the case.

When we entered the room, the first person I saw was Ricardo

Ruiz. He was taking a seat with two well-dressed men carrying briefcases. Could he have more than one attorney? I wondered. Moving into the row behind them were the two rough-looking men who always accompanied Ruiz. I was leading my little group to seats on the opposite side of the room when Ruiz looked up and met my eye.

He rose and executed an exaggerated bow. Gone was his animosity of the previous week, when he had attempted to bully the SPCA into giving up their petitions. The expression on his handsome face now was proud and self-assured, as if his victory this morning were a foregone conclusion. The two men sitting on either side of him watched me as I settled into my seat. Their faces reflected the usual curiosity and disdain common to the great majority of the city's male legal society. My standard reaction was to ignore their reaction, which was what I did now.

A moment later, seven men filed into the chamber and took seats at the front of the room. As the president of the council looked over the cases to be heard that morning, I felt a thrill of anticipation, as well as of fear. More than ever, I was convinced that the petitions alone would not be enough to change their minds about the bullring. Papa's so-called big bugs had decided that the arena would bring money into the town's treasury and eventually into their own pockets. As far as they were concerned, therefore, it must be allowed.

"Will I be asked to speak?" whispered Mr. Dinwitty, appearing nervous at the prospect.

"No, I'll present our case," I told him. "All you need to do is sit here and look relaxed."

"I'll do my best," he said, looking anything but relaxed.

Although the room was cool, there were beads of perspiration on his forehead, and the hand closest to my own exhibited a slight tremor. He raised a handkerchief to pat at his face, and as he did so, I actually saw his mustache twitch above compressed lips. Replacing the cloth in his pocket, he inhaled a deep breath as if to take himself in hand, then forced a smile onto his thin face.

"We have complete faith in you, Miss Woolson," he said, as much to bolster his courage as my own, I was sure. "I am certain that you will do your utmost to present our case in the best possible light."

"Rest assured, Mr. Dinwitty, I shall do my best."

I picked up the files I had removed from my briefcase, and Samuel gave me a reassuring wink as I waited for our case to be called. Mrs. Dinwitty's derisive frown was mitigated by Jane Hardy's confident smile, which clearly demonstrated her faith in my abilities. I said a quick, silent prayer that her faith in me would be justified.

One of the members of the council was reading from what appeared to be an agenda. His round head was bent over the document, revealing a shiny bald pate surrounded by a circle of light brown hair, much like a monk's tonsure.

After several minutes, he raised his head and called our case. He appeared startled when he saw me standing and making my way toward the lectern, which was centered in front of the council table. The men seated about him were regarding me with equal suspicion, whispering among themselves and shaking their heads as if in disapproval that I had been born female. Since I had taken care to indicate my gender when filling out my request for this hearing, I wondered why they were regarding me in such obvious surprise.

Once again, the president of the council glanced down at his agenda. "I took this to be a misprint," I overheard him say to the man seated to his left. "But she really is a woman. What is the world coming to?"

"You are Miss Sarah L. Woolson?" the other man inquired, seeming impatient to be done with this charade.

"I am, sir," I said, arranging my papers neatly in front of me, waiting patiently for the council to digest, and ultimately accept, that I was indeed a woman.

The first man, whom I took to be the council president, once again took control of the hearing.

"I see that you previously submitted signed petitions on behalf of the San Francisco office of the Society for the Prevention of Cruelty to Animals. You also presented a list of written objections to the bullring construction which has been proposed by Señor Ricardo Ruiz. Is that correct?"

"It is, sir."

He eyed me skeptically. "Are we to understand that you are a licensed attorney in the state of California, Miss Woolson?"

"I am, sir," I answered, weary, if resigned, to the seemingly never-ending need to recite my legal qualifications. "I passed my California State Bar examination eighteen months ago, and have been practicing law in this city since that date."

He studied me from beneath wire-rimmed glasses perched at the end of an unfortunately bulbous nose, the pores so prominent that I could make them out even from where I stood.

"I see," he murmured. "Would you please inform us why you have requested this hearing? *Briefly,* Miss Woolson. We have a full agenda this morning."

"Of course, Mr. . . ."

"Shaw, Miss Woolson," he replied a bit testily.

"Yes, Mr. Shaw. New information has come to my attention which disputes Señor Ruiz's title to the land he claims to own in San Francisco's Mission District."

Having prepared myself for his outburst, I did not flinch when Ricardo Ruiz flew to his feet and unleashed an indignant stream of Spanish. No translator was required to understand that his comments were not meant to be cordial.

Mr. Shaw glared at Ruiz, demanding that his attorneys instruct him to remain quiet until he was called upon to rebut my accusations. Ruiz looked at me furiously, then finally yielded to his lawyer's admonishments and curtly resumed his seat.

"Please continue, Miss Woolson," he directed.

I cleared my throat. "We do not contest the fact that Señor Ruiz's father, Javier Ruiz, purchased landholdings in southern California, as well as here in San Francisco."

Shaw made a dismissive sound in his throat and shuffled irritably in his chair. "If Señor Ruiz's land claim is not in question, then why are you here wasting our time, Miss Woolson?"

Once again, I suppressed my annoyance, answering calmly, "If you will allow me to continue, Mr. Shaw, I will endeavor to explain why I have requested this hearing."

"Very well, go on," he told me abruptly. "But take care that you confine your comments to the matter at hand. This council has no time to listen to frivolous female nattering."

I heard a loud gasp of indignation from somewhere behind me—Mrs. Hardy's, I suspected—and a wave of laughter and whispered comments rippled through the room, some of sympathy, far more from satisfaction that I had been put soundly in my place.

"Very well, Mr. Shaw," I said evenly, "I shall come directly to the point. Señor Ruiz does not hold legal title to the Mission District land, where he plans to build his bullring."

This time, the noise that filled the room was more raucous. Ruiz was again on his feet, gesturing with his arms and loudly protesting my claim in a mixture of Spanish and English. His two attorneys were attempting to calm him, while Mr. Shaw shouted to be heard over the fracas.

When he had finally regained control of the room, Shaw turned back to me. "Miss Woolson, I warned you against squandering the council's time. Not five minutes ago you said you were not here to dispute Señor Ruiz's land claims. Either explain yourself, or let us get on with valid city business."

I referred to one of my papers. "I'm sure that you recall the Board of Land Commissioners, established by the United States Congress in 1851? Their job was to settle land claims inherited from the period of Mexican rule."

"Of course, of course," Mr. Shaw said dismissively. "What of it?"

"Under the terms of this act, any individual who claimed a title derived from the Mexican government was given five years to prove his claim."

I looked toward Señor Ruiz, who half rose from his seat and waved a sheaf of papers at me. "And that is just what my father did. Here is proof that he was granted title to his lands."

"Yes, señor, that is correct as far as it goes." I opened a new file. "I have been able to locate the land claims Señor Javier Ruiz originally submitted to the Board of Land Commissioners in 1852. They were for a considerable number of acres in southern California—where I understand the Ruiz family had long maintained rancheros—along with the much smaller land parcel located here in San Francisco's Mission District."

"Yes, Miss Woolson," Shaw pressed. "Please get to the point."

"I am attempting to do just that, Mr. Shaw." At his curt nod, I continued. "Although the Board of Land Commissioners ratified all of Señor Ruiz's deeds, their decision was challenged by local city and county governments. Like a great number of other claimants, Señor Ruiz was forced to appeal his case to the district court, and eventually to the United States Supreme Court. It took nearly twenty years for the matter to be resolved."

Ricardo Ruiz once again stood and waved his deeds. "You say it yourself, señorita. I hold in my hands the land claims my father was finally able to obtain after so many years of fighting your *lastimoso,* your pitiful court system."

"I'm sure you do, señor," I said before Mr. Shaw could intervene. "However, I believe if you examine the deeds, you will find that whereas the southern California property was finally ratified, the San Francisco property, located in the Mission District, was never confirmed by the Supreme Court."

"Are you able to prove this accusation, Miss Woolson?" Shaw asked me, displaying the first glimmer of interest since I had stepped to the podium.

"I am, Mr. Shaw," I said. "I have here documents indicating that Señor Ruiz's father spent most of those twenty years attempting to gain legal title over his vast holdings in southern California. The land he owned here in San Francisco undoubtedly seemed insignificant by comparison, and was not as rigorously pursued."

"Never!" Ruiz shouted before his lawyers could restrain him. "My father harbored a deep love for San Francisco."

"That may be true, señor," I replied equably. "However, he apparently loved his many thousands of acres in the Los Angeles area even more, because that is where he concentrated his time, and the considerable outlay of money necessary to pay for lawyers, additional surveys, court appearances, and transportation expenses to bring himself and his witnesses into this country from Mexico."

Mr. Shaw directed his gaze to the flurry of activity going on between Señor Ruiz and his attorneys as he rifled angrily through the deeds.

"Señor Ruiz, bring me those papers. *Por favor,*" he added as an afterthought, and in dreadfully pronounced Spanish.

"What nonsense is this?" Ruiz demanded. "I don't comprehend."

One of his lawyers said something to his client, then took the documents from him, rapidly examining each one in turn. He stopped and pulled out a paper, then handed it to his fellow attorney to inspect.

"Well, Señor Ruiz?" said Shaw, watching the two men as they bent their heads over what I took to be the deed to the San Francisco property.

One of the lawyers finally explained something to his agitated client, then stood and carried the entire sheaf of documents to Mr. Shaw.

"We appear to have a small problem, Mr. Shaw," the man said with a relaxed smile, an expression that I was certain fooled no one in the hearing room, since his face was red and glistened with nervous perspiration. "Señor Ruiz has in his possession all of the southern California deeds, as he has pointed out. However, we appear to be missing the one relating to the San Francisco holding."

Shaw had been going through the deeds while the man spoke. Finally, he held up a heavy, slightly yellowing document.

"Here is the deed issued to Señor Javier Ruiz by the Mexican government," he said, then pointed to the rest of the papers.

"What we need to see is the deed which was eventually validated by the Supreme Court, like the rest of these."

The lawyer gave a little chuckle, as if this were but a minor detail that could be easily resolved. "I realize this, Mr. Shaw. That is why I am requesting that we postpone this hearing for one month, to give Señor Ruiz time to locate the missing document. He fears he may have inadvertently left it at his hacienda in Mexico City."

Mr. Shaw gave the man a sharp look, then turned to consult with his fellow council members. After several minutes, he turned back to the attorney.

"Because of the seriousness of this matter, we have decided to grant your request to postpone this hearing for one month. At that time, it will be incumbent upon Señor Ruiz to present a properly executed deed to the San Francisco property, issued by the United States of America. Is that understood?"

"Yes, sir," the lawyer said. He reached for the documents he had shared with the council and returned to his seat. Once again, he leaned over to explain the situation to his client, who had turned very red in the face.

"Excuse me, Mr. Shaw," I said. "I have not yet finished presenting my evidence against Señor Ruiz's bullring."

Shaw glanced at me as if I were a pesky fly that refused to go away. "What is it now, Miss Woolson? This hearing has been officially postponed."

"Before this case is held over," I continued doggedly, "I must inform the council that I have come across evidence of adverse possession in regards to the Mission District property. This may make the question of Señor Ruiz's locating the San Francisco deed, if it exists, a moot point."

Shaw looked confused. "Adverse possession? What are you talking about?"

"It's very simple, Mr. Shaw," I told him. "Under the doctrine of adverse possession, if a person openly occupies land that belongs to someone else, and does so for a designated number of years, the

309

title shifts to the occupier. The original owner effectively loses his right to the land."

Once again Ruiz was on his feet, shouting out in Spanish, while his attorneys attempted more or less unsuccessfully to defuse his outburst. At the same time, the city council members had their heads together, obviously trying to digest this latest bombshell.

I continued speaking, raising my voice in order to be heard over the din. "Since Señor Javier Ruiz has been deceased for the past nine years, and his son Ricardo Ruiz has neither constructed a building on the site nor resided on the property, the land reverts by law to those individuals who have been living there, secure in the belief that the land legally belonged to them."

The council appeared to select one of its fellows as spokesperson. "I am familiar with the doctrine of adverse possession, Miss Woolson," said a tall, thin man seated at the far end of the table. "However, in order to use this argument, it is necessary to determine how long an individual has lived on the land in question, and if he has paid taxes on that property."

"Yes, sir," I agreed, pulling documents from yet another file. "In order to address that question, I have obtained files from the Hall of Records, containing details of various individuals who have resided on the property for the required five years or more, and who have also paid their taxes in a timely and orderly manner."

The man looked surprised. "Really? I would be interested to hear what you have learned about these people, if you please, Miss Woolson."

Starting with the small general store located on the east corner of Twenty-third and Harrison Streets—which had been there for twenty-two years—I listed the eight homes and businesses whose owners could claim they had resided on their plot of land for over five years and who had dutifully paid taxes on said land.

"I have made copies of these documents for the council," I said. "The originals, of course, can be found in the Hall of Records."

Closing the file, I continued, "As you can see, even if Señor Ruiz is successful in finding the properly executed deed to the San Francisco land he claims to own, it will still be impossible for him to construct a bullring, or any other edifice, for that matter, on this acreage, until the adverse possession question has been settled."

The stir in the room grew louder, and the council members put their heads together for yet another hurried discussion.

I glanced over at Ruiz, to find him glaring at me with an expression of open malevolence on his flushed face.

"You will not stop me!" he shouted, raising his fist threateningly. "Despite your stupid laws and your female obstinacy, I will build my bullring."

After ruling that the city council would review the information I had submitted, and instructing Señor Ruiz to find the deed to his property, if he was able, Mr. Shaw called the next case to be heard before the council, and I returned to my place.

Samuel squeezed my hand, and Mr. Dinwitty was fairly dancing in his seat with excitement and relief. Mrs. Hardy was grinning at me as if I had just been elevated to sainthood, and even Mrs. Dinwitty was smiling, one of the first satisfied expressions I had ever seen on her arrogant face.

Samuel and I arrived at the jail shortly after noon. When we were shown into Mortimer Remy's cell, I was forced to bite my tongue. The poor man looked terrible. He had not shaved since he had been arrested, and his beard was coming in almost completely white. His eyes were sunken, his hair was uncombed, and his skin had an unhealthy pallor. He had been in jail for four days, but his appearance made it seem more like four weeks.

He insisted that I take my usual seat on his cot, while he stood with Samuel beneath the cell's solitary barred window. We spent several minutes discussing what was happening at his newspaper in his absence, then our talk centered on his case. I related what Eddie had learned the previous day when he, Fanny, and I canvassed the streets located in the vicinity of the California Theatre.

"Some boys actually saw Aleric being struck and forced into a carriage?" he asked, astonished. "That's wonderful news! Surely this proves that I had nothing to do with his death?"

"It might if we had any way of identifying the mysterious driver," Samuel told him. "The boys told Eddie that it was too dark to get a good look at the man's face."

"But I don't own a Dearborn carriage," he protested. "I own no carriage at all. I never have."

"The police must consider the possibility that you borrowed or rented one, Mr. Remy," I said, hating myself for dampening the hope that had flickered in his tired eyes. "However, they're going to question your neighbors today about seeing a Dearborn. It's decorated with a distinctive design, which may make it easier to remember."

Remy shook his head, sighed, then stiffened his spine as if determined to put up a good front. "What about my neighbors on the Hill? Has anyone come forward to say they saw me in my cottage last Wednesday night?"

"The police are interrogating everyone who resides on that side of Telegraph Hill today." I smiled, hoping to lift his spirits while at the same time crossing my fingers that George had indeed been able to commence the search. "I am committed to knocking on every door, Mr. Remy. We shall not give up until the entire neighborhood has been queried."

This time, Remy's smile reached his eyes. "You are a wonder, Miss Woolson. I realize all too well that I have saddled you with an extraordinarily difficult case. As you have pointed out, the evidence against me is largely circumstantial, but it is nonetheless compelling."

"You mustn't give up, Mortimer," Samuel said. He was trying his best to appear confident, but I doubt that his friend was taken in by the act.

I was struck by a sudden thought. "You know, Robert keeps

saying that given the disparity of the victims, this case makes no sense. I'm beginning to believe he's right."

"What are you suggesting?" asked my brother.

"Everyone seems to think that you and I being shot at has nothing to do with Dunn's, Foldger's, and Aleric's deaths. But they may have everything to do with them. What if we're looking at this from the wrong perspective? I think we must go back to the beginning."

"You mean the night of Wilde's reading?" asked Remy.

"Exactly," I said. "We're missing something here, I just can't put my finger on it. However inexplicable, that's when it all began. If we could just—"

There was a sudden commotion in the corridor outside Remy's cell. We heard the sound of men talking, then the door was flung open with a clang. To my surprise, George Lewis stepped inside.

"We've found a witness who claims to have seen two men digging a grave on Telegraph Hill last Wednesday night," he told us without preamble.

"Who is it?" I asked, feeling a surge of hope. "What did they see?"

"It's that Sullivan woman, the one who was wet-nursing the Dunn baby. Officer Turner got her to admit she'd seen the men last Wednesday night, then she panicked and slammed the door in his face. She's locked herself and her children in that house, and refuses to have anything to do with the police."

He looked at the two men. "Sorry about this, Samuel, Mr. Remy, but Mrs. Sullivan insists she'll speak to no one but Miss Sarah."

"Of course," I agreed hastily. "We must go there at once."

"I was hoping you'd say that," George said, looking relieved. "I've got the police wagon waiting outside."

313

CHAPTER TWENTY-FOUR

In the end, Samuel and I rode in Eddie's brougham to Telegraph Hill. It was far more comfortable than the police wagon, and George knew that the boy was bound to follow him at any rate. Since each of the vehicles was pulled by a single horse, however, we were forced to once again park and ascend the Filbert Street Steps on foot.

Before leaving the jail, I had jotted a quick note to Robert explaining where I was going, then asked one of the officers to deliver it to him at Shepard's law offices. I decided it was the least I could do to avoid another lecture and, I admit, to ease his mind.

I could hear the sound of Mrs. Sullivan's boisterous children long before we reached her cottage. Requesting the men to stand back, I walked onto the cluttered porch and knocked on the door. After a few minutes, the woman's frightened voice came from inside.

"Who is it?"

"It's Miss Woolson, Mrs. Sullivan," I replied. "Sergeant Lewis said you wished to speak to me."

The door was opened the barest crack, and I could see her fearful eyes inspecting me. Satisfied that I was who I claimed to be, she pulled the door open far enough for me to squeeze inside, then quickly closed it behind me. As on the occasion of my first visit following Claude Dunn's death, the cottage was filled with small children and several dogs, all seeming to be fighting over a rather mangy rubber ball.

"I'm that glad to see you, Miss Woolson," she said, clearing a path toward the only two chairs in the room. "Them police came here again, askin' more questions."

"I understand they wanted to know if you saw Mr. Mortimer Remy last Friday night," I said.

She regarded me nervously. "The thing is, Miss Woolson, I did see somethin' that night, but it warn't Mr. Remy. Leastwise, I don't think it were him. 'Course, it was dark, so I can't be sure."

My pulse quickened, but I kept my voice calm. "What did you see, Mrs. Sullivan?"

"Mr. Sullivan said I wasn't to say nothin'," she told me, pitching her voice so low that I had to lean closer in order to hear. "He don't hold with coppers. He'd be right huffy if he knew I were tellin' you what I seen. But it don't seem right not to tell someone, you know?"

"I think you'll feel a good deal better once you have, Mrs. Sullivan. And I promise that I won't tell your husband about our conversation."

"I had a feelin' you was to be trusted, Miss Woolson, and my feelin's is usually right." Once again she lowered her voice. "I seen two men diggin' over there past Tull O'Hara's place that night. I knew the minute I seen 'em they was up to no good. They had a lantern, but had covered it with somethin', so it didn't give off much light. But I was up feedin' our little Gracie, and I seen it bobbin' around over there like a big firefly."

"Do you have any idea what they were digging?" I asked.

"Not at first, then I seen 'em lug over somethin' heavy, like a man's body, drop it in the hole, and throw dirt onto it." She stopped to yell at two of the boys, who were teasing one of the dogs with a stick. "Pulled me curtains shut real quick, so they wouldn't see me watchin' 'em."

315

"Do you have any idea who the men were, Mrs. Sullivan?"

She shook her head. "Like I said, it were too dark to tell for sure. I remember thinkin' at the time that one of 'em might be Tull O'Hara, but I got no idea about the other feller. Both were wearin' dark clothes, and their caps was pulled down low so it were hard to see their faces."

"Did you by any chance see a Dearborn carriage parked near the men, Mrs. Sullivan?"

She thought for a moment, no easy task with children running and shrieking all around us. Suddenly a baby started to cry in another room, and Mrs. Sullivan wearily got to her feet.

"Now you mention it, seems to me I did see a carriage parked out on the road," she said, starting toward what I assumed was a bedroom. "Can't rightly say if it were a Dearborn, but it were small and black, and pulled by just the one horse."

"Could you make out any design on the side of the carriage?" I asked.

She shook her head, obviously anxious to get to her baby. "It were too dark to see much more than just the shape of the buggy. I'm sorry, Miss Woolson, but I gotta tend to little Gracie."

I had barely stepped outside when I was hit by the strong smell of smoke. It seemed to be billowing in from across the road in waves so dense that my eyes began to sting. Holding my handkerchief over my nose, I turned back and banged on Mrs. Sullivan's door, warning her of the fire and saying she should gather up the children and take them down the hill.

Once the terrified woman and her brood were safely out of the house, I was at last able to make out the source of the fire: Tull O'Hara's house was ablaze!

Coughing, I made my way closer to the shack, my first thought to find Samuel, George, and Eddie.

"Miss Woolson," a voice called out. I saw a man approaching me from down the hill. He was almost upon me before I saw through the smoke that it was Emmett Gardiner. "Do you know if they were able to get Tull O'Hara out of the house?"

"I didn't know he was in there," I said, my heart catching in my throat at the thought of the typesetter being trapped inside that inferno.

"I saw him about an hour ago when I was going down the hill. He . . ." He paused, then went on, "He was pretty drunk, I'm afraid. Perhaps that's how the fire started, a cigarette or cigar left unattended."

Three more figures were appearing out of the smoky haze, and I was grateful to recognize them as my brother, George, and Eddie. Their faces were blackened with soot, their eyes red-rimmed and watering, their clothes torn and soiled beyond repair. They were coughing and gasping to draw in air. I ran over to my brother.

"Samuel, are you all right?"

He wiped a hand across his forehead, succeeding only in creating a fresh trail of grime across his face. The sling on his left arm was torn away, and he was holding his injured arm tightly across his chest. I could see that he was in pain.

Catching my worried look, he protested, "I'm fine, Sarah. Don't fuss. We tried to see if anyone was inside, but—" Once again he started to cough, then went on, "It was useless. The place went up like a tinderbox."

Poor Eddie looked as though he had gone swimming in a bin of coal dust. Even through the black grime staining his face, however, I saw the glint of excitement in his eyes.

"It were hotter'n blazes in there, Miss Sarah. We done our best to get to the old geezer, but you couldn't see nothin' but fire and smoke. And the roof was fallin' down on our heads."

I looked from Samuel to George. "You think Mr. O'Hara was in there?" I asked, raising my voice to be heard above the shouting, falling debris, and whinnying of frightened horses.

The welcome clanging of a fire engine could be heard coming up the hill, thankfully pulled by two strong horses. Mere minutes after its arrival, men were passing buckets of water hand to hand

and throwing them onto the blaze, but it was obviously too late. O'Hara's dwelling was doomed; the firemen were laboring now to prevent the inferno from spreading to other houses on the block.

My brother shook his head. "If O'Hara was in there when it started, he's gone now. No one could have lived through that conflagration." He nodded a hasty greeting to Emmett Gardiner, then indicated that George wanted to talk to me in private.

"Excuse me, Mr. Gardiner," I said, and followed Samuel and George up the street until we were far enough from the fire to find a faint stir of fresh air and could be heard above the din without shouting.

"What did you learn from Mrs. Sullivan?" George asked, wiping rather futilely at his eyes. "Did she really see two men digging on the hill last Wednesday night?"

"She insists she did, and I believe her. She was up feeding her baby and saw the light from a lantern across the way. According to her, the two men dropped something heavy into the hole, then covered it up again." I hesitated. "She thinks one of the men might have been Tull O'Hara."

George grunted in disgust. "Why in tarnation didn't the woman tell us this a week ago? We might have been able to catch the devils then and there."

"Her husband didn't want to have anything to do with the police," I told him. "But when your men came to her door today and started asking questions, she felt guilty about keeping what she'd seen a secret. And that's not all, George," I hurried on. "She claims to have seen a small black carriage parked near the men. It was too dark to tell if it was a Dearborn, or to make out any design, but it seems too much of a coincidence not to assume it's the same one Eddie's friend saw abducting Aleric."

George nodded. "You're probably right. That would be how they brought the body here. You say she thinks one of the men was O'Hara? What about the other bloke?"

"Unfortunately, it could be anyone," I said grimly. "According to her, he was completely average looking."

318

"You realize, of course, that she could be describing your client," George said. "He and his typesetter burying their archenemy. It makes sense."

Naturally, I had already thought of this. Still, no matter how well it might seem to fit together for George, I would never believe that Remy could commit cold-blooded murder, not just once but three times! Not to mention shooting at Samuel and me.

"I think this damn hill is cursed," Samuel said, staring at the furor going on down the road. "Starting the night I was shot marching down the hill after Wilde's reading."

"Oh, dear Lord!" I interrupted, staggered by the realization that had flashed into my mind. This was what I had been struggling all day to remember. And now that I had finally put it together, it seemed too horrible to countenance. Three murders. No, I thought, *four* murders, for surely Tull O'Hara's death was no accident. Despite the heat from the fire, I felt an icy shudder. Samuel and I could have easily been included in that number.

"What is it, Sarah?" my brother said, staring at me. "You look as if you'd just seen a ghost."

"Oh, Samuel, I think—I truly think I may have done just that."

George had also seen the look on my face, but before I could say anything else, Stephen Parke came running down the hill, his eyes wide with fear.

"Whose house is on fire?" he cried. "Was Isabel— Has anyone seen Isabel?"

"It's Tull O'Hara's house," I told him. "And we haven't seen Isabel. Isn't she at her home?"

"No, she's not," he said, some relief showing on his face, but not enough to erase the lines of concern. "She should have been home over an hour ago. There are piano students waiting inside for their lessons. Her father came to my house looking for her. Then when we saw the smoke—we feared she might be down here."

I felt a stab of my own fear. "Did Mr. Freiberg see where she went after she left the house?"

"No, he didn't."

"Did she mention why she was leaving when she had students arriving?"

"A policeman came to the house asking questions," Stephen said. "Something about seeing Mortimer Remy last Wednesday night. According to Mr. Freiberg, she rushed out shortly after he left."

"And she said nothing about where she was going?" I could no longer hide my trepidation. "Think, please. It's important."

He stared at me as if just now comprehending that something was very wrong, and that it concerned Isabel. "Miss Woolson, you're frightening me. Why are you asking all these questions?"

"Just tell me if she said anything to her father before running off," I all but shouted.

"I don't think so." He hesitated, then said, "Hold on, I think he said she mentioned something about a carriage, although I don't see what that can have to do with—"

But I had heard enough. More than enough to have my worst fears verified. "Hurry, all of you. There's not a minute to lose!"

"Wait, Miss Sarah," George called out. "Where are you going?"

"This way, George," I threw back to him over my shoulder. "And bring some of your men."

Without waiting for a reply, I started half running up the hill, praying that we would not be too late. I could hear the men following behind me, some of them still asking questions. I ignored them all. I had but one focus, to reach Isabel Freiberg before she came to harm!

I slowed down when we reached her house, telling myself there was still a possibility I could be wrong. Perhaps Isabel had returned and even now was inside conducting a piano lesson. One look at her father's frightened face, however, told me that I was not wrong. She had not come back, and she was still in mortal danger. Without stopping, I hurried on.

Everything appeared so normal when we reached the top of Telegraph Hill that once again I experienced a flicker of doubt. It was nothing more than wishful thinking, of course, but I so desperately wanted to believe that I was imagining things too horrible to be true.

Out of breath, I stood for a moment looking up at the lovely mansion, perfectly situated with majestic views of the San Francisco Bay, Alcatraz and Angel Islands, and Marin County beyond. Even after several trips to the Hill, I realized this was the first time I had actually been to Mrs. Montgomery's home. It was built in the Italianate style, with a Corinthian column–supported central porch flanked on either side by stone stairs, a wide balcony, and double-hung windows perched above.

By now, I had a considerable group following in my wake: Samuel, Eddie, Stephen Parke, Solomon Freiberg, Emmett Gardiner, and of course George Lewis and several of his men. Other neighbors had also joined the procession, until I was reminded of the Pied Piper of Hamelin.

There was no need to mount the stairs and knock on the elegant front door. Abigail Forester swept out of the house and onto the porch as if she had somehow anticipated our arrival. I was shocked by her appearance: her face was chalk white, her mouth opened as if she wanted to scream but could not find the necessary breath, her pale eyes wide in horror. The house cap she wore was tilted to one side, and wisps of white hair flew in disarray about her head. Her small hands fluttered to her mouth and then to her bosom, unable to remain still.

"Oh, my, Miss Woolson," she cried, then stopped when some of the men started toward her. "No, don't, please, stay where you are. Oh, dear. What am I to do?" With a flurry of skirts, she disappeared back inside the house.

"Why did you bring us up here?" George asked. "And who was that?"

"That's Abigail Forester, Mrs. Montgomery's sister," I told him. "And we came here because Isabel Freiberg is somewhere inside that house."

He looked surprised. "What leads you to think that?"

"There's no time to explain now, George," I told him, keeping

321

my eye on the door. "We must find some way to get inside before Studds harms her."

Samuel took hold of my arm. "Sarah, you can't possibly think Mrs. Montgomery has anything to do with this. What reason could she have for killing Aleric, or Dunn and Foldger, for that matter?"

"The only one she truly wished to kill was Jonathan Aleric. You weren't the target the night of Wilde's reading, Samuel, he was. But he stumbled, remember? And when you bent over to help him, the shot hit you instead. We can only be grateful that it didn't kill—"

Mrs. Forester once again appeared at the mansion door. She was pushing her sister, who was seated in her wheelchair, holding little Billy in her lap. Abigail did not attempt to wheel the chair down the ramp that had been built into one side of the stairs, but instead the two women remained on the porch, posed dramatically above us like players on a stage.

At once, every eye fastened on to Katherine Montgomery; her strong, assertive presence was always the more dominant of the two women. Today, however, the elderly widow's face was scarcely less pale than her sister's, and her usually clear eyes appeared distant and dull with resignation.

She surveyed the crowd gathered before her, then said, "It has gone too far. Tull O'Hara should not have died. He was a stupid man, but no one deserves to die like that." She did not raise her voice, but somehow her words carried across the front garden so that everyone could hear.

At the moment, I was not interested in Tull O'Hara, grisly as the fire had been. "Where is Isabel, Mrs. Montgomery?" I demanded.

The old woman sighed. "She is here. Inside the house with Bruno."

"Is she all right?" Stephen started to move forward despite Abigail's appeal to stay back.

"She is fine, Mr. Parke," the widow told him. "For the moment, at least. But my poor Bruno—I fear Bruno is not himself."

"What does that mean?" I, too, had walked closer to the stairs, fighting the urge to take them at a rush and see for myself that Isabel was indeed all right. For her sake, I had to remain calm. "It's over now, Mrs. Montgomery. Surely you must see that. You cannot allow Bruno to hurt her. It will only make matters infinitely worse for him."

She sighed. "I am aware of that, Miss Woolson." There was a sound from above her head, and she turned to look up as one of the balcony windows opened. "Unfortunately, I seem unable to convince him of this inevitability."

"I don't understand," Stephen said, his face twisted in anxiety. "What's all this about Bruno Studds? And why is he holding Isabel in there?"

"She remembered the Dearborn," I told him, never taking my eyes off Katherine Montgomery and the baby. I did not dare attempt to pull him from her arms. "Bruno is afraid that she'll tell the police what she knows about the carriage, and who owns it."

Stephen looked at me, panic growing in his eyes as he struggled to comprehend what I was saying. "The Dearborn? For God's sake, woman, what are you talking about?"

"Miss Freiberg evidently saw our carriage during one of her visits to our home, Mr. Parke," Katherine Montgomery said, her voice uncharacteristically flat and devoid of emotion. "She came here to inquire if one of our neighbors might have borrowed, or perhaps even stolen, the buggy. It sounded exactly like the one the police were describing, you see, and she feared they might think we had been involved in Mr. Aleric's murder. Which, of course, we were."

"Katherine, please," begged Abigail, wringing her hands in distress. "You can't have had any part in this dreadful business. Tell them it's all a terrible mistake."

"But it's not a mistake, dear," Mrs. Montgomery told her sister quietly. "Bruno merely acted as my arms and legs, since they have been useless for so many years. He has always been fiercely protective of me, and of course of my dear son, Lawrence. I don't think it has occurred to him yet that I will be hanged. As will he, of course."

"It's unfortunate that Claude Dunn proved to be such a poor shot with a revolver," I said.

George was staring at me. "Are you saying that Claude Dunn shot Samuel? But why?"

"Because he needed money to tide them over until Lucy could go back to work after the baby was born," I said. "I assume Dunn must have performed other 'jobs' for you at one time or another?"

She nodded. "He was an exceedingly greedy and selfish man, unfit as a husband, and already demonstrating that he would be equally unfit as a father."

"Everything seemed to go wrong for you from the beginning, didn't it?" I said.

She gave a rueful smile, the merest curve of her thin lips. "Yes, perhaps I should have aborted my plan the night your poor brother was shot instead of Aleric. But I had waited so many years to punish that dreadful man for stealing my son's brilliant book. *An Uncivil War*—my lovely boy had mailed me excerpts during his time with General Grant, so I knew that it was his work."

"But you didn't possess enough evidence to prove it in court," I said.

"Unfortunately, no. The pages he sent were but odd passages here and there. Nothing substantial enough to convince a judge that he had been plagiarized."

"So, when Aleric showed up unexpectedly at Mr. Wilde's reading, it must have seemed as if fate had gifted you with the perfect opportunity to seek your revenge."

"I suggested to Mr. Remy that he allow Bruno to escort his guests down the hill," Mrs. Montgomery admitted, "so that it might appear that Aleric had been shot by accident. As you have undoubtedly heard, Miss Woolson, residents on Telegraph Hill are prone to shooting at the wildlife, even at night."

"You also wanted to ensure that no suspicion fell upon Bruno,"

I said. "He obviously couldn't have taken the shot when he was walking our group down the hill."

"Yes, Claude was happy enough to do it for me, but then, as I say, he would do anything for money. When Lucy died, however, he demanded that I pay him a great deal more cash for his silence." She sighed. "Bruno found a more . . . expeditious way to silence the miserable man. Unfortunately, we did not learn until several days later that he had sold the story to that disreputable reporter Ozzie Foldger."

"Who was about to publish the entire sordid affair in the *Tattler*," I finished for her. "So, of course, Bruno was required to silence him as well."

"Yes," she replied somberly. "As I say, it has gone too far. I must add that it was never our intention to harm you, my dear Miss Woolson. Bruno was instructed to merely scare you off the Hill. You really are extraordinarily nosy, and your questions were beginning to worry me."

Stephen Parke was practically in Sergeant Lewis's face. "For God's sake, do you hear what she's saying? The man up there is a cold-blooded killer. You've got to get Isabel out of there!"

Just as George and his three men started to move to the stairs, the second window above the porch flew open, and Bruno Studds stepped onto the balcony, pulling Isabel out behind him. One large arm was clasped around her slender waist, the other held a revolver to her head.

There were audible gasps and a few muffled screams from the crowd, and George immediately signaled his men to stop. Everyone, in fact, suddenly became as still as statues, terrified to move for fear that the deranged-looking man on the balcony might shoot the poor girl he was holding, or even shoot at one of them.

His mistress was watching him from her wheelchair. Her eyes reflected a peculiar mixture of sorrow and pride. At that moment, I realized that she loved Bruno Studds as a friend, even more than she depended upon him as a loyal servant.

"Bruno, stop pointing that gun at poor Isabel, and come down from there at once," she ordered. "There is no need to harm her."

"She's gonna put you in prison, Mrs. Montgomery," the man answered, pressing the gun even more firmly against the young woman's forehead. "Can't let her do that."

"I'm afraid it's too late, my dear. Everyone knows now what we have done. It's best if you turn your gun over to one of these policemen, and then you and I can accompany them without a fuss."

Mr. Freiberg had come to stand beside Stephen. His face was pale, and when he raised his hand to the man on the balcony, it was trembling. "Mr. Studds, please, let my girl go. She is all I have."

Stephen took a step forward, but Bruno saw him and shouted, "Stop right there, Parke. I swear I'll shoot her. And you, too, if you come any closer."

Abigail held both hands to her mouth, her eyes huge with fear and brimming over with tears. "Don't let him hurt her, Katherine. She is hardly more than a child. Oh, dear, oh, dear. I don't understand any of this. Lord have mercy, what is happening to us?"

"Calm down, Abigail," her sister told her, but I noticed that her eyes had also grown more intense, less certain now of the power she wielded over her manservant. "Bruno, I am telling you that harming Isabel will do neither of us any good. Killing that larcenous villain Jonathan Aleric was one thing, but injuring this innocent young girl is clearly wrong. Please, come down from there before anyone else gets hurt."

Undoubtedly frightened by all the noise going on around him, little Billy Dunn chose that moment to start crying. Without looking away from Bruno, the elderly woman tried to quiet the infant, jiggling him in her arms and murmuring soft assurances. He only cried louder, adding more confusion to the already tense scene.

I was horrified to see Bruno's eyes gleam insanely as he stared at his mistress. "I can't let her go, Mrs. Montgomery. She's gonna tell the police if I do. I, ugh—"

Isabel had suddenly jerked her head backward, hitting Studds

326

on the nose and causing him to fire off his revolver. Thankfully, he had stumbled and the shot went wild, but Stephen took advantage of the distraction to leap up the porch stairs and into the house through the open front door. He must have flown just as quickly up the inside staircase, because a moment later he appeared behind Studds on the balcony.

"Isabel, run!" he shouted, pushing her through the open windows and back inside the house.

Bruno came at him like a wild animal. The two men struggled on the balcony, arms and fists flailing, hard punches thrown as well as received, blood spurting from both their faces. Stephen was the other man's junior by a good twenty years, but Studds was powerfully built and accustomed to performing physical labor, while the younger man worked at a desk as a writer.

There was a horrified cry from a woman standing below, and I held my breath as Bruno managed to push Stephen against the balcony railing. Despite the younger man's struggles, Bruno was winning the fight, inching Stephen's feet slowly off the ground, forcing his head farther over the railing.

"He's going to fall!" a man shouted.

"Someone help him!" cried another.

George and his men had already followed Stephen into the house, followed closely by Emmett, Samuel, and, of course, Eddie, despite my shouts for him to stay where he was. One of the officers came back outside a moment later, leading a badly shaken Isabel Freiberg. Her father was instantly by her side, the two embracing and sobbing in each other's arms.

There was another scream, and all eyes flew back to the balcony. Stephen was fighting desperately with the other man to retain his balance. Bruno was pushing him inexorably over the railing, ever closer to the stone porch lying below them. For a terrible moment, I was certain all was lost, then Stephen managed to break the other man's grip long enough for his feet to once again touch the ground.

Suddenly, the gun went off for the second time, piercing the stunned silence that had fallen over the crowd as they watched the life-and-death struggle taking place above their heads. Stephen cried out in pain, and a bright red stain began to spread across his right side.

Seeing the blood, Bruno gave a gleeful laugh and went in for the kill, once again attempting to lift Stephen up and over the balcony railing. Still, the younger man refused to give up. Despite his wound, he fought valiantly to break the other man's hold.

"Bruno, don't!" screamed Mrs. Montgomery.

Seeing her attention focused on the struggling men, I dashed up the stairs and took the baby out of her unresisting arms. As I did, Abigail gave a little cry, rolled her eyes, and fainted. A man hurried to her side, managing to ease her plump form to the ground.

Above me, Stephen used his knee to kick Bruno hard in an area where I knew it would cause severe pain. The bigger man howled, allowing Stephen the moment he needed to break free and away from the railing. George and his remaining men burst through the window and onto the balcony. While the police officers subdued Bruno, Emmett and Samuel helped the gasping writer down the stairs and onto the manicured lawn in front of the mansion.

The first one to reach him was Isabel, looking far more frightened now than she had been while fighting for her own life. Kneeling on the grass, she gently took Stephen's head in her lap and brushed the hair out of his face, while George attempted to staunch the young man's bleeding. One of the patrolmen had been sent down to the police wagon in order to fetch a two-horse ambulance that could make it up the hill.

"Help will be here in a few minutes, my darling," Isabel told Stephen, showering his face with kisses. "You're going to be all right, I promise. And I will never leave your side again." She glanced up at her father, who was watching the two, his expression softer than I had ever seen it. In that moment, I think, Solomon Freiberg finally recognized the face of true love.

I heard someone hurrying toward us and saw that Robert had arrived. He stopped in astonishment, taking in the crowd, a battered Bruno Studds being led away between two policemen, and a bleeding man lying wounded on the grass. Finally, his incredulous turquoise eyes rested on me and the infant I held in my arms.

"Good God, Sarah! What has happened here?"

"Far too much to even begin to explain to you at the moment, Robert," I told him. "It all happened so fast. I doubt that any of us has had time to draw breath, much less put our thoughts in order."

"Never mind," he said, coming to stand beside me. "You look completely knackered, and so covered in soot and ash that I know you must have been involved with that fire down the hill."

When I didn't answer, he gave me a rueful smile. "You truly cannot be trusted on your own. Might as well expect my landlady's cat to keep a promise as to ask one of you."

He sighed, and as hard as he was trying to look cross, I knew it was a sigh of relief. "But at least you're safe, and in one piece. The story can wait."

Placing his arm around my waist, he gave me a little squeeze. "Besides, you look far too charming cradling that baby in your arms to be subjected to one of my lectures. I'll save it until later."

CHAPTER TWENTY-FIVE

Mortimer Remy was released from city jail the following morning. Samuel, Robert, and I were on hand to escort him back to his home in Eddie's brougham.

We made a jubilant foursome, despite Eddie's eccentric driving. I honestly doubt that anything short of an actual collision could have dampened Remy's exhilaration.

"I owe my life to you, Miss Woolson," he said. Although he'd insisted on paying a generous fee for my legal services, his smile would have been more than an adequate reward. "You did everything you said you would, and a great deal more. But I cannot understand how you came to suspect Katherine Montgomery of being the villain behind all those murders. For years I have known her to be a fine woman, and the most gracious of friends."

"I believe that at heart she is a decent woman," I said. "But a mother's love can be all-consuming, and Mrs. Montgomery adored her only son."

"This was the child she had with her first husband, Giraud Tilson?" Samuel asked.

I nodded, pondering the irony of the situation. "Evidently, Mr. Tilson passed away when Lawrence was a child. Since Mrs. Montgomery goes by her second husband's name, Jonathan Aleric never knew who she really was."

"I never met the boy, but I understand he was everything a mother could hope for in a son," said Remy. "According to Abigail, he was handsome, brave, and blessed with a rare literary talent which exhibited itself when he was still quite young."

"You say that Aleric stole the lad's manuscript when he was with him at Vicksburg?" Robert asked.

"Mrs. Montgomery is convinced that he did." I said. "Of course, at that point his notes were in the form of a journal. I have to say that I believe her. Given Aleric's dismal record in school, I think it's most unlikely he could have penned such an extraordinary book."

"And he never published another thing, which also argues against him being the author," Samuel put in, gingerly adjusting the position of his left arm, which was back in a sling. "By the way, did I hear Mrs. Montgomery say she suspected Aleric of being responsible for Lawrence's death?"

"Before the police took her away, she told me that her son had discussed Aleric in some of his letters home," I explained. "He knew the lad was maintaining a journal of his experiences in the war, and had even taken it to read once without Lawrence's approval."

"Obviously he was impressed," Remy said.

"I'm sure he was," I agreed. *An Uncivil War* is an outstanding example of writing, by anyone's standards."

"But that doesn't necessarily mean he wanted to kill young Tilson," Samuel pointed out.

"No," I replied, "but according to Mrs. Montgomery, her son was convinced that Aleric attempted to shoot him during a skirmish with Confederate troops. If Lawrence had died, I suppose it would have appeared that he had been struck by enemy fire."

Samuel gave a soft curse. "As he eventually was. Which left Aleric free to steal Lawrence's journal, and then publish it as a book after the war."

"To great acclaim," Remy added bitterly. "I cannot help but feel sorry for Mrs. Montgomery."

"Yes," I replied. "Despite what she's done, it must have been a terrible ordeal seeing her son's work published under another man's name. And powerless to do anything to disclaim it in court."

Robert looked disgusted. "Even if he wasn't responsible for Lawrence Tilson's death, the man was a complete scoundrel."

"You'll get no argument on that score from me," Remy said with passion. "I wouldn't have actually killed the bounder, even if I was tempted to do so on more than one occasion, but I would be lying if I claimed to be sorry that he's gone." He studied me expectantly. "But you still haven't told me how you came to suspect Katherine Montgomery. Please do share the workings of your remarkable mind with us lesser mortals."

Samuel snorted and Robert guffawed almost in unison, but they couldn't quite disguise their curiosity to hear my response.

Smiling to myself, I said, "Actually, some of the indications were apparent the night Oscar Wilde visited Telegraph Hill. Although there was no reason to pay particular attention to them at the time. I thought nothing of it when I saw Mrs. Montgomery speak to Claude Dunn after the reading. Of course now we know she was offering to pay him to kill Aleric as he walked down the hill, but then it just seemed mildly curious. And, of course, Dunn had no real alibi after he left the gathering for his own home."

"Like most of the other guests," my brother put in. "They all insisted that they'd gone straight home and seen nothing."

I nodded. "That's right, so he didn't stand out as particularly suspicious. Most misleading, of course, was the fact that he shot you instead of Aleric."

Samuel gave a self-deprecating little smile. "When he stumbled and I bent over to help him."

"That's what you get for being a Good Samaritan, Samuel," said Robert. Despite his attempt to keep his tone light, his face sobered when he studied my brother's injured shoulder.

"You're right, though," my brother said. "It sent us off on the wrong track right from the beginning. I hardly knew Dunn, so it never occurred to me that he might be the shooter."

"I still don't understand why he agreed to do it," said Remy. "Did the man have no scruples?"

"Apparently not many," I replied. "After his poor wife, Lucy, died in childbirth, leaving him with an unwanted son and the loss of what little income she'd brought in, the man was desperate. Blackmailing Mrs. Montgomery must have seemed an easy way to support himself."

"But couldn't Mrs. Montgomery have simply turned the tables on him?" Remy asked. "After all, Dunn was the one who fired at Aleric."

"She could have done that," I said. "But then she would have been forced to admit to her own part in the plot. Dunn knew that as a prominent member of San Francisco society she couldn't survive such devastating publicity—assuming the police didn't send her to jail. And he was right, although not in the way he expected. Rather than accede to his demands, and risk the very real possibility that the blackmail might go on indefinitely, she and Bruno decided to silence him permanently."

"But he had already sold the story of Aleric's plagiarism and Mrs. Montgomery's long-seething desire for revenge to Ozzie Foldger," Samuel noted. "Of course without mentioning that he had been hired to actually pull the trigger."

"That must have come as quite a shock," Robert put in. "Those two thought they were in the clear, only to find that they were about to become front-page news."

"But wasn't Dunn taking a real chance that Mrs. Montgomery would be so angry that she'd simply tell the police the truth about his role in the affair?" asked Remy.

I thought about this. "Probably not. As with the blackmail, in order to refute Foldger's story she would have had to admit that she hired Dunn to kill the publisher. The foolish man gave Mrs. Montgomery little choice but to murder him and squelch the newspaper article."

We sat in silence for several moments, contemplating this. Then the carriage hit a sudden bump, causing us all to jump in our seats and breaking the somber mood.

"Probably the most telling information came when I visited Isabel Freiberg's house after Dunn's death," I went on. "As Robert can verify, Abigail Forester is something of a chatterbox. That morning she mentioned that Mrs. Montgomery's only son had died during the march on Vicksburg. Of course, I was immediately put in mind of Aleric's book, but I was far from making any sort of connection between the two. Abigail also bragged that her nephew was a talented writer, that even as a child he had penned some beautiful poems. Her sister seemed unusually upset when she shared these innocent reminiscences with me. Even at the time I found this strange. Then, of course, I saw Bruno Studds deep in conversation with your highly unsocial typesetter, Mr. Remy, which was a considerable surprise."

Remy's face fell. "Poor Tull. For all his faults, he was a loyal employee. He'd been with me since we launched the newspaper, you know?"

I nodded sadly. "I suspect O'Hara spotted Bruno digging on the Hill beside his shack. When he went to investigate and saw that it was Bruno burying Jonathan Aleric, he probably lent Studds a willing enough hand. But after you were arrested for the murder, Bruno must have feared Tull would reveal who really shot Aleric in order to save you, and the newspaper."

"So, the villain set fire to his house?" Remy said angrily.

"Yes. Finally that was too much, even for Mrs. Montgomery. And, of course, when Bruno took Isabel, that provided the final straw. But even she couldn't get Bruno to stop." I paused, remembering the maniacal expression on Studds's face as he held the gun to Isabel's head on the balcony. "By then, I think he was beyond the ability to reason."

"He could have easily killed Stephen," Samuel said, obviously sharing my thoughts. "By God, it was a near thing."

"You know, you provided me with the final piece of the puzzle, Samuel," I told my brother with a smile.

Robert laughed. "All right, I'll humor her, Samuel. What magic words did you say that resulted in her sudden flash of genius?"

"Very funny, Robert," I said, unable to repress a laugh. "The night before the fire, Samuel was telling me what he'd found out about Aleric. He mentioned that he'd been a poor student in school and, lacking any practical skills, joined the Union army when he got out of jail. I was too tired to realize it at the time, but I think something clicked in my mind when he said that.

"The next day, after Bruno set fire to O'Hara's house, Samuel said he was beginning to believe that Telegraph Hill was cursed, starting from the night he was shot marching down the hill after Wilde's reading. It was hearing the word *marching,* I think, that finally helped trigger that all-important connection: both men had served under General Grant at Vicksburg. After that, everything else just fell into place. I only wish I could have put it together sooner."

"Don't sell yourself short, my dear," said Remy. "I am still in awe of your deductive abilities." He paused, then went on, "But why did Bruno shoot at you?"

"She was asking too many questions," Samuel told him. "After that second visit to Telegraph Hill, Mrs. Montgomery worried that Sarah was getting too close to the truth, and wanted to frighten her away. Unfortunately for her, she was dealing with the wrong woman. My little sister does not frighten easily."

Eddie stopped the brougham on Sansome Street just short of the Filbert Street Steps. Remy said he did not mind the climb. In fact, he claimed he was looking forward to enjoying the lovely day, as well as his newfound freedom.

He bade the men good day, then opened the door and stepped out of the carriage. Once he was on the street, he reached back inside the carriage and took my hand, bringing it gallantly to his lips. Ever the perfect southern gentleman, I thought, even as I felt a slight flush creep into my cheeks.

"I can never thank you enough for all that you have done for me, my dear. You are amazing. Absolutely amazing. I shall always remain your most faithful servant!"

One month after our first appearance before the city council, Mr. and Mrs. Dinwitty, Mrs. Jane Hardy, Samuel, and I entered City Hall to hear the final verdict on the SPCA case against Ricardo Ruiz's proposed bullring. As before, the seven city council members filed in and took their places at the table set up in the front of the room.

Across the aisle from us, Ricardo Ruiz sat flanked by his two attorneys and, of course, his usual henchmen behind him. The Mexican's handsome, aristocratic face was as dark as a thundercloud when he glanced over to where the five of us were sitting.

"He appears very angry," Mrs. Hardy said, trying to hide a smile. "I believe that bodes well for our cause, don't you agree?"

"I do indeed," I answered, returning the man's rude look with a polite smile. He instantly turned his head to speak angrily with one of his lawyers.

Mr. Shaw, president of the city council, was looking over what I took to be the day's agenda. After a few moments, he cleared his throat and called our case. I stood, as did one of Ruiz's attorneys, but neither of us was called to the podium.

"Señor Ruiz," Shaw said, turning his attention to our adversary, "have you been able to locate the deed for the San Francisco property issued to your father upon his appeal to the United States Supreme Court?"

Ruiz's attorney gave Shaw a blasé smile, looking for all the world as if this matter were hardly worth the effort to comment.

"Unfortunately, my client has been forced to postpone his trip back to his native Mexico because of pressing business matters, Mr. Shaw," the lawyer said. "But surely it is a mere formality. As we demonstrated during the initial hearing, all of Señor Ruiz's California deeds are in order."

"Not the deed in question," Shaw told him. Shifting in his chair, he addressed Ruiz directly. "You were given one month to locate the proper title to that land, Señor Ruiz, yet you have failed to do so. Have you anything to say before the council rules in this case?"

Ruiz immediately got to his feet, his manner that of an important individual forced to deal with an inferior assembly who obviously did not know what they were doing.

"Señor Shaw," he began, his accent making his erudite voice seem even more striking. The man could certainly turn on the charm when he was so motivated, I thought. One had to give him that. "My family is well-known throughout Mexico. For over sixty years, we have owned property in California. Our claim to the land parcel here in San Francisco cannot be in question. My late father always intended that we should erect a monument to our illustrious family in this glorious city, and I am here to carry out his wishes."

He swept out a hand in my direction. "This woman, this Señorita Woolson, dares to stand in my way. She, who calls herself an attorney, attempts to prevent me from fulfilling this sacred obligation." He paused to look knowingly at each member of the council. "Come, gentlemen, we are men of the world, are we not? My bullfighting arena will bring great prestige, not to mention considerable income, to San Francisco. Are we to allow this naïve young woman to stand in the way of progress? I have already taken steps to correct my father's temporary oversight in obtaining what truly amounts to no more than a mere slip of paper, from your Supreme Court. I have petitioned them to issue me the deed in question in all possible haste."

He smiled imperiously around the room at large, then at the seven councilmen. "There, gentlemen. I believe that should settle the matter to our mutual satisfaction."

I was flabbergasted to see several council members nodding

their heads in amiable agreement. Furious, I stepped uninvited to the podium before any of them could respond to this shameful display of chauvinistic pomposity.

"Mr. Shaw, members of the council," I began, ignoring the seven pairs of eyes regarding me with displeasure. "Señor Ruiz may feel this matter has been settled, but I disagree. It certainly has not been settled to my satisfaction, or to the satisfaction of the SPCA. There is the small matter of the law, which he appears to consider beneath his notice."

I heard a noise coming from Ruiz's seat and hurried on. "This council gave Señor Ruiz one month to produce a valid deed for the property he claims to own in the Mission District. He has not done so. Moreover, even if he were to miraculously deliver such a properly executed title to the land in question, it would not be legally binding due to the matter of adverse possession, which I previously brought up before this council. To refresh your memories, neither Señor Ruiz nor his father has ever resided on that property, nor has either man erected any house, business, or farm there."

Behind me, Ruiz was demanding to be heard. In front of me, Mr. Shaw was banging his gavel. I paid no heed to either of them. I pulled out the sheaf of documents I had brought with me and waved them at the seven pompous men seated before me.

"Also in order to refresh your memories, I have here the necessary city records to prove that the owners of at least eight businesses and private homes within the boundaries of this property have fulfilled the obligations required to qualify for adverse possession. They have resided on the land for over five years—some of them for more than twenty years—and have dutifully paid taxes on these properties."

I took a moment to let my eyes rest on each member of the city council. "If, by any extraordinary possibility, this body finds in favor of Señor Ruiz, I shall personally ensure that all eight of these individuals sue the city of San Francisco for gross injustice, and for generous financial compensation."

Ordering Ricardo Ruiz's attorneys to quiet their client,

Mr. Shaw and the other six members of the city council put their heads together to confer. Five minutes later, the San Francisco City Council officially ruled in favor of the Society for the Prevention of Cruelty to Animals.

There would be no bullfighting ring constructed in the Mission District, or in any other area of the city if I had anything to say about it!

The following week, Samuel's book, which chronicled crime in San Francisco since the Gold Rush days, was accepted by Moure and Atkins Publishing House. There was a great deal of excitement at the Woolson house, and despite the death of his sister, Papa decided we must have a party to celebrate.

Mortimer Remy had been invited, as well as Robert, George Lewis, and two very special guests, Mr. and Mrs. Stephen Parke. The two had been married in a beautiful ceremony, which Samuel, Robert, and I attended. I don't think I have ever seen two happier people. Although I would never admit it in front of my mother, that afternoon I thought perhaps the institution of marriage was not so intolerable after all. At least for some people, I thought, and for a moment rather wished that it were possible for me to be counted among that number.

Perhaps the happiest news of all was that the couple had taken in little Billy Dunn to raise as their own son. It was unlikely they would ever be rich, at least by society's definition of the word. But they would be rich in love, which as far as I was concerned would be to enjoy wealth beyond measure!

Our entire family was present for the party, even my eldest brother, Frederick, and his wife, Henrietta, whose attendance, under the circumstances, could hardly be avoided. To my surprise, they both behaved remarkably well. Evidently, having a published author as a brother fell within the bounds of acceptable social achievements.

The man of the hour was beaming with pride, all the while

attempting, mostly unsuccessfully, to appear humble. I suspected that he was secretly still pinching himself when no one was looking. After all, it wasn't every day that a writer's fondest desire was realized.

Now that Mrs. Montgomery was awaiting trial on multiple murder charges, the literary foundation she had established was temporarily in limbo. I say temporarily, because her sister, Abigail, seemed to have discovered a surprising inner strength beneath her fluffy exterior and had expressed a desire to see the Butter Ball Literary Competition continue in her nephew's memory.

Because of her age and frail physical condition, Katherine Montgomery would most probably be spared the capital punishment she had predicted, although I wondered if spending the rest of her life in prison might be an even worse punishment. Bruno Studds would not be spared the hangman's noose, although his lawyer was attempting to plead insanity. But this was an extremely difficult defense to prove and would more than likely fail. Frankly, I hoped it would. The lives of four human beings, no matter their moral vicissitudes, must in the final analysis count for something.

Unfortunately, my brother Charles had been called away to handle a medical emergency, but Celia was circulating about the room, helping my mother cope with the enthusiastic guests, while our maid, Ina Corks, passed around finger food, and my father was practically bursting his vest buttons with pleasure and pride at his youngest son's accomplishment. Reporter or no, all of Papa's expectations about my brother following a legal career seemed to have dissipated like the morning fog wafting over San Francisco Bay.

"Well, he did it," Robert said as he handed me a glass of punch. "And the first time out of the gate, too. You must be very proud of him."

"He has genuine talent, Robert, and this is a dream come true for him. I'm so thankful that he persevered and followed his own path in life. He was never cut out to be a lawyer."

"Just as you weren't cut out to be a wife and mother, Sarah?" His voice was soft and just a bit wistful.

"It isn't that I don't want those things." I paused, trying to find words to explain. "I just don't see a way to obtain them and . . ."

"Fulfill your own dream," he finished for me.

I sighed. "Yes. Society, contemporary standards, other people's expectations . . . It's difficult to be true to oneself, particularly if you're a woman. Look how hard it was for Samuel, and he's a man."

"If you weren't such a damn good lawyer, I'd try to argue the point with you." He let out his own sigh. "Unfortunately, or perhaps fortunately, at least for your clients, you're one of the best attorneys in town."

He looked down at me, his blue-green eyes sparkling in the glow of gaslights. "Someday, I hope to use another form of persuasion on you, my dear," he added, his Scottish r's rolling nicely as he bent his head closer to mine. "One that even you might find difficult to resist."

Suddenly, I found it impossible to swallow. "I, ah, that is, after Mortimer Remy and the SPCA cases, my firm is actually solvent, at least for the next six months." It was such a pathetic change of subject that I blushed in embarrassment. I had no idea why he had the power to wreak such havoc on my otherwise sensible emotions. "I wish you would reconsider joining me, Robert. Together, we would make a formidable team."

"I have no doubt of that. Of course, if the money you have just brought in is to last six months, it will be necessary for one of us to forgo regular meals, not to mention a roof over his head."

He smiled, his eyes twinkling now. "Let me see, Campbell and Woolson, how does that strike you?"

"I'm sure you mean Woolson and Campbell."

"Hmmm. How about Campbell and Campbell? I think that has a very nice ring to it, don't you?"

I attempted to reply to this astonishing suggestion, but no sound issued from my throat. For one of the very few times in my life, I appeared to have been struck speechless.